THE PIPER IN THE WIND

By Anne Hepple

THE PIPER IN THE WIND

by

ANNE HEPPLE

The clouds are blown across the sky—
The piper in the wind goes by.

GEORGE G. Harrap & CO. LTD.
LONDON   SYDNEY   TORONTO   BOMBAY

And the vessel that he made of clay was marred in the hand of the potter: so he made it again another vessel, as seemed good to the potter to make it.

Jeremiah xviii, 4

First published August 1939
by GEORGE G. HARRAP & CO. LTD.
182 High Holborn, London, W.C.1

Reprinted: August 1939;
November 1939; *July* 1940;
April 1941; *May* 1941;
October 1941; *July* 1942;
May 1943

Reset and reprinted October 1943

Reprinted: September 1944; *July* 1946
August 1947

THIS BOOK IS PRODUCED IN
COMPLETE CONFORMITY WITH THE
AUTHORIZED ECONOMY STANDARDS

COMPOSED IN GARAMOND TYPE
AND PRINTED BY JARROLD AND SONS, LIMITED
NORWICH

MADE IN GREAT BRITAIN

CONTENTS

BOOK I

BOOK III

BOOK I

And the vessel that he made of clay . . .

CHAPTER I

"SIGH NO MORE, LADY"

WHEN Hagar Thorne's father took her out driving in the dog-cart behind a new mare and the beast shied and ran away and Hagar was thrown out against a stone wall, not only was her face broken, but her heart too; for, you see, her face struck the wall, and in one instant proud, pretty Hagar was gone for ever, and Earle Johnson, the young squire and Hagar's sweetheart, couldn't stand the sight of her altered, wounded face, and left her and went off to South Africa; so when this story opens both her face and her heart had scarcely healed scars.

Her face had mended very well; the scars cutting her cheek were fainter now, though her mouth would always look awry, but her pink-and-white prettiness was entirely gone. Instead of that charming little flower-face, there was a pale, thin countenance, with a bang of black hair to cover a great jagged mark across the brow, dark, lonely eyes, and that queer, awry mouth.

Her heart had mended too, fairly well; unlike a new pot from the Potter's hands, it did not ring quite so quickly and merrily back, perhaps, when flicked with the fingers of life, but it was quite a good pot for all that—good for years and years to come; fit still to hold laughter—and a few tears, though never so many as once it had.

When she was twenty-five Hagar's father died. He had been a Yorkshireman and a parson, and there was just his life insurance for Hagar, which would bring her in a few pounds a year, but do practically nothing towards keeping her, so

Hagar decided that, as she wasn't clever at anything but housework, she would be a housekeeper.

In her mind's eye she saw a quiet little Midland vicarage in the country with herself at the head of it, mothering and looking after a nice, white-haired old minister, much as she had mothered and looked after her father, and it was while these pretty dreams were still occupying her head that she saw an advertisement in the papers:

> Wanted, a housekeeper, gentlewoman preferred, but not essential. Large family, invalid mother, one servant and other occasional help. Apply to JAMES PEREGRINE, The Falcon's House, Breckan.

It was not all that Hagar wanted, but it was the only advertisement for a housekeeper in the paper that day, and she thought it would do no harm to apply for further information, so she wrote that very afternoon to Mr James Peregrine, asking for further particulars about the situation, and giving some about herself. "I am a good plain cook, and have until recently kept my father's house. I am sober and honest, and a member of the Church of England." She bit her pen-handle for a long time after that, decided she hadn't any more outstanding qualifications, and signed herself "Yours faithfully, Hagar Thorne."

Three days later a letter arrived, among others, for Hagar, with a large black seal with a falcon on it, and a twopenny stamp instead of a penny one.

Hagar opened it, read it, read it again, read it three times, and decided that somebody else not essentially a lady would have to do for Mr Peregrine.

Then she read the other answers to applications, sighed a little, thinking two of them might suit for earning a living, and turned back to the one with the black seal.

It was such a very queer letter. "Mad," was Hagar's reaction to it. "The man's mad," said she.

Then she read it again.

Among other things it said, "I have seven devils, but three are not of my begetting, but acquired," and, "I hope you are not easily intimidated and do not wear home-knitted stockings," and, "What, I fear, we require is not so much a lady housekeeper as a saint and termagant rolled into one."

There were other things, but those were the worst.

"Mad," repeated Hagar. "As mad as a hatter." But she read the letter again.

Now if Hagar's mother had not been half an Irishwoman and half a gipsy things might have turned out quite differently; but when you have one half of good, stubborn Yorkshire blood—taking all in, but giving nothing away—with a dash of Irish and a dash of gipsy in the other half, you get something a little out of the ordinary run. You get, in fact, Hagar.

Hagar had no idea she was anything out of the ordinary run, nor had she been up till the present; the cautious Yorkshire blood had always been on the top, like cream. All her life Hagar had been quietly taking things in and giving nothing away—except her heart, of course, which she had given to Earle Johnson, and which had fallen and got broken as he handed it back to her; but we are not talking of hearts just now—just heads and suchlike.

Now as she read the letter for the fifth—or was it the sixth?—time, slowly weighing it all up and deciding against it, the quick Irish wit and the gipsy adventurer were stirring underneath; it was as if a few bubbles bubbled up from them and burst above the cream.

After all, whatever else this situation sounded, it didn't sound dull.

That was what was the matter with the others: very suitable and all that, but they sounded so dull, so dreary.

She thought of the manse and the nice, white-haired old clergyman, and suddenly they too seemed just the least bit—well, uninteresting.

At that moment a precept of her old Yorkshire father's came into her mind, "Thou must not fear life." How often he had said it to her in the beloved dialect, "Thou must not fear life, Hagar."

As she remembered these words they were suddenly like the call of the blood—like the sound of the hunting-horn to the hound that has lain asleep, like the beat of drums to the warhorse. Metaphorically Hagar neighed, metaphorically she started up and gave tongue—actually she went and got the penny ink-bottle from behind the bust of Archbishop Cranmer and sat down to write a letter.

Who was afraid of life? Not she, Hagar Thorne. Hadn't life done all it could do to her? Hadn't it? Well, what then? Was she afraid of seven devils? Not she. Not Hagar Thorne. Not on your life!

Besides, that letter roused her curiosity. Who were they, these Peregrines? What were they like? What lay behind that strange epistle? She must see the writer of that queer letter— Mr James Peregrine. She must see the devils. She had less curiosity about the invalid wife. After all, there was much of a muchness about invalid wives. Still, it would be interesting to see the person who could possibly have married anyone as mad as Mr Peregrine. Possibly she was mad too. . . .

THE VICARAGE
HIGH WICKERING
YORKSHIRE

MR PEREGRINE

DEAR SIR,
    I have much pleasure in accepting the post at the salary mentioned. I can do white starching and am a good needle-woman, and consider my stockings my own affair.
                                        Yours truly,
                                        HAGAR THORNE

That happened in November. At the beginning of December Hagar, having packed up and sent on her trunk the day before, said good-bye for ever to the Vicarage, High Wickering.

Not without sadness, not without a few tears leaking down into that well below our hearts into which are gathered all our unshed tears; but Hagar's tears have little to do with this story, which, as it turned out, had more use for her sensible head and her twisted, humorous mouth.

She gathered a late and hard-bitten monthly rose from the bush below the parlour window, left some milk for the cat—a good mouser which the incomers had taken over—and buttoned the green baize cover on to the parrot's cage.

The parrot she was taking with her. Not that she liked the parrot—an ill-natured old harridan whose presence in the Vicarage everybody had long deplored—but what can one do with a parrot? Nobody wants a parrot, especially a parrot who cannot even swear in English, but it does it so literally and efficiently in parrotese that there is no mistaking what she means. Nobody wants a parrot who sulks and mopes, a parrot who bites and scratches, a parrot who—well, nobody does want a parrot. Yet one cannot ruthlessly slay a parrot. In any case, does anybody know how to kill a parrot? Nobody does. Nobody ever killed a parrot. Nor can one lose a parrot; it is quite, quite impossible. One cannot even open its cage and say, "Begone, dull care!" (meaning the parrot), because even if it wasn't much too wise to be gone the whole district would bring it back again the next morning.

Hagar solved the problem in the only way it could be solved. She took it with her.

"If there are seven devils already," said she to Jane—the parrot was called Jane—"they'll never notice you."

"Keep your d—— face away from my d—— cage," said Jane, or words to that effect.

So, with her shabby case, her umbrella, and her sad little winter rose in one hand and her flamboyant parrot in the other, Hagar set off to seek her fortunes.

The train was a little late in arriving at Breckan, a little lost town on a river among the Northern hills, and when Hagar descended on to the platform she looked a little eagerly up and down to see if anyone had come to meet her. No one had. There was no one in the station, in fact, except a shepherd with two dogs, a nonagenarian—at least, that was what Hagar thought he was—a few porters, and a forlorn-looking girl wheeling a wagon with a pile of sandwiches and some sweets. Hagar asked her if she could tell her the way to the Falcon's House.

"Turn to your right," she said, "and ask when you come to the Highgate."

It was a grey day in December with a hint of snow in the air, and the woolly clouds all matted together like a blanket that has been boiled—without a mesh for the sun to peep through —and cold. "The owl for all his feathers was a-cold," quoted Hagar to herself, and drew her black coat with the astrakhan collar more tightly round her.

Breckan, as she came out of the station, certainly seemed to her the dullest town she had ever seen, and the most uninviting.

"Of course, I couldn't expect them to meet the serving wench," she said to herself a little drearily, as she looked up and down the drab street. Before her was a church with a bit of paper-strewn grass and one tree in front of it, to the right a broad, practically empty thoroughfare with a few spindly plane-trees caged round by iron bars down one side of it.

She turned and made her way along it. Rounding a corner, she came on a view that cheered her up a bit. In the middle of the road there was an old stone gateway, and beyond it a funny cobbled street with red-roofed houses—all ups and downs and ins and outs—at the end of which was a town-hall with great broad steps and stone pillars and a clock in the middle; the whole place, red roofs and cobblestones, the rounded window of an apple shop, the pig hanging at the pork-butcher's door, the deep eaves of the fishmonger's, the horse-trough near the George Inn, all jumbled together, gave her an impression of medievalism, of fairy-tales, of something left over from long ago, that was decidedly pleasing; a snowflake fluttering down and catching on a creaking signboard, the rattle of a gig coming through the archway of the inn, a message-boy with a huge basket on his arm, all added to her feeling of having got by mistake into one of Hans Andersen's tales—there was even a gutter down which a toy soldier might sail in a little paper boat.

Seeing a friendly-looking, stout man with whiskers and wide trousers standing at a shop door, she again asked her way to the Falcon's House.

"Up ze yard," said he, and pointed to a small opening between his chocolate shop and a stationer's.

Surprised, Hagar looked at the narrow opening. It had "Featherbed Lane" chiselled in queer old letters on a stone above it, the inner walls were whitewashed, and it looked as if it led to some very poor quarter of the town; to strengthen this impression she saw sticking out from a low doorway a few yards up the narrow passage a notice—"Michael Moon, Cobbler."

"My goodness!" said Hagar to herself. "Do the Peregrines live up a yard?"

For one moment she thought of going back home. Then she remembered that she had no home. She had nothing but thirty-eight pounds a year and a parrot; her boats, in fact, were burnt.

Still she hesitated. Hagar had always lived in a large manse with garden and shrubbery and orchard and so forth all around it. As far as her experience went, only the very poor and shabby lived up yards. What had she let herself in for? She had really expected the Falcon's House to stand alone and on a height somewhere outside the town. Falcons built on mountain-sides and sea-crags, didn't they?

"Falcon's House! My hat!" said she to herself. "It's the first time I've heard of falcons building in a crowded little yard in the middle of a town. Some folk should study natural history—the Sparrow's Nest or the Canary's Cage seem more like it. However, here goes!"

But as she ducked into the yard and stumbled over the rounded cobbles her old father's precept was a decided comfort to her: "Thou must not fear life, Hagar." Whatever came she wasn't going to be daunted—'dauntoned' was how her father put it—a good word!

On her left were storerooms or warehouses, and on her right low, whitewashed cottages with nasturtiums planted between the cobblestones and attached to the walls by strings; the nasturtiums were nothing now but a gelatinous mass of pale green and brown at the foot of the strings, but a few dry leaves still clung to the latter and waved forlorn-looking flags in the air. Past the cottages the yard suddenly ended in a high wall built right across it; over it there hung some straggly cushions of aubrietia, and here and there pellitory-of-the-wall had settled in crannies of the stones. Three steps led up to a green door with a brass handle which shone out of the general darkness like a blink of sunlight.

"Thank goodness for the bit of brass," said Hagar to herself, for, being Yorkshire, she liked brass; not money (though, of course, again being Yorkshire, she had no objection to that), but real brass, shiny and cheerful.

Now, ever since she was three or thereabouts doors had fascinated Hagar. Passionately she had wondered what Johnnie Dorry had seen when he "went up three steps and in at a little doorie." Now at last she was to know, for here before her were the three steps, and here was the little doorie.

She turned the handle, opened it, and gave a little gasp. There before her was the loveliest December garden she had ever seen. A real garden, not a suburban place of neat crazy paving, ending circle-wise round a sundial or a bird-bath. Nor a pergola and a rockery with a cement rabbit at one end and a gnome with a wheelbarrow at the other—very nice and all that, but lacking the essentials of a real garden: mystery, age, and smell of secret places, the hint of years of seeding and climbing and tangling, the memories of the struggle with frost and snow and drought and rain.

This garden had all that; it had been a garden, it seemed, for centuries. Snowdrops would ring their bells all over it, in groups and drifts, in February; in March crocuses would come marching unafraid, with spears erect and golden armour gleaming, across the grass and forming battalions under the pear-trees. Blossom would drift and fall through the sharp May sunlight; lily of the valley would come up year after year between the wall and the pile of old flower-pots; larkspur and poppy, pansy and dusty miller, clove pinks and none-so-pretty would flower in their due seasons; lavender and rosemary and bee-balm and lad's love would scent the warm afternoons, and mignonette and tobacco flowers the evenings.

Now as Hagar stood and peered through the door the trees were leafless and the borders brown, except for an ancient cedar that stood at one corner of the grass, and the great untidy masses of jasmine against the walls whose green twigs were starred over with bright yellow stars; but Hagar knew that there would be sweet secrets all over such a garden—clumps of violets under an apple-tree, a group of Christmas roses, naked and pure against the brown soil, a thrush among the holly-berries.

Indeed, as she lingered she heard one trying over a few notes in the chill December air—or was it a starling's mimicry? Ah, no, the starling could never touch that sweet, deep note —and there he was in the crook of the lichened apple-tree, looking not unlike a wet frog with his bright, speckled breast and yellow, triangular beak.

With a lighter heart Hagar took her way up the path.

Before her was the queerest house she had ever dreamed of. It began with a low two-storied bit in the middle: three windows under a low roof, then three beneath them, but one of the latter was a French window opening on to the garden. At one side the red-tiled roof went up again to a point where a square, squat addition had been built on. At the other side a round tower soared away up to a pepper-box top and a weathercock, with windows of every shape and size all round it. The walls of the house were coloured, under the deep red tiles, a pale saffron yellow, and covered with straggling stalks of Virginia creeper and clematis. This yellow tinge gave the effect of sunlight through the soft veil of snow that now began to fall lightly over the garden, and was increased by the silver-gilt light that sparkled already from some of the windows.

"The lamps are lit," thought Hagar, and then remembered —"oh, no, it will be gas."

Feeling still more lonely out there in the snow and the darkening garden, she moved up to the only entrance she could see, the French window, and tapped lightly on the curtained pane.

There was no answer.

She tapped again.

There was no answer.

She tapped a little louder.

There was a sound of footsteps, and the door opened.

CHAPTER II

"WITH EYES FULL OF LAUGHTER AND SONG ON THEIR LIPS"

OR, rather, the French window opened. Before Hagar stood a girl, to all appearances quite an ordinary girl; she looked about sixteen or seventeen, but Hagar was to learn, was really twenty. She had wide blue eyes and fair hair plaited into two plaits and crossed round her head above her pink-cheeked, ingenuous face.

"Good afternoon," said Hagar. "I'm Hagar Thorne."

The girl did not answer. She stared at Hagar for a moment, then, flinging the windows wider, she left her and ran across the room, where she opened a door and shouted, "Rachel! Penny! Perry! She's come!"

Then she rushed back to Hagar.

"Are you *really* Miss Thorne?"

"Yes—why really?" said Hagar.

At that moment the space behind the girl seemed to fill with laughing faces, all looking at Hagar, not unkindly, but with a perfectly frank curiosity.

This put Hagar on her mettle. Ever since her accident she had hated above all things to be stared at.

"Why are you so surprised?" she repeated. "Didn't you expect me?"

"Oh," said the round, fair girl, "because you are not a bit like her—is she?" And she turned to the others.

"No, Marion, she's not," they chorused together. "Not—one bit like her!"

Hagar stared in her turn.

"Like who?"

"Miss Hagar Thorne."

"But you've never seen me before."

"Oh, no," said Marion, the fat and fair one, "but we guessed at you from your letter—you know, honest and sober and a good plain cook and no legs."

"No legs!" Hagar gasped.

"No. You were so prim about the stockings, we thought you must be like the Queen of Spain. You remember what the courtier said when a subject wanted to give her a present of stockings—'The Queen of Spain has no legs.'"

"We thought," a thin little girl with short hair said now in a low, deep voice, "you would be very stout, with red face, forty-five, and—what else?" She turned to the others.

"Butter-coloured hair," said the tall one, "and a bosom."

Hagar thought it was now her turn. "And you are the seven devils, I suppose, or, at least"—for she saw they were not seven—"four of them," and she smiled.

Now Hagar had the queerest smile; her mouth trembled a little at first, or twitched is perhaps a better word, then suddenly broke into a quick, sad smile, and as suddenly stopped. She had smiled like that ever since her accident, for, after her face healed, when she smiled one side of her mouth lifted a little higher than the other because of a scar. She had noticed

B

this once when she caught a glimpse of herself in a mirror, and for long after whenever she began to smile she remembered her awry mouth and stopped. The pain about it was over now, but the habit remained. When she laughed, too, she always put up two fingers and held one side of her mouth —for long the Peregrines were to wonder about that.

As she smiled now the group drew back to let her cross farther into the room; then, as she came fully into the light, the tall girl said quickly, her voice soft with sympathy:

"Oh, you have hurt your face!"

"I had an accident," said Hagar briefly. "It spoiled my beauty, but did not affect my working capabilities."

At twenty-five Hagar could look at it like that.

They were silent, and Hagar glanced round. This was evidently the dining-room; it was shabbily but comfortably furnished in mahogany, with old wainscoting round the room and portraits in heavy gold frames. She was tired, and wondered if they were going to give her any tea, and where Mr and Mrs Peregrine were.

"Can I see your mother, or your father?" she asked. "And then would you show me my room?"

"Oh," said Marion quickly. "Yes, we will take you up, but first I'll introduce us. I'm Marion, the eldest, and this is Rachel"—turning to the slender, brown girl at her side—"she's next to me; and this is Penny; she's the youngest of us"—pushing forward the thin little girl, who had fine corn-coloured hair—"and this is Perry: he's the boy."

"Is that all?" said Hagar. "I thought there were seven of you."

"That's devils," said Marion; "they include Paulie: that's our cousin; Beenie: she's the maid of all work, and a besom— and Mrs Brown: she's the cat."

But still Hagar did not get taken to her room. Perry's eye now caught the huge cage enveloped in green baize.

"What's that?" he asked.

"It's a parrot," said Hagar.

At that there was a general and joyful babble of questions.

"Whose parrot is it?"

"It's mine."

"May we see it?"

"Certainly—you can have it if you like."

Hagar undid the buttons and exposed an angry Jane to view. Jane had been going to swear, but when she saw all the faces she subsided and closed one eye.

There came a chorus of "Oh's."

"She's winking at me," said Perry.

"Did you mean it?" asked Penny softly. "Did you mean we could have her?"

"Yes, I did—and welcome. You and Perry can have her."

"But don't you love her?" asked Penny with raised brows.

"No," said Hagar, "I don't; she's a bad-tempered old besom. That's why I had to bring her—nobody else would have her."

"Oh, but we'll love her," said Penny; and then she and Perry said, "Pretty Polly," both at once.

"She's not Polly," said Hagar. "That's her one distinction. She's the only parrot who isn't called Polly. Her name's Jane— she's a devil."

"That's eight devils now, then," said Perry. Like Penny, he was very thin, a boy of thirteen or fourteen, she thought.

Suddenly Hagar felt very hungry—and where was Mr Peregrine, and where was Mrs Peregrine? There was no sign of either or of a meal, though it must be tea-time.

"I'd like to go to my room and have a wash and a brush up," she said, "and then I must see your parents."

She caught a glance that passed between Marion and Rachel, but had no time to wonder about it. In a moment her case and her umbrella were seized and taken from her, and the whole company propelled her across the room, through a hall, and up a broad staircase, chattering merrily.

On the first landing they stopped before a door. Marion looked at Rachel, and Rachel looked at Marion and nodded.

Hagar was turned round and propelled farther up the stairs. On a little square landing they stopped before another door. Like the one in the outside wall, it was up three steps, but this really was a "little doorie," one of the smallest doors Hagar had ever seen. It was narrow and arched at the top and was in a deep recess.

"I think we'd better tell her first," said Marion.

Rachel nodded. Marion was evidently the eldest, but Hagar noticed she always referred things to Rachel. Now she went on, "You see, if you were what we expected, and what Father said you would be from your letter, we were going to give you the buff room; it's quite nice, but haunted. But if you were 'the Unexpected,' and we liked you, then Rachel said she would give you her room in the tower—you'll love it! This is it!"

She threw open the door, and Hagar looked into the quaintest of rooms—a darling of a room. It was round, but had jutting-out bits with windows; it was small, and it was infinitely friendly and cosy. A log fire glowed in the small, old-fashioned grate; there was a little bed, a low arm-chair, a tall-boy, a writing-table, and heaps of cushions. The curtains and chair covers and bed cover and cushion covers were all of bright, shiny chintz, a chintz with a trellis-work and flowers and green paroquets. Two branched candlesticks stood on the mantelpiece and lit up the room with their six candles.

"Oh," said Hagar, "what a lovely room! But of course I cannot take Rachel's room; the other room will do quite well for me. I'm not afraid of ghosts."

"I am," said Marion—"of all kinds, sad ones and merry ones; but our ghost hasn't begun to haunt us yet——" She stopped, looking at Rachel.

"Yes," said Rachel now, "this is your room."

"And where will you sleep?" asked Hagar.

"She'll sleep with me to-night," said Marion, "and to-morrow we'll start and put the tower room right. Rachel's always wanted it. Will you just keep your things in your

trunk to-night? We'll have great fun to-morrow putting the
rooms right. Can you paper and paint?"

"Oh, yes."

"Do you like peat-reek?" said Rachel now.

She went forward, and with a small pair of tongs lifted a
bit of peat off the fire and waved it in the air, the blue smoke
trailing after the tongs.

"Sniff," she said.

Hagar sniffed.

"Oh, yes, I do like it. I've never smelt it before."

"How long will it take you to be ready for tea?" Perry
put in now. "I'm hungry."

"Just a few minutes," said Hagar, thankful for the mention
of tea, and Perry ran away downstairs, and the three sisters
turned to go.

"I do," said Hagar to Rachel, "thank you for your lovely
room, but is it all right? Does your mother not mean me to
have the other room? Would——" She stopped, seeing the
girls look at one another again.

"You'd better tell her, Marion," said Rachel.

"Our mamma is dead," said Marion.

"Oh," said Hagar, completely taken aback. Then, recovering herself, "But the advertisement said——" She paused.
Of course, the advertisement said she was an invalid.

"She died two weeks ago," said Rachel.

"Oh, I am sorry," said Hagar. And now she noticed that
they were all, like herself, in black; it did not seem to affect
their high spirits.

"Should we have written and told you?" asked Marion.

"Well, it would have been usual, wouldn't it?"

"Yes, I suppose so, but . . . the circumstances were unusual." Rachel spoke stiltedly, as if quoting, and Marion
put in:

"You see, we didn't like her."

"What!" said Hagar, completely shocked.

Then Penny spoke in her deep, low voice.

"She was a great trial," she said, looking very small and serious.

"You see," said Marion, "we've had enough of mothers—she was the third!"

"Oh, she was your stepmother!" exclaimed Hagar, relieved.

"Yes," said Marion. "The second."

"You don't mean the second stepmother," said Hagar, getting mixed. "The other would be your own mother."

"Oh, no," said Rachel. "That was Janie. We are so sick of mothers we never call our own one 'Mother'—just Janie. She died long ago. We've had two mothers since then. We called them 'Mamma.'"

"And so," said Marion, "when Mamma died, and we said should we write to Miss Thorne, our father said, 'No, just let her come. If she doesn't like us she needn't stay.' You see, under the circumstances our father hated writing letters about it."

Hagar was about to say, "What circumstances!" but stopped and said instead, "Where is your father? Oughtn't I to see him?"

"He's in the shop," said Marion. "You'll see him later. Do you mind having tea in the kitchen?"

"Not I," said Hagar. "I like kitchens."

"Oh," said Rachel, "so do we. You see, it's Beenie's day out, and we always make tea ourselves in the kitchen on Beenie's day out. Oh, Marion, your flapjacks!"

Marion turned and fled. Rachel and Penny went hurtling after her, and Hagar was left alone. She looked round the room and tried to make something of her impressions of this strange introduction to the Peregrine family, but her brain would not work.

"They are just as queer as I thought they would be, but jollier," she said to herself, and left it at that. Perhaps she would understand them as time went on. Meantime she had a hunt for a bathroom, found it, and washed, and changed her dress, wondering as she did so if she should have told Mr Peregrine her age. Evidently he expected an older woman.

Still, twenty-five was quite a good age, and she was sure she looked about thirty-five, so perhaps it would be all right, for she was going to stay.

She had made up her mind. Marion was plump, and seemed kind and simple. Rachel was cleverer; she was sure of that—the clever one of this queer, gay, pathetic family. Why pathetic? She did not know. She just felt they were pathetic, especially that funny little thin Penny with her fair, short hair and deep, soft voice. Marion was the prettiest, but Rachel was more attractive, not at all pretty, but unusual— that was the word for her. So slender and brown, with her dark skin and red hair. Usually red-haired people had very white skins, but not Rachel. She was all brown—nut-brown skin and ruddy, beechen hair, with straight eyebrows over long, brown eyes.

Hagar had got so far in her cogitations when a tap came at the door and Penny came in.

"I've come to take you down to tea," she said, and held out her hand for Hagar's.

They were crossing the landing when suddenly she stopped, and, throwing two thin, stick-like arms around Hagar, she said:

"I like you. I like your face and your twisty mouth. Stay with us, will you? Will you promise?"

Hagar hugged her back.

"I like you too," she said. "Yes, I think I'll stay."

"Will you not mind about Mamma?"

"No, it's all right."

Penny hesitated as if she was going to say something else, then seemed to think better of it.

"Rachel said I wasn't to talk," she said, and then suddenly, as children will, changed the subject.

"Jane likes Perry and me," she announced, and continued to discuss the parrot till they reached the kitchen. Here a square deal table was spread with a red-and-white checked cloth laid cornerwise. A great jug of jasmine had been set in the middle, and the table was laden with plates of new bread and butter, pots of jam, grocer's cake, and a plate piled with burnt pancakes—evidently Marion had been too late to save the flapjacks.

On the bars before the huge open fire stood a brown teapot and a brass kettle. In front sat the red-haired Perry with a large toasting-fork, toasting new bread. On his knees he balanced a huge black cat.

"This is Mrs Brown," said Marion. "She is our cat. We've a dog too, but he's out. Tell Hagar about Robert Burns, Perry."

But Perry seemed shy now. He did not speak; but, as Hagar was to discover later, it was not shyness that kept Perry silent for long periods at a time, but merely the fact that he was usually far away on some imaginary quest of his own.

Hagar enjoyed her tea. She was hungry, and there was plenty of thick bread and butter and grocer's strawberry jam. The kitchen was warm and cheerful, and everybody talked together. There was no appearance of Mr Peregrine. Indeed, so elusive was Mr Peregrine that Hagar began to wonder if there was any such person, or if this queer family had just made him up.

She was still wondering when bedtime came, for when the girls took her up to the tower room and left her late at night no Mr Peregrine had yet appeared.

CHAPTER III

"AND ONE MAN IN HIS TIME PLAYS MANY PARTS"

STILL doubtful as to whether there was or was not a Mr Peregrine, Hagar rose the next morning. The first thing she did was to pull up the blind in the front window of her tower room, and there yet another surprise caught at her heart and took her breath away.

She had complained coming up the yard that falcons did not build their nests in the middle of a town, but made their eyries on the mountain-sides and rugged cliffs. Well, the Falcon's House, to her amazement, was true to type. From her window she looked across a river, far below, to a wide expanse of snow-covered country and distant hills; beneath her the wall of the tower went sheer down to steep crags, whence sloping grass and whin-covered banks spread to the waterside.

So great was her surprise that it took her a few minutes to orient herself. Then she realized that the town must be built high up above the river, and that the Falcon's House must stand on a small promontory jutting out at this point, so that, while the back was within a few yards of the middle of the town, the front was several hundred feet above the surrounding country.

"Oh, you lovely house!" exclaimed Hagar, addressing the walls. "I offer my humble apologies for complaining because you were up a yard. To find you, as a surprise, at the top of Featherbed Lane is just perfect. . . . Now, I wonder why Featherbed Lane? It seems such an anachronism, if I've got the right word."

She hadn't; but anyhow it was a nice long one, and as there was no one to tell her it was Featherbed Lane for the simple reason that, before the Falcon's House was built, it had been a convenient spot at which to empty old featherbeds and other rubbish over the cliff, she got on undisturbed with her dressing.

The sound of a bell in the depths below made her realize that she had slept in. She put off no more time, but finished brushing her hair and nipped downstairs.

Outside the dining-room she heard a man's voice, and paused a moment. So there really was a Mr Peregrine!

As she opened the door she caught sight of a large, stooping figure outlined against the French window and caught what he was saying.

"I ought," said Mr Peregrine, "to have been a monk."

Immediately and devastatingly Hagar knew that this was a mistake. Nobody, thought she—no, not an angel from heaven —could have resisted the reply—and pat it came from a gaunt old woman who was putting plates of porridge round the table.

"Happen thou would have made a much better monkey, James Peregrine," said she, and without a doubt, as Hagar had realized in one enveloping glance, there was something monkey-like in Mr Peregrine's appearance.

He might have been of average height, but stooped from the shoulders, and his extraordinarily long arms looked as if they could easily have swung him up into the topmost branches of the family tree. His face too, with the long upper lip and the small, bright, too clever eyes under the bushy brows, had something of the monkey's pathetic, thwarted over-intelligence about it.

Just now, as the servant-woman spoke, two lines of stern disapproval indented themselves deeply from nose to mouth, while above them his small, bright eyes laughed at Hagar through the ambush of his hairy eyebrows as he turned towards her.

"Miss Thorne, I presume."

"Yes," said Hagar.

He waved a hand from Hagar to Beenie.

"I gather you two have not met as yet. Allow me to introduce you—the new broom to the old: Miss Hagar Thorne, Miss Tabitha Muckle—but we call her Beenie, because it's a sort of generic name for Scots maids! You'd better make friends with Beenie, Miss Thorne. She's the only enduring thing among us—and has a tongue like a file—eh, Beenie? This is the lady housekeeper, Beenie. I hope she won't be another thorn in your flesh."

"I warrant as how I can stand onything in this house efter what I've stooden already," she said, and immediately, hearing her accent, a strange mixture of broad Scots and Lancashire, Hagar felt, for all her ungracious words, a warm glow of friendliness for the older woman.

For that, indeed, is the effect of those warm, homely accents of the North of England—Yorkshire, Lancashire, Northumbrian. The sound of them to those who have been brought up among them is like the sound of home, and breaks down barriers with a lightning stroke.

Beenie, however, did not wait for any reply, but, picking up her tray, went out of the room.

Mr Peregrine took no notice of her departure, but went on to Hagar, as if it were she who had compared him to a monkey.

"I dare say you are right. I might have made a first-class monkey, and only a very second-rate monk. Still, as even a second-rate monk I should have escaped the cares of a family . . . and even as a monkey my trials would have been less. My offspring would have taken after me—that's to say, they would have been pure monkey without any mixture of devil, angel, or Lowland Scot. As it is, God knows whence they got their characters. Not from the Peregrines, who are devils, but sound, businesslike devils, with a mixture of hawk—and there an end! Not from the Turtletons, who are fat as wood-pigeons, solemn and smooth-spoken, and destined to be lord mayors and wet-nurses. No . . . they must be . . ." He stopped, and then added in a mild voice, "I hope you haven't been frightened off already, Hagar?"

The use of her name surprised Hagar, but the last sentence was said so kindly that she could not complain or stand upon her dignity. Anyhow, this did not seem a family in which it would be of any use standing on one's dignity.

"Oh, no," she said, "I like them."

"So do I," said Mr Peregrine, "though not immoderately."

As Hagar had nothing to say to this he resumed his cogitations.

"No, not immoderately. You will not find that I am the proud parent, nor the fond one—far from it, though I made a concession in the matter of stockings. 'I hope,' said Rachel, on hearing you came from Yorkshire, 'she won't wear home-knitted stockings, two plain and two purl.' Whether this was a natural conclusion to arrive at on hearing the place of your birth I cannot say. I merely state facts. I hope my reference to stockings was not considered to—ah—to verge on the immoral?"

"Good gracious!" said Hagar.

"Just so—the proper comment, if I may say so. But about the family. You will find them frank and outspoken to the point of—ah—to the point of——"

"Yes, I understand," said Hagar. "I've met them."

"Of course, of course; and no doubt you will also find that, whatever else they are, they are not dumb, driven cattle. You recall the words, 'Be not like dumb, driven cattle; be a hero in the strife'?"

He blinked at Hagar through his hairy eyebrows, and for the life of her she could not tell whether he was just a gas-bag, or whether he was talking so that he could observe and sum her up, or whether he was laughing at himself all the time. He went on:

"Not that I'd put them down as 'heroes in the strife' either. So far, and so far only, they take after me, who, you will have noticed, am not built in the heroic mould—'a thing of shreds and patches!' Otherwise, I cannot conceive where they got their characters. High-handed with life, that's what they are. They'll take everything hardly, you mark my words!"

He was interrupted in his remarks by the door of the breakfast-room creaking and then slowly opening inward. For a moment there was no visible cause for this, and then a small boy of about six slowly crawled into the room on his hands and knees.

"What the devil are you up to, Benjamine?" demanded Mr Peregrine, breaking off in the middle of his high-flown meditations.

"I'm the cat," said Benjamine.

"Oh, are you?" said Mr Peregrine. "Well, 'all the world's a stage, and one man in his time plays many parts,' but there's no use in overdoing the thing. Get up at once and behave like a Christian. What's that in your mouth?"

"It's a mouse," said Benjamine. "I caught it in the cellar." And his freckled, disarming face was turned up to Mr Peregrine, with the remnants of an old teddy-bear dangling from his small white teeth.

"Put it down at once," said Mr Peregrine, "or we shall carry this affair to its logical conclusion and make you eat the mouse—it's all you'll get for breakfast."

Benjamine crawled across the floor, scratched up the mat with his fore-paws, hid the teddy-bear underneath, and then scratched it back again. Benjamine was evidently nothing if not thorough.

"Never mix your metaphors, Benjamine," said Mr Peregrine now, having solemnly observed this disposition of the mouse. "It's a very serious literary crime. Cats don't bury their mice. It's dogs who bury their bones. Where are the others?"

He turned to Hagar: "Benjamine lives near here, and has attached himself to the family. He is always in and out."

By this time he and Hagar were seated, one at each end of the table—Hagar facing the French window, where she had been waved into a seat—and had started on their porridge. Hagar, too, was wondering where the rest of the family could be.

"Rachel," said Benjamine, "is pulling out Penny's false tooth."

"The devil she is!" said Mr Peregrine. "And when, pray, did Penny get a false tooth?"

"Oh, we just call it the false one," said Perry, who had now come in, "because it has two black spots on it like a domino."

"The connexion seems vague," said Mr Peregrine, "but why pull it out? Was it because, having lost a domino, you needed another?"

Before Perry could answer the door burst open and Marion rushed in, and without a word of greeting sat down to her porridge.

"Where are the rest of you?" asked Mr Peregrine.

"They'll be here in a minute," said Marion. "I was

pretending to be the nurse, but I had to rush off because we're going to paper Rachel's room, and I'm to go for the paper. Rachel's the dentist, or at least she's told Penny she's the doctor, but as she has a country practice she had to do tooth-extracting in her odd moments. She is the anæsthetist too —she's just given Penny the gas."

"What?" gasped Hagar, turning round to Marion and starting up.

"Oh, it's all right, Hagar. Rachel just put a pillow-case over Penny's head and turned on the gas for a minute to get the right smell. Rachel wanted everything done in order to distract Penny's attention. She tied the thread to Penny's tooth before she gave her the gas so that no time should be put off during the period of unconsciousness."

At that moment a piercing yell rang through the house which made Hagar jump from her chair and Mr Peregrine drop the knife and fork with which he was now tackling his ham and egg.

"My God!" he groaned, and then picked his knife and fork up again. "What's that?"

"That's Penny," said Marion. "The tooth's out!"

The words were hardly out of her mouth when the door banged open and Penny, with a flaming face, upon which sat an outraged and indignant expression, rushed into the room and went bang into Hagar, where she drew up, sticking her head on to Hagar's shoulder and performing a war-dance with her feet. She was followed by Rachel in a striped pyjama jacket. Rachel threw her arms round Penny and began to comfort her, while explaining to her father. "We made it all up, and I acted the dentist to make some fun and get Penny's loose tooth out—it's been hanging by a thread for days."

"Well," said Mr Peregrine, "is the tooth out?"

"No," said Rachel, "the thread broke."

"The forceps slipped," corrected Mr Peregrine. "Come here, Penny," he went on. "Let's see the tooth." Penny went over to him and opened her mouth as wide as it would go.

"Aha," said Mr Peregrine, "I see the domino—this one, isn't it?" And he touched it with his forefinger.

"Uh-uh," said Penny.

The next moment another appalling shriek, compounded of surprise, rage, indignation, and reproach, rent the air, then at its height suddenly changed into a sort of grunt.

"It's out!" said Penny.

Benjamine immediately ran forward, picked the tooth from the floor, and put it in his pocket.

"The quack," said Mr Peregrine with quiet satisfaction, "sometimes succeeds where the fully qualified practitioner with all his paraphernalia fails—eh, Rachel?"

And as he blinked at his daughter, his subtle eyes laughing, his mouth staid, Hagar suddenly and surely knew that, in spite of what he had said about his family, he adored them, and that it was from him they got all their different characters. For Mr Peregrine himself was not one person, but a score rolled into one. He had as many sides as a diamond has facets, and each of a different colour. Before breakfast was over she had seen the literary man, the artist, the tragedian, the buffoon, the thinker and the clown, the staid elderly gentleman and the whimsical elf.

Which of them all was the real Mr Peregrine? It was to be long, if ever, before she knew.

CHAPTER IV

"MATTHEW, MARK, LUKE, AND JOHN"

MR PEREGRINE was the head of Peregrine and Turtleton, Booksellers and Stationers, and his shop was the one that Hagar had seen in the Highgate at the bottom of Featherbed Lane. There had been Peregrines and Turtletons, Booksellers, in Breckan since, as Marion said, "before the Flood," and when an ancestral Peregrine had fallen in love and married a Turtleton, and so domestically as well as in business joined the two firms, their respective fathers had connived together and built the Falcon's Nest for the young couple. The date 1793 had been written in darker tiles on the red roof, but as this did not show far enough for the Peregrines the figures had been tarred in black tar, and at every spring-cleaning since the tar had been renewed, so that from far across the river the date could be seen on the red-tiled roof, except, of course, when a veil of snow lay over everything, as it did this morning, when Hagar, having watched Mr Peregrine's broad figure departing down the garden under a huge umbrella, turned to Marion and said:

"Now show me over the house."

They all showed her over the house, from the attic, where the pears and the apples were stored, down to the kitchen, where Beenie was monarch of all she surveyed. Then up again by the tower stairs to the room that was to be Rachel's at the top, a real eyrie with windows that looked over town and country from north, south, east, and west. They showed her the Victorian drawing-room, with the bead and woolwork hassocks and chairs, the white marble mantelpiece, the gilded clock, the wax fruit under glass domes, the grand piano, and the bulrushes in a painted drain-pipe. Then Mr Peregrine's den, which they called "Papa's Parlour," not because that was the name they gave their father, but because their grandmother had called it "Papa's Parlour" when her children were young, and "Papa's Parlour" it had remained ever since. It had a faint atmosphere of Mr Peregrine about it: Shakespeare and churchwarden pipes, a desk covered with jumbled papers and new editions of the classics, a peat fire, and Mrs Brown, the cat, curled up in the warm depression Mr Peregrine's 'bahootie' (Rachel's word; she collected suchlike Scotticisms) had left in the arm-chair. On the mantelpiece a globe depicting the pathway of the heavenly bodies, a poacher's net wrapped round two sticks, and a bit of Chelsea ware depicting a shepherd and shepherdess. But what surprised her most of all was to find Jane, the parrot, comfortably ensconced at one side of the fireplace.

"Father likes the parrot," said Penny, "so we've lent her to him."

Then they showed her the "Corndollies' Cupboard," where an old corndolly still sat on a top shelf, and the "boley-hole," a funny room that sat all by itself at the top of a little staircase off the main one, and had been the nursery ("but we always called it the boley-hole"), and was now the girls' own comfortable, shabby old sitting-room, where they held their 'confabs' and pursued their hobbies.

Before one door they paused.

"This is the room we were going to give you if we hadn't liked you," said Marion.

"Ah," said Hagar, in a sepulchral voice, "the haunted chamber!"

"Yes, but it's not haunted yet. We just think it will be. It's where our stepmothers slept—all of them."

"Two's not so very many," said Hagar.

"It's an awful lot of stepmothers," said Penny.

It was a large room with a cold smell and Nottingham lace curtains, and looked out into the garden. Hagar liked the tower room much better, and said so.

"And now we'll show you the front of the house and the turtle and the falcon," said Marion.

The front door opened on to a narrow stretch of grass with huge, ivy-clad walls to right and left and a low one in front covered with wall plants. In the middle of the latter was a little gate, and from it a narrow path ran along the top of the crag and then went zigzagging down to the river. In each of the other walls were big doors. One opened on to a yard with a stable, and so on, while the other was the main entrance to the house, by which Hagar was supposed to arrive the night before when she surprised them by tapping on the French window.

c

The front of the house itself was full of whimsies. The wide drawing-room windows were flanked on either side by round windows like portholes, and the front entrance had been made by chopping a piece out of a corner and putting the door underneath the angle. At the left of the door rose the tower, soaring up past the main roof to its red-tiled, pepper-pot top.

Hagar now saw that there was in front a projection at either side topped by a carved figure.

"That's the family coat-of-arms," said Rachel, with a smile.

Hagar saw then that on one side the figure was that of a turtle-dove on its nest, while on the other a falcon poised on a rock, wings raised as if for flight.

"Oh," she said, "I see now—the peregrine falcon and the turtle-dove."

"Exactly," said Rachel drily.

"And," said Marion, "we are the result of the mixture— the fierce wild falcon and the home-loving turtle-dove."

They all giggled.

"A fat pigeon and an old crow would have done just as well," said Rachel, and as she spoke Hagar realized two things —that there was something embittered about Rachel, and that, besides looking somewhat like a monkey, Mr Peregrine going down the snowy garden that morning in his black morning-coat with rounded tails had looked not unlike an old crow from behind—certainly more like a crow than a falcon.

"Well, that's the house," said Marion. "Do you like it?"

"I love it," said Hagar; "it's a house of parts—a house that knows things, a house that's lived, a house that has secrets of its own."

"And of ours," said Rachel.

"Come on," said Marion, "let's start the papering."

That was a suggestion after Hagar's own heart. She loved putting houses to rights. Everything to do with a house enchanted her; she liked papering and painting and white-washing, sweeping, scrubbing, and polishing. She liked

cooking meals, whether it was preparing a lordly turkey or
using up scraps of mutton; and she loved making jams and
jellies, marmalades and chutneys, and was in her element with
a batch of bread to get ready for the oven, scones for the girdle,
and cakes for baking.

As a matter of fact, she had been secretly delighted to notice,
the night before, the lack of a real housewife at the head of
affairs. The new baker's bread, the grocery cake and jam, the
burnt flapjacks at tea, had appalled her Yorkshire flair for what
a tea-table should be, but had also given her a thrill of pure joy,
for here there was work for her to do—here she was needed.
She'd soon change all that. She'd show them how a house
should be run, and teach the girls too—Marion anyhow. She
had not such hopes of Rachel. Rachel did not seem to have
the makings of a housewife. Not that she thought any the less
of her for that, or any the more—to each one his talents!
Rachel looked as if she might write poetry or study the higher
mathematics. Hagar was not quite sure whether she'd ever
love Rachel as she felt she was going to love Marion; there
was something about Rachel—a holding back, a stillness, a
reserve that might mean anything; and then there was her
tongue. Hagar was sure Rachel could be very, what they used
to call at school, *sarcastic*.

Then there would be Beenie to conquer. Beenie, one could
see, was a good worker of the rough-and-ready kind, and had
been there a long time, and Beenie was prepared to stand no
nonsense: one would have to walk warily with Beenie; she
would have to be *managed*. Not that that prospect daunted
Hagar. She had managed a Yorkshire parish and a Yorkshire father, and it is a well-known fact that if you can manage
a Yorkshire father you can manage anything—even a Lowland
Scot.

As Hagar, metaphorically, surveyed her battle-ground,
which included dusty mantelpieces, fried eggs with frills of
brown lace round them, burnt bacon, and Beenie's aprons,
and armed herself for the fray she remembered how there had

been one snag in her engagement to Earle. He was rich and had hated to see her doing housework. "Once we are married," he used to say, "there'll be none of that for you"; and she had never been able to make him understand that she liked housework—indeed, he seemed to think there was something slightly shameful in such a confession. Well, that needn't worry her now. She was no longer a lady, but a working housekeeper with plenty of work to do.

Having got so far in her cogitations, she saw the girls off upstairs with a pile of paper and a pail of batter, and set off to interview Beenie about the meals for the day. No use hesitating. She must begin as she meant to go on, even if she felt in her bones that Beenie would be like a hedgehog at the moment with all her prickles out. She was.

"I think, Beenie," said Hagar to the broad back presented to her as she entered the kitchen, "we'd better arrange about dinner before I go up to help the girls. What time do you usually have it?"

"Round about one," said Beenie, "and the denner's arranged."

"That's good," said Hagar. "What are we having?"

"There's the kail and there's the cold meat," grunted Beenie shortly. "Now go thy ways out of my kitchen. I hev my work to do."

"Eh, mon," said Hagar, "I du lik to hear thee talk."

Beenie, completely taken aback, turned round and faced her. Hagar, with a broad grin on her face, nodded at her.

"Be'st thou from Lancashire?" said Beenie.

Hagar shook her head. "A Yorkshire tyke," she said.

"However has to gotten here?" Beenie, she was to find, usually talked Scots, but could drop into her childhood's Lancashire when it pleased her.

"That's a long story," said Hagar; "but here I am to earn my living. I'll tell you all about it some day if you don't get me turned away by not letting me do the work I'm paid to do—that's the housekeeping and the cooking. You can't do all the work of this house single-handed, so we'll divide it between us. What do you like to do—the cooking?"

"Eh, you hev me there, lass, as fast as a thief in a mill. Cookin's a thing I never did shape to do, but that French hizzy turned all our stomachs, and it mun be done."

"All right," said Hagar. "I'll do it. So that's that. Now get your kitchen redd and leave the dinner to me, and in the mornings I'll come down and cook and set the breakfast, and that will leave you free for your firesides. What part of Yorkshire do you come from, or is it Lancashire?"

In a few minutes Beenie and she were deep in Yorkshire and Lancashire reminiscences. Beenie was won. Hagar, passing between pantry and kitchen, prepared rissoles from the mutton and made a sweet, and whenever Beenie seemed captious she reminded her in the most barefaced way that they were both Midland folks and far from 'whoam,' or she hummed a line of *On Ilkley Moor baht 'At*, and so she got through the first and most difficult hour with Beenie, and, though they were to have a few skirmishes later on, the battle was practically won, in spite of the fact that Beenie had really lived more in Scotland than in Yorkshire, Hagar's home.

Mounting the stairs a little later, she entered the tower room to find Marion standing on a chair on a table very busy slapping a new strip of paper on to the wall with the whitewash brush.

"What I don't understand," she was just saying, "is why so many people don't do this for themselves."

"Perhaps the reason will be apparent when you've finished," said Rachel, and Hagar could not but join in the laugh, for it was plain to be seen that if Marion's well-meant but ruthless efforts were continued the last bit of paper would have to be fitted in like a piece in a jig-saw puzzle.

Hagar took things in hand, and by dinner-time—at one punctually: Hagar was having no "round about one"—the ceiling was done and the paper up. It was a low room, and the deep embrasures for the windows were all of dark polished wood, so there really wasn't much paper to put on.

"Now," she said, as they all washed in the bathroom, "we'll scrub it out this afternoon, and by to-morrow we'll get the furniture in, and then we'll start preparing for Christmas. Is the mincemeat made?"

"We always buy it, and the plum-pudding," said Marion.

"My certes!" said Hagar. "It's time you had a house-keeper."

"Couldn't we make cakes one afternoon?" said Rachel. "Because the Wotherspoons are coming to tea on Sunday."

"Oh," said Hagar, "we'll have to make some cakes then. Who are the Wotherspoons? Are there many of them?"

"Four," said Marion. "Matthew, Mark, Luke, and John. Benjamine is a relative of theirs, and spends a lot of time there, and he often comes too."

"Gracious!" said Hagar. "Matthew, Mark, Luke, and John!"

"Yes," said Rachel. "Their father was a very pious man."

"And I always think of them," said Penny, "when I say the prayer that Naomi taught me:

> Matthew, Mark, Luke, and John,
> Bless the bed that I lie on."

"Who was Naomi?" asked Hagar.

"'Is,' not 'was,'" said Rachel. "She's French."

"Oh, the 'French hizzy'!" said Hagar.

"Yes." There was a pause. Hagar felt something uncomfortable in the room. Then Penny said:

"She married Matthew—and Matthew wasn't hers. Matthew was Marion's, wasn't he, Marion?"

"Don't be silly," said Marion, cheeks flaming. "I wouldn't have had Matthew, not if he'd been made of——"

"Beaten gold and precious stones," put in Penny.

"And is Naomi coming to tea?" asked Hagar.

There was a silence then.

"No," said Marion. "Neither Matthew nor Naomi will be coming. Naomi never comes here . . . nor Matthew now. . . ."

"You see——" said Penny.

"Hold your tongue, Penny," said Rachel, and turned the subject away from Naomi. "You see," she said to Hagar, "though we call them 'Matthew, Mark, Luke, and John,' Mark is really the eldest, and Matthew the second. I expect their father only began to think of the four Evangelists after Luke and John were born; they are twins."

CHAPTER V

"TROUBLED ABOUT MANY THINGS"

THE dinner pleased Mr Peregrine so much that he was most affable when Hagar suggested that he and she should have an interview before he went back to the shop, to talk about 'ways and means,' as Hagar put it. Everything had been so casual so far that she felt, as she told him, more like a guest who had dropped in than a grave and responsible housekeeper.

Pinned down to essentials, Mr Peregrine proved that he could talk sense for a few minutes at a time, which Hagar had doubted, and discussed her duties, the housekeeping allowance, and allied matters in a way that made her see that after all he might be a very good business-man beneath all his peculiarities. Up till then she had been wondering how in the world he ever managed to run a shop.

She was quite glad, too, when he asked her to come along with him and see the shop.

"You can then kill two birds with one stone," said he, "for that, I can see, is how you prefer to kill your birds, Hagar. You can see the shop and get your monthly housekeeping allowance; you can also meet Anthony—another bird for your bow and arrow."

"Who's Anthony?" asked Hagar.

"God bless my soul! Haven't they told you about Anthony?"

"No; we've been too busy about the house to talk about anybody outside."

"Anthony is the industrious apprentice," said Mr Peregrine. "Go and put your hat on. This must be seen to at once. We can't have you not knowing Anthony. I have him marked out for one of the daughters of the firm. Perhaps you'll be able to help me to choose one for him."

"You'd better let him choose for himself, I should think," said Hagar drily. "It would be less trouble in the end."

She ran and put on her round astrakhan cap and an old astrakhan coat that she'd hung in the hall to be ready for emergencies, and they went off together, through the snow-covered garden and into the narrow yard, where Mr Peregrine let himself into one of the store-rooms by a key.

Hagar saw that here was evidently no little country stationer's shop, but a large business in everything in the bookseller's and stationer's line. They passed through rooms lined with shelves full of boxes and parcels, and with stairs into lofts above them, and then through a room lined with new books, and then a lending library before they reached the shop.

"Are you a reader?" asked Mr Peregrine.

"Not what I expect you'd call one," replied Hagar frankly, "but I love reading books of travel on Sundays."

"Good gracious!" said he. "Do you only read on Sundays?"

"No," said Hagar, "but I like reading books of travel on Sundays. It's such a stay-at-home sort of day."

Mr Peregrine had no chance to make a comment on this, for a young man at a desk, seeing them, came forward to speak to him. When he saw Hagar he hesitated for a moment, just long enough, however, for Hagar to take him in. He was very slight, she saw, and tall. He had straight, untidy dark hair, and his pale face had the look of an early Victorian gentleman's by reason of the very slight touch of black 'sideboards' at either side of his cheeks.

"I can just see him in white nankeen breeches, a blue coat with brass buttons, and wide-brimmed tall hat," she said to herself; "and, my goodness, isn't he shy?" For his grey eyes, meeting hers, had immediately and hurriedly passed over them and fixed themselves on his employer.

Had Hagar known it, this was not so much shyness as an extreme sensitiveness on Anthony's part; he had at once seen the scars on her face, and, terrified that she might think he was looking at them, had passed his glance on to Mr Peregrine.

"Well, Anthony," said the latter, "I've brought Miss Thorne over to say 'How do you do?' It seems she's been nearly twenty-four hours in the house and never heard of you —a sad state of affairs in view of my well-known machinations to marry one of the daughters off to the successful apprentice. Well, well, here we are—Miss Hagar Thorne, Mr. Anthony Truett."

Anthony bowed, but said nothing.

"How do you do?" said Hagar, feeling a little shy, as she always did when confronted with young men. Then, as he looked a little confused, she guessed that neither had he heard anything about her till this moment.

"I'm the new housekeeper," she explained.

"Yes, yes, the new broom," said Mr Peregrine; then added, after a slight pause, "And possibly, for all we know, the new besom."

Then Anthony's eyes met Hagar's as they both laughed, and, in spite of the shyness, she thought she liked Anthony.

There was no time for anything more, as a customer came into the shop, and while Anthony went to attend to him Mr Peregrine took Hagar to the till and counted out the month's housekeeping money.

"And as it's Christmas and you'll be wanting to give us all indigestion here is a little extra for the provision of seasonable fare," and he gave her an extra ten-pound note.

"Well, whatever Mr Peregrine is he isn't mean," said Hagar to herself, putting the money into the little leather bag she had brought with her, and which was to be alluded to for ever after, had she but known it, as "Hagar's Money-bag."

With another glance round the shop, which looked bright and cheerful with its shelves of books and displays of Christmas cards and calendars, fountain-pens, books, annuals, and other Christmas wares, she turned and made her way back through the store-rooms to the door by which she had entered: but instead of turning homeward she ran off and bought a few necessaries for the cake-making afternoon they were going to have before the arrival of the visitors to tea.

"They always come at five," Marion had said, "in the gig, two before and two behind."

"And who's the fourth?" asked Hagar.

"Mother Wotherspoon," said Rachel. "She's a dear old lady." And they all laughed.

"I bet Mother Wotherspoon's a dragon," Hagar thought to herself, remembering the laugh, as she hurried back with the parcels.

She found the girls in the kitchen with a huge fire on and the oven going. Beenie might not be a good cook, but she kept the flues clean, and although other parts of the house might leave much to be desired, her kitchen was speckless.

Hagar was too used to Yorkshire and country servants generally to worry about that; she knew that the kitchen came first with them, the kitchen and the brasses, and was always thankful there were people who thoroughly enjoyed cleaning and blackleading firesides, and thought their hands a second consideration to the shining grate, the twinkling brass, and the whitewashed hearth. The Falcon's House had none of the modern amenities of stainless taps and enamelled stoves and white tiles; but for all that Hagar liked it. It was what she had been used to in the old-fashioned manse.

Beenie, it appeared, had a friend in one of the houses down the yard who came from "Blackstone Edge way" like herself, and with whom she loved a gossip in her free time, so, hearing that her kitchen was to be filled with cake-makers, she'd "stepped down the wynd," as she called the yard, "to have a crack with Mistress Brearley."

Hagar, a born leader, soon had them all busy, for not only was she making scones and "fancies," but had started preparations for a Christmas cake—what she called "a keeping cake"—and had Penny and Perry busy stoning raisins, peeling almonds, and cutting up citron and lemon peel.

"Tell us about the Manse, High Wickering," said Marion. "Did you keep a cow?"

"Yes," said Hagar, "and we had ducks and geese and a pond and a sexton and a horse called Charlie," and she started to entertain them with tales of the Manse and her father, who had been quite an elderly man when she was born, and more like a staid, indulgent grandfather than a father to the small girl.

When she had finished a highly diverting tale about the sexton and his prize pig Rachel said, "Now it's our turn. What shall we tell you about?"

"The French hizzy," said Hagar at once. "She prejudiced Beenie against me; but I can't help thinking she might have been all right if allowances had been made for her being French. Did she make nice French dishes for you—what my father used to call 'kickshaws,' and that sort of thing?"

There was a pause, and then Marion said, "You tell her, Rachel."

Penny and Perry had departed to look for apples in the loft, so there were only the three of them in the kitchen.

"Oh," said Hagar at once, "please don't talk about her if you'd rather not. I didn't think she might be a person you didn't care to talk about. It was just Beenie calling her 'that French hizzy' that set me on about her—and I've never met a French woman. But let's talk about something else."

"No, let's tell her," said Marion. "She'll hear all about it sooner or later. You do it, Rachel."

"We liked her," said Rachel, and paused.

"I still like her," said Marion.

"Then you oughtn't," Rachel turned on her. "She stole Matthew from you."

"No, she didn't. Mat and I were just friends," returned Marion hotly. "And you know she is fascinating."

"She didn't fascinate me," said Rachel. "Well, are you going to tell Hagar or shall I?"

"I think you had better," Marion returned.

"All right. I'll begin from the beginning, and then it will be easier."

"Yes," said Marion, "and don't forget about *Helix pomatia*."

"What's that?" asked Hagar. "Is it French?"

"No, it's Latin," said Marion. "It means the edible snail." They both joined in with Hagar's ringing laugh.

"Come on. Tell me about the edible snail."

"Well, Mamma asked our father what she should give Mademoiselle for her supper on her first night, and Father said a dish of *Helix pomatia* would be suitable and economical, as, he had heard, the French Sisters—who were here before the present nuns—had introduced them into the convent garden. Perry overheard him, and went and looked up *Helix pomatia* in the encyclopædia, and then he and Penny and Robert Burns —our dog—raided the convent garden the night before she came——"

"And did they get any?"

"No, the nuns caught them, and sent Perry and Robbie home, but kept Penny as a hostage. The nuns said they'd gone into the garden to steal the fruit, and when Perry got home and told Father about the edible snails he said they were misbegotten devils, but he laughed so much he was nearly ill."

"And what about Penny?" asked Hagar.

"Well, you see, they'd found about twenty snails, but they didn't know if they were pure bred or mongrels or what, so Penny had put them in her pocket till Perry could look up the diagrams in the *Encyclopædia Britannica*. Father went for her, and was shown into a very cold, rigid sort of room, and a very tall, stern nun came—she was the Mother Superior—

who looked, Father said, as if she'd never once laughed in all her life.

"She said the children had been an annoyance to them for weeks—it was only days, but never mind—peering into the garden at all hours, and that they had known they were after the fruit, which was just ripe, so they'd kept a watch and caught them red-handed. Indeed, she was sure the little girl had some of the stolen fruit in her pocket, because she had kept her hand in it ever since they'd caught her, and screamed and kicked when they tried to take it out. Well, Father heard it all out, and then Penny was sent for.

"'Penny,' Father said, 'you will now lay on the table the fruit you have stolen from the convent garden.' Penny didn't want to, because it was a sworn secret between her and Perry, but Father said, 'I'll hand you over to your mamma for punishment if you don't.' She always beat us, you know. So Penny put her hand in her pocket and brought out twelve snails, one after the other, and all a little bit squashed, and laid them on the green baize table.

"'Helix pomatia,' said Father, when she'd finished. Then he looked at the Mother Superior and said, 'We have a French lady coming to the house, and rumours had got abroad that the ingredients of a favourite dish of the French were to be found in the convent garden—heirlooms from the late sisterhood. . . .'

"Well, he paused then, and suddenly the Mother Superior's face all broke up and she laughed and laughed. She knew all about Helix pomatia, and now she and Penny are great friends. She calls her 'the edible snail.' That's partly because Penny always crawls so slowly to school. She goes to the convent school now."

"And poor Mademoiselle never got her snails?" asked Hagar.

"No; but Marion looked up how to cook them in a French cookery book in the shop, and used a glass of prawns instead. Nobody liked them, so Father made Perry and Penny eat them as punishment for all the bother they'd given. Mamma was ill again then. Not that we were sorry about that. We were always glad when she had what Mademoiselle called 'the megrims,' and kept her room."

"I wonder you called her 'Mamma' when you disliked her so much," said Hagar.

"Father insisted," said Rachel. "He said when he'd gone to the trouble to provide a mother for us the least we could do was to call her Mamma. So we did it to oblige him."

"I think you are rather hard-hearted," said Hagar, "talking about megrims in that light way. After all, she must have been really ill, since she died in the end."

There was silence for a moment, then Marion said:

"But you see, Hagar, she didn't die. I mean not just like that. She killed herself."

"What!" exclaimed Hagar, completely aghast and staring at the girls.

"Yes, she did. She took an overdose of her sleeping draught. It was because of Mademoiselle."

Hagar said nothing. She just stood staring at the two girls in the darkening kitchen. She felt they were all on too dangerous and tragic ground for her to precipitate any more revelations by injudicious questions.

"She thought Father liked Mademoiselle," said Marion. "But——"

"Yes, I know what you are going to say—Mademoiselle married Matthew. Mamma said that was just because she had to leave the house and wanted to be near Father. It was a very sudden marriage. We all think Matthew was rushed into it. He's much younger than Naomi."

"I don't," said Marion quickly. "I don't think he was rushed into it." And Hagar saw that her face was very white.

"That's enough," she said now, quickly. "Here are Penny and Perry, and it's nearly four and the tea is set."

"But, Hagar," said Marion, "we want to talk about it

to some one. Let's talk about it to you some other time. You see——"

She paused, for Penny and Perry came into the kitchen shouting that they wanted their tea at once because they had important preparations to get on with for Christmas.

CHAPTER VI

"THE GOOSE IS GROWING FAT"

THURSDAY, it appeared, was usually a half-holiday in Breckan, but as Christmas was so near the shops were going to keep open.

"Are you Scots or English in Breckan?" Hagar asked them next morning at breakfast. "Do you keep Christmas Eve and Christmas or Hogmanay and New Year?"

"Both."

"All!"

A chorus of explanations arose that Breckan, being a Border town, was a mixter-maxter of Scots and English, and so both days were holidays and both were celebrated.

"But," added Penny dolefully, "we've never had a real Christmas or New Year since our own mother, Janie, died. Stepmothers don't hold with Christmas."

"They're beasts," said Perry, who instead of eating his porridge like a Christian was planning a series of fortifications and moats in his plate, the latter flooded with milk.

"Sup your porridge," said Marion, who was evidently used to Perry's military tactics. "Your drawbridge has broken down, and anyhow if you don't you'll grow up skinny and never be able to wear the kilt."

Perry had informed Hagar the night before that, whatever the rest of the family were, he was a Scot, and got his carroty head from the Red Douglases. His name was Peregrine

Douglas Peregrine, and he would like her to call him Douglas. Hagar tried, but it was a hopeless attempt. Perry could never really be anything but Perry.

"Well," she asked now, "what are we going to do about Christmas? It's time we were making plans."

"Let's have a real Christmas," said Penny. "Anthony is coming on Christmas Eve, and we'll ask Mark then too, and Luke and John can come next morning with Mother Wotherspoon. The Wotherspoons always give us a huge big turkey. They will be bringing it on Sunday when they come to tea."

This met with a chorus of general approval, but Hagar put in a word for authority.

"But what about your father? He may not want to have a big party to dinner, especially when you are in mourning."

"But we're not mourning——" began Penny, when Marion hushed her down, and then went on herself: "Oh, but Father will. He just loves filling the house with people, but our stepmother would never let him. They made her head ache, she said, especially the Wotherspoons. You'll see he'll be as pleased as anything."

Marion proved to be quite right. Mr Peregrine fell in at once with the idea of having Anthony Truett and Mark for Christmas Eve, and all the Wotherspoons to dinner. He was, as Hagar had already found out, a man who loved to talk, and the more there were to talk to the better he liked it; but he was a hospitable and generous soul as well, and liked keeping open house.

So after midday dinner preparations were at once afoot, for, as Hagar severely remarked, they had not made any of the preparations that should have been started *months* before. Everything had to be done within the next two or three days.

Rachel said that a meeting should be immediately called to discuss the question, and they all gathered in the little "boley-hole" up the stairs to write down lists of what was to be done, what was needed, and the different tasks to be allotted to each.

Marion was told off to do the shopping, Penny and Perry to go to a wood they knew of to bring in holly; Rachel was to finish her room in the turret, and Hagar to go over the cupboards and chests to count the dishes and the silver and linen herself, so as to become familiar with what they had in the house and to make any additions she might think necessary. They were all to meet at tea and after tea. The plum-puddings and the mincemeat were to be made in the kitchen, with all hands on deck, except Beenie, who was going out to a *soirée* in connexion with her church.

Hagar thoroughly enjoyed her afternoon. She loved going over cupboards and drawers and making lists, and the cupboards and chests in the Falcon's House were worth going over, for they were full of lovely things. When a family has been prosperous for a generation or two it gathers together a surprising quantity of stuff, and as Hagar counted the old French wine-glasses and rummers, the piles of yellowing napery, the fruit dishes and coffee cups, as she sorted out the silver in the canteen and the baize-lined drawers, and looked over the dinner-sets, the tea- and coffee-sets, the sets of porridge bowls and finger-bowls, she realized that here was not only an old family, but a family that a generation or two ago had been of large and generous size. An old dinner-set for eighteen looked as if it had been in careful use for years, and another old ironstone set, in glowing shades of plum and blue, had vegetable dishes that were more like large fruit dishes without lids than present-day vegetable dishes, all looking too, though the colours were unfaded, as though they had seen yeoman service.

By tea-time she had a fairly good idea of what most of the cupboards and chests contained; but she was tired of standing on her feet, and glad when Beenie thumped on the big brass gong to let them know that Mr Peregrine was in and the tea on the table.

D

It was pleasant in the big room with the French windows. Beenie, with her Yorkshire training, was generous with the fires, and the flames leapt and glistened in the polished steel of the grate. Through the French windows the snow-covered garden looked still and magical, with the moon rising over the whitened twigs of the apple-tree and glistening on the snow-laden branches of the cedar.

Penny and Perry had already returned with glowing cheeks and huge bundles of berried holly, some of which they had already wreathed round the gaselier over the table.

There were no small table-mats in the Falcon's House. The huge mahogany table was covered with gleaming white damask, and on it the coloured tea-set, the bright green butter-dishes like vine-leaves, the crystal dishes of scarlet jam, looked cheerful and gay, and Beenie's piled plates of toasted tea-cakes had each had a bit of berried holly stuck in them as if they were plum-puddings.

Hagar took the place that had been allotted to her, opposite Mr Peregrine and behind the group of teacups, and had lifted up the teapot before she noticed that the family had increased. At the far corner on her left a big, dark boy of sixteen or seventeen was seated. He looked shyly across at Hagar, and then stood up as Mr Peregrine introduced them.

"This is my seventh devil," said he, "Paul Turtleton. He doesn't look like a Turtleton outwardly, but, unfortunately, he has all their virtues. Paul, this is Miss Hagar Thorne."

Paul contented himself with a smile across at Hagar.

"No," she thought to herself, "he is not like the Peregrines. He's more solid and slower; but I like him." And as these thoughts passed through her mind she suddenly realized that she liked all this queer family, every member of which had a charm of his or her own, that she was glad she had come among them and felt already one of them. She longed to be accepted by them as one of themselves, to be identified with them.

"I feel already," she said to herself, "that the Falcon's House is my home. It's 'our' house, not 'their' house, and it's 'us,' not 'them,' in my heart. Oh, I do hope they are beginning to think of me like that."

And as if in answer to her thoughts, queer, sharp little Penny said, "You must like our Hagar, Paulie."

Again his eyes met hers, and he grinned his shy boy's grin, but said nothing.

"Paul and I will take our time to get acquainted with each other," said Hagar. "I'm a Yorkshire woman, and I can't be rushed." And she smiled her quick and awry smile at Paul.

"When will the Wotherspoons be coming on Sunday?" asked Marion.

"About three," said Paul. "Everybody's coming."

"Matthew too?" Marion flushed up scarlet.

"Oh, no," said Paul. "I mean everybody at Bowchester. Mother Wotherspoon too, and that beastly little kid Benjamine. He's going out there to-day."

"Don't you like Benjamine?" asked Hagar.

"No," said Paul.

"Young Benjamine is not always a favourite of the family," said Mr Peregrine.

"He's an only child and an awful little devil," explained Paul.

"Oh, he's just spoilt, I expect," said Hagar, who liked little boys.

"The only little boy I like," said Penny, in a superior voice, "is our Perry. I don't like all the rest."

"I'm not a little boy," said Perry.

"Yes, you are. I mean, you're not grown up."

"Yes, I am. I'm going to leave school soon."

"You are a red-headed, argumentative Scot," put in Mr Peregrine, who always took Penny's part, "and if you don't look out you'll grow into a haggis-eating Highlander in a kilt."

"Well, I'll like that," said Perry, who never forgot that his mother had been a Highland woman and that his real name was Peregrine Douglas Peregrine.

"So will I," said Penny, who would fight to the death with

Perry herself, but always flew to his side if he was attacked. "Can you make a haggis, Hagar? Beenie can't."

Hagar had to confess that she had never made a haggis, but added that she was willing to learn, whereupon Mr Peregrine gave them all a learned dissertation on the haggis, which continued till the last toasted tea-cake had disappeared. After tea they all repaired to the kitchen, where, after washing up the tea-things for Beenie, they started on the plum-pudding and mincemeat.

Everybody joined in, and though Mr Peregrine had departed through the snowy garden after tea to the shop, which was being kept open till late on these nights before Christmas, Penny announced that she was going to go for him and Anthony Truett and Miss Jenkins and Barty Lough to come and stir the pudding and wish a wish. Miss Jenkins, it appeared, was the librarian and head assistant, and Barty the message-boy, a particular favourite of Penny's.

"First we'll get the decks swept for action," announced Perry, who was being a sailor for the nonce, "and then pipe all hands aboard for the pudding."

Hagar was soon in her element. She loved cooking, especially cooking on a large scale and for a party.

In a twinkling she had donned a big cooking apron, and from her store had also arrayed her assistants in white aprons, Paul and Perry meekly lifting arms while she tied the strings round their chests.

"Overalls are all right," said she to the girls, "for housework, but I do like a clean white apron for cooking."

Perry immediately seized on the opportunity not only to be a cook, but to be the "head *chef* of the Waldorf-Astoria Hotel," and produced for himself a tall *chef's* cap made out of kitchen paper which so intrigued Penny that nothing would do but she must have a *chef's* cap too.

So it was a merry party of cooks and *chefs* that stoned raisins and chopped apples and peeled almonds and sliced up lemon peel and citron.

Paul decided to preside over the scales and do the weighing out, which, he said, needed a steady-going Turtleton and not a flighty Peregrine, who was as likely as not to mistake ounces for pounds and teaspoonfuls for cupfuls. In the intervals he would beat the eggs.

Penny decided to make the breadcrumbs on condition that she could have all the crusts for her birds, while Perry stoned the raisins on the understanding that he could eat one in twenty.

Hagar, looking at the solemn, red-headed Perry, religiously counting his twenty raisins, simply loved the young boy. She knew already that he would not eat a single raisin beyond the allotted number, and when there was any doubt the pudding, not himself, would be the gainer.

Penny she already adored, but everybody loved little, thin Penny with her quick, warm heart and her capacity for pain. Looking at her standing on a stool and struggling between her conscientious attitude to the pudding and her love for everything that could boast of a feather, as she examined the crusts and wondered if she might leave that small bit of white crumb for Peter, the robin, Jenny Wren, or Snowflake, the blackbird with a white feather in his wing, Hagar felt that she could leave her suet-chopping just to go and hug the small, thin match of a body in the big white apron.

"Oh," she thought quickly, "I hope there will always be somebody to love and take care of small, sweet Penny," and it was as if some fear had leaped out at her from the future telling her to guard little Penny.

But, if so, it was all forgotten the next moment, as she listened to the merry chatter and joined in the teasing that was going on.

Hagar presided over the two large clay dishes at the end of the table, in one of which were the contents for the pudding and the other the mincemeat. Paul at the other end weighed out and measured, advised Perry, and helped Penny to decide which was really crust and legitimate food for birds, and which was crumb.

"'Tell us exactly what you were doing last Christmas at this time," said Marion to Hagar, in a pause in the chatter, "and then we'll tell you exactly what we were doing."

This suggestion was greeted with a hail of enthusiasm, and Hagar, always willing to oblige, looked at the calendar, then at the clock, and started off:

"Last year at this time . . ." She paused.

"Don't tell us if it hurts you," said Penny quickly.

"Oh, no," said Hagar. "It's about Mrs Applethwaite and my father. You would have loved my father. He was six feet two and very broad, and he was always falling out with Mrs Applethwaite, who was our tiny housekeeper. She was very short and dark—just like a little black hen—and she had a mania for tidiness, and my father was very untidy. Just before Christmas Jenny Applethwaite and I were in the big Vicarage kitchen plucking the geese."

"Geese—did you have more than one goose?"

"Yes, we always had two—or three. You see, my father invited such a lot of people to come and have dinner with us, we were never sure how many there would be, so we had plenty of food."

"And did you have to take the feathers off yourselves? Didn't the poulterer sell them dressed?"

"No, there were no poulterers. We raised our own, and so we had everything to do."

"Yes—now go on—what was the kitchen like?"

"It had a stone floor and a huge range and a large hearthrug made out of old pink hunting-coats——"

"Oh, lovely!"

"And from the rafters there were sides of bacon hanging and bunches of dried sage and camomile flowers, and in the corner was the corner cupboard with the tea dishes, and against the wall the big white wooden dresser with the dinner dishes all arranged on the shelves, and in the corner Father's boot-jack and fishing-rods and hook for pulling on his hunting-boots, and in the middle of the floor the huge table scrubbed white with soap and sand—like the dresser—and then spread with newspapers to catch the feathers. We were each plucking a goose, and in front of us were huge piles of feathers. On the dresser were pots of newly made lemon curd waiting to be covered. Can you see it all?"

"Oh, yes—yes, Hagar, do go on."

"Well, it was a very stormy night, with a high wind blowing snow and hail over the moors, and Jenny Applethwaite had just been saying to me that she wouldn't be surprised if we were snowed up for Christmas, when the door opened and Father appeared. To get in Father had to open the door wide, for he was a big man. As he flung the door back to the wall a great gust of wind came thrashing over the moor and full into our kitchen. Up went the feathers, all over the place— it was like a snowstorm in the kitchen—and up went Jenny Applethwaite's temper. But there was some excuse for Jenny that time. Everywhere there were feathers. They stuck into the pots of lemon curd, they fell into our hair, into the stock-pot on the fire—they lay in clouds on the floor and over the chairs; but worst of all were Jenny and Father. Jenny had on a black woollen dress, and the white down stuck to it as if glued on, and Father's grey homespun suit was wet, and his beard and hair were wet, and the feathers all seemed to fly at him like iron filings to a magnet. He looked so funny with his beard all stuck with feathers that I laughed and laughed, and that made them both cross. Jenny ran from the lemon curd to the stock-pot, trying to keep off the feathers, and puffing and nagging like an angry little black hen, and Father stood trying to pick the feathers off his wet beard, and they stuck to his fingers, and then he tried to blow them off or wipe them off, and all the time he kept shouting—danging feathers and danging women and sending them all to Jericho."

"But he was a clergyman. Did he really get cross?"

"Bless you, yes, as cross as two sticks, but it was all over in a twinkling, and then he began to laugh, and we both laughed till we ached, but Jenny wouldn't see the funny side. She shooed us both out of the kitchen. Now you tell me what you were doing a year ago to-night."

There was silence for a moment, and then they all broke out, arguing about what happened, until Rachel suddenly said:

"I know what happened. That was the night our step-mother said that Naomi or Paulie had put something into her coffee and made it bitter—do you remember?" She turned to the others, and met with a chorus of assent.

"Tell Hagar about it, Rachel, and how Paul made her sick with the mustard."

"Our stepmother always hated Paulie," said Rachel, "because she said he had no right here, and should be sent to a home—didn't she, Paulie?"

"So I should," said Paul.

"Oh, no," another chorus rose at this. "You're our very own cousin, and a Turtleton, and this house is for Turtletons and Peregrines. Father says so. They all have a right here."

"But what about the coffee?" asked Hagar.

"Paulie was helping us to make the supper because Beenie was out, and Naomi—that was Mademoiselle—was so slow, and he carried in the coffee in big cups on a tray. All the saucers were set on the table, and we boiled the coffee with milk in a big pan, and then poured it into the cups on a tray, and Paul carried it in.

"Our stepmother took a drink of hers, and then she said it had a funny taste and that Paulie was trying to poison her. We were all mad with rage when she said that, and sat screaming at her—everybody was screaming, and she screamed back; but Paul suddenly jumped up and tasted the coffee, and then he flew to the kitchen and came back with a glass of warm water and mustard, and he said in a low, sepulchral voice to Mamma, 'Drink that or you may die,' and she got such a fright she drank it up, and was dreadfully sick. And Paulie said afterwards he just did it for fun—did you, Paulie?"

Paul had glanced at Hagar, and as he did so she realized that Paul was older than the others, not in years, but in his mind, for his glance held anxiety, as if he was wondering how she would take this story so frankly and guilelessly poured out by the others. But he only said, "Of course it was fun. I thought it would do her good to be sick—the old——" He paused.

"The old beast," said Perry.

"Hush!" said Hagar.

"But you see, Hagar," said Marion, "she really was what Perry says. She used to do such beastly, mean things. She knew Paul wouldn't complain, because he was so grateful to Father for taking him in, and so she used to try to starve him. She would give him all gristle and bone off the meat, and then she would say, 'There's not very much pudding—do you want any, Paul?' and of course Paul always said he wasn't hungry, and we found that he had only one blanket on his bed in the middle of winter, and—oh, lots and lots of things. You see, Paul never said anything. We just had to find out. And she did such cunning things. She hated us too, but not so much as Paul."

"But how unhappy you must all have been!" exclaimed Hagar suddenly.

"We were all miserable," said Rachel darkly. "*Miserable!* Right up till a few weeks before you came. Then Naomi went away, and our stepmother died, and things got better. We used to be happy before Father married her, and when she went out we would all get together and be a little bit happy then. Naomi too was nice then, but she hated our stepmother too. She always tried to send Naomi away, and she had nowhere to go."

"And you liked Naomi?"

There was silence for a moment; then Penny said:

"We used to like her, but then she got funny, didn't she, Perry? And we never knew when she was going to be angry; and then she married Matthew, and we couldn't love her after that—because Matthew was Marion's."

"He wasn't," said Marion, "and *I* still like Naomi."

"We've sent her to Coventry, anyhow," said Rachel. "But she doesn't want to come here any more."

And then they began to argue about whether Naomi stayed away because she didn't want to come or because they had sent her, as Rachel said, to Coventry.

In the midst of all this talk, which had been continually interrupted with questions about weighing out ingredients for the puddings and the mincemeat, the stirring stage was arrived at, and Penny flew off to bring in Anthony Truett and Miss Jenkins, Barty Lough, and various other assistants from the shop to stir the pudding and wish a wish. Even Mr Peregrine had to come, and entertained them all by telling a gruesome story about three wishes that were fulfilled which produced such delicious thrills of horror in Penny and Perry that he had to promise to tell them ghost stories on Christmas Eve.

CHAPTER VII

"HERE'S RUE FOR YOU"

OH, what fun!" exclaimed Marion and Rachel to a suggestion from Penny. "Yes, let's have Anthony to tea. You know, we terrify him by making him think we agree with Father that he has to marry one of us, like the industrious apprentice always does; but we like Anthony."

"I love him," said Penny. "He can marry me if he likes."

"You're too young," said Rachel. "Why, goodness! Anthony must be twenty-eight or thirty."

"I don't care," said Penny. "I like him just as he is."

"But he won't stay as he is," said Marion. "By the time you are twenty he'll be quite old—nearly forty."

"No, he won't," said Penny, who always defied the inevitable with vigour and conviction. "I won't let him."

"That's the spirit," said Hagar cheerfully. "Now let's have

the second best tea-set out—the one with buttercups. It will go nicely with the sprigs of winter jasmine, and I'll put some yellow icing on these little cakes."

"That's not the second best," said Marion. "The second best is the Crown Derby, with the blue sprigs and the gold bands and the queer little birds, and the very best is the green Rockingham, but we only use it for weddings or great family affairs."

"Well, we'll have the buttercups," said Hagar, "and we'll put yellow candles in the old Sheffield plate candlesticks with the three branches. I saw some yellow candles in the grocer's, just old white wax ones, but they looked yellow. Penny can slip over for them." She got out her money and gave Penny, who was already dancing with excitement, sixpence, and she flew off for the candles.

Marion turned and gave Hagar a hug. "Oh, I do like you, Hagar," she said. "It's so lovely to have somebody with the party spirit. Mamma would never let us have parties and put out our pretty things. Naomi used to want to, but she wouldn't let her. Naomi and Mamma were always quarrelling."

Rachel had left the kitchen and flown off to set the tea. The snowy December afternoon was darkening, and there was only the firelight in the kitchen.

"Perhaps your Mamma didn't feel well enough," said Hagar, opening the oven-door to take out the last batch of small cakes, and shutting it again on the huge Christmas cake, which was to bake slowly for hours.

Marion was silent for a moment. Then she came and put her arm round Hagar, watching her as she began to ice cakes that had already cooled off.

"Hagar," she said, "you won't believe any stories you hear about Naomi, will you?"

"What kind of stories?" asked Hagar, pausing with the icing bag in her hand. She felt something mysterious behind Marion's words, and wished she knew more than she did. She felt that of all in the house Marion was the most likely

to talk to her. Rachel was too self-contained, and Perry and
Penny too young, while she could not conceive of Mr Peregrine
confiding in her. Yet if she was to be one of them and help
them it would be better for her to know all that was troubling
them, for that they were troubled she could feel. There was
something in the very atmosphere of the house that was dark
with secrets.

"I'd like to tell you, Hagar. I'd like to tell you all about it,
though Rachel said we were never to tell you. But that was
before we knew you. I think she wouldn't mind now—now
we can trust you."

"Yes, you can trust me," said Hagar. "I feel already that
I'm needed here, that I'm going to be one of you, part of the
family, and that your troubles will be my troubles too."

"Yes, that's what I feel; and you're so—so *steady*, Hagar,
as if you had come through things and they hadn't downed
you."

"Yes, some day I'll tell you about that too."

They could hear Rachel getting the teacups out of the
cupboard, and in the distance the garden door banging as
Penny sped back with the candles.

"But we've no time just now," she went on. "We must
wait for a quiet hour together, and then you can tell me
what I'm not to believe about Mademoiselle Cuendet—Mrs
Wotherspoon, I should say."

"Yes, I just wanted to say something before Beenie begins
talking. She hated Naomi. Her name was Nahomi Cuendet.
She spells it with an 'h.' But she is Mrs Wotherspoon, of
course, now she has married Matthew."

Hagar looked at her. There was something in her voice that
caught her attention. It wasn't just stating a fact—or, rather, it
was just stating a fact, but very carefully, with no expression
—too carefully.

Just then the door burst open, letting a gust of frosty
air sweep into the kitchen, and Penny danced in with her
six candles.

"Do let me put them in," she said, breathless with her run, her little nose pink from the frosty air. "Let me put them in and light them. Anthony is coming. Father said he had to, and he's coming for *all* Christmas Day. Oh, Hagar, couldn't we ask him to come on Christmas Eve and stay all night? He just lives in lodgings, and Miss Gunter—we call her 'Miss Grunter'—is a real mean woman. Beenie says she'd skin a louse for its tallow."

"*Taisez-vous*," said Marion. It was evident they'd picked up some French phrases from Mademoiselle. "You're not to repeat Beenie's low sayings."

"Well, I won't if you'll ask Anthony to come on Christmas Eve—I promised faithfully, Marion."

"All right, I don't mind," said Marion, "but we must ask Hagar."

"And your father," said Hagar.

"What is that?" asked Rachel, coming in. "Oh, what fun!" she immediately exclaimed on hearing Penny's proposal. "But we must ask somebody else too. Let's ask Mark, as we said before."

"Mark's so sulky," said Marion. "I'd rather have Luke and John."

"Luke and John can't come. They always go to their old granny's with their mother on Christmas Eve; but Mark won't go because she told them all if they didn't come oftener to see her they'd get none of her money. Mark has never gone back."

"You shouldn't chatter so much, Penny," said Rachel. "It's not good manners to talk about other people's private affairs."

"But Luke and John told me," said Penny. "They just laughed; they didn't say it was a secret. They said they went, and Mark was just *silly*."

"Well if you go on chattering your visitor will be here before the tea's ready. Get the candles lit, Penny and you finish the table, Rachel, while Marion toasts the tea-cakes. Oh, sakes! I hope there's enough butter. We've used such a lot for the cakes! I'll go round and light the lamps."

"The gas, you mean," cried Penny, as they all sped off on their duties. "It *is funny* to hear you talking of lamps, Hagar."

"Doesn't it look pretty?" said Penny, surveying the table as Hagar went in to see to the finishing touches. "Oh, I do hope Anthony will like it!"

Thin little Penny herself was looking her very plainest, if ever that piquant little face could be called plain. Her fair hair had been wetted and dragged back off her forehead, showing the comb marks, but leaving a soft little silvery fringe of down where the roots of the hair left her brow. It was plaited into a short, hard little plait and tied with a red ribbon. Her cheeks and little nose were pink from a scrubbing with Sunlight soap, and the gap where her tooth had been made her lisp slightly. Luckily that would soon fill up, as it had been a sort of extra tooth squeezed in, or perhaps left over from her first teeth. Her mouth, however, with its very short upper lip, was irresistible. Never to her old age could Penny be plain with a mouth like that; even the absent tooth could not spoil its charm. Her dark blue eyes were too big still for her face, and in the candle-light looked darker still under the long, straight lashes.

The table looked attractive and welcoming with its branched candlesticks and yellowish candles, the twigs of jasmine in glasses which showed the stalks, the green and yellow cups and saucers, and the hurriedly iced cakes, all set off by the large window behind showing the snow-covered garden, the rime-lined branches of the apple-tree, the gleaming grey sky with its touch of silver, and the new moon rising over the cedar.

As they looked out the little green door opened and Mr Peregrine—like a blackbeetle, thought Hagar, walking on its hindmost legs—came through, followed by the tall, slightly stooping figure of Anthony.

Penny flew to the French window and began hopping in her slippers across the crisp snow. Hagar called her to come back, but in vain; but Anthony, seeing her, strode off in front of her father, and, putting his hands under her arms, swung her in a couple of long swoops over the snow into the candle-lit room, where she hung on his arm, pointing out all the beauties of the table.

"Well, well!" said Mr Peregrine, surveying it with his hands behind him, under his black coat, flapping the tails up and down. "Quite a party; but where are the guests?"

"You and Anthony are the guests," said Penny. "We did it all for you. You mustn't eat that yellow cake with the walnut on it, Anthony, because it's my particular cake. Hagar said so."

But Anthony had turned shy now and only smiled. Hagar, glancing at his slight dark face in the shadowy candle-light, thought he looked more than ever like an escape out of the eighteenth century.

"I wonder why he wears those slight dark lines at the side of his face," she thought. "They make him look older. He can't be more than twenty-six, now I see him closer."

She was relieved from all conjecture, however, by Penny, who now paused on an assault of the walnut cake to ask, point-blank, "How old are you, Anthony?"

He looked across the table, smiling at her, hesitated, and then said, "Twenty-three."

They all started in surprise. Even Mr Peregrine glanced with raised eyebrows in the direction of his assistant.

Penny had licked her fingers and was now counting on them.

"That's eleven years older than me. You were eleven years old when I was born, Anthony."

"Yes, and I felt grown up then," he said, "when you were a baby, Penny. I'll soon be an old man."

"It's because you wear these funny little sideboards," she announced. "Why do you? Do you like them?"

He glanced across at Mr Peregrine. "I had to look older," he said, "to get a job."

"Bless my soul!" said Mr Peregrine. "I thought you were twenty-eight or thirty. I've a good mind to send you packing." But his small brown eyes were twinkling with fun.

"Oh, but you couldn't do without him," said Penny anxiously. "You know you couldn't. I've often heard you say you couldn't carry on without Anthony. Hasn't he, Marion and Rachel?"

"That's enough of the secrets of my prison-house," said her father. "He'll be asking for a rise in order to get married if we're not careful."

"Oh, no, he's going to wait for me, aren't you, Anthony? You know you said you would when I asked you."

Anthony smiled across at her, his dark eyes serious, his mouth closed, as Marion quickly put in:

"That's no way to talk, Penny. You are just a child. Anthony will be married long before you are grown up."

To Hagar's complete surprise—she had been pouring out the tea and fully occupied, so that she had been only half listening—the tears suddenly sprang into Penny's eyes.

"He won't! He won't!" she cried. Then she rose from her place, and, running round behind Anthony, climbed on the rung of his chair and put her arms round his neck.

"You won't, won't you not, Anthony? You'll wait for me, won't you? You promised; you know you did."

"Of course I'll wait," said Anthony. "But don't hang me. I'll be one of those hundred and fifty beaux you told me about."

"This is most embarrassing, Anthony," said Mr Peregrine now, still twinkling. "Another case of the hawk and the turtle-dove, with my daughter, I regret to say, in the rôle of the hawk."

But Hagar thought it was quite time she put her oar in. Anthony Truett did not look the least embarrassed. His glance at her was a little inquiring and queerly sad, she thought, but not at all confused as he took Penny's hands and gently loosened them from round his neck; but she sensed an appeal in it.

"If I were you I'd have my tea, Penny," she said mildly, but with a slight hint of authority in her voice. "You know we have the mince-pies to make."

"And that's much more important than your marriage," said Perry, who had been silently and diligently sampling all the cakes. "Anyhow, nobody's going to run away with Anthony. He isn't a ladies' man."

Both Marion and Rachel rose to this sweeping accusation.

"How do you know?" asked Marion indignantly. "Anthony would be quite nice-looking if he'd shave off those silly little black lines at the sides of his cheeks."

"Anthony doesn't like women," said Rachel. "He's what they call a misogynist—aren't you, Anthony?"

"So am I a misogynist," announced Penny solemnly, and at that they all went into peals of laughter, and tea proceeded amidst fun and jokes.

But Hagar, watching Penny, was not too easy about her.

"I hope that Anthony Truett knows what he is about," she thought to herself. "Penny is so childishly serious and would be so easily hurt. She's made of that fine clay that is so easily marred and broken."

She watched the little scene that was going on now. Anthony Truett was standing by the mantelpiece, leaning down a little and smiling at Penny, who, shadowy and pale in the candle-light, with her hair escaped from its tight plait and sprayed out round her head in a silver shine, which, caught by the firelight, made her look like a little taper herself, was standing on a stool measuring her inches against his slender height.

"Look, Anthony! I've only to grow the height of the stool to be up to your shoulder. Will that be big enough for you?"

He did not answer; he lifted her down with his mouth very tight and his eyes grave. Then, as she looked up, he smiled very gently down at her.

E

"I think that should do, Penny. Could you manage it in ten years, do you think?"

"Ten years! Oh, Anthony, what a long time for you to wait."

"Oh, but I'm good at waiting."

"And then what shall we do?"

"I'll stand at the crossroads, Penny, and wave to you as you pass me by."

CHAPTER VIII

"WHEN DICK THE SHEPHERD BLOWS HIS NAIL"

ON Saturday, market-day at Breckan, John Wotherspoon, in town with a half-score of beasts, brought a message from his mother that since Bowchester was coming to the Falcon's House on Christmas Day the Falcon's House must go to Bowchester for tea on Sunday.

Bowchester (the Camp of the Bowmen, pronounced "Bowcassel") was the farm of the Wotherspoons. The farmer had always been called "Bowcassel" in accordance with Border custom. Matthew, who had quarrelled with his mother when he had suddenly married Naomi and, taking the little money he had, gone to a small sheep-farm in the hills named Goslaw (Goose Law—the Hill of Wild Geese) with his bride, was called "Goslaw," and Mark Wotherspoon, who farmed the place for his mother, was called "Bowcassel" by the farming fraternity. The twin sons, Luke and John, were also employed on the farm, which was a big place, and a great deal of quarrelling went on, as Hagar was to learn, because the two younger men had been at an agricultural college and wished to introduce new methods and run the farm solely to make money.

Mark hated this. He loved the farm passionately. It had been in the family for ages. They even claimed that the

Wotherspoons had been the original bowmen of the camp and they still practised archery in their spare time. Although the farm belonged to Mrs Wotherspoon for life, it would pass on to the eldest living son at her death, so she could not leave it to her younger sons, though she adored her twin sons, and was heart and soul with them in all their new ideas. She had come from a money-loving Yorkshire family, and had none of Mark's sentiment about the place, but would have ruthlessly ploughed up old pasture-lands to grow potatoes, cut down the old woods and spinneys, and rooted out the flowers that spread themselves by the stream or clothed the bits of marsh and fenland where Mark loved to take his gun for snipe or wild duck or passing wildfowl.

Mark had accepted the invitation for Christmas Eve, since his maternal grandmother, who had retired on her widowhood to a house in Breckan, was something of an old miser, and also now on the side of the twins. Old Mrs Waugh had thought to tame Mark by threatening to leave him out of her will, showing thereby how little she understood him, for Mark had never gone to her house since she had voiced her threat, and would otherwise have spent the evening alone at Bowchester. Not that he would have minded that, but he liked Mr Peregrine and all the family at the Falcon's House, and had been deeply hurt when Matthew had married Naomi. They had all thought that Marion would be Matthew's choice. Unlike his mother and brothers, however, Mark still saw a good deal of Matthew, and the two were in absolute sympathy about the farm.

Hagar had gathered a little of all this before they started on the Sunday drive to the farm, for this was in the days before the War, and motor-cars were a luxury only for the very rich. The Peregrines drove out to Bowchester in a wagonette, carrying two in front and six behind. Mr Peregrine was no horseman, so Anthony, who seemed always at hand, had been called in to manage the pair of heavy carriage-horses. Anthony's father had been a wealthy squire, who, instead of looking after his estate, had spent all his time in the library studying the Greek classics. When Anthony was seventeen years old his father had gone bankrupt and then died. Everything had been sold over their heads, and he and his two sisters thrown on the world to earn their living. One of the girls had married and gone out to Africa, taking her sister with her, and Anthony had grown sideboards and obtained—on the strength of them, Mr Peregrine declared—a post as assistant with Peregrine and Turtleton, Booksellers and Printers. No doubt he had inherited his father's bookish tastes, for he had been an entire success, and was practically at the head of the firm—at least, so Mr Peregrine frequently declared, saying that he himself was only the nominal head. As a matter of fact, his was the business mind, while Anthony ran all the other side of the huge affair.

Perry was destined to follow his father, so there was no real chance of Anthony ever being the head of the firm; but he seemed quite content to carry on as he was in his quiet, retiring way.

Whenever a hitch occurred in the Peregrine family Anthony was called in, and Anthony always seemed ready to be at their beck and call.

He had been brought up with horses, and had ridden and driven and hunted until the *débâcle* in his father's affairs, so the management of two staid, fat carriage-horses, while presenting insuperable difficulties to Mr Peregrine, in no wise disturbed Anthony. He picked up the empty vehicle at the inn, and drove round in style to the front door of the Falcon's House, wearing a grey topper—which had belonged to his father— and looking more than ever as if he had stepped out of the eighteenth century—or so Hagar thought.

He climbed down, helped Mr Peregrine to the front seat, and the ladies in behind, swinging Penny up to sit bodkin between himself and her father, and stowing Robert Burns— Robbie, the dog—to balance things at the back, where the rest sat facing one another, Hagar, Marion, and Rachel at one side, Paulie, Perry, and Robbie, and a present of a basket of fruit and sweets at the other.

Then Anthony picked up the whip, and with a flourish they were off, bowling along the deserted Highgate and over the bridge into the country beyond.

A thin coating of snow still lay over the countryside. There had been frost the night before, and trees and hedges were covered with rime. There was cat-ice in the ruts along the road, which Mr Peregrine called "the turnpike," and thin ice on the pools and farm ponds which they passed on their journey.

Hagar loved it all—the snell air in which the horses' breath made clouds of frozen steam, the stiff white grasses at the verge of the road, the black rooks in the elms, the robin's red breast in the frozen thorn, the clear blue sky, the sheep in their wattled enclosures, looking yellow against the snow, the quacking ducks crowded in a pond where the water was dark and free from ice under the bending willows.

Rachel talked more than usual, telling Hagar stories about the places they passed, pointing out the Bride's Brae, where the newly made bride, riding behind her bridegroom, was thrown from the horse and killed; the long row of trees where all the men of a village had died of the plague and been buried on a ridge in the fields, a tree above every grave.

"And they were all cobblers," said Penny.

Hagar laughed, but Anthony assured her it was true. Every Border village in those days, as they often are to-day, was famed for one particular trade—bootmakers in one village, tailors in another, fly-making for fishing in another, and violins in another. Many years after this Hagar was pleased when a Border village, pointed out to her long before by Rachel as famous for its gardens and gardeners, won the first prize for sweet-peas in a competition for all Britain promoted by a famous London daily.

But they did not pass the gardening village that day, which lay on the other side of the river.

It was a long drive, but at last Penny jumped up and pointed out a high chimney.

"There's the chimney of the threshing-mill at Bowchester," she cried, and they turned off the road to bowl down a narrow lane which led to the entrance.

As they passed a little three-cornered spinney the old farm-house came into view, built of weathered red bricks with slated roof, in which stonecrops grew. It was a picturesque and ancient house, and Hagar felt at once a warm sympathy with Mark, who wanted to keep it as it was, and had played hell with his brothers, who had been keen to take away the old ha-ha and increase the size of the front garden by sloping it down to the stream, and stick an excrescence on at the side of the house in the shape of a garage, with a bathroom on top. A garage and bathroom had been managed at the back, and were the source of constant grumbling, because of some slight inconvenience, but the beautiful lines of the house were left and the wavering dip of the roof; steps had been made down from the old ha-ha, and the wall, filled with old-fashioned wall plants, remained. You could sit in the sun there, sheltered from the wind, and watch the tennis players on the new court.

"Oh, what a lovely house!" said Hagar. "I wouldn't let anyone alter a line of it if it were mine. It looks as if it had grown there and *belonged*."

"Yes," said Marion, "and Luke and John wanted to put up a sort of 'ye olde English' garage building at the side and take away the ha-ha, and lay out the grounds with sundials and lily-pools and rose-pergolas, and Mother Wotherspoon was all on their side. She has no sense."

"Yes, she has," said Rachel. "She's what you call a pushing, sensible woman; but she has a lot of the wrong kind of sense, and so have John and Luke. Yet to look at them you'd say they had all the poetry and that sort of thing in them, and Mark was the staid, dour, commonsensical Northumbrian."

As she spoke they turned in at the open gates of a grass-bordered drive with immense old trees on it, and stopped in front of the house as two laughing young men came out to welcome them.

"Ahoy, Anthony!" they shouted. "Where did you get that hat?" and began to sing in charming light tenors, "Where did you get that hat?"

A stout woman came bustling up behind them, whom Hagar at once recognized as Mother Wotherspoon from the girls' description, and began to scold her sons for singing comic songs on Sunday and hospitably to welcome her guests.

She was a tall, handsome woman, broad and stout in contrast to her slender sons, who were only of medium height. She wore a black serge dress with a cream satin front, and her thick grey hair was parted in the middle above her broad, weather-beaten face; instead of slippers she wore fine elastic-sided boots, and on her wrists she had black knitted cuffs with bright steel beads ornamenting them.

She greeted the girls warmly, and gazed quizzically at Hagar as she shook hands with her.

"I hear you're a Yorkshire woman too," she said, "but, my certes, you don't look it! We run to beef and brawn in Yorkshire."

Hagar laughed, putting her two fingers nervously up to her mouth.

"What's happened your face?" said the forthright woman immediately. "Ye look as if ye'd been in the wars."

CHAPTER IX

"EIN FICHTENBAUM STEHT EINSAM"

AT that moment a tall, broad man came out, and you saw at once that if Mrs Wotherspoon had not given her character and temperament to her eldest son she had certainly presented him with her looks. There was no mistaking them for mother and son—the same bigness and breadth, though he overtopped her by inches, the same long, weatherbeaten face, the same thick hair, but in his case dark and untidy-looking beside her neat parting and plaits and his brothers' smooth, varnished heads.

He saw Hagar standing, slight and pale, the dark, wind-blown fringe partly hiding the scar on her forehead, but the healed line at the corner of her mouth standing out pink as it always did when sudden nervousness distressed her. She did not blush at such times—she became if anything paler; but all the lines of her scars deepened and stood out red on her ivory skin.

He thought her, standing there with the deep red mouth in the creamy face, the dark, wind-blown hair, the brown, suffering eyes and shrinking mien, as she tried to hide the scarred cheek with her thin brown fingers, the most witching and lovely thing he had ever seen, and at once spoke out before she could answer.

"Mother," he said, "they are all freezing with cold. You take them in, and I'll go round to the stables with Anthony."

Mother Wotherspoon's hospitable heart was at once all eager to comfort and warm her guests. She left the subject of Hagar's scars, and hustled them all upstairs to a huge bedroom with a glowing fire to take off the outdoor wraps in which they were muffled; then led the way, talking all the time, downstairs to the dining-room, where tea was laid on the shining damask of the great mahogany table, and Luke and John were waiting for them, ready to laugh with and tease the girls and Perry, and eager to put Robbie—clasped tightly in Penny's arms—through his tricks.

Robbie was a Scottie with bright brown intelligent eyes and a flair for the tricks which Penny had patiently taught him.

"Make him say his ABC, Penny," they demanded, clustering round, while Mother Wotherspoon hustled off to hurry in the tea. The small boy, Benjie, now crept out from under the sofa where he had hidden to pinch the girls' ankles, till the suggestion of Robbie's tricks was too much for him and brought him out. He shook hands with a grubby paw, and then shouted, dancing with excitement, "Make him do his tricks, Penny! Make him do his tricks!"

"No," said Penny to the boy. "He's shy, and he doesn't like boys except Perry; but he'll do them after tea. He likes strong tea with cream and sugar in it."

"He likes me," shouted Benjie. "He *must* like me."

"No animals like you, Benjamine," said a deep voice, as Mark came in with Anthony and Paul. "You tease them too much."

"But I won't tease him. I won't pull his tail. Let me give him his tea, Penny, and then he'll like me."

"Penny must give him his tea herself," said Anthony. "She knows how he likes it. Besides, you teased him before at the Falcon's House, and dogs always remember."

At Mark's heels a bull-terrier bitch had walked in, and now there was a diversion as Robbie set up a shattering series of barks and growls, though Sally, at a word from her master, had lain down with calm dignity, head on her forepaws and an expression that clearly said, "That yelping morsel of shaggy wool is beneath my notice."

"Oh!" Hagar exclaimed at once on seeing the bitch. "A bull-terrier! We always had a bull-terrier at home."

Mark looked at her. "Then you like the breed?" he said, stooping to wind a finger round Sally's ear.

"Oh, yes." She paused. "I wished so that I could bring Shadow with me when I came to Breckan."

"Why didn't you?" asked Penny at once. "We should have loved him."

"He was too old and set in his ways. He had had his own snug bed and his own arm-chair in the chimney-corner for twelve years. He couldn't have settled in a strange place. Old Sam Morton, the vet, said he'd break his heart and die. It was kinder to put him down. He'd moped, anyhow, since Father died."

"You had him put down?"

Hagar nodded. She didn't like to speak about that.

"There's no dog like a bull-terrier," said Mark quickly. "Once a bull-terrier has got you, you're spoiled for other dogs—eh, Sally?"

"It makes me like Sally just to look at her," said Hagar, recovering herself. "Shadow was white too, but with a black patch over one eye."

Sally turned her back and curled herself up against Mark's boot. Sally, it must be confessed, was, like most bull-terriers, a one-man dog, and took not the slightest notice of anyone else, whatever their blandishments. Robbie, on the other hand, though Penny came first, was a friendly soul, and ready to be pally with anyone who took notice of him, though he'd only do his clever 'tricks' for his small mistress. Every one loved amusing Robbie—he was irresistible; but only Mark adored Sally and knew her matchless worth. Sally never showed off. She had no tricks, but she read Mark's every thought, did the most amazing and wonderful things as occasion arose, was utterly without fear, and when she turned and showed fight was unconquerable. Since only death would have made her give in, or, rather, beaten her, she did not know what it was to give in. She never bit, yet she was the terror of tramps or evildoers. The hair rising along her spine and her deep, warning growl was enough to keep them paralysed with fright, while she stood within a yard or two, daring them to move until Mark appeared.

Mark had told her in one curt word that she was not to interfere with Robbie, and nothing would make her interfere with him. She would walk away or retire under the sofa if the other dog teased her, or, driven to extremities, would give a warning growl or a snap with her sharp teeth. That was enough for any dog.

Tea was a real Northumbrian farmhouse tea, with toasted muffins and tea-cakes, hot scones off the girdle, home-made bread and butter, with jugs of rich cream, and plum cake and custard pies, jams, jellies, and preserves; a ham was on the sideboard for those who wanted it, and a silver stand with little hanging pails of brown eggs. Penny always had an egg for the delight of lifting the little pail by the handle from which it swung and eating it with a little silver spade for a spoon. She would have loved a little silver pail and spade of her own, but, alas! there was just the set of twelve and Mother Wotherspoon could not break the set. Anthony haunted the antique shops of Breckan to try to find one for her, but had never been successful; and on Easter Sunday Mother Wotherspoon always sent her a dozen eggs and a little pail and spade to eat them with, which had to be duly and carefully returned when the last egg had vanished.

Hagar, amid the general noise at the big table, soon lost her shyness. As the stranger and honoured guest, she was put on Mark's right hand, where he sat at the foot of the table and looked after her with shy carefulness. They were instantly aware of each other, but Mark was much too shy and Hagar much too engrossed with other things to realize it. They talked about bull-terriers, and she wondered why the girls called this big, shy man dour and ill-natured, and, seeing Rachel glance at him once or twice with a curiously intent look, wondered if she were secretly in love with him.

As for thinking of love in connexion with herself, such a thing would never have entered Hagar's mind. She had been too deeply hurt in her young love to recover. This vessel that the potter had marred would not easily be made into another vessel. Her broken face and heart would always show their healed wounds. Perhaps she was too sensitive of her scarred face, but the shock of seeing it swollen and ugly and criss-crossed with hideous stitched lines had left her for ever conscious of it. She could not see it as it was now, and, in fact, always avoided mirrors if she could, so it was always an effort to her to meet strangers.

Mrs Wotherspoon did not help matters, for no sooner was

tea over than she drew Hagar aside and began asking again what had happened to her face.

It was nothing but kindly curiosity, and Hagar realized that as she drew her shrinking thoughts together and satisfied the inquisitiveness that was like salt on raw wounds, for she could not bear to talk of the accident, and was always terrified that she would be seized again with one of the terrible bouts of weeping that for long had been a nightmare to her, since at first they had broken the wounds and earned her such grim scoldings from the doctor and such frightful self-torture, because her old father had more than once broken down and wept too, with the hard and terrible sobbing of the old and strong.

"I was thrown from a dogcart," she told Mrs Wotherspoon. "and caught my face on the breeching of the harness, which had brass ornaments on for the horse fair; then I struck a stone dyke as the horse fell, and we rolled over together, and I got stones and sand in the open wounds. That is how the scars are so bad."

"Good gracious, lassie! How old were ye?"

"Nineteen."

"Were you driving yourself?"

She shook her head.

She never told her or anyone that her father, an abstemious man, had had a glass at the fair which had been too much for him and made him unfit to drive the spirited beast, already nervous with the trappings on its harness.

"No," she said, "some one else was driving. Perhaps it would have been better if I had had the reins to hold on to; but it is all so long ago, and I don't really remember much about it, because I was unconscious for a long time afterwards."

At that moment Mark came into the room, and saw Hagar sitting upright, her face white, with the lines of her scars showing red, and, knowing his mother's insatiable curiosity and inquisitorial ways, at once came to her assistance.

"Would you like to see the horses?" he asked, then flushed,

though it was hardly discernible on his brown skin, thinking
perhaps she did not like horses since her accident. "Or the
cows?" he added rather lamely, then remembered with relief
the garden. "The Christmas roses are out," he said quickly.
"Would you like some to take home?"

"Oh, yes, I'd love them," said Hagar, relieved to get away
from Mother Wotherspoon's questions. "There are two out
at the Falcon's House, but that's not enough for a bowl, and
they would be lovely for Christmas."

"Ours are always earlier than the Falcon's House ones,"
he said. "We'll get a basket in the hall."

Once he got her away, however, he had not much to say.
It was Hagar who did most of the talking, telling him stories
about her beloved Shadow, how she missed him, about their
garden at the Yorkshire vicarage, and from that on to the
cows and pigs, the horses and the collies, the geese and turkeys
and hens they kept, and, finding his silence and occasional
remarks full of sympathy and understanding, went on to
describe her father, half farmer and half vicar of his parish,
with an inborn love of farming, hunting, and shooting that
his calling could never entirely eradicate.

"Do you like farms too?" he asked. "And the country?"

"Yes, I can't help it," said Hagar. "It's born in me.
Especially old-fashioned farms like this," she continued innocently, forgetting for the moment the remarks she had heard
about his brothers' up-to-date methods. "And I like old-
fashioned gardens too, where things are left alone a little, like
here and at the Falcon's House."

He had gathered twenty or thirty blooms of the Christmas
roses for her by this time. As he put them in her basket he
smiled down at her.

"I like the old ways best too," he said. "Thee and me
would get on, Hagar."

He had smilingly used the old Yorkshire and Northumbrian
way of speaking, and she laughed back.

"Sure-ly," she grinned shyly, the fingers going up to her

mouth and pronouncing the word in the Yorkshire way, "sure-ly."

Then Penny came running up to join them and to ask for some roses for Anthony.

"His housekeeper never puts flowers in his room," she said, "so I give him some every week."

They had a happy evening. Discovering that Hagar was an adept at a quaint harmonium in the house, having played one at the choir practices at home, where she had been organist, and choir-master, and Sunday-school mistress, and everything else except vicar and sexton perhaps, but even ringing the bell or tolling it on occasion, they soon got her on to play while they all sang lustily the hymns that Mother Wotherspoon would only allow on Sundays. Marion had a lovely voice. Hagar also sang, while Rachel joined in with a deep contralto and Penny a sweet childish treble.

To end up Anthony sat at the piano with Penny on his knee, and they sang *In the Sweet By-and-by* together as a part-song. But Rachel wasn't pleased at that.

"That's Matthew's and Marion's hymn," she said to Anthony. "Nobody can sing it like Matthew and Marion. You and Penny can't."

"No," said Anthony, a little distressed, "of course we can't. Penny and I will have to find another hymn we can sing in parts."

"I'll sing you the *Robin's Song*," said Penny at once, always willing to oblige, but Mrs Wotherspoon would have none of the *Robin's Song*.

"Only songs in praise of the Lord in this house on the Sabbath day," she said severely, and then supper was announced, and after a hearty meal of cold chicken and one of Mother Wotherspoon's famous pressed tongues they all climbed merrily into the wagonette and started home through the moonlit, snowy fields.

"Did you enjoy it, Hagar?" asked Marion.

"Every minute," said Hagar heartily.

"Mark likes you," said Marion. "He hardly ever speaks to anyone, and he actually gathered Christmas roses for you. How did you like Mother Wother?"

Now that Hagar was one of the family they were dropping the "Mother Wotherspoon" for the "Mother Wother" they familiarly used among themselves.

"I think she is very kind," said Hagar, "but I'm a little afraid of her."

"You're not the only one," they chorused, and then Penny's small voice chimed in:

"I believe in taking bulls by the horns," said she. "Don't you, Anthony?"

"I do not," said Anthony. "I believe in taking to my heels."

Anthony, indeed, had been very quiet all the afternoon—but then Anthony was always quiet.

CHAPTER X

"LET HOLLY HAVE THE MAISTERIE"

GREAT preparations went forward for Christmas. It seemed that the Peregrines, not having had what they called a "proper" Christmas for years, were determined to have a real Christmas this year. Nature seemed to sympathize with them for once. Although there was not much snow, there were a few showers to make a white world, and then the frost came and held, so that there was skating on the long skating ponds behind the walls, which were really parts of the moat that had once surrounded the town.

Whenever they could get away the family were off skating. Even Mr Peregrine and Anthony found time after the shop closed to skate in the moonlight, and Hagar was dragged down willy-nilly to show them how to do the figure eight, her one accomplishment. There they met the Wotherspoon men, and many happy parties arrived for tea and supper. Beenie, amid much grumbling, was in her element, for she dearly loved parties and preparing big "spreads," as she called them, as long as she had not the actual cooking to do, and Hagar saw to that.

The house was decorated from top to bottom with holly and mistletoe, looking-glasses were turned into snowstorms with dabs of whiting and "A Merry Christmas" printed on them. Hagar would never allow the shortened form of 'Xmas' to be used, for her father had hated it, and she loved to keep to his admonitions when she could.

Perry, Paulie, and Penny made an expedition on their own to Bowchester woods and brought back a Christmas-tree and great logs to burn on Christmas Eve. The tree was decorated and stood ready to be lit up in a corner of the drawing-room.

Secret presents were prepared for the family, and parcels made up for Bowchester and all those employed in the shop, besides other friends of the family.

Hagar loved Christmas too. She knew all about old Christmas customs, and entered into the spirit of it all with her whole heart.

On Christmas Eve the largest log was to be burnt while they sat and told ghost stories in the firelight and drank mild punch.

The pudding and mince-pies were ready, the brandy bought to set the former on fire and to provide for the game of snapdragon, which the Peregrines had never heard of. The turkey was stuffed, and the sausages and ham on the pantry shelves. Marion was to make and decorate the trifle all by herself, and Penny was to supplement it with a decorated jelly, whose ingredients were supposed to be a great secret.

Mr Peregrine was as happy as the younger ones, and continually coming in with parcels containing almonds and raisins or sweets or boxes of preserved fruits and wonderful crackers.

A pudding for the birds was made by Penny of suet and nuts and bird-seeds, and stood in its basin ready to be turned out on Christmas morning. It was anathematized by the old gardener, Duffie, who said it introduced all kinds of strange plants into his garden besides charlock and other weeds of the devil; but that did not worry Penny, with whom the birds came first, particularly the blackbird and the robin, who came at her call, the latter alighting on her fingers and her head. There was a tom-tit too, called Joseph, and a blue-tit called Mary, who flew down from the old apple-tree whenever she appeared in the garden.

A stocking was made to be filled with titbits for Robert Burns and another for Mrs Brown. Even Jane, the parrot, was remembered, and a stocking prepared to be hung on the stand Mr Peregrine had bought for her Christmas present.

Every one in the house was, of course, to hang up a stockings Penny had fished out her father's largest sock and put a loop on it to hang round the handle of his door, and one of Mark's great stockings and an old one of Anthony's had also been borrowed.

"I do think," said Penny, at the end of all these preparations, "Santa Claus will have to bring an extra bag with him for pets and grown-ups."

"I think myself you are overtaxing Santa," said Hagar, "but go ahead. Better overdo old customs than underdo them is what I say."

"Me too," said Penny. "I like old customs too. I like everything that's old."

"Including an old sweetheart," put in Rachel's sharp tongue.

"Anthony's *not* old, isn't he not, Hagar?"

"He's younger than I am," said Hagar, "so it would ill become me to talk of him being old. All the same, you'll be wanting a younger sweetheart when you grow up, Penny."

"I will not then. I only want Anthony. I'm surprised at you, Hagar," with much dignity. "You said people ought to be faithful to one sweetheart all their lives."

"Did I?" said Hagar, with a slight sigh, then went on quickly, "I meant grown-up people, and the real thing."

F

"Anthony's grown up," said Penny, "and I'm old for my years. Mother Anthony at the convent says so."

It was tea-time on Christmas Eve. The girls had come in from helping to decorate the church, and all the family was gathered round the tea-table. Mr Peregrine was glancing at his youngest daughter, his bright eyes regarding her with some apprehension beneath his thick, drawn brows.

"The industrious apprentice," he said, after a moment's cogitation, "seems to be in need of some protection from the daughter of the Leech. Do I understand your intentions are to marry him willy-nilly, Penelope?"

"But Anthony likes me," said Penny. "He isn't willy-nillying."

"A new word," said Mr Peregrine, wiping his mouth and putting down his table napkin, "but none the worse for that. Still, if I may say so, Penny, I think you'd better content yourself with loving your family and such outsiders as the birds in the meantime."

"Anthony's not an outsider. He's one of the family."

"Then that's all right," countered Mr Peregrine, "since you cannot marry one of the family—even at the age of twelve." This floundered Penny for the moment, but Paul, who had been sitting quiet, suddenly spoke up.

"Cousins can marry," he said, a little truculently, and then suddenly flushed up and began confusedly buttering a piece of bread already buttered.

"Not in this family," said Mr Peregrine, decidedly glancing at his nephew. "The Peregrines and Turtles are too much mixed up already. Are you by any chance a rival of Anthony's?"

Paul from red turned a sickly white.

"No," he said, in rather a sulky voice.

Penny at once jumped up and, running round the table, clasped him firmly round the neck with two sticks of arms. "But you do love me, Paulie, don't you? Oh, Paulie, don't you—I mean brotherly love?"

Paul pulled her round on to his knee, seemingly relieved at this turn in the conversation. "Of course I do, you silly-billy. You're my best little sister. Here! That's my almond icing!" For Penny had made hay while the sun shone by grabbing the icing he had saved off his cake for a final *bonne bouche*, and the discussion ended up in a tussle.

All the same, Hagar wondered just why he had flushed so hotly after the outburst. She glanced at the other girls, but they were both evidently entirely unconscious. She was to be enlightened later on, however, by Marion.

"Isn't Paul silly?" she said, as they put the finishing touches on the big Christmas cake. "He has started *mooning* about Rachel, and she's older than he is—*months* older."

Hagar laughed. "Months don't make much difference," she said. "What about Rachel?"

"Rachel can't be bothered with him," said Marion. "Besides——" She stopped, then changed the subject. "What are you going to wear to-night? Do you think I should put on my green velvet?"

"No, keep that for to-morrow. Wear your old red silk frock. It looks Christmassy. Rachel is going to wear that orange woollen one with the embroidery. Penny is putting on the white silk that you tried to dye pink, to save her new one for to-morrow, and I'm going to dazzle forth in hodden grey."

"Oh, it is lovely to be out of black!" said Rachel. "But grey is nearly as bad. Won't you wear a coloured frock to-morrow? Wear that blue one I saw in your wardrobe. Mark likes blue. I know he does, because he liked my old blue dress I used to wear before Mamma died."

"She remembers what Mark likes," Hagar thought to herself. "Well, *I* won't wear the blue." Aloud she said:

"Mark liking *you* in blue is a very different thing. I think you would look pretty in blue, Rachel. Haven't you a blue dress? I'll give you that one of mine. It will be old-fashioned before I can wear it, and it will easily let down. I could do it in two ticks. It doesn't matter to Mark Wotherspoon what I wear. Im' wearing my grey silk dress. My daddy liked grey, and he's first with me."

"Don't you like Mark?"

"Yes, I like him quite well. I can't understand his mother liking the other two better, but, of course, I don't know him. He's just one of the Wotherspoons to me—the big one!"

"*I* think Mother Wotherspoon has never liked him since he was thrown from his horse and became lame for a while. She hates anything like that. She kills anything on the farm that becomes what she calls a 'lameter,' and Mark knows that quite well."

"Was he very lame?" She stopped. She hated people asking about her face, and never showed curiosity about other people's disabilities. Besides, if Rachel was secretly fond of him it might hurt her to have it referred to by anyone else. "I'm sure you must be mistaken about his mother," she went on. "He's not a 'lameter' now—that's an old Yorkshire word." She tried to turn the conversation. "I noticed Mrs Wotherspoon used lots of Yorkshire words, and sometimes she leaves out 'the' just like Yorkshire people do."

"Yes," said Rachel musingly, going back to Hagar's question. "He was thrown trying to save Jenny Nichols at the hunt, whose mount ran away with her. He caught it, but his own horse stumbled, and he couldn't save himself with having two to control, so he went down and broke his leg, and she got off scot-free—the little silly! It is funny, Hagar, both you and Mark having accidents with horses."

"I expect Mother Wotherspoon will never like me," said Hagar. "I'll be a 'lameter' in her eyes."

"Oh, well," said Rachel, "nobody really minds Mother Wother."

"Oh, I'm not distressing myself," laughed Hagar. "I'll never come much in Mother Wotherspoon's way."

Rachel laughed too. "She might want to have you put down if you did, the old tartar."

Mr Peregrine would be late that evening because Christmas Eve was a busy time in the shop, but he was letting Anthony, who hadn't anything to do with the actual selling or serving of customers, away early. He and Mark arrived about the same time, 'got up to kill,' as Marion remarked, though both of them were in their sober Sunday best, tall, slender Anthony wearing easily his black coat and striped trousers, but Mark looking too broad and big for broadcloth and finery.

"You should have come in your *everyday* things," said Penny, with whom to think was to speak. "I like you best in breeches."

"Then I'll go home and change," said Mark solemnly, "or Anthony will put my eye out with you, Penny. He looks like a Prime Minister."

"Anthony always looks nice," announced Penny. "He looks nice in breeches too. I've seen him riding."

"Then my last hope is gone," said Mark, and he caught Hagar's eye and smiled to her, "but I've got my breeches, Penny. I rode over and stabled the mare at the Red Lion."

The girls were all in party clothes, even if they were their second best, and made a gay bunch as they conducted their visitors up the stairs to see their rooms, with the glowing fires, and over the house to admire the decorations.

Then they all sat down to supper of a huge pigeon pie, its pastry decorated in Hagar's best style, mashed potatoes and turnips, followed by jellies and sweets and creams of a plainer make than the morrow's extravagances, since Hagar had said they mustn't have too much rich food the night before Christmas.

"Rich or not, it's a feast for the gods," said Anthony, and as they were all hungry everything was enjoyed amidst laughter and chatter. Mr Peregrine had slipped from the shop for supper, but had to eat it quickly and go. The rest, however, lingered and took their ease, till Beenie looked in and asked if they were never going to finish and let her get "redd up for the morn."

They all helped her to clear, and would have helped with the washing up, but Beenie had got her friend Mrs Brearley in to help her, and shooed them all out of her kitchen and shut the door on them.

"Away wi' you," she cried, "and see you get to your beds at a decent time o' night like honest Christian folks."

They put the log on the drawing-room fire, turned out the lights, and drew round the hearth.

"Now," said Penny, with delighted expectant shivers, "tell us a ghost story, Hagar."

So Hagar told them the story of *The Long Pack*: of the lonely house on the moor where the servant-girl was left alone to keep everything safe while her master and mistress were gone; of the eerie arrival at sunset of the packman with the long, queer-shaped pack which he begged her to keep for him for the night; right on through all the hair-raising horrors of the stirrings of the pack—like breathing—the terror of the lonely girl when she realized there was *a man in the pack*, who was to let in his fellow-sinner to rob the house; the boiling of the huge kettle in the candle-lit kitchen; and so on through all the thrill of that old Northumbrian tale to the triumphant, cunning outdoing of the villain by the brave girl, till in the dawn she stood on the steps and blew the whistle that was to tell his accomplice the coast was clear, but was to bring him into the trap she had prepared for him. They shivered and shook and triumphed with the girl, and then begged for more.

"That wasn't a ghost story," said Penny. "Tell us a real ghost story, Hagar."

But Hagar had no intention of frightening Penny with ghosts. *The Long Pack* as she told it, for she missed out some of the more awful and eerie bits, was thrilling but not too frightening, for the servant-heroine girl rose to every occasion and got the better of the packman all the way through. So she told them the story of *The Golden Leg*, which ends by making every one jump and then go into gales of laughter at the way they have been taken in.

Then Anthony told the lovely story of the girl-mother with the baby who appeared one Christmas Eve all over the countryside and was taken for Mary with the Christ Child in her arms by the simple folk, and Mark told a story his Irish nurse had told him about the fairies and the cows; and then they turned up the lights, poked the fire, and sang Christmas carols till the clock struck, and clear in the moonlit air came the voices of the real carol-singers, who stood outside in the garden, their lanterns glowing orange and yellow on the pure blue-white of the snow.

"Hark! the herald angels sing."

After that excitement had died down Hagar sang in German the Christmas carol her old German governess had taught her—*Stille Nacht, heilige Nacht* ("Still the night, holy the night"). Then they all took their candles from the hall table, for the uppermost rooms were still lit by lamp- or candle-light, and suddenly Mark and Anthony, prompted perhaps by Paul and Perry, discovered the mistletoe cleverly hung and hidden in the rafters, and all the girls were kissed by all the men, and Anthony held Penny above his head and then kissed her on both cheeks, and Mark, stooping over Hagar, said rather shyly, "I'd need to lift you up too," and then, taking, like Penny, the bull by the horns, he quickly lifted her up and kissed her cheek, and then hurriedly busied himself with his candle.

Mr Peregrine, arriving at the moment, insisted on also kissing everybody under the mistletoe, Hagar getting a fatherly hug with the rest. She was beginning to be less shy with him, partly because she was gradually becoming aware that all his bluff and talk were used to hide from the world a sometimes rather lost and bewildered soul.

CHAPTER XI

"FAMILY AFFAIRS AND SHIPS AND THINGS"

IT was on Christmas Day that Hagar had her first real talk with Paul. From the first she had recognized in Paul a steadiness and character far beyond his years, that among the changeable Peregrines he stood for something solid and enduring that would not be swayed, as they were, by the blowing winds of temperament. He had less charm than any of them, but was a more trustworthy chronicler, since you felt at once that Paul would look at things objectively and as they were, apart from his own feelings. The rest of them were all of the subjective temperament, that views everything through its own spectacles, rosy-tinted or black, as they happened to be.

To all of them their stepmother had been a villainess of the deepest dye, but, though she had been unkindest of all to Paul, he put in a word for her now and then, and would sanely correct Rachel or Marion when they were indulging in their highest flights of oratory about her cruelty and meanness.

On Christmas morning the whole family, except Paul, Hagar, and Beenie, had gone off to church with Mr Peregrine, who was a great churchman. Paul did not belong to the Church of England. The Turtletons had been Wesleyans, and Paul, without being enthusiastic, occasionally attended the Wesleyan chapel, though he was not above accompanying his uncle or the girls to church if they made a point of it.

On Christmas Day, however, he said he would stay behind and help Hagar by setting the dinner-table. He was clever with his hands, and could arrange flowers, fold table-napkins, and set a table beautifully. He could cook too, and while the rest might make a spoon or spoil a horn, Paul's dishes could always be depended on to turn out what they were meant to be, whereas Rachel's gravy, for instance, might turn out either gravy or dishwater, and on one momentous occasion, which she was never allowed to forget, had turned out a pancake! Or so they said.

It was a lovely frosty morning, and as they all went chattering through the garden, Penny bringing up the rear hanging on to Anthony, Paul turned to Hagar, who was smilingly watching them from the window, and said:

"You've made them so happy."

"Oh, but they are happy dispositions," said Hagar. "I just love them. I do love people who are made happy over little things."

"You're like that yourself, Hagar," he said. "You can't think what a difference you have made. They were all so downed under poor Aunt Adeline."

"Well, she wasn't kind to them, or to you either," said Hagar.

"She had her troubles," said the boy. "I'd like to tell you about that—the truth, I mean. I expect you'll hear all sorts of stories, and if you don't know the truth you won't know what to believe."

"That's true enough," said Hagar, "but I don't like curiosity about other people's family affairs. You mustn't think I'd ever want to pry into what happened before I came."

"No, but you are one of us now, and I'd like to talk to somebody about things. I get worried myself about them."

"All right," said Hagar, "if you think your uncle wouldn't mind my knowing."

"Oh, no," said Paul. "I expect he'd like to talk to you himself. He worries under all that play-acting, and he thinks I'm too young. He just play-acts with me too."

"Well, come and help me to polish the glasses, and then you can set the table while I see to the cooking."

They were having an early dinner, as that would leave them all free for the afternoon and evening. They had decided only to open letters and unpack their stockings on Christmas morning, and to leave the tree to be lighted and the parcels

all to be opened when the darkening came on, by which time
Hagar would be free to join in the fun and festivities, for
Hagar, of course, was doing all the last-minute cooking and
the superintending, and would have her hands full till the
large Christmas dinner was over. Not that there wouldn't be
plenty of help forthcoming. They had each and all offered
to stay at home from church, though they were eager to go,
loving the decorations and the music of the Christmas service;
but the responsibilities were all Hagar's, and she never meant
to forget it, however much they were inclined to pet and spoil
her and make her one of themselves.

There had been great hilarity over the stockings, which had
been stuffed, so to speak, with jokes, Mr Peregrine finding
a grand silk umbrella in his—he dearly loved his old cotton
one, with one rib unattached to the cover, and would never
buy another. Anthony's stocking had contained, among
squeaking pigs and so forth, a false beard as a finish to his
slight sideboards, and Mark's a selection of farmyard animals
ranging from cows to hens, because he hated any kind of
new machinery, tractors and incubators and suchlike, that
did away with animals at their natural functions. The girls
had not escaped a laughing reminder of some idiosyncrasy,
and even Hagar had been presented with a pincushion in
the shape of a hand with two fingers outstretched in her
well-known gesture, about which they had now begun to
tease her.

As Paul and Hagar started on the glasses he said:

"Didn't you wonder why no one wrote and told you Aunt
Adeline had died before you came?"

"I did rather," said Hagar, "but I gather there was some
accident."

"Yes, she took an overdose of her sleeping draught"—he
paused—"at least we think so."

Hagar paused in the polishing of a glass to look at him.

"*Think* so?"

"Yes. This has been on my mind a long time, Hagar. You

remember the girls talking about the coffee that she said was poisoned?"

"Yes."

"Well, it did taste bitter. That's why I got the mustard—not for a joke."

Hagar stood staring at the boy.

"What do you mean, Paul?"

"I don't know." His young brows were drawn together in a frown. "You know, Aunt said Naomi was trying to poison her, but she was always saying things like that; she hated Naomi. You see, Uncle was sorry for Naomi, and would not have her sent away. At least, he said he would not have her dismissed in disgrace as Aunt wanted; she was always wanting to turn her out of the house there and then, and Uncle said if she went she must get proper notice and stay until she had found another post. You see, Naomi had no home and no friends."

"Did you like Naomi? What did you think of her?"

"Well . . . she was French, and terribly changeable. She would be awfully kind and sweet and then fly into rages; but she was always kind to Uncle, putting his slippers to warm and seeing his room was tidy and the fire bright, and reading to him when his eyes hurt—you know, he reads too much, and the doctor said he mustn't read in artificial light—or she played chess with him."

Hagar knew all about that, for they all took turns in reading to Mr Peregrine in the evenings or they played chess with him, though he complained all the time of what duds they were.

"She was a clever chess player. I think Aunt Adeline was jealous, but she was never kind to Uncle James herself. She was always nagging and being sarcastic, and she laughed at him in front of us. But she wasn't well. She had a very red nose with indigestion, and Beenie said she drank, but she didn't. Well, I went and tasted her sleeping draught, and it tasted just like the coffee. That worried me, Hagar. I asked Naomi about it, and she said yes, she did put a spoonful in,

because she thought it would make Aunt sleepy, and she'd go
to bed and leave us in peace. Aunt Adeline was in a horrible
temper that night and making everybody miserable. I'm sure
that was all Naomi did. She wasn't wicked, and was really kind
sometimes—then we did like her." He paused a long time.

"Yes, Paul."

"Well, Beenie hated Naomi too. She said Naomi meant to
make mischief, and that she wanted Uncle for herself. Beenie
didn't like Aunt either, but she simply hated Naomi, and does
still. Well, another time Aunt said her coffee tasted bitter,
and Beenie tasted it, and then they both said Naomi had tried
to poison her, and there was a terrible row, and Naomi ran
away to Bowchester. Mother Wotherspoon couldn't bear
Aunt Adeline either, and she and Naomi were friends then.
Well, the next thing we heard was that Naomi had secretly
married Matthew, and Mother Wotherspoon was furious.
She always wanted Marion for Matthew, and never thought of
Naomi marrying him, because she is much, much older.
Mother Wotherspoon says she is nearly forty. She was so
cruel to Naomi that Matthew took her away to a little sheep-
farm he has in the hills, and they live there now.

"Well, one day Naomi came here for a box of things she
had left, and that night Aunt died from an overdose of her
sleeping draught, and Beenie said she poisoned her. But she
couldn't have, you know, because she was away home hours
before it happened. There was a terrible scene that evening,
because Aunt said that Uncle had asked Naomi to come for
her box, instead of just sending it to her, and I think Aunt
just took too much of her sleeping draught when she was
excited and miserable. Of course, Beenie is too faithful to us
ever to say anything like that outside the family, but we are
afraid she might say it to you, so I said to Marion I'd tell you
the whole story the first chance I got. We wanted you to
know all the truth before Beenie could say anything."

"Did Marion like Matthew?"

"Oh, yes. We all thought Matthew *belonged* to Marion.

Once we weren't sure if it was Rachel or Marion, he seemed to like them both so much, and then it turned out to be Marion. They weren't engaged, but every one knew they loved each other, and Naomi did too—but he married Naomi. Marion always sticks up for Naomi, but I think it's just that she can't bear us to think that Matthew could do anything wrong."

"Poor little Marion!"

They were both silent a moment.

"So that's why you did not tell me that Mrs Peregrine had died?"

"Yes. We were afraid you wouldn't come. Uncle wouldn't speak about it."

"Well, I'm glad I know all about it. I think with you, Paul, that your aunt had been worked up into a state of such excitement she couldn't sleep, and had perhaps taken another dose of her draught. It's the natural explanation; but people like Beenie love dramatizing and making the worst of things. They just can't help it. I know the type. But she is faithful and honest and a dear soul, and she means well. The best thing it just to try to forget it all and leave the past to the past. We have all the future before us, and we are going to be happy and make this a happy home for every one in it. Marion will recover. One gets over these things. So now," she ended up cheerfully, "let's all enjoy our Christmas Day, shall we?"

"There's just one other thing, Hagar," he said shyly.

"Yes, what's that?"

"It's Rachel who was most hurt. Rachel feels things most." He paused. "Hagar—you'll help me with Rachel won't you?"

"Help you? Yes, of course, but . . . how do you mean, Paul?"

"Well, you see, I'm going to marry Rachel."

"But——" She stopped.

"Yes, I know, we are cousins, but I'm going to marry Rachel all the same," he said stubbornly and quietly. "I just thought you'd better know."

He was silent for a moment, then laughed at her surprised face.

"What about that turkey?" he said.

"Oh, goodness!" exclaimed Hagar, and flew off to the kitchen, leaving the surprising Paul to get on with the table.

CHAPTER XII

"THE PIPER IN THE WIND GOES BY"

MRS WOTHERSPOON had a cold, and had not come on Christmas Day, but after breakfast Luke and John had arrived, and they joined the family as they came home from church, with glowing cheeks and pink noses. Mr Peregrine, sporting his new umbrella, had insisted on a walk after church, and a walk they had had.

Now they were all dying of hunger, and Hagar just had time to slip upstairs and change into her grey silk dress before Beenie brought in the turkey. The grey silk sounds very old-maidish—as Hagar meant it to—but it really was a very pretty frock, with a bodice laced with grey cords over a cream silk front, and a full skirt, which made her seem small and as light as thistledown on her feet. Her black hair was brushed till it shone, and because it was a party she had put a tiny touch of colour on her pale cheeks, which made her look young and gay and set her dark brown eyes sparkling.

"Isn't Hagar pretty?" they all chorused when she appeared, and her slender fingers went up to her mouth as she laughed and shook her head.

Marion looked adorable in her green velvet, and dark Rachel very attractive in her straight orange frock, while Penny in her new white silk and patent-leather slippers looked frail and sweet.

Mr Peregrine, looking more like a distinguished rook than

ever in his morning-coat and dark grey trousers, carved the turkey, an enormous bird, at the side-table, while Perry and Paulie helped Beenie to serve the other dishes. Mr Peregrine came out in all his glory as a host. He joked with every one, and then joked with the turkey's ghost, which was supposed to be in some paradise of its own.

It was a real old English Christmas dinner, with no modern frills. There was turkey and stuffing and sausages and bread-sauce and boiled ham and mashed potatoes and sprouts.

Then Hagar disappeared for a few minutes to make sure the brandy was warm to pour round the pudding. The room was darkened, and Beenie came triumphantly in, bearing the flaming dish of blue flames. A cheer went up, and Mr Peregrine recited what he called an "Ode to the Pudding," but which consisted for the most part of a sepulchral intonation of "the flames they crept in, and the flames they crept out!"

Anthony got the ring straight off, and gave it to Penny, and got her threepenny-bit in exchange—he'd need it, said Mr Peregrine, if he didn't succeed in escaping from his youngest daughter's clutches.

Paulie, Penny, Perry, and Mark went manfully on through the mince-pies, but the rest held back for the trifle and Penny's wonderful jelly, which was a work of art in all the colours of the rainbow, but hadn't much taste. Anthony, it must be recorded, denied this. He said it tasted "of rose leaves and Penny"—but nobody took any notice of these delusions. Perry said it tasted of *Helix pomatia*, but this witticism was treated with the silence it deserved. Hagar, who had forgotten the Latin name of the famous snails, wondered what on earth he meant.

After dinner they all retired to the drawing-room for a well-earned rest, except Robbie, who performed every one of his tricks. He said his ABC, which consisted of giving a bark for every letter Penny said till she came to Z, when he growled, then jumped down from the table for his biscuit. He died for the King and lived for the King, and sat demurely looking at a biscuit on the floor till the word 'Yes' was said, when he snapped it up. He begged, and threw up a biscuit from his nose and caught it, and as a crowning feat walked about three steps on his hind-legs.

"All done by kindness, ladies and gentlemen," said Perry. "And biscuits," growled Paul in the background, which ruffled all Penny's feathers.

"He doesn't do it for biscuits. He does it for love, and because he's so clever. He just gets a biscuit."

They had drunk healths and pulled crackers and made speeches till they were tired, so the new books and the cards came out to be examined till tea-time, while Mr Peregrine frankly lay down on the sofa in Papa's Parlour and snored.

Then Mark had a brain-wave, and suggested they should build a snowman in the garden. There was plenty of snow for that, and in five minutes they were all in the garden enthusiastically building a snowman which everybody said looked exactly like Mr Peregrine, which was not really surprising, seeing they had purloined his old umbrella, his most ancient topper, and his pipe for finishing touches.

It was while he was hunting for a carrot for a nose in the out-house that Perry came on a couple of their old sledges, and nothing would do for them then but to have them out and sledge down the steep slope at the front of the house that ran down to the river. Every one had to join in. So, bundled in woollies and fur caps and cravats, they careered back and forth, up and down the hill till Beenie came to tell them it was six o'clock and tea was ready, and that sledging was no "wark" for Christmas Day, whereupon they put Beenie on a sledge, and not only took her down, but hauled her up again—all hands to the ropes!

Tired and in glorious spirits, they poured into the dining-room for tea, and then, as luck would have it, a little note of dissension crept in.

Mr Peregrine had evidently taken the opportunity of the

quiet afternoon on the sofa to ruminate on affairs in the family. No doubt he had been worrying about his seven devils and their adherents, and had been thinking out ways and means of setting things to rights. His sharp little eyes took in everything. Though no one had mentioned it to him, he had seen Paul's preoccupation with Rachel, and had noticed his quick words about cousins marrying. Penny's alarming thinness and her cough, not to speak of her adoration for Anthony, were there for all the world to see, and no doubt he knew all about Marion and Matthew, though no word of it had ever crossed his lips.

"He is preternaturally sharp," Hagar thought to herself, listening to him as he began to discuss their futures, without a hint of what really lay behind his decisions.

"How would you like to go to Germany to school for a year or so?" he electrified them by asking Penny.

Penny stopped with her cup half-way to her lips to stare at him as this new idea presented itself to her.

"Oh, Daddy!" she began, breathless with excitement. "Do you really mean it? Is it because I told you about Dolly Mein's sister being at school in Germany? Do you really, really mean it? When would I go? Would I go to the same school as Clara Mein? Would you take me to Germany? Oh, Daddy!"

The questions poured out. Penny was always one for adventures, and had instantly thrilled to the word 'Germany,' which before the War meant fairy-tales, wild swans flying, snow-laden pine-trees, sledges drawn by reindeer (a mix-up from Santa Claus), little hares bringing Easter eggs, houses looking as if they were made of gingerbread and icing, song and romance.

Her face was white, her eyes starry with excitement. "Is that my Christmas present?" she asked. "Am I really and truly to go to Germany?"

"Well, now, steady on, steady on," said Mr Peregrine. "I'm thinking about it. That old fool Dr Merriman said to me the last time he came in to play chess that a year in the south

G

of Germany wouldn't do you any harm. He said they lived on *Sauerkraut*, whatever that is, and fat pork and hot chocolate and cream, and would feed you up till you looked like a little roly-poly pudding. The old scoundrel can't play chess for nuts, but I dare say he knows what he is talking about when he is by way of being a physician."

Penny jumped up and ran around to hug him, so he took her on his knee and held her thin little body close to him. "How would you like to be a little German roly-poly?" he asked her.

"I should love it. I like being fat. I'd love to have hands like Dolly Mein. She hasn't any knuckles, just dear little dimples."

Her eyes fell on Anthony.

"But what about Anthony."

"On sober reflection, I don't think we can send Anthony to a girls' boarding-school in Germany," said Mr Peregrine solemnly, "unless, of course, we dress him up in petticoats and pass him off as a girl. There have been such cases. What do you say, Anthony?"

"I think perhaps I'd be better employed staying at home and writing letters to Penny," said Anthony.

"Hum—hum . . ." Mr Peregrine appeared to ruminate, then shook his head. "Quite impossible! Quite impossible! I'm afraid you'd come under the category of 'young men'— strictly forbidden in boarding-schools."

Before anyone could speak he suddenly changed the subject.

"Well, nothing's settled. You girls can talk it over with Hagar." He turned to John and Luke, who had been enjoying themselves with the rest.

"Now we are discussing futures," he said, "what about that agricultural college for Paul? He seems keen on going to South Africa to join his Turtleton cousins out there. They want him to be a little older first. A year or two at the college might be a good thing."

They all joined enthusiastically in a discussion of the college,

Paul with glowing eyes. He was keen on going out to the colonies and farming there. The freer life appealed to Paul, who had no use for books or a sedentary life, and spent a great deal of time at Bowchester.

It was in the middle of all this that the note of dissension slipped in.

"And what about me?" said Perry. "I want to be an airman."

This bomb created the explosion. Flying in those days was a rarity, hardly to be considered by sensible folk.

"Airman! Airman!" shouted Mr Peregrine. "What the devil are you talking about, Perry. You follow me in the business. God bless my soul! You're my only son, aren't you? You'll be Peregrine of Peregrine and Turtleton's."

"I don't want to be an old bookseller," said Perry, pushing out his lips. "I'm going to learn to fly."

"You are going to do as you're told. Who is to carry on the business, I'd like to know? Hold your tongue, sir."

But Perry was not so easily silenced. He had evidently been brooding on this for a long time.

"Anthony can carry on the business."

"Anthony is not a Peregrine."

"He likes it. You're always saying yourself he is your right hand. Why can't Anthony carry on Peregrine and Turtleton's?"

"Enough of that!" Mr Peregrine rose, glowering. "You are my son. You are the only Peregrine left. You'll carry on the business, and your sons after you."

He pushed back his chair and marched out of the room.

"Oh, Perry," said Marion, who had evidently been in his confidence, "what made you speak about flying to-day? Now you've spoiled our Christmas!"

"I don't care." The tears were in his eyes. "I won't be a bookseller and stand in a shop all day. I hate it! I hate it! And I won't. Nobody will make me."

"Well," said Hagar cheerfully, jumping up, "you're just a

schoolboy yet, you know. There's lots and lots of time before you need settle about that. Let's go and have games in the drawing-room now and unpack the parcels."

The tree was lighted and glowing in its corner, with piles of packages under it.

In the excitement of unpacking them all was forgotten. Mr Peregrine came in smiling, all his bad temper gone.

"I remember," he said to Hagar on the quiet, as he helped her to undo a string, "when I was Perry's age I wanted to be a lion-tamer in a circus. He'll get sense as he gets older."

"Of course he will," said Hagar, but she wondered. Perry was a strong-willed, queer boy, not one to be driven the way he did not want to go.

After the parcels were unpacked pandemonium was let loose. Luke and John had seemed to Hagar rather colourless young men, but they came out of their shells with the first game, and proposed and carried through the maddest romps. They turned out the lights and played at hide-and-seek all through the house. They played at blind man's buff and kiss in the ring, and then dressed up and had charades.

Then more mistletoe was discovered hidden in an unexpected place by Anthony, who held Penny above his head to see it and then kissed her on each cheek.

Hagar was standing watching them and smiling, when suddenly she felt an arm round her, and there was Mark smiling down at her and then up at a tiny piece of mistletoe swinging above her head among the holly.

"Custom must be indulged with custom, or custom will weep," he quoted, as he bent quickly and kissed her wounded cheek.

"Oh, you shouldn't," said Hagar, as she put her two fingers up to cover the scar and pushed him shyly away. Once under the mistletoe was quite enough, she thought.

At that moment Rachel held up her hand.

"Hush," she said.

A little wind had risen, with a threat of snow in the air. It moaned round the house, shook the door, piped sadly through the keyhole, and went whistling softly on.

"Listen," said Penny, her eyes wide—"it's the piper in the wind. He always goes by when anything is going to happen."

As they stood there quiet and listening there came the sound of wheels, which, even as they waited, stopped at the door. The next moment there was a knock and Hagar stood looking as Marion opened the door. A little snow blew in, and then a whitened figure stepped inside and enveloped Marion in a hug.

"We just stopped to wish you ze merry Christmas," said a voice. "Matthew wished not, but I say yes. Peace and good-will."

"Naomi!" thought Hagar instantly.

"Come in, Naomi," said Marion. "Come in, Matthew."

Glancing round, Hagar was instantly struck by Rachel's attitude. She was shrinking back against the closed door of the drawing-room, her face deathly white, her eyes staring.

But in a moment she recovered herself and came forward, and then they were all shaking hands and wishing one another a happy Christmas.

"Have a drink," said Paul, playing host in his uncle's absence. Mr Peregrine had retired to his own room when the games commenced.

They surged into the drawing-room, drinks were poured out, and introductions made.

"This is Hagar," said Marion to Naomi.

"She come in my place?" laughed Naomi, and shook hands.

"How do you do?" said Matthew. He stood very still and quiet, watching Marion, who, with flushed cheeks and over-bright eyes, was talking all the time, rapidly and nervously. Hagar was shocked to see how young he was. He looked little more than a boy, rather like Mark, nearly as tall, but slighter and much more handsome, less rugged, less set. "Terribly boyish," she thought sadly, "to be the husband of this bouncing Frenchwoman, plainly so much older than himself."

His thin brown cheeks had still the curves of youth, and though his brow was already lined under the boyish tuft of dark hair that had fallen over it, the blue eyes were young as spring, young and bewildered and full of pain.

"Naomi," he said, after a few minutes, "I think we should go now." He looked round at the company, plainly embarrassed and ill at ease. "We just wanted to wish you all a happy Christmas," he said.

"And break ze ice," Naomi added, "and ask you all to come and see us."

There was a moment's awkward pause. Then Marion said: "Yes, of course we shall."

Instantly Naomi turned to her.

"You will come, Marion. Come soon and stay with us. It is lonely for me out there in ze hills at Goslaw when Matthew goes out with ze sheeps; he goes out so much in winter. Promise, Marion. You are all ze friends I have."

"Yes, I promise," said Marion. "I'll come."

"And Rachel." Naomi looked across at Rachel, who stood proudly aside in the shadows, her back against the wall, her head up, her eyes blazing with resentment in her paper-white face.

But before she could answer Matthew put his hand on his wife's arm and spoke again:

"We should like to see you all," he said quickly, "at any time. Good night, Marion. Good night, everybody. We must really go."

He guided his wife swiftly towards the door as every one called out, "Good night" and "A happy Christmas!" Everyone except Rachel, who stood back, still and proud and white, her hands clenched, her head thrown back, saying nothing.

Hagar looked at Naomi, laughing still and carrying things off; unmistakably a Frenchwoman, with her sallow face, thin nose, highly coloured cheeks, and short black fringe curled on her forehead—her body too stout for her thin face. As they came under the light of the hall lamp Hagar saw her glance resentfully at her husband and caught her full face as she lifted her chin; a subtle face, an experienced face, that might hold witchery, that might become engaging with a smile, that might harden into ruthlessness.

In a moment they were gone, and the door closed behind them. No one made any comment. The sound of the wheels died away, and then the soughing of the wind fell on their ears, rising and falling, eerily whistling through the keyhole and shrilling over the roof.

Then Rachel gave a short, hard laugh from her corner in the shadows, and spoke at last.

"The piper in the wind goes by," she said.

BOOK II

Marred in the hand of the potter

CHAPTER I

"TO BE YOUR VALENTINE"

AND I a maid at your window, to be your valentine." Penny had picked up the words from her Shakespeare, and was gaily singing them to a tune of her own as she ran up the winding stair to Rachel's little turret room.

It was well into February—St Valentine's Day. The snow-drops were out in drifts in the garden, in clumps under the apple-tree, nodding in the borders, climbing the old mossy steps that led beneath laburnum and lilac to the fruit and vegetable garden, where Perry kept his tame rabbits and Penny her guinea-pigs, and where much innocent discussion went on as to their mating.

"Do you think if I had two husbands for Maria," Penny anxiously asked Anthony, "I would get baby guinea-pigs any quicker?"

"I'm afraid there would be tiffs," said Anthony. "I'd stick to one."

"But Maria must have some babies before I go to Germany." A prolonged sigh. "Oh, I should love some dear little guinea-pigs. Will you look after them for me, Anthony?"

"Not in my lodgings," said Anthony hastily, thoroughly scared at this idea.

"Oh, no! I couldn't trust them with Miss Gunter. You could come and visit them here and see that Perry wasn't neglecting them."

"Certainly," said Anthony, on a note of relief. "I'll send messages to tell you how they are getting on."

"There'll be hundreds before you get home," said Perry

104

cheerfully, having had more experience than Penny. "We'll have to put them down."

"You will not, then!" Penny flew at Perry and grabbed his hair. "You will not! Not if there's hundreds and thousands and *millions*!"

Anthony left them fighting it out tooth and nail. He foresaw that if he stayed he would certainly have to promise to preserve the lives of the millions, and Anthony could not bear to break a promise to Penny. Discretion in this instance was certainly the better part of valour.

The question of the guinea-pigs had been settled in some amicable manner, into which it were better not to inquire too closely, and now Penny was on the way to rouse Rachel with some directions about the rooks which she had awakened to hear cawing in the group of elms at the corner of the vegetable garden.

Mark had unfortunately presented Paul with a rook rifle, and Penny, after vainly trying to extract a promise from Paul not to shoot anything with it, had suddenly realized there might be danger to the rooks in the elms.

She knew that Paul would do anything for Rachel, so Rachel must be persuaded that the whole garden, including the elm-trees, must be a "Sanctuary for Wild Life"—a great idea, and a grand-sounding phrase into the bargain.

The little turret-room was now Rachel's own sanctuary, a lovely room if one didn't mind draughts and whistling winds in winter, for it was round in shape, with windows facing every direction, and shaken by all the bitter blasts that came sweeping in from the sea, howled down the river valley, or tore across the country from the Cheviot Hills.

Rachel loved blasts and storms, and was never happier than when, snug and alone, she heaped up the glowing fire with wood she gathered from the river-side and seashore—tales of wrecks and floods clinging to them—or pieces from the jealously guarded sack of peat with which she was yearly presented by a shepherd friend among the hills.

She always locked her door—solitude at times was a craving need in Rachel's nature—so Penny had to bang ruthlessly some time before it was opened by a sleepy Rachel, who was, however, good-natured about it, it being one of her tenets that people who were aristocrats of the mind—among whom she wished to be—always wakened up good-humoured and with their minds alert and tempers under control.

" It's a great thing to be philosophical," Anthony had remarked on hearing this. "It helps other people to put up with us."

Penny, however, was wise enough not to have come unarmed against a sea of troubles. She held something behind her back, which she now produced with a flourish, as though it had been the main cause of her thunder at the door.

"There's a letter for you and a little packet—and oh, Rachel, I think it's a valentine."

Valentines were out of fashion and practically unknown at the time, but Mr Peregrine in going over his stock had unearthed a few ancient ones and a bundle of the hideous coloured slips that used to be called 'off-takes,' and which had really killed the pretty custom of the valentine.

The little square packet certainly looked exactly like a valentine, and as Rachel took it and got back into bed, after poking up the fire, which had smouldered all night, Penny climbed on to the eiderdown and sat down beside her.

"Do open it and let me see it, Rachel. I'm dying with curiosity. Have you got a sweetheart? Do you think Mark sent it? Would you like Mark for a valentine? Marion hasn't got one, for I looked to see; but Matthew couldn't be Marion's valentine now, could he? Can married men not be valentines? I'm sure Matthew doesn't like Naomi as well as Marion, because——"

"Be quiet!" said Rachel. "You mustn't say that."

"Why mustn't I say it?"

"Because Matthew has married Nahomi Cuendet, so of course he must love her better than anyone; that's why he

married her. You must never say that again, Penny. Do you
hear me?"

"All right, I won't; but I can *think*, and I think——"

"You must learn to keep your thoughts to yourself; and
anyhow, you are just a little girl, and don't understand, and
nobody cares what you think."

"But I do understand, because I love Anthony. Oh, Rachel,
aren't you going to open it and let me see?"

"Not just now." Rachel pretended to yawn. "I'm sleepy.
I'll let you see it afterwards."

"Do you want to see it first by yourself? I would if Anthony
sent me one, but there isn't any for me; but there's a little box
for Hagar. Oh, Rachel, I'm simply bursting with a secret.
Will you keep it if I tell you?"

"What mischief have you been up to now?"

"Not mischief, really and truly. It's a real secret, but if you
want to know it very, very much I'll tell you."

"All right, fire away. I see you'll burst if you don't tell
somebody."

"Yes, I expect it would just burst out of me, I'm so excited.
I sent Anthony a valentine!"

"Goodness, you little goose! What ever did you do that for?"

"Because he'll love to be my valentine for a whole year, and
I'm going to Germany, and I won't see him for months and
months; but he'll be my valentine all the same. Oh, Rachel,
it was a lovely one, with paper lace all round it and a little
painted silk pad in the middle smelling of attar of roses, and
a heart and two hands clasped on it, a lady's hand with lace
round the wrist and a gentleman's hand with a sort of cuff and
a wreath of pink roses and violets in a circle, and it said:

> " Roses are pink,
> Violets are blue,
> If you will have me,
> I will have you.

Isn't that lovely?"

"Very," said Rachel drily.

"Do you think Anthony will like it?"

"Oh, I dare say he's silly enough about you to like anything you do. All the same, it was a very bold thing to do. However, I expect he'll just laugh over it. He knows what a sentimental little goose you are."

"Anthony and I are going to be *betrothed* when we are older." Penny loved a fine new word. "At least, when *I* am older," she continued, getting a bit mixed up.

"Do you expect him to stay twenty-three till you catch up?"

"Oh, no, I'm not so silly. But there's one thing," she added triumphantly. "He has stopped growing, and I'm still going on, so he'll can wait till I am up to him."

"Be able to wait—not 'will can,'" corrected Rachel. "Well, skedaddle! I'm going to get up."

"Oh, but there's something else I want to ask you."

And she plunged into the main reason of her early visit. She was going to make all the garden—and the elms—into a "Sanctuary for Wild Life," and would Rachel help her? Perry had promised not to trap birds with a riddle and a stick in the garden, and Beenie and everybody had promised to rescue the blackbirds caught in the strawberry nets and to feed the birds in winter, but Paulie wouldn't promise not to shoot with his rifle.

"Goodness! What's the use of a rifle if you promise not to shoot with it? You are a silly, Penny."

"But not in the garden. Will you ask him to promise not to shoot in the garden, Rachel? He won't if *you* ask him not to."

"Oh, yes, I'll do that," said Rachel, "and I'll see that he keeps it too."

"Nor the rooks in the elms?"

"Of course not. I wouldn't let anybody shoot the rooks in our rookery. What an idea!"

Penny flung her sticks of arms round her sister and gave her a hug.

"Will you promise me something in return?" asked Rachel.

"Yes, I'll promise *anything*."

"You should never say that. However, this one is easy. Don't say anything about my valentine—not till I tell them myself."

"All right, I won't." Penny hesitated, making a big concession. "And I won't ask to see it myself. Do you think Anthony will show you mine?"

"No, I don't. Not if I know Anthony. Now off you go."

And she playfully ran Penny out of the room and locked the door behind her.

Once alone she slipped back into bed, took the small white packet from below her pillow, and quickly tore off the coverings. Penny was right. It was a valentine. Not quite so ornate as that of Penny's description, but the real old-fashioned affair with paper lace and scented flowers. She turned it slowly over with a puzzled expression till she came to a tiny inscription in a corner, "from Paul."

Instantly she threw it on the floor, all interest in it gone. Then she picked up the torn wrapping and examined the address again.

"Of course, I forgot," she said slowly to herself. "They do write alike."

Another rap at the door made her pick up the discarded valentine and open the door.

It was Hagar this time with two cups of tea.

"Penny said you were awake," she said, "so I thought I'd steal two cups out of Beenie's teapot. There's a letter from Germany for your father, and Penny's jumping about like a hen on a hot girdle waiting for him to come down and open it; and Marion said to tell you she had a letter from Naomi asking her to go there for Easter; and Paul has shot a starling, and Penny has put the Bishop's curse on him—or it sounds like that, anyway. I think that's all the morning news. Oh, yes, and the rooks are building in the elms, and I've had a box of primroses."

"And I've had a valentine," said Rachel, "from that great silly Paul. Isn't he a goose?" And she held out the valentine for Hagar to see.

"Gander, you mean," said Hagar, who was a stickler for the etiquette of the sexes. "You shouldn't make fun of Paul loving you, Rachel. He's so serious about it."

"Of course I'll make fun of him. It's just calf-love, and he must be laughed out of it. Why, he's just a boy, and he's heaps younger than I am. It's just silly."

"Paul is over sixteen, getting on for seventeen, and old for his years. I don't see Paul being laughed out of anything."

"Well, I'll be glad when he goes to college, and then gets shipped off to Africa. I used to like Paul. Paul and I were such friends, but I can't be bothered with him since I grew up and he turned into such a *simpleton*."

"Don't you make any mistake—Paul is no simpleton."

They had finished their cups of tea over Rachel's fire, and now Hagar got up to go.

"The breakfast bell will be ringing in ten minutes," she announced. "Hurry up, Rachel, or you'll be late."

"You haven't told me whom your primroses were from," said Rachel.

"I don't know. There isn't any card or anything with them; but they are lovely ones, and the very first primroses."

Hagar had a shrewd guess that Mark had sent the primroses, because she had said to him how early they were in Yorkshire, but she did not want to say anything about that to Rachel.

CHAPTER II

"LOVE AND VAIN-LONGING LINKED HAND TO HAND"

THE letter for Mr Peregrine was to say that since Clara Mein had left a year ago the school had been taken over by a new proprietress—Fräulein Trainer—and that she would be delighted to have Penelope as a pupil, and was sure she would be very happy with them. They had moved to another house, Das Glockenhaus, which stood in the middle of a large garden, and they had their own vegetables, fruit, etc. There were thirty pupils, and more were expected after the Easter holidays. Fräulein Trainer would be pleased to meet Penelope anywhere her father decided upon. She spoke English herself, and had an English governess (also a Frenchwoman for French), and would do all in her power to make his daughter's stay in Germany a happy and profitable one.

"Sounds all right," said Mr Peregrine. "What do you say, Hagar?"

By this time Hagar was not only considered one of the family, but an indispensable one, to be consulted and confided in by each and all. Had Americanisms reached England by that time they would have said, "What Hagar says goes," for that was the truth of the matter.

Hagar was older than any of them, except Mr Peregrine, and really, Hagar sometimes thought, she was even older than Mr Peregrine, who could never be depended upon to be *staid*.

"Somebody has to be staid in a family," Hagar often assured herself, "and as nobody else is—except Paul, and he's so young —I've just got to be so myself."

Instead of getting older-looking, however, to suit this eminently praiseworthy ambition Hagar looked younger than ever she had done since her accident. The lines of her scars were gradually fading out, and though she still held her fingers to her mouth, and it still went crooked when she laughed, it was an adorable crookedness, as more than one man had discovered. Mr Bell and Mr Buglass—in the shop—had both made her offers, and Mark Wotherspoon never missed coming to tea on Sunday nowadays. Hagar liked Mark, or, rather, she regarded him with a little fear, which made her keep him at a distance.

She was convinced now that Rachel was secretly in love with Mark, and, as she considered herself definitely on the shelf, and (rather amusingly, if she could have seen it in that light) a sort of mother to the girls, she did all that she could to throw the two together and make Mark see what was so eminently the proper thing for him, a match with Rachel.

Mother Wotherspoon also had her eye on Rachel, who, she thought, would "bring Mark to his senses," since Rachel had no sentimental leanings towards old ways, and was interested in all the new ideas Luke and John were so keen about. Possibly she would have liked her better for either of her two younger sons, but neither of them showed the slightest interest in the Peregrine girls, except a brotherly hail-fellow-well-met attitude, as far from sentiment as anything could well be. Marion had also had her share in convincing Hagar that she was right about Rachel.

Since Naomi and Matthew had called on Christmas night they had had several quarrels about Marion's accepting Naomi's invitation. Rachel was implacable, and stood out against Marion's having anything to do with Naomi.

"She stole Matthew from you," she said bitterly. "She knew Matthew was yours, but she made him marry her because she had nowhere to go, and because she thought he was rich. She always talked about the 'rich Wotherspoons.' You should have too much pride to go near her."

Of Matthew's side of it she never spoke.

One day, when she was trying to get Marion to say she would not go, she went too far, and gentle Marion turned on her.

"Naomi didn't steal him from me," she said, with angry tears in her eyes. "If Matthew Wotherspoon doesn't—didn't —want me I don't want him. I wouldn't be like you and let a man see I was in love with him, and pining for him, when he showed plainly he didn't care for me. That's where *my* pride is, not in blaming Naomi—so there!"

Rachel had gone so deadly white Hagar was afraid she was going to faint. Marion saw too how sharp the sword was she had planted in Rachel's heart, and ran to her and put her arms round her.

"Oh, Rachel, I'm sorry. I didn't mean it. I was just angry. Oh, I hate the Wotherspoons. Don't let us quarrel about them, Rachel. I love you better than all the Wotherspoons put together."

"No, you don't," said Rachel, holding herself stiff and proud. "We are both in the same boat except that Matthew still loves you and . . . and no one ever cared about me. I am just the fool in the play, the poor cat in the adage—a damned mewling Ophelia—'Get thee to a nunnery!'" Suddenly she broke off. "Leave me alone! Leave me alone!" she said fiercely, and pushed Marion aside and ran off, banging the door behind her.

Marion broke into weeping, and Hagar threw down the stockings she was mending, and, putting out her arms, clasped Marion and drew her on to her knee, big as she was, in the big arm-chair.

"Poor Marion!" she said. "Poor little Marion! Just have a good cry, my pet, on old Hagar's chest, and then we'll laugh to-morrow."

It was an old saying of her father's with which she often comforted herself—"We'll laugh to-morrow."

"Sometimes it's the day after," she thought, "and sometimes it's years, but we all laugh on some to-morrow. Broken hearts heal." But before Marion had her cry out Rachel came rushing back. She carried Mrs Brown, the cat, and, putting it on Marion's knee, she laughed a little unsteadily.

"Here are the two poor cats in the adage come to cheer you up, Marion. Let's make it up, or Hagar will think we are two love-lorn maidens, whereas we're just two sillies. Do be friends. I'm sorry for what I said."

Marion came round at once. Her nature was lighter than Rachel's—at least, it seemed so then . . . while the Potter held His hand.

Often, looking in the glass after her accident, Hagar had quoted to herself the old words made familiar from her father's lips, "The vessel that he made of clay was marred in the hand of the potter." Now as she looked at Marion and Rachel she hoped they would not too be marred in the making. Marion so far was all right in spite of her hard experience; her nature was still sweet and unspoiled; but there was a secret bitterness about Rachel that broke now and then through her reserved pride.

"If only it would come all right between her and Mark," she thought, "all might yet be well." And there and then she made up her mind to try to *do* something about it, though what to do she did not know.

Since she came to the house and had instantly taken to them all she had felt herself responsible for them, and had taken the troubles of the whole family on her slender shoulders.

Now, as Mr Peregrine turned to her at the breakfast table and asked her what she thought about Penny and the school, she felt, a little vaguely, that she would have liked to know more about Fräulein Trainer, and she wished that the school had not changed hands since Clara Mein had been there. Clara had been immensely happy at the old school and had loved the headmistress, to whom it belonged, Frau von Putlitz.

"I think," she said at last, "that you should go with Penny, Mr Peregrine, and see the school and Fräulein Trainer for yourself. I wouldn't send her with Mrs Laurie now the school has changed hands."

Mrs Laurie was an acquaintance who was going to Germany on a visit, and it had been suggested that she should take Penny to school when Mr Peregrine had finally decided that she was to go—a conclusion he had come to almost as soon as his old friend Dr Merriman had spoken of Germany, since he was worrying at the time, not only about Penny's health, but about her attachment to Anthony and her loudly declared intention of marrying him. She was only a child, and Anthony was dealing with her in the most delicate and sensible way possible. Anthony was a gentleman through and through, but she was too young for that sort of thing.

He had confided in Dr Merriman, and they had put their

heads together and decided on a school in Wiesbaden in
Germany. It would be good for her delicate constitution at
the moment and give her a complete change of environment
and thoughts.

He sat thinking over what Hagar had said. Hagar was
always sensible; perhaps she was right. He dearly loved his
Penny, and would run no risks of her not being happy.

"Well, well," he said at last, "we'll see."

But Hagar was sure he had decided to go. He would enjoy
the trip himself, for he loved change and variety.

"I'm going to stay with Naomi and Matthew at Goslaw,"
said Marion now. "I promised I would at Christmas, and
I've got a letter this morning asking me when I'm coming."

"Well, talk it over with Hagar," said her father.

"*I* don't think she should go," exclaimed Rachel. "She
ought to have more proper pride."

"I have, so far, always observed," said Mr Peregrine, who
much preferred wordy philosophizing to making decisions,
"that *pride* is an attribute of the Peregrines, *proper pride* of
the Turtletons. The latter have always reproached the Peregrines for not having *proper pride*, while suffering loudly at
the same time from the disdain of their co-partners. It seems
that now the boot is on the other foot, since from all outward appearance I should have said that you, Rachel, were a
Peregrine, and your sister a Turtleton. There must be something wrong somewhere—eh, Rachel?"

He blinked across at her, his too clever eyes bright with
meaning, and went on, "May I also suggest that too much
enthusiasm in the cause of others is a mistake in tactics; people
begin to wonder if we have a secret wound of our own.
Excuse my propensity for quoting, but, in the words of the
vulgar, a nod is as good as a wink to a blind horse."

He began meticulously to fold up his napkin as though he
had no more interest in the words of the vulgar. But Rachel
had suddenly gazed at him in a startled manner and flushed
a slow, painful red.

"'That's what I think," exclaimed Marion, hurriedly stammering a little over the words. "I think it's far prouder really not to mind things than to show you care."

"Well, I wouldn't be a mat for people to wipe their feet on," countered Rachel, recovering herself as the blush receded, leaving her paler than ever.

"The hawk and the dove are at it again!" Mr Peregrine smiled blinkingly across at Hagar, who could not help smiling back, the remark was so apt, for thin, fiery Rachel with her dark red hair standing up from her brown forehead above the eagle nose, looked at the moment very like an angry hawk, while soft, deprecating Marion, with her gentle dove-grey eyes, looked uncommonly like a plump, disturbed pigeon.

"I do wish you'd stop fighting about Matthew," put in Perry now. "Girls are always fighting about men."

This brought the wrath of both his sisters down upon his head.

"Nobody's fighting about Matthew," they exclaimed together. "You mind your own business, Peregrine Peregrine."

"It's *Naomi* we are arguing about," continued Marion "Little pitchers should be seen and not heard."

That was a grand opening for Mr Peregrine, who straightway went off into a dissertation about mixed metaphors, proverbs, pitchers, and long ears, bringing in, of course, the Peregrines and Turtletons, the former, he declared, being famous for their big noses, the latter for their big ears.

"Well, you have both a big nose and big ears, Father," said Rachel, with her sharp tongue, "so you must be as much Turtleton as Peregrine."

"God forbid!" said Mr Peregrine, forgetting in his perturbation his strictures on mixed metaphors. "An my ears flap it's the donkey in me, not the dove."

And he got up and began to shout for Beenie and his umbrella.

After that morning things seemed to Hagar to move very quickly. In no time she seemed to be packing for Penny, while Marion, who had decided to go to Goslaw a few days after Penny and her father left, was equally busy with her preparations.

Rachel absolutely refused to help Marion, who was always trying to get round her by asking her advice rather wistfully about clothes and such small matters, as though in that way she thought she might make up for discarding it on the main point. But Rachel was adamant, always too busy with Penny's things to take any interest in Marion's.

And, indeed, there was a lot to do for Penny, who was to be away for a year at least without coming home. Winter and summer clothes had to be discussed, bought, and packed, her name marked or sewn on to every article. A list of necessities had come, and included sheets, table-napkins, towels, and table silver—knife, fork, spoon, and napkin ring (with her name engraved on them).

"You'd think," said Rachel, "they hadn't an extra thing in the house—fancy taking your own soap!"

Soap was not on the list, but they had been advised to take soap for the journey, and Clara Mein had cautioned Penny to take some toilet soap to school if she was particular. "You only get that yellow kind for washing clothes," she warned her. Penny didn't care what soap she used, but Marion and Hagar tucked in a box of the scented soap which had called forth Rachel's derision.

Every one had given her presents. Anthony arrived with a beautiful leather writing-case fitted with paper in her favourite colours, and with robins and blue-tits and squirrels or flowers on every sheet and her name in a little circle. There were pens and pencils and wafers and sealing-wax (in every colour), a box of nibs she fancied, postcards and rubbers and everything she could possibly need. "Penelope Mary Peregrine" was stamped in gold on the outside of the case, which, he said, he offered in the spirit of a saint and a martyr, since she would not be able to write to him on it. Mr Peregrine had well drilled into them that letters to or from young men would most certainly not be allowed, and she would have to content herself with messages in the family epistles.

Paul gave her fur-lined gloves, in anticipation of the hard and snowy winters, Perry a pin-cushion in the semblance of Mrs Brown (who was a black cat), which was instantly and with due ceremony baptised Mrs Brown. Rachel gave her a diary fitted with tiny lock and key, Marion a very grand autograph book, and Hagar a little old carved chest with wrought hinges and lock, packed with goodies, but destined to hold her private treasures in the prying world of schoolgirls.

Mr Peregrine gave her a necklace of seed pearls to wear with her white silk party frock. All the Wotherspoons sent gifts, even Naomi remembering her with a funny little French bag to swing from her waist and carry her handkerchief, so there was a great deal of packing to be done and many visits of farewell and thanks to be made. But at last all was ready. Mr Peregrine's ancient bag was packed, and the conveyance ordered to take them to the station in the morning.

Anthony had, of course, to spend the last evening with them, and was measured once again against Penny on her stool. She seemed less fragile in her school dress, but so small-boned and thin she still looked a childish nine or ten and very young to be going so far away. Hagar, looking at her, thought Penny would never really grow up; she would keep that childlike nature to the end—childlike in all except her love for that quiet gentleman Anthony, who, looking down at her with a tender, rueful smile on his gaunt, dark young face with its quaint sideboards, seemed to be saying a long farewell to something very precious.

"How many inches is that, Anthony, I have to grow?"

"About seven should do, I think." He was very serious, as became so grave a calculation.

"Will I be—just as high as your heart then?"

"You're there already, Penny," smiling down at her.

"You'll be sure and wait for me?"

"I promise not to grow another inch."

"And you won't marry Alice Smythe or Janie Peters?"

These two young ladies of the town she considered her rivals, since they made excuses to come to the shop and see Anthony.

"I won't marry anyone, Penny."

"I do wish I could stay and look after you."

They all laughed, and he picked her up and swung her round.

"You must grow heavier too—a wind would blow you away. Try to catch me up in weight too, and come home as plump as a little partridge."

"And you promise to marry me?"

"If the winds don't blow you away from me, Penny."

He was with the family party when they saw the travellers off on the following day, waving a large white handkerchief till Penny's little, tear-stained face faded into the distance and for him, it may have seemed to Anthony, for ever into the past.

CHAPTER III

"SOK AND SEIL IS BEST"[1]

THE Sunday before Marion left home for Goslaw the Wotherspoons all came over to the Falcon's House. Hagar had thought they might not pay their usual visit, as Mr Peregrine was away, but they arrived in full force, Mother Wotherspoon sitting in front of the large gig with Mark and the two younger sons precariously balancing themselves behind, for Mark liked to drive a spirited beast, and sped them over the roads like a whirlwind.

"We came in a whirlwind, in a whirlwind to heaven," they both chanted, as they entered the parlour arm-in-arm, pretending to stagger with exhaustion.

[1] The ploughshare and simple country happiness are best.

Hagar could never understand the bitter fights that went on at Bowchester, for Luke and John always seemed so good-natured and full of fun when she saw them and as if they hadn't a care in the world.

But "that was all she knew," Rachel assured her. "It's well enough for them to be good-natured," she said; "they are four to one with their mother and her money and their grandmother and her money on their side. Mark has to fight a lone hand."

Still, Hagar found it difficult not to like the two youngsters, and Mother Wotherspoon was always friendly enough in a way, though Hagar was sure she did not trust her where Mark was concerned. It was plain that she wanted Rachel for Mark, and that the little "working housekeeper," as she was careful to call her, would get short shrift if she aspired to the hand of a Wotherspoon.

Penny had always manfully corrected her when "Mother Wother" thus spoke of Hagar.

"Hagar isn't our working housekeeper," she would say. "Hagar is a *lady*. She is a real lady. Her father was a vicar and a *dean*, and she was engaged to a gentleman who would have a title when his uncle died. Daddy says a vicar is socially far above tradespeople like us. She had nearly added, "And farmers," thus quoting her father exactly, but a natural politeness restrained her.

"Hoity-toity!" said Mother Wotherspoon. "Well, I hope she isn't afraid to work, for that's what your father engaged her for."

"She loves working," returned Penny. "Real ladies are not afraid of work."

"Teach your grandmother to suck eggs," said Mrs Wotherspoon witheringly. "Most of them are afraid of soiling their fingers."

For Mrs Wotherspoon's pride was the pride of the yeoman farmer; she had no illusions about being considered a "lady," though she felt herself an equal to any lady in the land, and meant no son of hers to "demean" himself by marrying a "sort of servant lass," whatever her forebears might be.

She kept an eye on Mark, listened if he spoke to Hagar, and always tried to intervene if she suspected him of trying to get Hagar to himself for a few minutes. She was honest enough, however, to admit to herself that Hagar gave him no encouragement and tried as hard as she did herself to interest him in Rachel.

Their reasons, however, were very different.

Hagar thought Rachel was secretly in love with handsome Mark, but Mrs Wotherspoon wanted Rachel because she thought she would be a good influence, and that, once safely married to "a lass with so much sense," he would quickly settle down and come to her way of thinking.

Mark obstinately refused to have anything to do with his mother's match-making schemes. Though he got little chance of being alone with Hagar, his eyes continued to follow her, and he made such hay as he could whenever his sun happened to shine.

That Sunday he was in luck's way, or perhaps he forced that lady's hand, for after tea he innocently proposed a walk, and cheerfully went off with the others when Hagar said she had the supper to see to and would stay in.

Mother Wotherspoon, after seeing them off, said she would pay a call on Mrs Brearley, Beenie's friend, who was also an acquaintance of hers from Yorkshire days, and a great gossip. Whenever Mrs Wotherspoon wanted to know how the land lay at the Falcon's House she paid a visit to Mrs Brearley, and now she wanted to hear all the details about Marion's visit to Naomi and Matthew, with which Beenie would have primed her friend, for the girls were saying very little about it.

She had not been gone many minutes when Mark appeared at the kitchen door.

"I thought you'd gone for a walk to the Needle's Eye," said Hagar, none too pleased.

"Well, my leg began bothering me a bit."

"Oh, I'm sorry. I thought it never bothered you now."

"Oh, yes, it can—on occasions," he said quietly, with pauses between the phrases. "It still has its uses."

Hagar looked up quickly. There was the faintest hint of a smile about the corners of his sternly moulded mouth.

"My, you're a deep one," she said to herself, with an irresistible inward laugh (though she told herself she was very much annoyed with him).

"Well, you had better take a book and read in the parlour till they come back. Your mother has gone to call on Mrs Brearley for a few minutes."

"I know." He looked round the kitchen rather helplessly. "Can I help you to dry plates or something?"

"No," she said, her confidence beginning to slip away. Somehow she always felt shy with Mark. He made her feel self-conscious.

He took a towel that was lying on the table and picked up a plate, which he began to rub, holding the plate in one hand and the towel bunched up in a lump in the other as though he were polishing a bit of harness.

"Put it down," she said. "Anyone can see you never dried a plate before in your life."

"I can learn," he said.

"You don't need to learn. Drying plates will never be part of your job."

"I don't know," he said, and then was quiet for a few minutes as he rubbed the towel round and round.

Hagar wondered if it would be any use speaking of Rachel. Would he resent it? Had he never thought of Rachel except as the girl who had played with him and whom his mother had an eye on for him? Would it be possible to waken a different interest from that? She knew that many a man would be immediately interested in a girl if it were hinted that *she* liked him, but Mark was such a dark horse.

Anyhow, here was an opportunity; she would try.

"Rachel will miss you," she said. "I wish your leg hadn't

bothered you." She spoke lightly; she didn't want to give Rachel away—just to hint to him there was another side to the question than the 'suitable match' which no doubt his mother harped on and which was likely to put any man off. It was very difficult. "I don't understand how match-makers go about it," she thought. "I suppose they sing the praises of each to the other, but that's no use to me. Mark knows Rachel better than I do."

"Oh, no, Rachel won't mind. In fact, she made it easy for me."

"Oh, dear!" thought Hagar. "How stupid men are. Of course she would make it easy."

"I've got something for you," he said. "Rachel knows about it."

"Perhaps you told her about the primroses too," thought Hagar. "You great big, long *lump* of stupidity!" Which was anything but fair, since the last thing Mark was was a *lump*.

"Guess what it is."

"Pussy willows."

"Quite cold, especially the pussy."

"Well, it can't be dog-roses. Mr Wotherspoon, really and truly you mustn't bring me flowers. I'm the housekeeper here, not"—she smiled—"one of the young ladies. You might lose me my place." He was very serious, rubbing the plate round and round uselessly, too serious to be really impressive; he might be laughing at her. "I mean it," she went on. "Mrs Wotherspoon, your mother, doesn't like me to be encouraged —I'm quite serious. She might try to put Mr Peregrine against me. Besides . . ." She paused, and boldly took the plunge. "It might hurt Rachel. I mean, I don't know, but it *might*— don't you see, you have always been such friends, and I'm just an outsider. I know it's just because I talked about primroses and pussy willows and made you think I was homesick for them, and it's very kind, but——"

She paused for breath and to collect her wits, which were getting rather scattered.

"It isn't pussy willows."

"Oh!"

"I'll go and fetch it. Is that plate dry enough?"

"Dry! You've nearly rubbed the pattern off!"

But he had gone. In a few moments he opened the kitchen door again, and came in carrying one of those large baskets with two lids and a peeled wand to keep them fastened.

"It's a hen!" she gasped. She had announced to him, when talking of farming, that she would love to try a setting of eggs under a clocker at the Falcon's House, so that eventually they might have newly laid eggs for breakfast.

"It's a clocker!" she reinforced her statement. Well, after all, a clocker wasn't so bad as primroses and pussy willows; there was something definitely unsentimental about a clocker. Even Mrs Wotherspoon must acknowledge that a clocker was a suitable object to present to a working housekeeper.

But she had hardly got so far in her ruminations when Mark took the wind out of her sails.

"A *clocker*!" he exclaimed, astonished. Then he put the basket on the table and, leaning back, roared with laughter. "Oh, Hagar!" he said. "You funny little piece! Who but you would think of a clocker!"

"But I'd like a clocker."

"You can have a dozen clockers if you want them, and a dozen settings to put under them, but how the deuce did you come to think that I'd give you a clocker? This is a *present*."

"Well, I'm disappointed," said Hagar. Then, curiosity getting the better of her, she asked, "What is it?"

"For heaven's sake don't guess again," he said, pulling out the wand that closed the basket and opening the lid at one side.

A little, quaint, roguish head popped out with a black patch over one eye.

"Oh!" said Hagar, quite overcome, and, kneeling straightway on the floor, she put her arms round the basket, the quick tears coming into her eyes. "Oh, Mark! Oh, the lovely dear, the pet, the darling! Look, he has a patch over one eye!

Shadow had a patch over one eye. Is he for me? Do you mean it? Will you give him to me? Is he one of Sally's puppies?"

With her hands still round the basket she lifted it gently on her knee.

"Oh, how I love him! I just couldn't refuse him—I couldn't. Look, he is licking my hand—— But should you give him to me?"

"I've given him to you. I wanted to give him to you when nobody else was about so that he would understand at once that you were his mistress and not get confused. Here, Samuel —I called him 'Samuel' because he's so wise. He's going to be as wise as his mother—not clever at tricks, you know, but wise; he shows signs of it already. But you can call him what you like."

He lifted Samuel out and put him on Hagar's knee. "There, Samuel, that's your mistress. You understand, old chap, don't you? That's your missis—your missis, Samuel. You're to do everything she says, and look after her and take care of her." He looked round for something of Hagar's, pulled her apron strings and loosened them, and, putting the apron on the table, lifted the pup and put him beside it with his paws on it.

"Guard, Samuel! Guard for Missis."

Samuel sat solemnly blinking up at him, too young to really know his duty yet, but evidently anxious to understand.

"He'll come on. I'll help you to train him. You must be firm with him, and you can give him a cuff, but never hurt him; bull-terriers are too sensitive to be struck."

"As if I would!" Hagar was indignant.

"But you mustn't spoil him. If that Benjamine comes over here keep the pup out of his way. He'll look after himself when he's older, but Benjamine is a little devil to tease animals, and he's always about here."

That was true. The spoilt only boy was a frequent visitor, as his parents lived near, and Penny was not here now to chase him off the premises with loud war-whoops and frightful threatenings.

Mark had brought Samuel's diet sheet and a round puppy basket for his bed. He went and got it from under the seat in the gig, and they made the small dog comfortable in his own quarters.

Hagar's conscience was still a little troubled over Rachel, but Mark reminded her that Rachel did not care about dogs, anyhow, and it was Marion who looked after Robbie and Mrs Brown for Penny, with the somewhat intermittent aid of Perry, who had pets of his own, but was not above taking Robbie for his walk occasionally, whereas Rachel liked to walk alone.

"That's another thing I wanted to talk to you about," said Mark, who had now sat down in the kitchen and was watching Hagar as she prepared the supper, it being Beenie's Sunday out. "I wish you wouldn't try to help Mother about Rachel. She thinks if I married Rachel it would completely change me about the farm, because Rachel is on her side about all the things we differ over. Nothing will change me. That's why I cannot ask any girl to marry me just now. I've nothing to offer her."

Hagar looked at him, surprised. He had got hold of a piece of string and was knotting it and re-knotting it as he spoke, his eyes fixed on his hands—long, lean hands, browned with the weather and stained with toil.

"You know the farm is Mother's. At least, it's as good as hers, for it is run on her money, and she wants to turn it into one of those new efficient machine-run concerns—machines for hatching eggs, machines for milking cows, machines for separating the milk and making the butter, machines for ploughing the land and reaping the corn, machines for every damned thing, while men and horses can go to the wall! They don't matter—flesh and blood doesn't matter—everything has to be sacrificed for machinery!" He spoke with such deep and sudden bitterness that she began to understand something of the terrible quarrelling that was going on at Bowchester. The knuckles stood out in his clenched hands as he suddenly tautened the thick twine and with an outward wrench broke it in his fingers. "I won't have it!"

"Oh, Mark!" said Hagar sadly, and could say no more. She too loved horses and all the old ways on a farm.

"I'll farm in the old ways like my fathers did before me, with men and cattle and horses doing the jobs they were meant for. It's against nature to milk the poor cows with machinery and light lamps—have you heard of Mother's latest idea?—to make the hens lay because they think it's still daylight." He laughed fiercely. "And they are not even to be allowed to follow their natural bent and bring their young out of their eggs as God meant them to do. No clockers permitted! Dip the poor wretches in water or set them where they cannot sit down—they are only hens! All they are good for is laying eggs! Make the poor brutes into egg-laying machines, and kill them off when they give out! What are men? A machine can do the work of half a dozen, a machine is more precious than a man—turn them off to starve!"

He was talking to himself now as much as to Hagar. "There's your new methods for you. Well, I'd die rather than turn Bowchester into a godforsaken machine-run place like that!" He looked up and said, his voice suddenly gentle:

"That's how it is, Hagar."

"Couldn't you leave, Mark, and have a little place of your own?"

"Desert Bowchester? No, Bowchester's mine. Matthew is the only one that thinks as I do, but Matthew is a sheep-farmer; he's all for sheep. The farm's mine—with no money to run it!"

"Didn't your father . . . think about that?"

"My father loved the land and the old ways. He couldn't foresee all this. He'd turn in his grave if he knew what they want to do. Drain the bit of fenland where the snipe comes and the wildfowl make their nests, cut down the spinney where the fox has his lair and the brock his den, turn the Hagg woods into money, and drain the old curling-pond where the village men have had their bit of sport for hundreds of years—make money, money, money! As if there wasn't enough for a man's simple needs without spoiling the countryside and depriving his neighbours or himself of their bit of sport and fun! I tell you, Hagar, I'm sometimes nigh despair. It's because you understand I like to talk to you. You're the only one that does. I felt it in you the first time you came that Sunday and innocently talked the way my heart answered—of things my heart was full of—like it were to burst."

"I'm sorry, Mark. Oh, I'm so sorry about it all."

He looked up to her and smiled.

"So now you know. I don't want anyone to match-make for me. When the time comes, when I have something to offer, when it would be fair to a girl, I'll do my wooing myself—I'll——"

He stopped. The kitchen door had opened, and Mrs Wotherspoon stood there, staring at them, a frown gathering on her face.

"What are you doing here?" she said to Mark, in a tone that made the colour rise in Hagar's cheeks.

"That is my business, I think, Mother," he said quietly.

She flushed up, drawing down her brows and tightening her lips.

"I'd have you know it's my business as well. I'll have no hole-and-corner on-goings under my nose; just understand that, the both of you."

She was ugly in her anger, her face a dull purple, her voice coarse and vulgar.

He stood up.

"You will have to apologize to Miss Thorne for that, Mother." His voice was quiet but authoritative. "I'm not making love to her, nor is she setting her cap, as no doubt you would put it, at me. I came back here to give her the puppy, and to ask her to stop her attempts to back you up in getting me to marry Rachel. You must have seen for yourself she is trying heart and soul to help you, and I want you both to stop it. I'm quite capable of wooing a woman for myself without either of you interfering."

He spoke the last sentences roughly, almost rudely, but Hagar saw he had done the right thing to remove his mother's hateful suspicions of an underhand intrigue.

Mrs Wotherspoon was honest enough with herself to acknowledge that he spoke the truth about Hagar trying to help her with Rachel and Mark.

Her anger had been against them both for the moment, but it was really Mark she suspected of being attached to Hagar. She had never seen a sign of attraction on Hagar's part—could not have done so, indeed, since Hagar had never shown the least sign of interest in him except on Rachel's behalf.

Mrs Wotherspoon felt she had made a mistake, not only in her momentary suspicions, but in her tactics, and, being a fair woman in her way, and a clever one, at once climbed down and apologized—as far as it was in her nature to apologize.

"Well, it gave me a start," she said, "seeing you there, deep in talk like a pair of schemers, but if that's what it's all about I'm willing to take back what I said." She turned to Hagar. "I'm sorry, Hagar. I think you're an honest lass and fond of Rachel, poor lassie. It's bad enough for us all to have had one Peregrine girl thrown over and insulted by a son of mine without the other being treated the same way. It fair upset me to think that exactly the same thing was happening all over again."

"It's all right, Mrs Wotherspoon," said Hagar, smiling. The last thing she wanted was a quarrel with Mother Wotherspoon, so close a friend of the Peregrines. "I dare say we did look a pair of dark schemers, but I was only being scolded and put in my place for trying to be a match-maker." She spoke friendly and innocently enough, but she had caught the underlying warning, and though she resented it could not but admire the swift cleverness of the old woman, who in making her apology had managed to subtly put Mark in the wrong, hinting that he was treating Rachel exactly as Matthew had

I

treated Marion, "and with the 'working housekeeper' too," she added smilingly to herself.

Just then the others came in, and for the rest of the evening Mrs Wotherspoon was her motherly self and could not be kind enough to Hagar.

As she put on her bonnet to go away the real reason of her visit came out. As in a woman's letter, the important thing was kept to the postscript.

"I hear you are going to Goslaw," she said to Marion.

"Yes, Mother Wotherspoon, I'm going on Tuesday," said Marion.

"Do you think you're wise?"

"Yes, I do. Rachel thinks I shouldn't, but I think we should get over all that unfriendliness now. Matthew and Naomi are married, so why not be friends? I always liked Naomi, and I still like her, and Matthew and I will *always* be friends. We weren't engaged or anything, just friends, so he was quite free to marry Naomi if he liked. I wish you would forgive them too, Mother Wotherspoon. Matthew is unhappy about not being able to come home because you won't receive Naomi, and about your never going to see them at Goslaw."

"I don't need a callow lass like you to tell me what's right to do, Marion," returned the grim old woman, "and *you* think well before you go to Goslaw; that's my advice to you. It's a dangerous thing to play with fire, and damped down flames can easily spring up again and wreak havoc, so take to heart an old woman's words and bide in your own home. As for that Naomi, she'll never enter my door, nor will I enter hers —a French snake if ever there was one. Your ma was no friend of mine, but she was right about that maddymoiselle, as she called her—a heathen Papist! It's safest to have no truck with the likes o' them."

She hooked on her cloak with a snap, kissed the girls round, and departed. She had had her say—Marion could take it or leave it.

CHAPTER IV

"AFAR IS A FAERIE LAND"

PENNY and her father, like the true adventurers they were, set off to enjoy themselves. Adventure to the real adventurers needs no far travels. Some people will get more adventure in a bus ride to the next village than others who take a round-the-world tour. Mr Peregrine and his youngest daughter were of the first persuasion; everything was an adventure, even the Channel crossing—neither of them would have dreamed of being sick. Sick! My goodness! With so much to enjoy? Not they. They stood as near the prow of the ship as they could get, lashed by the spray and the salt wind, Penny screaming to her father and he growling enthusiastically back, forgetting in his enjoyment to play a part.

There was a fog in the middle of the Channel, and they enjoyed even that, sniffing up, like war-hounds, the sense of danger.

Penny made friends with a lady who told her that *Das Glockenhaus* meant "the House of the Bells," her first lesson in German.

They entered Germany two of the most callow innocents abroad it was possible to imagine. Neither of them knew a word of German except that *Das Glockenhaus*—heaven knows how they pronounced it!—meant "the House of the Bells." They were immensely proud of it, but it was not calculated to help them much.

They got over the money difficulty by Mr Peregrine's holding out a handful of strange coins and allowing waiters, hotel-keepers, cab-drivers, and suchlike to pick and choose. Clara had told Penny privately that all she needed to do anywhere on the Continent when driven to extremities of a private nature was to say in a loud voice, "Vattercloset." She passed this valuable information on to Mr Peregrine, who not only said it, but roared it. Their journey was, it must be said, a sort of triumphal progress from one 'vattercloset' to another, but they arrived safely at their destination, after staying a night at the Dom Hotel in Cologne, where they also saw the cathedral and bought a bottle of eau-de-Cologne from "Farina, the real and original makers," in some *Strasse* or other.

Mr Peregrine had an insular idea that one must not drink water on the Continent, so poor Penny suffered terribly from thirst, which the gassy 'wassers' he bought her only seemed to increase. She even tried her father's lager beer, but loathed it; in the end she took large draughts out of the hotel bedroom water jug and damned the consequences, with entire success.

They arrived on a Saturday, and drove straight from the station to the school at Das Glockenhaus, and asked for Fräulein Trainer.

After a few minutes a stout woman came in and welcomed them in excellent English. She wore a dark blue cotton dress with white spots and a little collar and cuffs of starched *broderie anglaise*, and mittens on her plump, mottled fingers—her plump hands always looked cold. She had an absolutely round face with a three-cornered little nose planted exactly in the centre. It was pink. Her eyes were round, cold, and blue, and her eyelashes and scant hair were the colour of pale yellow butter. Her hair she wore parted exactly in the middle, showing her pink scalp, drawn down on either side of her brow, and gathered into a little round bun at the back.

She was all enthusiasm, welcomed Penny to Das Glockenhaus and Germany, and said that unfortunately she had arrived at holiday time, but she would meet all her schoolmates the following Monday morning. She assured Mr Peregrine that she would be a mother to his motherless daughter, an assurance which left Penny cold—she had already had her fill of ladies who wanted to be a mother to Mr Peregrine's motherless daughters.

Penny knew that she did not quite like Fräulein Trainer, but she kept that to herself; it was no use worrying her father now. So she smiled and allowed herself to be kissed, standing sedately at Fräulein Trainer's knee. Fräulein sat facing Mr Peregrine and listening to all he had to say about Penny's health and comfort with nods and becks and wreathéd smiles.

They were given cups of watery tea and creamy cakes, and then conducted, for Mr Peregrine's benefit, on a tour of the house and garden. It certainly was a lovely house, with large hall, broad, shallow staircase, and big rooms sparsely furnished and with large white monuments of glazed white tiles in the corners which, Penny discovered to her surprise, were stoves. She had taken them for some kind of cupboard or wardrobe.

The bedrooms had eight or nine little beds in each with white sheets and immense red feather quilts—or so they appeared—on top which were buttoned into white covers. Each bed had a chest of drawers, which, as Fräulein pointed out, had each its own lock and key. Penny did not know then how much that lock and key—not on her own chest (they promptly disappeared), but on the others—were to mean to her in the future. The house stood in its own large grounds, with fruit-trees and pine-trees with grape-vines climbing up them, and flowers and vegetables—altogether a lovely garden. Everything in the house was as clean as a new pin, and Fräulein herself looked as if she had been scrubbed with a scrubbing-brush and yellow soap and then polished.

It all looked eminently satisfactory; the classrooms were large with pleasant windows, all the floors of pale yellow polished wood where not a germ could have found a hiding-place. There were large verandas where, they were told, the girls took tea and did their needlework in the summer. It certainly looked bare with no carpets or hangings, but that was to be expected in a school.

The bill of fare was gone into: hot coffee, rolls and butter, at eight, rolls and fruit at eleven, a plentiful two-course dinner at one, coffee and bread and butter and preserves or cake at four, and a varied supper that might consist of soup, or pancakes, or *Dicke Milch* (sour milk) with brown sugar and bread or sweet puddings.

Mr Peregrine thought it all very satisfactory, and left Penny to go to his hotel.

He was travelling back the next day, having seen the school and the headmistress, and Penny safely installed.

As soon as he was gone Fräulein said she would take her and introduce her to the mistresses, who would now be in the dining-room.

Penny found them sitting round a lamp at a polished table sewing, while one of them read aloud from a book she held in her hand. There was a Scots girl, Miss MacAlpine, a French-woman, Mademoiselle Jeune, and Fräulein von Schell. They were introduced, and Fräulein Trainer took her seat at the head of the table, and the reading went on. It was in French, Fräulein explaining that they read an English, French, and German novel in turn.

Penny was glad to have supper and go to bed. She found she was to sleep in a little bed in one of the larger rooms with Miss MacAlpine, the English governess. She supposed that on Monday all the other beds would fill up, and went off to sleep without much talk.

Next morning her father came to call for her, and took her for a drive round the town and to his hotel for lunch and tea. It was glorious weather, and they thoroughly enjoyed them-selves. Penny had enjoyed her supper of potato pancakes the night before and her breakfast of delicious coffee and rolls, and told her father all she could of the school. She liked Miss MacAlpine and Fräulein von Schell and Mademoiselle Jeune, and thought she might like Fräulein Trainer when she knew her better.

Mr Peregrine was leaving at half-past seven that evening. He came to the school with her, and they bid each other good-bye. At the last Penny clung rather desperately to him and nearly sobbed out her wish that he would take her home again with him, but managed to control herself, while Mr Peregrine, wiping her eyes with his large silk handkerchief, thought to himself that she was sure to be homesick at first, but would soon get over it when all the other girls came back.

He produced a present of a large box of chocolates, got her face fairly dry, and left her with his own heart rather sore. Still, it was the best thing for her, and she had been so keen to come, and Dr Merriman had been rather afraid of the Northern spring for her lungs—that cough of hers had lasted too long. She would soon get over her homesickness in the company of her schoolfellows, who would be back to school in the morning.

"I do hope they don't go away every week-end," Penny had said. "Do you think they can all be weekly boarders?"

"I shouldn't think so," said Mr Peregrine. "Didn't Fräulein say something about some feast or fast day or something?"

"Yes, I expect that's it," said Penny.

"And some of them are sure to ask you to go home with them if there are weekly boarders," he assured her hopefully. "That will be great fun."

"Of course they will." Penny had suddenly cheered up. "Clara had such fun in Saxony staying with her school friend Bertha Gross."

The other mistresses were spending the Sunday night out, but Miss MacAlpine had stayed in to look after her when she came back.

Miss MacAlpine seemed very young to Penny to be a school-mistress. She was a pale, stoutish girl with dark blue eyes, brown hair, and freckles.

"I'll help you to unpack," she said now to Penny, whose corded trunks still stood unopened in the bedroom. "Once your things are in your drawers you'll feel more at home. I'll race you up the stairs."

"Won't Fräulein Trainer mind?" asked Penny, as they arrived breathless in the big, cold room.

"She is out at church, and then she goes to supper with Frau Pfarrer Grein—that's the minister's wife. Every one takes their husband's title in Germany, so she is Mrs Minister Grein."

They both laughed, and then Penny opened her box of chocolates, and they each had a chocolate.

"Don't eat them up too quickly," said Miss MacAlpine, as Penny pressed her to take more. "You'll find you like one when you come to bed."

This seemed eminently reasonable to Penny, who loved to munch sweets in bed, and the box was carefully closed, and they started to unpack. It was cold in the room, for it was still early spring, and though everything was much further on than at home, the evenings were chill, and there was no fire in the big stove.

CHAPTER V

"WHEN SICK FOR HOME"

AT last everything was put tidily away, dresses and coats being in the *garde-robe*, a room fitted with pegs on the landing, and they were ready to go downstairs.

"Daddy will be away," Penny said, looking at the little watch Anthony had brought to the station as a parting gift, a little gold watch which fastened to her dress with a gold brooch in the form of a lovers' knot. " The train started at half-past seven, and it's nearly eight."

"Supper's at eight on Sunday. We just have time to wash and tidy up. Do you like ground rice pudding?"

"No," said Penny, "not very much. Is that what we get for a sweet?"

"It's all you get," said Miss MacAlpine. She had a Scottish accent and a wide smile with big teeth.

"Nothing else but pudding!" Penny stared.

"No. You'll get used to it; there's cinnamon and sugar to eat with it."

At that moment the bell rang, and they went down to

supper. On the table was a cloth and spoons, and in front of Fräulein Trainer a large white shape turned out like a blanc-mange and sprinkled over with cinnamon.

"Goodness!" thought Penny. "It's cold. I do wish there was something hot. Perhaps we'll get some hot coffee."

But there was no hot coffee. There was nothing but the pudding, with a little sugar and cinnamon sprinkled over it. Penny was hungry and could have eaten more than her first serving, but was not offered a second helping and did not ask, as none of the mistresses did.

"I expect they've had supper out," thought Penny, "and then they are all mistresses. I expect the girls will eat more." And she remembered the chocolates with thanksgiving.

After supper they read and sewed again till bedtime, but this was an English evening, and Penny enjoyed the story they were reading—*Kenilworth*, by Sir Walter Scott. Luckily they had just begun it.

"We'll have to start you on needlework to-morrow," said Fräulein Trainer. "What can you do? Plain sewing? Knitting? Embroidery or crochet?"

"I should like to learn to embroider," said Penny, who was admiring the lovely work Fräulein von Schell was doing in coloured silks.

"We'll go into town to-morrow then and buy some linen and silks, and Fräulein will teach you."

By bedtime Penny was feeling very homesick again, and she was glad when good-nights were said and they took their candles up to bed.

It was as they were undressing that the great shock came.

"Homesick?" asked Miss MacAlpine, seeing Penny's efforts to hide the tears that would well up in her eyes.

"A little," she said bravely. "You see, it's sort of lonely without the girls. It will be better to-morrow when they are all back. It will be fun when all the beds are full, won't it?" And she looked round the row of cold little empty cots.

"The beds?" said Miss MacAlpine, looking up surprised.

"Yes," said Penny, puzzled at her look. "The room will be full of boarders, won't it?" She counted. "There are eight beds, not counting yours. There will be nine of us, won't there?"

"But"—Miss MacAlpine was staring at her—"don't you know? There are no boarders."

Penny was sitting on her bed taking off her slippers and stockings. She stopped with a slipper in her hand. "No boarders?" she faltered incredulously. "Oh, yes, Fräulein Trainer said there were between thirty and forty girls. I remember her letter. She said she was sure I'd be happy with all her girls; there were between thirty and forty now, and she expected the numbers to be largely increased after the Easter holidays. There must be some girls."

"There may be some boarders coming after Easter," said Miss MacAlpine. "I do hope so; if she said that perhaps there are. In fact, I think there are sure to be—it isn't long to wait, you know."

Penny was still staring at her in absolute dismay. There must be some mistake. What could Miss MacAlpine mean? Perhaps she meant there were none in this room, that they were all in the other rooms.

"But the others—the thirty or forty—are they all in the other rooms, you mean?"

She had seen at least three rooms all full of little tidy, empty beds. Miss MacAlpine shook her head. "No, there isn't a single boarder—just you. You are our first. Are you sure Fräulein Trainer said thirty or forty boarders?"

"Yes, I'm positive—at least"—she paused—"she said girls, but that's the same thing, isn't it?"

"She must have meant the day girls," said Miss MacAlpine. "There are thirty-two day girls."

"Day girls! Do you mean girls that just come for lessons in the day and then go home?"

"Yes. Didn't you really know?"

Penny shook her head, all her castles in the air tumbling round her ears, all her dreams of the fun in a world of happy, romping schoolgirls. She could not believe it, she simply could not believe it, that there weren't any girls—none at all; that she was alone in this big, dreary house with four mistresses and no one of her own age, no girls. She wouldn't believe it; she couldn't believe it.

"It's not true!" she gulped at last. "It can't be true. She said there were all those girls. My daddy thinks there's lots of girls, and Hagar and Marion and Rachel all think there's a lovely big school full of girls. Clara said so too. There were nearly a hundred girls with Clara when she was at school, and this is the same school. What do you mean? Where are they all? There must be some girls. There must! There must!"

"You poor child!" said Miss MacAlpine, coming over and sitting on the bed beside her and putting her arm round her. "I never dreamt you didn't know. When you spoke of girls I thought that you meant the day girls. That is what Fräulein Trainer must have meant—the day girls."

"Then there aren't any boarders? There aren't any at all? There's nobody coming to-morrow?"

"Just the day girls."

"Then I can't stay—I can't!" She jumped up as if she would begin to dress there and then. "My daddy must take me away——" Then she remembered. Her daddy was gone. He was away, travelling back to England.

There was no way to get in touch with him to call him back. She was alone, left stranded in this great, empty house, without another girl to speak to, with no companions, not one—alone. She shuddered, and then began to tremble so violently that Miss MacAlpine got alarmed and, lifting her up, folded back the sheet and tucked her into bed with the huge feather *plumeau* over her.

"There, childie," she said. "Get warm and go to sleep. It won't seem so bad in the morning."

She sat beside her a while, then put out the lights and crossed to her own bed.

Then the tears came and overwhelmed Penny. Stuffing her handkerchief into her mouth, she tried to cry quietly, but the sobs broke out and shook the bed. She sobbed and sobbed in the darkness.

By and by she felt her *plumeau* lifted, and a warm, comforting figure crept into bed beside her and cuddled her up close.

"Are you homesick? I'm homesick too," said a voice that sounded very young and forlorn in the darkness. Penny flung her arms round her, and they clung to each other and cried and cried till they cried themselves to sleep. All Miss MacAlpine's defences went down as she sobbed out to Penny. "It's so difficult keeping it up—being a schoolmistress, I mean."

They wakened with the first dawn and lay talking together.

"Call me Mallie when we're by ourselves," said Miss MacAlpine. "That's what they called me at home. I thought there were girls here too when I came, but, you see, I never thought of asking Fräulein Trainer. I just naturally thought there would be a lot of boarders, as it was a boarding-school and with that grand prospectus showing the big house and everything. I'm not a real governess, you know. I'm here as what is called an 'au pair' pupil. I give English lessons and help generally in return for board and German and music lessons, but Fräulein Trainer calls me her English mistress and says I mustn't be too friendly with the girls. I'm the only English teacher, though I came here as assistant English mistress, and thought I was just to help a resident mistress. You and I will stick together. We're the only English girls here."

"How old are you?" asked Penny, too forlorn to be polite. "I thought you looked quite grown up with your hair up and those spectacles on. You look younger now, though, with your plaits hanging down."

"I'm sixteen—nearly seventeen," said Mallie. "My mother and father died, and I was going to be a governess, so I came here to learn German. As I couldn't afford the fees, I teach instead."

"Are there really and truly no boarders?"

"No, not a single one. You see, they all left when the old lady gave up the school. Fräulein Trainer was a governess there, and I don't think the girls liked her. She is always saying boarders are coming, but they never appear, and we were all so pleased when you really turned up. Perhaps some more will come now."

"Do you like it here?" asked Penny.

Mallie hesitated. "Well, it's good for me, because there has been no one to speak English with, and one learns very quickly when one must talk German all the time. You'll learn quickly too; in a week or two you'll understand nearly everything they say and will be able to talk a little, and you won't be so lonely as I was, because you'll have me to talk to. I cried every night in this big, lonely room, all by myself with all these ghostly beds and nobody in them."

"I wish my daddy hadn't gone—I'd ask him to take me away. I hate it. I wanted a real boarding-school with lots of girls and fun and having secret parties at night and all it says in books about boarding-schools."

"I know. Never mind; perhaps lots will come now you are here, and Fräulein Trainer will be awfully kind to you, I expect, she's so pleased to have got you. It's been awful for her having no boarders. It's nearly a year now since she began."

"I'm the first swallow," said Penny, who shared her father's propensity for quoting, "but one swallow doesn't make a summer. I don't like Fräulein Trainer; she smarmed over me in front of Daddy, but she has funny eyes. Do you like her?"

Loyalty evidently struggled with Miss MacAlpine's natural frankness. Besides, she was in a very different position from Penny, a real pupil paying large fees. She hesitated.

"She's had a hard time," she said at last, "and I'm sorry for her. I think she'll be awfully good to you. I know she is going to take you to the Kursaal Concerts and the Opera House and everything. Cheer up! One gets over homesickness."

The sun was coming in to the window by this time, and after all she was in the Germany of her dreams, and it was nearly Easter—there would be more girls after Easter. A tiny corner of the grey cloud lifted.

"I'm glad I have you," she said, giving Mallie a hug. "I'd have *died* without you."

CHAPTER VI

"WHEN I AM OLD AND WEARY AND WORN"

WHAT a bother," said Marion at breakfast. "There's a letter from Granny Wotherspoon; she says I must go over and see her at once."

They all called the old lady Granny Wotherspoon, though her name was really Waugh.

Granny Wotherspoon was one of those ancient ladies who are always getting on with their dying, but never quite accomplish it. Possibly she enjoyed the fuss she created, or perhaps she did feel the end was near; in any case, she had called "Wolf!" so often she was in danger of not being believed when he really came to carry her off.

"Well, you don't go to Goslaw till this afternoon," said Hagar. "You'll have time to slip along this morning. After all, she's ninety, isn't she? It's not beyond the bounds of possibility that she is near her end, and you'd be sorry afterwards if you hadn't gone."

"Marion was always a favourite of hers," said Rachel. "She almost went up in flames when Matthew married Naomi, and has never 'goamed' him since. That's her own word."

"It means 'never acknowledged his existence,'" said

Marion. "I like old Granny, but I wish she'd forgotten my existence to-day. I have so much to do."

"I expect she's heard you were going to Goslaw and wants to stop you," Rachel went on. "Granny hates Naomi, who used to try to suck up to her because she knew Granny was an old miser and had hoards of money. I expect she thought Matthew, who used to be her favourite, would get heaps of it, but he won't get any now. Granny wouldn't let Naomi touch a penny of her money. Luke and John will be the rich ones, now Mark has disdained her old money and told her he wouldn't knuckle down to her for it. I'm just warning you, Hagar," she laughed mischievoulsy across the table at Hagar.

"Hagar wouldn't marry *anybody* for money," exclaimed Marion.

Hagar laughed. "How do you know?" she asked. "Perhaps I'll set my old cap at Luke or John and become a baby-snatcher now you've told me where the money goes."

"I wish she'd give me some money," Perry announced solemnly. "It would be very useful for me to learn to fly."

"You're to go into the business," said Paul. "*You'll* have plenty of money. Now *I* really need it to buy a farm in Rhodesia."

They plunged into schemes for spending old Granny's hoards, and thoroughly enjoyed themselves till breakfast was over and Marion went off to put on her outdoor things.

"I'd better go at once," she said, "and get it over, but I hate listening to her calling Naomi names, and if she says one thing about Matthew I'll bite her."

"Grandmothers have large teeth," Rachel reminded her, "the better to eat up little Red Riding-hoods. You'd better take your pot of honey with you," she continued after a moment's pause, a slight bitterness in her voice, but left them to deduce the meaning for themselves.

"Rachel's making one of her deep remarks," said Perry, spearing a pat of butter.

"Rachel can buy any one of this family at one end and sell

them at the other," said Paul, instantly rising to any suspected criticism of his beloved Rachel.

"O what can ail thee, knight-at-arms——" began Perry, when a well-directed roll cut him short.

"You needn't think that the mantle of Elijah has fallen upon you, Perry, now Father isn't here," said Rachel ruthlessly. "You're just being a donkey."

And that ended that little breeze.

Marion found old Granny sitting up in bed and looking very frail. Her tongue, however, was as forthright as ever, though she sometimes had to gasp for breath.

"So you're determined to go and stay with that wily bitch," she said, as Marion kissed her and sat down by her bed.

"Granny Wotherspoon, you're a bad old lady, using words like that."

"I'm too old to pick and choose my words to suit your ears. She's a bitch, and if you don't know it now you will some day. You've had proof enough of it already—big softy that you are."

"Well, if I'm a softy what do you want to bother about me for?"

"Because I like you, that's why. Aye, Marion, I've aye liked you best o' the bunch. You're the pick o' the basket, and though I may call you a softy, fine I know it's only on top, there's more grit underneath than in any Peregrine o' the lot—or Wotherspoon either. That's why I wanted you for Matthew. A young gander like him needed a *woman* to guide him. Eh, well——"

"Matthew's not a young gander."

"There ye go, arguing with me, though we both know better. Will you listen to my advice?"

"Not if you say I'm not to go. I'm sorry for Naomi, Granny. Everybody is against her, and Mamma and Beenie made up such lies about her."

"That's as may be—not that I believed all that poisoning nonsense your ma talked of. Sheer spite that was. Anyhow, that friskmahoy is too fond of her own skin to risk it, and was too keen on getting Matthew to lose her place near him. Your father, pshaw! All stuff and nonsense! James Peregrine may be a fool in some ways, but he's decent through and through—a *good* man, your father, Marion, though, like you, he covers up the sound, good stuff with a lot of palaver. Never you believe a word against your father."

"As if I would!" said Marion indignantly. "Our father's the best man in the world."

"Well, well, lay your feathers. I'm not saying he isn't. I'm just saying there was nothing in your silly stepmother's daft talk. She never *thought*, that one; she just opened her mouth and let the nonsense dribble out of her. It was Matthew, poor goat, with his handsome face, that besom fell for, and Matthew she got, the viper! If I had had anything to do with her I'd soon have set fire to her kilts. But that wasn't what I wanted you here for. Get me my keys; they're under my pillow."

As Marion hunted for the keys she went on, "If you'd married Matthew, Marion, I'd have left him the lion's share of my money. Poor Matthew! I was aye fond of the laddie. He and Mark——" She stopped. "A thrawn devil, that Mark. Do you think there's anything between him and this new lass you've got in—I never can mind her outlandish name? Martha [Mother Wotherspoon] tells me they're gey and greet."

"No, there's not. Hagar is a darling. She wants Mark to marry Rachel."

The old woman's sharp eyes pounced on her.

"Aye, aye . . . What set ye to fancy Matthew, Marion, when Mark was there? He may be a dour chiel, but he's older and a stronger man than Matthew, though Matthew has the looks. Could you no think of Mark now?"

Marion laughed. "Goodness, no! Besides, Mark never looks at the side of the road I'm on, but I wish he and Rachel would marry, and Mother Wotherspoon wants Rachel to. I'm going to be an old maid, Granny."

K

"Aye." Granny didn't disclaim this. "Aye, but it would be a great pity. Have you got those keys?"

"Yes, here they are."

"Well, go over and open the bottom drawer in my kist. You'll find a tin box under my flannel petticoats. Bring it here."

Marion found the box, a little steel deed-box, and brought it over to her.

"That's for you, Marion. You're to open it when I'm gone, and say nothing about it. It wasn't your fault you lost Matthew. You're a good lassie, Marion, and a kind one, and I don't intend you should lose what you would have shared with Matthew. I don't hold with putting everything in these banks that may go back on you at any minute. Your share's in there, and nobody knows about it. Nobody kens what I got. I could aye keep things to mysel'; that's where Yorkshire blood tells."

She was pulling a key off the ring as she spoke, while Marion sat and gazed at her, utterly taken by surprise.

"I may be gone when you get back, and anyway you never know when you might need it."

"Oh, Granny, I can't take this! I—it doesn't seem fair. You keep it, Granny; you may live for years and years yet." She smiled. "You may need it yourself if the bank goes back on you."

"Not I. I don't put all my eggs in one basket. Now take it and say no more about it. You've suffered enough through the Wotherspoons. You're not going to lose everything. You'd have had a bit of money to spend through Matthew getting his share if you'd married him. Do you think I'd let that French hussy get what should have been yours? I'm no that daft. Na! Na! Right's right, and that's yours."

"But, Granny——"

"But me no buts. I'd leave it to you anyway, but I like giving it to you myself. You never know when you may need it. Now take it and give me a kiss, love. It's a real pleasure to me to give it to you—the only bit of real pleasure I have in it now."

Marion put both arms round the old woman and kissed and kissed her, holding the frail body in her arms.

"Oh, Granny, you are too good to me. I feel I can't thank you. I can just love you. I'll take it, but, mind, it's still really yours. If ever you want it back I'll bring the box and the key just as you've given them to me. I'll never open it——"

"Well, unless you are in some desperate need, my bairn, don't open it till I'm gone, but, mind, if you need it it's yours now."

"All right, Granny, and thank you, darling Granny, a hundred million times." The tears were in her eyes. She wished she had been kinder to the old woman, had visited her often, had never spoken impatiently of her, and wanted to convey all she felt, but words seemed so useless.

"Eh, now, say no more." She put the key in Marion's hands, patted it, and folded the fingers over the key. "You'll have to be going now, and, to tell the truth, I'm tired and maun take a rest. Good-bye, love. God bless you!"

"Good-bye and God bless you, Granny."

She rose to go. Then the old woman caught her hand and held it, gazing at her with unfathomable old eyes.

"You do what your heart tells ye. Do what your heart tells ye. Dinna forget I said that and gave ye my blessing."

"No, I'll always remember every word you've said."

"That's right. Now off you go or ye'll have some of them coming up to shoo ye out. Put that box under your cape"— Marion had on the big golfing cape of tweed, lined with tartan, she was wearing for her journey—"and let none see it." She dropped into broad Yorkshire. "Thon's a secret between thee and me, but thou's just startin' on the road, and I'm nighin' th' end, and, eh, lass! I'm weary—weary and worn."

CHAPTER VII

"GIVE ME A STAFF AND A CROOK"

A COLD March wind was blowing when Marion arrived at the little hillside station which lay surrounded by the steep slopes of the Cheviot foothills, grey now in the dusk of a dull afternoon, drawing to its close.

As Marion stood looking about a wedge of geese flew high overhead, and the young stationmaster standing beside her remarked, following them with his eyes, "Aye, there'll be an oncome; they're flying afore the snow."

Marion shivered. She didn't like snow in March. Patches of it lay so long, "waiting for more," said the old people. "It'll no go till it has company."

As she watched the flight of the geese across the hillside she saw the trap coming down the rough road with Matthew in it.

"There's Goslaw," said the man, giving him the name of his farm. "The auld mare likes to take it easy."

In a few moments the trap, a two-wheeled gig, drew up, and Matthew climbed down. He looked a little broader, she thought, in the rough grey shepherd's tweed he wore, with an old black and white tartan plaid thrown across his shoulders and fastened with a kilt pin under his armpit.

"Well, Marion, here you are," he said. "I'm sorry I wasn't in before the train; the mare picked up a stone. Is that all your luggage?" glancing at her trunk and smaller case. He seemed more natural and himself than he'd been at Christmas.

"Did you expect me to bring another trunk with all my dance frocks?" asked Marion, laughing.

"Lord, no! I just meant had you got it all out of the van. There's not much dancing in the hills—eh, Jock?"

"Eh, I wouldn't say that," said the man. "You should have brought the wife to the grieve's weddin'; they danced till fower o'clock i' the morn."

"And you are getting married yourself, Jock. I'll have to bring Miss Peregrine over to dance at your wedding."

They were strapping the luggage on behind, and now Matthew lifted Marion up and swung her in, then climbed up behind her, and turned the mare's head as he shouted good-night.

"How far is Goslaw?" asked Marion.

"Oh, the matter of a few miles, but it's a rough road, and Jenny's not so young as she was—like you and me." He turned and smiled at her. "But you look younger than ever —Grandmamma, what pink cheeks you've got!"

"The better to bluff you with," she answered, laughing. "I'm getting on."

"Grandmamma, what blue eyes you've got!"

It was an old game of theirs, but she picked up her cues more slowly, and he went on:

"You ought to say—now what ought you to say?"

"The better to see through you with."

He laughed. "That's what you used to say—in the old days. Now it should be, 'the better to——'"

"That's not playing fair," she broke in. "You're taking my turn."

"All right. Grandmamma, what a red little nose you've got!"

"The better to smell the supper with—oh, Matthew, I'm starving. Has Naomi got the pot boiling?"

"She has a snipe 'on the spit,' as Penny would say, and watercress salad and potato straws, *à la* something or other, preceded by what she calls a *pot-au-feu* and followed by a *ragoût*—a real French meal, I was to tell you, as far as she could make one in the hills."

"Clever girl—I wonder you haven't got fat, Matthew, with all the lovely things Naomi can cook. Do you remember how Beenie used to scorn her 'French messes,' and how any left-overs always mysteriously disappeared?"

He laughed.

"Rather, and the *Helix pomatia* and everything. . . . How is Penny liking Germany?"

"Father isn't back yet to tell us. I expect she's in her element. She always wanted to go to a large boarding-school and be 'Penelope of the fifth form' or something like that, and, of course, she was over the moon about going to Germany and walking straight into Grimm's fairy-tales. You should have heard her going on about sledge rides and pine-trees laden with snow and wild swans and goose girls! We had to keep reminding her it would be summer when she got there, or spring anyhow, and that she wouldn't see much of Big Klaus or Little Klaus or witches or gnomes at school."

"Oh, well, she'll have little Gretchens, won't she? And the little hares that bring the Easter eggs—a very far-fetched way to get eggs, to my mind. If it had been squirrels now. Squirrels at least build nests."

"She would have liked to take a guinea-pig with her, but Father put his foot down on the guinea-pig—so to speak."

He laughed. "Funny little Penny. And the cough—was it better?"

"No, but Dr Merriman says she'll soon get rid of it. We teased her about coming back a little fat Gretchen. Anthony said we'd roll her downhill from the station."

"Anthony and she are still playing the knight and his lady?"

"Rather. He just worships her, and Penny has the ring he got in the plum-pudding tied on a bit of thin cord round her neck—little goose."

"Well, you never know. Anthony knows how to wait."

"He won't get off waiting if Penny can help it. She reminded him every day that he was to wait and marry her—no coy maiden about Penny."

They were on their old easy terms before the little sheep-farm lying in a lirk of the hills came into sight, with the blue peat smoke curling up from the chimneys and the sheepfolds lying round it.

"Oh," said Marion, "I know I'm going to be happy here. How lovely it looks! See, there's Naomi waving at the door!"

She waved enthusiastically back. The gig turned away from the little rushing burn they had been following and drew up before the door of the low, cottage-like building.

In a flood of French and English Naomi met her, calling her by all sorts of French endearments, and insisting on Matthew's seconding her.

"No, I don't think she's the least like a cabbage or a cauliflower," said Matthew, "and nothing will make me say so. An apple now—I'll go as far as an apple." He put his hands on Marion's shoulders and ran her into the house.

"There now," he said. "What do you think of Naomi's decorations, and can you smell your supper?"

"The poor infant's starving," he said to Naomi. "We must feed her at once."

If Naomi had ever been jealous of Marion there was no sign of it now. It may have been that she was so desperately lonely she was glad to see anyone, or she may have thought that with the advent of one Peregrine the rest would follow, and that she and Matthew would again be received in the two families at the Falcon's House and Bowchester, but, whatever the reason, she welcomed her and fussed over her with what seemed genuine warmth.

Matthew took the head of the table as they sat down with one at each side of him, and a merry meal was soon in progress.

It was a strange supper for the farm kitchen of a shepherd's house, and Matthew said so.

"Porridge and milk would be more in the setting," he remarked, laughing, to Marion.

"To-morrow for ze porridge; to-night we feast," said Naomi.

They had a happy evening together. Matthew and Marion had always been great pals as well as lovers—in fact, their love-affair had only been in its first stages when Naomi came on the scene, but their happy association had started when they were children and gone on for many years. They drew each other out, had the same sense of humour, a sort of special variety of their own, and each was at their best in the other's company. They had an endless store of old jests, teasings, quips, and conversational turns and twists, often understood by none but themselves, and they kept Naomi laughing by resorting to them and then explaining them to her.

There was the "stroke down and stroke along, stroke down and stroke along," which indicated that any particular story, pun, or rhyme, was their own special possession, utterly unintelligible till explained that a stroke down and stroke along made twice with a pencil formed an enclosure, which imaginary enclosure staked a claim on pun or joke for the one quick enough to say it first.

Their talk that night was full of these reminiscences of childhood, and their young, gay laughter rang through the kitchen.

"But how Mattoo can laugh!" exclaimed Naomi more than once. "He is so solemn always, this husband I have got."

"I expect it's being so much with the sheep," said Marion. "Sheep are such solemn creatures." Which immediately re-started an old argument about sheep, for whom Matthew claimed an intelligence far above the ordinary in animals.

"I do not like zheep," said Naomi. "They smell, *mon Dieu*! I smell zheep all the day, and Mattoo, he too smell of zheep—phui!"

"Good, healthy smell," said Matthew.

When he went out with his lantern Naomi took Marion up to her little room with the attic windows and helped her to unpack, exclaiming over the new frocks she had acquired, asking questions about Rachel and Penny and all the family, not forgetting her old enemy Beenie or the new addition, Hagar.

"But what for a name—Hagar! Do you like Hagar?"

"We love her," said Marion. "She is so dear and funny. She is only a little older than we are, but she has taken us all under her wing as if she was a little black hen with a lot of Buff Orpington chickens or a clecking of ducks. I'm sure if she *were* a hen with ducks she would get drowned trying to swim after them. Dear, darling Hagar! And she's so competent you wouldn't know the house——" She stopped, remembering the confusion in Naomi's reign.

"I do not like her," said Naomi. "She has ousted me."

This was just like Naomi, who was incapable of seeing anything but from her own personal point of view. Selfish and volatile, and never to be trusted, there was yet a sort of charm about her, a sunny warmth and friendliness when she was happy, that made one forget how quickly the storm clouds could roll up, how violent her anger could be, how ugly her subtlety and cunning.

She and simple Marion had always got on well because Marion was incapable of seeing through her, as Rachel did. She took her at her face value, and had always listened with sympathy to the tragic tales of loneliness and woe which Rachel had spurned with contempt.

The first days passed happily, with Marion helping Naomi in the kitchen and dairy. The little farm was practically self-supporting, and Naomi with her Frenchwoman's quickness had soon mastered all the details of scone-baking, butter-making, bacon-curing, and cheese-making, and it was a delight to Marion to help her, with the difference that she loved the farm work, while with Naomi it was a constant grievance. She did it, but she hated it, hated the primitive cottage, the loneliness, the distance from the gaieties she loved, the cinema, the dance-hall, the theatres, and the shops.

"Mattoo must give up all this," she said, and then began to try to find out from Marion what prospects he had of heiring money from his mother and grandmother. "They are so reech, and he is the favourite grandson," she kept repeating. "He must get ze money of the grandmother and some of his late father's."

"I don't know," Marion could only answer to all her prying

questions. "Mother Wotherspoon would never talk to me about her private affairs, you know, Naomi, and I don't know anything about his father's will."

"But you were almost——" she stopped. She had been going to say "almost betrothed," and to inquire if dowries and portions and money matters generally had not all been discussed by the two families before things came to a head, as in France, but she suddenly remembered that she had always pretended to look upon Marion and Matthew's affair as a joke to be brushed aside as a funny little girl and boy friendship of no consequence whatever.

So she stopped and began to grumble about what she called Matthew's secretiveness. "He tell me nozzing," she said fretfully, "nozzing."

That was the only fly in Marion's ointment at the moment. Naomi was continually grumbling to her about Matthew, about his secretiveness, about his love for sheep and sheep-farming, his lack of ambition, his refusal to see his mother and insist on his 'rights,' his shutting her out of his business affairs.

"It ees not like that in France. Ze husband and wife run the beezeness together. The wife always keep the accounts and manages the money—always."

"You'll have to get used to English ways," said Marion. "Matthew doesn't mean to shut you out; it's just the different customs you are up against. My father never discusses the business with us. We don't know if he's rich or just comfortably off or anything, and I'm sure he never talked to my stepmothers about it."

"The English are mad," reiterated Naomi. "But I *will not* have it."

At first she was careful to leave Matthew alone in front of Marion, but as they became more familiar she forgot all her good intentions and began to nag him unmercifully. Matthew always retired into silence and said nothing, which occasionally roused her to bitter anger. The storm broke, and she would scream like a virago in French and English, her English always

getting broken as she became excited. When she remembered
to take pains she could speak quite good English, but she was
lazy about it.

In many ways she was lazy, and she was getting too fat.
She would not walk anywhere in the high-heeled shoes which
she would not discard, and lay down and slept every afternoon,
and, as Marion grew more familiar with the ways of the house,
she took advantage of her good-nature to lie in bed and have
her breakfast brought up in the morning, starting it with
complaints of a headache, and then apparently taking it for
granted.

Matthew was not pleased.

"Naomi not down yet?" he would ask.

"No, she's having breakfast in bed this morning."

"But it's giving you a lot of work, Marion. Naomi and I
forget you are here for a holiday. I'm afraid we both put on
you. You were helping me with those lambs all yesterday."

"Oh, but I *loved* it! I love the lambs."

That was true. She was in her element petting the motherless
ones, keeping them at the fire till their poor wet wool all fluffed
up dry and warm, feeding them out of the milk bottle, teaching
them to suck it. It was all the greatest fun. "And," she went
on, "it's a chance for Naomi to have a few little indulgences
while I'm here. It *is* dull for her here, Matthew, and it does get
monotonous doing the same thing every day—and she does
enjoy breakfast in bed. I think they always have it in France."

Matthew would grunt and then recover his good nature,
and in a few minutes they would be laughing and happy
together.

So it went on for a while. Marion had come for ten days or
so, but it looked as if her visit would be prolonged, for neither
of them would hear a word of her going. Then another element
began to creep in.

CHAPTER VIII

"ACH, WIE LIEGT SO WEIT, WAS MEIN EINST WAR"

MR PEREGRINE had returned home with triumphant tales of the journey, of the beautiful schoolhouse, of the garden, of the kind lady at the head of Das Glockenhaus, and by the time Penny could draw her breath after her shock letters of congratulation were coming from home saying how pleased they all were that everything was so lovely, the headmistress so kind, the food so good; teasing her about becoming fat, asking which Gretchen was her 'best friend.'

Penny read them with the tears running down her white cheeks. If they only knew—oh, if only they knew!

At night Miss MacAlpine was "Mallie," but by day she had inevitably to return into Miss MacAlpine. Fräulein Trainer knew that the parents of her pupils supposed the Scots girl to be a dependable and efficient English mistress of fairly ripe years. Any descent into girlishness was frowned upon and met with instant cold displeasure.

"I hope you keep your distance with Penelope in the bedroom," she had said, "and do not become too familiar. Remember you are a mistress, and she is one of your pupils. If I hear of any maudlin friendship or lowering of your dignity you will go."

An idle threat, for she got too much out of Mallie and too cheaply to let her go. But Mallie didn't know that. She had her living to make, and she was terrified of leaving her job before the specified year was up and not getting a good reference.

So, though lonely, Penny had the comfort of Mallie's companionship and friendship at night and on the few occasions they were sent out walks together. During the day it was Miss MacAlpine with whom she had to deal, each of them afraid to show any interest in the other.

The walks together were few, for though Penny was sent a long walk every day, dreary in the extreme, it was with Mademoiselle or Fräulein von Schell she went. Fräulein Trainer was always called "Fräulein," but the little German aristocrat working for her bread and butter was always "Fräulein von Schell." Fräulein Trainer herself, however, never mentioned her name, possibly jealous of the 'von' that proclaimed her to be *hochwohlgeboren* (high-born) and of vastly superior birth to herself.

At first Penny could not understand a word that either of the mistresses said in her own tongue. Fräulein von Schell, retiring and conscientious, never spoke a word of English unless driven to a brief translation. Far otherwise was it with Mademoiselle. Here was a heaven-sent opportunity for her to learn English, and she took it under the mask of kindliness.

"I talk Engleesh, and you correct me—it will be fun, but ze *bear* must not know."

The "bear," needless to say, was her employer.

To homesick Penny, so seldom hearing a word of English through the day, it was all right. She didn't in the least see through Mademoiselle. She thought she was kind and funny, and she reminded her of Naomi—who had also never spoken French if she could help it—so Penny heard hardly a word of Mademoiselle's mother tongue, which may have been as well, as she was another of Fräulein Trainer's cheap acquisitions—a French-Swiss with an atrocious accent.

Every morning the little gate at the far end of the grounds had to be unlocked for the day girls, and it became one of Penny's jobs to do it. She loved it; it was the only time she was free from supervision, and she loved running through the garden, jumping down the steps, and, later on, picking up the burst, over-ripe apricots and greengages that fell and could be purloined before old Frau Trainer—Fräulein's mother—was sent round with her basket to pick them up.

For Penny was always hungry. She, who had had to be coaxed to eat at home, never knew now what it was to feel satisfied. They were all the same, but Fräulein von Schell and Mademoiselle had, at least, a little money to spend. Mallie had none, and though Penny was supposed to have pocket money it was spent by Fräulein Trainer, and she never saw it. It took many weeks to pay for the needlework, and after that there was always something else to which her shilling a week had to go.

For breakfast they had one roll and butter each. The 'bread and fruit' lunch was a dry roll and a withered apple or a few apricots or a couple of greengages.

For dinner there was usually a small plate of soup, and then Arabella, the maid, handed round a dish on which lay thin wafers of meat and another with the exact number of potatoes to give them one each. When they were large potatoes it was not so bad, but when they were small Penny would rise from table almost as hungry as she sat down and longing for tea-time. There was never any pudding. Such puddings as they got, large, icy-cold shapes of rice or semolina, were reserved for supper.

On one never-to-be-forgotten occasion Penny, coming last at the table, helped herself to two pieces of meat—there was always an extra slice which she had wondered that no one took.

She had hardly lifted it when Fräulein Trainer's cold voice cut across the table:

"Are you so greedy, then, you can't leave a little for the servants?"

Poor, sensitive Penny blushed scarlet all over her shrinking little body. To be so addressed with Arabella there, whose meat she was taking, plunged her into black depths of shame. She sat with the tears dripping on her plate, unable to eat her share for the lump in her throat.

Fridays were the most dreaded days. There was horrible boiled white fish for dinner with a sauce made of flour and water such as the girls had made for paper-hanging at home, and for supper there was nothing but a small soup-plate of sour milk with little dice of rye-bread in it and a sprinkling of sugar. With their coffee (without sugar) in the afternoon they had two slices of rye-bread and butter. This was all right when they were in the middle of the loaf, but they were long German loaves, tapering away to nothing at each end, and the two pieces were all they got, small or large.

No one dared ask for more. There was something about Fräulein Trainer that terrified them all. They starved and endured.

If it had not been for kind Arabella, the maidservant, the lot of Mallie and Penny would have been even worse, but Arabella, when she could manage it, sneaked up pieces of bread from the kitchen and put them in one of the empty chests, locking the drawer. She even sometimes put in a little enamelled teapot full of slightly warm weak tea.

This constituted all the 'secret feasts' Penny ever had at school—a few stolen bits of dry bread, sometimes with a scrape of butter or jam.

She never wrote home about it. In after years they were often, at home, to wonder why, but Penny couldn't have told them. It was just one of the incomprehensible things children and young girls do. For one thing, Fräulein Trainer read all her letters. They had to be taken to her unsealed, and she posted them. Penny had no stamps for letters herself, but might have got them from some one else if she had thought of asking for them, which she never did, as she simply never thought of writing home on the sly.

Then her father had gone home. In those days Germany seemed to her as far from Breckan as Johannesburg might have seemed to-day. A great gulf lay between her and home, and she wouldn't have wanted to upset them even if she had thought of it, but the fact is she never did. If she could have caught her father before he went home she would have poured it all out about the empty school, but once he was gone it seemed to her there was nothing to do but bear it till the time came for her release.

She had a formula to help her at night. Curled up in bed, she thought, "Now I'm going to sleep and not waken up till

I get home. I will think I waken in the morning, but that will just be part of this bad dream. I won't really waken till I open my eyes the first morning at Breckan."

For some reason this always comforted her, and she got to sleep after the first few weeks without crying.

She grew thinner and thinner, and the cough never left her, but when the warmer days of spring came in she was better. There was the stolen fruit and Arabella's crusts of bread, and sometimes she was asked out to a *Kaffeeklatsch* by one of the girls as she got to know them, but that was not until she began to speak German. Once started, she made tremendous strides, for she heard little or no English, and was soon chattering German as swiftly as English. Mallie and she often forgot and talked German together. It was easier when they had been talking German all day.

But that was all later on. In the meantime, while she wept and hungered in Germany, they read her sparse, dutiful letters at home, telling them how quickly she was learning German, how she had been to the concert and the opera and various excursions, for there was one thing about Fräulein Trainer— she could teach, and had ideas on education which were all concentrated on her one chick of a precious boarder. Penny read with her the pick of the German classics, both in prose and poetry; was taken to hear all the best music, of which Wiesbaden was a centre. She saw all the Wagner operas, and was taken to music festivals all over the district, for which Mr Peregrine paid for both her and Fräulein Trainer, who never gave the governesses a chance of accompanying Penny. She was taken to picture galleries, and had to read about the pictures and be lectured on their periods, their artists, and their excellencies. Statuary was the cause of many tears, as she stumbled through Lessing's *Laokoon* and other German classics on the subject—always in German. The only English she read was the *Breckan Advertiser* and *The Girl's Own Paper*, sent from home. Perry had also sent the *Boy's Own* till Fräulein's sneers made her ask him not to continue it.

Fräulein Trainer was efficient, but a cold, cruel woman, whom the lack of success with her boarding-school made almost fiendish with disappointment and absolutely ruthless about economy.

Her punishments were always lack of food, no supper, no afternoon coffee, no butter, or a lashing with her merciless, bitter tongue.

Mallie had a friend in Wiesbaden, with whom she spent her free afternoons and Sunday, sometimes, if permission could be got, taking Penny with her.

Fräulein Trainer's greeting when they returned was always savage.

"Well, have you fed yourselves full?" using not the term for human beings, but for animals, "*Haben Sie sich voll gefressen?*" Penny could never forget that. The coarse insult was eaten by acids into her shrinking soul. She insulted the English on every occasion she could, saying they had no pleasure but "feeding," that they all looked like cooks and stablemen. Sometimes Penny fired up, but she was quickly silenced, and she was so defenceless, while Mallie was in even worse case, as she would need a testimonial when she left, and was terrified of its being withheld.

Sometimes when she had been particularly cruel she would evidently get frightened that Penny would turn and get word home that would have her removed. Then she would "smarm," as Penny called it, round her, saying how fond she had grown of her, asking if she was happy, if she had everything she wanted and plenty to eat. "Yes, thank you," Penny would say to the last question, standing still and proud, knowing that Fräulein knew how hungry she was, that she remembered, too, how she had put out the fork to take another small piece of meat and been reprimanded and insulted before the maid-servant. Wild horses would not have dragged from her a request for more.

The pride of the two British girls infuriated Fräulein more than anything, causing her to become coarse and vulgar in

L

her efforts to break it. Once for some reason a slice of bread
was missing. Mallie was last, and Fräulein von Schell spoke
up. "There is a slice of bread missing," she said.

In awful silence Fräulein rang the bell, and then said:

"I suppose Miss MacAlpine would think herself starved if
she missed a piece of bread. The English are always stuffing
themselves."

It came up—one slice—and was passed to Mallie.

"No, thank you," she said, aching with hunger.

"Eat it—the servants have brought it for you."

"No, thank you."

"Then pass it to your compatriot."

"No, thank you," said Penny, passing it to Mademoiselle.

Mademoiselle took it and ate it. She had a nice thick skin
through which no insults ever penetrated.

"If Daddy knew!" thought Penny to herself. "If Rachel
or Marion or Paulie or Perry *knew*! If *Anthony* knew. . . .
If Anthony knew he would kill her."

It was a little comfort.

But none of them knew. They wondered a little sometimes
that she said so little about fun with the other girls, but when
she had said in her first letter there were no boarders Fräulein
had brought down the letter.

"There are boarders coming," she said. "You have all the
day girls for companions. Kindly write that letter again. It
gives an entirely wrong impression." And poor Penny labori-
ously copied it out again and never afterwards mentioned
boarders, so that when she mentioned girls by name they
concluded they were boarders. Penny had once been a great
letter-writer, but she had told them at home she was only
allowed to write on Sunday afternoons, so they put down many
of her omissions to lack of time, and there was, of course,
never a word about being hungry or unhappy.

DEAR DADDY,

There is a pink camellia out in front of the veranda where we
sit and sew in the evenings now it is so warm. Sometimes a

hornet comes and buzzes on the lamp. It is very like a big wasp. On Tuesday I went to tea with Julia Haverberg. They live in a big flat, and the floors are so slippery you sort of slide about from mat to mat. They bring whipped cream in a glass bowl, and you take a spoonful out and put it on the top of your chocolate or coffee. I had chocolate; it was lovely. I can now understand all the sermon in church; they sit down when they sing and stand up when they say their prayers. Please may I have a new pair of slippers? Fräulein Trainer will take me to have a pair made by a man she knows; they will cost five marks fifty pfennigs, which is about five shillings and sixpence. I enjoyed *Tannhäuser* very much, and Fräulein Trainer is going to try and get tickets for an afternoon concert in the Kursaal, where we often go to sit in the garden and hear the band. I now understand enough German to take all the lessons with the other girls, and am learning a long poem called *Der Ring des Polycrates*.

How are my guinea-pigs, and Robin, and Joseph and Mary, the tits, and Dixie and Robbie and Mrs Brown and Jane? Give them my love, and give Beenie a big hug, and hug yourself tight with both arms.

From your loving
PENNY

P.S. I am writing a letter to Marion and Rachel and Perry and Paulie, so will give them my love in it.

That was the sort of epistle. It sounded all right.

CHAPTER IX

"NOT KNOWING IN ANY WISE HIS OWN HEART AND WHAT IT WOULD SOME DAY SUFFER"

MARCH had come in that year with high winds and cold, bright sunshine, which continued, off and on, throughout the month. At the Falcon's House they kept up huge fires, for the wind sweeping from the North Sea was bitter, in spite of the sunshine.

"The icebergs are breaking up," the fishermen said, having an idea that it was cold at Breckan when the icebergs were loosened in the Polar regions in the spring. The garden at the back, however, was sheltered, and the crocuses painted patches of purple and lavender and gold on the grass and in the brown beds of the borders. Thrushes and blackbirds piped in the mornings from the old pear- and apple-trees, and the robin sang his clear little song from the rose-bush near the door.

Hagar had come in with a large bunch of little sweet-scented purple irises, and was arranging them in a bowl with some sprigs of forsythia one Saturday morning when she saw Mark coming up the garden. Saturday was market-day at Breckan, and one of the Wotherspoon men usually came in to lunch, but this was early, and she wondered what had made him come so soon in the morning. Usually at this time all the farmers and corn merchants were busy in the corn exchange or the cattle mart, buying and selling.

She thought Mark looked quite handsome as he strode up the path in the old rough suit of Lovat mixture he was wearing instead of the usual riding-breeches or the finer suit he wore to town, and, running from the room, she called for Rachel, who was up in her turret getting ready for a visit to the butter market to buy country butter and chickens for Sunday's midday dinner from the stalls of the farmers' wives.

Mother Wotherspoon always sent eggs and cream and butter when she had any, but she was short of butter for the moment, only making enough to serve her own household. Perhaps she had changed her mind, thought Hagar, and was sending the chickens they had ordered earlier in the week, but of which she had also been short. She would have told Mark to let them know early, before Hagar or Rachel went to the butter market in the old town-hall to buy from others.

But Rachel seemed in no hurry to see Mark. She often puzzled Hagar. Every one seemed to think that Rachel loved Mark, and Marion had hinted as much more than once in Rachel's presence, and Rachel had never denied it, just flushed up and either broken out into anger or turned away to hide the tears that sprang to her eyes.

Hagar thought it was probably because she thought Mark did not return her affection, and there Hagar had to leave it, because she was uncertain about that herself, for if Mark showed a real predilection for anybody she was bound to confess, had she faced it, it was for herself. But Hagar preferred not to face this, and in any case Mother Wotherspoon's words had sunk deep. *She* wasn't going to be another Naomi, not if she knew it!

But it wasn't chickens Mark had come to speak about. It was Marion. His mother had sent him to say that she thought Marion had been long enough at Goslaw. A friend of hers had been in from the hills, and she had gathered that there was 'talk.'

Mark had been told to tell Mr Peregrine, but Mark shied off that. It would be easier to speak to Hagar, so to Hagar he had come.

First he had to have a word with Samuel, who was all excitement at the sound of Mark's voice, but when Samuel had been reduced to comparative calm he plunged in.

"Marion not home yet?" he asked.

"No," said Hagar, a little anxiously, "but I think she will be coming home next week. Did you want to see her?"

"No, but . . . Well, the truth is Mother is getting worried. She had a call from that old gossip Belle Wynd, the porter's mother, and she said there was talk beginning about Marion. It seems Matthew took her to the dance at Jock's wedding without Naomi, and that started it, and she is out a lot with Matthew on the hills—well, you know what country folks are! Mother told me to tell Uncle Peregrine he was to send for her to come home, but I couldn't do that."

"Oh, no," said Hagar quickly, "don't do that."

"So I came to you, Hagar. We all come to you with our troubles." He paused and stood looking down at her. "Those small shoulders shouldn't have so much to carry."

In spite of herself she flushed up a little, but let the remark pass.

"I wonder what I should do?"

He wheeled an arm-chair round with one hand. "Sit down and we'll talk it over. I came early to catch you alone."

"Rachel will be down in a minute—don't worry Rachel about it."

"No. Like every one else, I'm worrying you."

He sat down on the arm of the chair beside her, and gently and rather shyly rested a hand on one of her shoulders. "Isn't that the way of it, child?"

His voice was so kind and low it made her heart beat quickly. For a passing moment she had thought of what it might be to have Mark make love to one—then resolutely put the thought aside. He was only being kind—and besides . . .

Up above she heard Rachel trilling a little ditty she had taken a fancy to:

> "O happy eyes, for you shall see
> My love, my lady, pass to-day.
> O happy, happy eyes."

Mark was evidently listening too, for he suddenly joined in the last line in his deep voice, "O happy, happy eyes."

"There!" thought Hagar to herself. "He's letting Rachel know he's here. It *must* be all right. He must want to see her, though he wanted, of course, to tell me what his mother said, and not worry Rachel about Marion."

"I'll tell you what I'll do," she said. "I'll write to Marion and say I'd like her to come back. There's been some trouble with Perry, who wants to leave school, but won't go into the shop. He wants to learn to fly, and Paul is going off to New-castle Agricultural College. I'll say we should talk things over."

"Paul had better keep away from there," said Mark at once, dour and dark-browed. "They'll soon take all the real farmer out of him and make him a master-mechanic——" He stopped, and put a big, shy hand on Hagar's hair and brushed it back.

"Nice hair you have, Hagar. It curls round into your neck like a little grebe's ruff. Have you ever seen a Slavonian grebe?"

"No." She shook her head under his hand, which still rested lightly on it.

"They come to the Seggy Swire sometimes—the bit of bog land by the Hagg woods my family wants to drain. You must come with me and see them next winter. Will you?"

"I'd like to see them," said Hagar, "but——"

They heard Rachel's feet pattering quickly down the stairs.

"—but Rachel——"

"Rachel doesn't like birds," he said, standing slowly up as she came into the room. "Do you, Rachel?"

"Do I what?"

"Like birds."

"I like them to eat. I suppose you didn't bring any chickens? I'm just going off to buy some."

"Yes, off you both go," said Hagar, standing up too. "I'm late with the round for the lunch. Good-bye, Mark."

She watched them go down the garden together, and caught her breath in a little sigh as Mark closed the gate behind them.

"How different Mark can be sometimes," she said to herself. Then she rushed off to the kitchen, where the large round of salt beef and the pease-pudding were already wobbling in the pot. A big midday dinner had always to be provided on Saturdays, as Mr Peregrine liked to ask one or two of his country customers to share the meal.

So Hagar wrote the letter, and Marion got it on a sunny March morning.

She and Matthew had been dancing with the daffodils through the sunny March days. At first when they met they were so happy just to be together that they had no cares. Nothing was said on either side; they had always been friends, happy in each other's company; they were young, and the wine of spring was in their veins. They laughed and they chattered, they teased each other and remembered—"Do you remember?" they kept saying, and laughed again.

"You were always giggling," said Naomi, but at first without rancour, they were so frank and unembarrassed and young.

The young lambs were on the hillsides, the heather was greening on the uplands, the larks sang, the burns chattered gaily, the wind chased the woolly clouds over the blue fields of heaven, the midges danced in the slanting sunbeams between the hazels and the peat-brown stream. Marion strode up the hills with Matthew, the dogs at their heels, the sheep in fan shape before them, the pipits rising and falling, trilling their music of the fells.

In the evenings they took their rods, and Matthew taught her to fish. Naomi would not come; she did not like fishing, but she made lovely dishes of fried trouts for them. She loved cooking, and was never too lazy to cook, enjoying the pleasures of the table with all the epicurean enjoyment of the French.

It was only very gradually that a new note crept into the dancing music of the spring.

At first it was hardly a note so much as a silence. A pause in the laughter, a thrill as he took the rod from her and their hands met, a glance as he stood fixing a fly, looking downward into her eager, upturned face, a sigh in a lull of the wind as he swung her over a burn, or held her hand to help her up a crag.

When a little of it crept into speech it was all very innocent.

"You are so lovely, Marion. You look like a wild rose, only the yellow stamens of your hair are in the wrong place —your hair is just the same yellow, and your cheeks the same pink."

"So are you, Matthew—lovely, I mean. I used to think you were a very plain boy with your freckles, but I think you are lovely now. You are such a nice nutty brown, and your nose is so straight, and your mouth so proud, and, Grandmamma, what white teeth you've got!"

"The better to bite your little nose off if you're cheeky to me—lovely!" He went into peals of laughter. "What an insult!"

"Well, handsome, then, but I hate that word—like Apollo, whoever he was, but with straight hair. I don't like men with curly hair."

"I do—I mean, I like curly hair. Grandmamma, what nice curls you've got!"

"The better—the better——"

"Ah, I've caught you napping this time. I'm one up!"

The game was to catch each other 'napping,' without a ready answer, and it had never to be a repetition.

"Well, grandmothers don't have curls."

"Yes, they do. You'll have curls when you are a grand-mother."

"I'll never be a grandmother. I'm going to be a great-aunt —Great-aunt Marion. Doesn't it sound nice?"

"I like Marion better, just Marion, Marion, Marion—'but I loved you better, Marion, riding through the broom.'"

Pause.

A lark would rise, singing, carolling through their silence.

"We've only got two little trouts, Matthew. We must get some more, or Naomi will give them to the cat."

Sometimes he would sing to her as they sat in the heather or trudged homeward, Marion often running beside him as he strode along on his long legs, the rods over his shoulder, the creel on his back.

> "The bird's in the bush,
> The trout's in the burn."

She would join in with him:

> "The sheep's in the meadow,
> The cow's in the corn.
> Thou's over-long in thy bed,
> Bonny, at morn."

They had always sung together. At school concerts a duet sung by Marion Peregrine and Matthew Wotherspoon had always

been one of the items on the programme. At five and seven
they had piped, Marion with a lisp:

> "Little brown theed, oh, little brown brother,
>   Are you awake in the dark?"

Or later, both dressed up to the nines in ruffles and furbelows:

> "Madam, will you walk,
>   Madam, will you talk,
>   Madam, will you walk and talk with me?"

they had brought down the house.

And every Sunday evening at Bowchester or the Falcon's
House they sang. Hymns at Bowchester, "There is a green hill
far away," "Oh, dearly, dearly has He loved, and we must love
Him too"; but at the Falcon's House the rules were not so
strict. Songs were intermingled with the hymns, Scots songs
and Irish songs and old English ballads. They all sang, but
Matthew and Marion had the sweetest voices, the truest ears,
till Matthew's voice broke; it had come back deep, but true
as ever.

Now they sang the old songs all over again.

In the evenings too they would sing while Naomi played on
the piano she had insisted on having at the cottage. She played
well, and, though she could not sing herself, she had taught
the Peregrine girls little French songs, and now Matthew had
to learn them too, and they sang in duet:

> "Malbrouk s'en va-t-en guerre,
>   Mironton, mironton, mirontaine,"

and all about the cobbler who had three coats.

She knew German too, and taught them *Wie einst in Mai*
long before it ever came to England as *As once in May* and *Aus
der Jugendzeit*, with its haunting sadness: "Yes, the swallows
still sing down the village street, but no swallow can take
you back to the days for which you weep"—but song is
untranslatable.

They were merry evenings, too, at first. Naomi could be good fun and very charming when she liked, and she was very keen on being at her best, for she wanted to be on a friendly footing again at the Falcon's House. At Bowchester too she wished to be on good terms, though that was more difficult; she hated Mother Wotherspoon, and could not keep her tongue from reviling her, but knew that there was where the butter lay for her bread, and that in her own interests she should try at least to hide her animosity and rancour and attempt a reconciliation.

She would have preferred Rachel or Penny as her means of getting once more into touch, for she had been intensely jealous of Marion at one time, partly because she was securing so good a match, and partly because it was handsome Matthew. But Penny was away and Rachel intractable, so she had to fall back on Marion, who in any case she was inclined to despise as being absolutely devoid of her own arts where men were concerned. Marion had easily been outwitted, and in any case Matthew couldn't have thought much about her when he was so easily beguiled out of their "silly, half-baked affair"—calf-love was soon got over and, once over, was done with.

But after the first week or so she began to wonder and be suspicious. Her manner subtly changed. Marion could not understand her, but put it down to Naomi's moods. She had always been changeable. There had never been a word between herself and Matthew that could make her feel guilty about Naomi. Naomi and Matthew were married; she still thought he loved Naomi, and was only fond of herself and enjoying her company because they were "friends," had been friends for so long—long and long before Naomi came on the scene.

In the last days it had been worse. She had often felt uncomfortable, so she really was pleased to get Hagar's letter. She was turning a little frightened of Naomi.

She did not know how much Naomi knew of that brief love-affair with Matthew, for, though their friendship had been long, and the family had always coupled their names together, she and Matthew had very gradually found themselves in love, and had hardly begun to think of any formal engagement. They understood each other; little had been said between them; it would all come in time. They were just happy and careless and free. Then Naomi had come, and very soon Marion was having little secret heartaches, which culminated in the terrible blow when she heard that Matthew and Naomi were married.

Her pride and her love had come to her rescue then. No one really knew that there had been any love-making between them. No one should ever know. She must not only protect her own secret wound, but save Matthew from reproach. She could not bear the thought of anyone knowing how badly he had treated her. They might guess, but not even that if she could help it. So she had strenuously denied there had ever been any under-standing, any engagement, between them, and to make it more feasible she had insisted on her affection for Naomi. That was partly pretence, though she had liked Naomi at first, but it was a pretence that she believed in herself. She *made* herself like Naomi, and, of course, in her love for him found all sorts of excuses for Matthew, the chief one being that he had only fancied himself in love with herself, and then when Naomi came found out his mistake.

She was too young and ignorant to know that in going to stay with them she was playing with fire. She had persuaded herself that she would always love Matthew in secret and never marry. She was going to be their friend and help them. When they had children she would love them and be their adored "Auntie Marion." In fact, she had had all a young girl's heroic, silly, ignorant dreams.

It had all seemed easy at first—till she discovered that she was all wrong about Matthew, that he loved her still, had always loved her. It had all been a tragic mistake. He told her about it one day, sitting on the hillside watching the sheep. She had laughingly gone off to meet him with a message that had come cancelling an earlier one that had been sent, asking him to ride into Fenton with a message for the doctor for a neighbouring shepherd's wife. It had been sent to him when he was watching sheep on the hillside, but Naomi had seen the doctor passing, and found he was going to the cottage, so Marion had gone to tell Matthew he was not needed.

She had urged Naomi to come too, for the walk would be good for her, but Naomi hated walking anywhere, and especially through the heather, in which she always imagined adders to be lurking ready to bite her ankles.

Matthew was on his way down with the flock, but on hearing the message sat down and took out his pipe for a smoke while the sheep grazed a bit longer, spreading his plaid for Marion to sit beside him. They were in sight of the house lying below, and for a while lazily watched Naomi in the distance, coming out to feed her chickens, to chase the pig out of the garden, to take in a basket of peats from the peat-stack.

"It is wonderful how Naomi has taken to the work of a farm," said Marion, "when she never knew anything about it before."

"Yes," said Matthew, "Naomi is very clever and quick, though, you know, she was brought up by her grandparents on a farm in France. That was after her parents died. She hated it, and, as she was very clever and did well at school, they managed to train her as a teacher. She hated that too, but after a year or two came to England as governess in a family, and then came to your father as housekeeper through knowing one of the nuns in the convent—but you know all that bit, of course."

"Yes, it was Sister Stanislaus, who had known her mother, but I didn't know about the farm. Naomi never liked to talk about France."

"No, she had some very unhappy times, poor Naomi, both then and later on in France."

They sat quiet for a time, watching the hill larks rise and fall, and then Matthew laid down his pipe, picked up a bit of heather, and began stripping it bit by bit.

"I've always wanted to tell you, Marion, how it was, and—to ask you—to ask your forgiveness."

"It was all right, Matthew. There was nothing to forgive. It was just a mistake about—about us. . . ." She paused, and then said bravely, "It was a good thing, really, you found out in time."

"Found out what?"

"That you didn't really love me."

"I'll always love you, Marion. It wasn't that."

She turned and looked at him, but he was gazing intently at the bit of heather.

"Well," she said at last, "it's all over now. Let's just keep on *always* being friends, Matthew. I couldn't bear that we shouldn't always be friends—you and me—and Naomi too."

"I married Naomi because——" He paused, pulling at the tough heather. "It's difficult to tell you, Marion, but I want you to know the truth, and then you'll understand, and we can always be friends, if you still want to."

He looked very young with his blown, untidy hair, his smooth, brown, boyish cheeks, and the wrinkled, anxious brows above the puzzled blue eyes. After all, he was still just a boy of barely twenty-two, a boy who had been caught in the net and forced into manhood when just out of his teens.

"Don't tell me if you'd rather not, Matthew. It doesn't matter—really it doesn't. I just thought you found it was really Naomi you loved."

"I want you to understand. It wouldn't be so bad if I thought you knew that—that I didn't mean to hurt you, Marion."

Neither spoke for a few minutes. He threw away the heather, picked up another piece, and began the same earnest stripping of its leaves and twigs with his shaking brown hands.

"You see, Marion, I—I—Naomi and I——" He suddenly turned and looked at her. "I was unfaithful to you once, Marion."

She flushed all over her face, and he put his hand over one

of hers as it lay on the grass. "Then that time Naomi came to Bowchester she said I must *marry* her because—because . . . You know what she meant, don't you? I—I can't say it."

"Oh!" She looked up at him, utterly taken by surprise. "But Naomi hasn't—Naomi isn't . . ." She couldn't say, either. Naomi had no child. They themselves were indeed little more than children.

"No, it wasn't true. . . . That is all. I just wanted you to know why I had to—how I couldn't help it—that I never wanted to hurt you."

"No, you couldn't help hurting me. Oh, Matthew, I'm so sorry—about it all, I mean."

"Will you forgive me, Marion?"

"Yes, yes, Matthew. I don't feel anything to forgive. It wasn't your blame."

"Yes," he burst out bitterly, "it was my blame. I did wrong, and I had to pay. And I wronged you too, only I never meant to. It wasn't love. I never loved anyone but you, but I went and made a swine of myself, and spoiled my life and spoiled yours, and God may forgive me, but I'll never forgive myself. I don't think He will either. He'll kick me into hell, where I belong for hurting you. Sometimes I feel I'd like to be burnt inch by inch, to burn it all out of me, to burn me clean so that I could start all over again——"

He stopped, let go of her hand, rose, and, holding out his own, pulled her to her feet. They stood for a moment hand in hand.

"Perhaps He will, Matthew, like Hagar says. I think it's in the Bible, about the Potter whose pot was spoiled that He was making, 'so he made it again another vessel,' but I forget the rest—something about it being quite a good pot, I think."

She smiled with her mouth all twisted, trying to keep the tears back.

"Dear, sweet, dear little Marion," he said, his boyish mouth trembling.

Then his young face grew stern and aged a little, with the lines deepening from nose to mouth as he tried to gain control, to tighten the lips, with the soft down of boyhood at the corners, into the firmness of manhood.

He dropped her hands and, turning, whistled to the dogs which lay guarding the sheep a little distance away, one sitting upright and alert, the other stretched out with its head on its paws, its bright, intelligent eyes on its master.

A meadow-lark rose, mounting upward on jubilant wings, carolling its careless song.

Marion watched it till the tears had all gone from her eyes, down into the well of unshed tears.

Then she followed Matthew where he had gone on down the hill after his sheep, and took hold of his hand, and so they went a little way, clinging to each other's hands, but saying nothing more.

CHAPTER X

"FOR GRIEF, ONCE TOLD, BRINGS SOMEWHAT BACK OF PEACE"

HAGAR came through the garden with a basket of purchases in her hand and Samuel at her heels. He was on his lead, which he intensely disliked, but put up with it, as it meant he would not be left behind to bemoan his fate while Hagar was shopping. He was as lively and mischievous as any pup could be, but an engaging young rascal. Hagar often wished Penny were there to see him. Penny would have adored him, and she was so good at training animals.

Robbie Burns missed her terribly, and was always disappearing under her bed. He knew he wasn't allowed in the bed, but paw marks and scraped back sheets and blankets betrayed his hunt for his mistress. When she wasn't to be found he got under the bed to wait, curled up in a ball. Like Anthony, Robbie knew how to wait.

Hagar had been buying things for Easter, though she did it with less heart because Penny wasn't there. In the short time they had been together Penny had coiled herself round Hagar's heart. She loved her, and was never quite happy about her. Perhaps the doctor had been right, and the bitter winds that swept the north-east town from March till the end of May were too dangerous for her delicate lungs, but she had seemed so young and defenceless to go among strangers in a far country.

The others had accepted her absence with cheerful acquiescence in what the doctor said. It was only Hagar who doubted. Still, she cheered herself up, Penny's youth would help her to settle down, and there would be lots of other young girls to have fun with and make merry with.

Hagar and Rachel had packed a large box with Easter eggs for Penny, chocolate ones and real ones, hard-boiled and dyed, small Easter cakes and buns, fluffy yellow ducklings and chickens, a huge home-made simnel cake, and presents from every one, including Anthony, who sent a lovely little satin egg on which flying swallows were painted over the words, "O Swallow, Swallow, flying, flying South, fly to her, and tell her, tell her, what I tell to thee."

No one could find any fault with that, thought Anthony, as he carefully washed his fine paint-brushes. Inside was a little round gold locket on a gold chain. The locket had her initials set in pearls and turquoises on one side, and had a tiny painted plaque of forget-me-nots on the other, also set round with pearls and turquoises. A very lovely gift for a little girl, but after all he had not been able to send his precious Penny a letter. Anthony was much too fine a gentleman not to have taken Mr Peregrine's hint and abided by his own unspoken but understood promise to regard it.

Inside the locket looked empty, though there were two frames waiting for miniatures, or a curled lock of hair, or what you would, but if you pressed the springs, as you would need

M

to do to insert the pictures, you found two small spaces, one at either side. In each of these Anthony had managed to set a half-sovereign behind the thin plates of gold. He could only hope that Penny, examining it thoroughly—she liked to be at the bottom of everything—would find them and buy herself some goodies. Gold was gold all the world over.

Penny's box had gone off to Germany days ago, and now Hagar was bringing in chocolate eggs and Easter offerings for the rest of the family, together with more fluffy yellow chickens and ducklings to decorate the Easter breakfast table. There was still Rachel and Perry to do these things for, and she hoped Marion would be home too. She had written to say she would come at the end of the week.

Paul would not be there. He had gone off to study agriculture at the college in spite of Mark's warnings of what would happen to him. Steady, confident Paul sympathized with Mark, and loved the country and animals too, but he intended to know all he could on the other side. As Mr Peregrine said, Knowledge was easy to carry about with you, and would not take up much room in the hold of the ship in which he proposed to sail to the Fortunate Isles. Being Mr Peregrine's, the idea had to be wrapped up in what Paul called his "high-falutin langwidge."

Rachel had been informed before he left that he would never change, and he had been laughed at for his pains.

"I know I just make you impatient," he had added, rather humbly.

"Then why don't you stop being so silly?"

"It's the nature of the beast," he said gruffly, and left it at that.

Among Hagar's purchases were some daffodils. They were beginning to come out in the garden, but Hagar liked to see them growing there. She arranged a few blooms in a shallow bowl with some bits of rock and moss, and climbed the stair to Rachel's turret with them to give her a surprise.

As she set them on the broad sill of one of the windows she saw that the bed was unmade. Rachel looked after her own room, but had had to hurry out that morning to take Mrs Brown, the cat, who had got a bone in her throat, to the vet, so Hagar pulled off the sheets and blankets to start to make it. As she lifted the pillows a square of cardboard fell to the floor. She picked it up and turned it over. It was a photograph of Matthew, and looked as if another figure might have been torn off.

For a second Hagar looked at it, wondering; then, thinking that Marion had perhaps sent it in a letter, she laid it on the dressing-table, and made the bed, and thought no more of it

She was amazed when later on Rachel came into the parlour, where she was busy arranging pussy willows and daffodils with white face and angry eyes.

"I wish you'd leave my things alone," she said. "I hate people prying into my private affairs."

"Prying!" exclaimed Hagar. "What do you mean? I only took up some daffodils and made your bed——"

As she spoke she suddenly remembered the photograph and mentioned it at once. "A snapshot of Matthew Wotherspoon fell on the floor, and I put it on your dressing-table. You're not angry about that, are you, Rachel?"

Her voice was puzzled. Why should Rachel be so angry? It was natural enough that Marion should have sent her a snapshot of Matthew.

"You'd no right to make my bed. I always make my own bed."

"Well, I'm sorry. But you are a funny girl, Rachel. Most people would be glad to have their beds made. I thought I was doing you a good turn." Hagar was rather hurt. "You'd better bring the daffodils down into the parlour, and I won't go into your room again when you are out. I apologize," she added stiffly.

Rachel stood looking at her uncertainly.

"It wasn't the photograph—an old torn thing," she said. "I suppose it had dropped on the bed. I just don't like *any* of my things being touched."

And at that moment Hagar knew with a queer sense of certainty and bewilderment that it *was* the photograph, and that it had been under her pillow, and that Rachel had torn some one off who had been standing beside Matthew.

"Well, I've apologized, but I do think you are being unreasonable and unkind, Rachel, and I resent very much being accused of prying."

She picked up her tray of scraps and leaves and walked out of the room, growing more indignant as the full force of the word came back to her. Prying! She, Hagar Thorne, to be accused of such a vulgar, hateful offence. Her pride was up in arms.

She went into the kitchen to busy herself with preparations for tea, but she could not help puzzling over the question why Rachel had been so upset. If it had been Mark she would have understood—but Matthew!

Suddenly the kitchen door opened and Rachel came in. It was Beenie's afternoon out, and the kitchen was empty save for themselves.

"I'm sorry, Hagar," she said. "You weren't prying. The daffodils are lovely. Thank you for making my bed."

"What upset you, Rachel? Was it Matthew's photograph? But why?"

Hagar in her self-imposed task to be a 'mother' to the girls was very conscientious. She thought she ought to get to the bottom of Rachel's deep resentment, and, besides, she was really fond of her, and couldn't bear a cloud of misunderstanding to rise between them.

Rachel stood with her back towards her, looking out of the window. She did not speak, and Hagar decided to take the bull by the horns, as Penny always so strenuously recommended. It might do Rachel good to turn on her and get some of the bitterness out of her heart, for it was spoiling her, this secret brooding over Mark.

"If it had been Mark, Rachel," she said, "I should have understood."

In a flash Rachel had turned round.

"Mark! Mark! Will you all stop bothering me about Mark! I don't care two straws for Mark Wotherspoon! As if I'd bother myself over that dumb, dour fish with his silly old notions about the farm! Shut up about Mark!"

It was exceedingly rude, but Hagar was too wise to bother about that. People are rude when their nerves are jangling.

"Well, what in the name of goodness is the matter with you?" demanded Hagar, still thinking a flash or two of lightning would clear the air. "What are you so bitter about, Rachel?"

"I'm not bitter."

"Yes, you are. If no one else will tell you the truth I shall. You are bitter, and you are brooding about something, and it makes you very disagreeable sometimes."

"Well, what about it?" Rachel flashed out, her face white, her eyes flashing. "Can't I be allowed to brood in peace? It's all I've got. All I've ever had, and you must grudge me it. I have to laugh and be merry so that you'll all be comfortable, and when I don't you all push Mark down my throat. Mark! Mark! Mark! It isn't Mark, if you *will* know—it's Matthew. There, now! I fling it in your face! It's Matthew—and Matthew is a married man, and Matthew was engaged to my sister—and Matthew doesn't care a button about me, even if he wasn't married to Naomi. It's Marion he wants—Marion! But he once—he once—he once—— Oh!" She choked, and, flinging herself down into Beenie's old arm-chair, burst into tears.

"Leave me alone! Leave me alone!" she cried out, incoherent and choking with sobs, but Hagar had not moved. She stood staring at Rachel, utterly amazed, the ground taken completely from beneath her feet. Matthew! The idea was so new she could hardly take it in.

"Matthew!" she said aloud at last. "Matthew? Why, Rachel——"

"Yes, go on." Rachel's voice came strangled between her

sobs. "Say it all! Say I ought to be ashamed of myself. I'm not ashamed of myself. He loved me first—he did! He did! And if it had been me *I* wouldn't have let Naomi get him. I'd have pushed some of her own poison down her throat, the liar! He should have had me to fight for him. I would have kept him if he'd been mine—oh, why should he have wanted Marion, who couldn't keep him—who wouldn't fight for him? Oh! Oh!" She turned in the chair and, burying her face in the cushion, sobbed and sobbed.

Hagar stood looking at her, her petrified astonishment gradually fading away.

So that was it. Poor Rachel!

She did not speak for a minute. At the back of her mind she was glad the outburst had come. Rachel was young, and this would pass. She had nursed and brooded over her wrongs and her unhappiness too long, lived in an atmosphere heavy with clouds and sultry with lonely suffering, but it had broken —the thunder had rolled, the lightning flashed, and the rains come. Hagar knew with an intuitive wisdom that the worst was over, and that Rachel would recover now it had all come out. How old was she? Eighteen. Hagar smiled to herself. At nineteen she herself had thought the world was ended for her because she loved a man who didn't love her, and now she had practically forgotten all about him, or only remembered him with a smile.

She went and got out the little yellow breakfast set she had bought for Rachel's Easter present, with ridiculous little yellow chickens with stumpy wings marching round the tea-pot and the china. She put the tray-cloth on the tray—its outlined chicken had still to be embroidered, but that didn't matter—and busied herself making a good, strong cup of tea, while allowing Rachel to sob out her grief in the chair. Then she pulled up a little table and put the tray on it.

"Let's have some tea, Rachel," she said.

"I don't want any."

"Well, I do. After all these storms and excitement and the

shock you gave me I feel like having tea. Look! We're going to have it out of your Easter present. I bought it for you."

Rachel looked at it with one eye from behind the soaked handkerchief.

"It's very pretty," she gulped uninterestedly. "Thank you, Hagar."

Hagar laughed.

"It's not meant to be pretty. It's meant to be funny—at least, it's meant to be both."

She poured out a cup for each of them, put cream and sugar in Rachel's, and stirred it ready for her.

"Drink it up."

She spoke in such an ordinary voice that Rachel wiped her sodden face and drank it.

"It is nice," she said.

"Do you like the chickens?"

"Oh, yes, I do. They *are* funny pets, Hagar."

"I thought you would. Now tell me all about Matthew. You know, I was terribly in love with a man too when I was nineteen. *He* wasn't married, and we were engaged, but he took one look at me after my accident, fled from the sight, and never came back. I cried and cried for him. I wonder I didn't think about Matthew when I saw that snapshot. I used to keep a photograph under my pillow too, I loved Earle so much. Oh, dear, it's terrible, isn't it, when we love men, and they don't care about us, or love somebody else? I thought I'd never get over it. I expect you feel like that too, poor infant."

"I'll always love Matthew—I'll never get over it; but I wouldn't mind if—if"—the tears came again—"if he were happy."

"I don't know. I knew Earle was perfectly happy. He got engaged to a pretty girl before very long, but that just seemed to make it worse."

"But what did he say? Did he just go and leave you and never say anything?"

She was getting interested.

"Well, he didn't *say* anything when he saw me—just how sorry he was and all that—but he wrote me from abroad, where he had gone straight away, and said he thought it was better to part, as his feelings had changed. He said it wasn't the accident—it had begun before—but he didn't like to tell me when I was so ill. He said he knew I would think him a cad——"

"Well, so he was! A cruel, hateful cad!" Rachel broke in.

"Oh, no, it was really better, or if it was cruel it was better for me to know it and get over it. He told a friend of mine he had been as much of a cad as he could so that I'd hate him and despise him and get over it, because he just couldn't bear to look at my broken face, and would only have hurt me if he had tried. You are better off in a way, Rachel. You needn't despise Matthew."

"But I do. I despise him for marrying Naomi, and that makes it worse."

"You'll have to get over it. There's nothing else to do. What happened when you found out it was Marion? Did you just get to know gradually? I think that must be even worse than getting the shock all at once like I did."

In a few minutes Rachel was telling her all about it, and as she talked Hagar knew it was all right; that time had already begun to heal the wound to her young heart; that she had been unconsciously keeping it up to herself, brooding and being bitter partly because she resented, or, rather, her subconscious self resented, having to bear it all alone, without any sympathy or understanding from others.

By the time the tea was all finished Hagar had got all the story, and Rachel had apologized for what she had said.

"I knew you weren't prying, Hagar. I just said it because I was so furious. I didn't want anybody to know about Matthew."

"Well, nobody will ever know but you and me. I was worse off there. Everybody knew and *pitied* me, and some girls who had been jealous, because he was what they called 'the catch of the neighbourhood,' rather enjoyed my being jilted and said things that stung."

Hagar wanted Rachel to sympathize over her case; it would be good for her. If she knew how thoroughly Hagar had been humiliated she wouldn't mind talking to her about her own trouble, and that was what Hagar wanted—to get her to talk, to get the bitterness that was spoiling her out of her system.

"My goodness!" she said frankly, when the cups were empty. "You do look a fright. Go and wash your face in hot water, as hot as ever you can bear it, and then in icy cold out the tap. That's the best thing when your nose and eyes are all swollen up with crying. We'll say you've got a bit of a cold, if need be, but I don't think it will. Let's dye the eggs to-night after tea when Beenie is out. I got a basketful of whin blossom when I took Samuel out yesterday, and there's onion skins, and I wondered if you had any coloured rags—bits of velvet are very good. Now I must set the tea."

She hadn't said a word of sympathy, and she didn't mean to; it would only make Rachel cry again with self-pity, and she had had her cry out. She must be cheered up and interested and talked to casually about Matthew and not allowed to brood.

Luckily a letter came from Penny by the post that arrived at tea-time in which Mr Peregrine was so interested he paid no attention to Rachel. And Perry had his own preoccupations too. He had been finding out more about flying, and was wondering how to introduce the subject to his father.

Penny's letter, as usual, was full of her doings, but told them little about herself. The last sheets were rather stilted, as if she had been wondering what to say, a strange state of mind for Penny, who had always so much to divulge to the world, so many opinions to state, so many adventures to relate.

"Penny used to be a better letter-writer," said Mr Peregrine. "I wonder if talking so much German is making her stilted in her own language—reading *Wallenstein*, she says. We'll have an intelligent little miss made out of our Penny if she stays there long."

"'Then don't let her stay," said Hagar quickly. "I couldn't bear Penny altered."

"You express my feelings exactly," said Mr Peregrine. "'To paint the lily' and so forth——"

"Father," put in Perry, "if I left school and just learned to fly——"

And the conversation went off on to flying.

But if they had only known their guess about Penny wondering what to say had been exactly right.

Mallie had been ill, and had fainted one day in a shop while out with Fräulein Trainer and Penny. They had been to a famous dish market and wandered for some time looking at the peasant ware, and Mallie, on going into the shop, had sat down, and when Fräulein had reproved her for sitting down when she herself, an older lady, was standing she had closed her eyes and slid off the chair in a dead faint.

Fräulein had made the best of it, being very hearty and proclaiming how she had stood on her feet in the market till she was tired and faint too, but wouldn't give way to it, at the same time professing great care for Miss MacAlpine and ordering a cab to take her home, though Mallie protested to the last, saying she was all right and could walk, knowing quite well she would have somehow to find the money to pay for the cab. Penny was sent back with her, and as Mallie was shivering she drew a hard, wooden arm-chair, the only one in the place outside Fräulein Trainer's own rooms, up to the stove and got a shawl and wrapped it round her.

Then Fräulein arrived back and the storm broke. Mallie was ordered away from the stove, asked if she thought herself an invalid or an old woman to sit wrapped in a shawl, accused of malingering, and told to get on with her work. White-faced and frightened, Mallie humbly apologized and said she must have eaten something that disagreed with her—a grand opening for Fräulein, who talked about people who over-filled their stomachs and so on, till Penny turned and said Mallie didn't over-fill her stomach, and in her turn came in for a brow-beating.

In writing home she described the dish market, and then went on to tell how Miss MacAlpine, as she always called her in her letters, had fainted in a shop.

Fräulein Trainer had come down with the letter in a fury of rage, and ordered Penny to rewrite all the last sheets and leave out any mention of Miss MacAlpine. So, frightened and distraught, Penny had rewritten them, but all her lively description of the scene had fled. She could not write naturally under these circumstances. No wonder Mr Peregrine thought she was growing stilted—Penny was growing not only stilted, but subdued.

CHAPTER XI

"I WILL PUT MY HOOK IN THY NOSE AND MY BRIDLE IN THY LIPS"

INSTANTLY when Marion came down from the hill that afternoon with Matthew and went into the kitchen she knew that Naomi was in what the North-country folk called 'bad fettle.'

She did not speak to Marion's greeting, but banged the kettle farther on to the fire.

"You've taken your time," she said then.

"We sat on the hill and watched you," said Marion, smiling. It was rather a crooked smile, for she had felt a terrible revulsion against Naomi after Matthew's revelations, which, however, she was trying to hide. "We saw you feeding the hens and chasing the pig and getting the peats for the fire."

"I dare say," said Naomi, "it was very nice sitting in ze sun and watching me do all ze work, when my head aches."

"Oh, Naomi," said Marion quickly, "I'm sorry. I would have hurried back to help you if I had known."

Naomi did not answer, and an uncomfortable silence

followed, broken at last by Matthew, who said, "If your head is bad would you not like to lie down?"

"I prefair not to lie down."

Neither of them believed in Naomi's headaches, which she could adopt or throw off as the occasion suited her, but it was best to humour her when in one of her moods.

"We could pull the sofa up to the fire, and you could rest while I do anything there is to do. There's not much this evening."

Marion only meant that it was not one of their big days such as washing or baking days, but Naomi seemed determined to take offence.

"Oh, no, there is never much to do in ze shepherd's cottage. It is all so easy as water running off ze cat's back."

Marion laughed good-naturedly.

"You mean the duck's back, Naomi; you've got it awfully mixed, but I know what you mean, and I don't think that. I think you work awfully hard, and I've told Matthew how clever I think you are to have learned it all so quickly—haven't I, Matthew?"

"What is the matter, Naomi?" asked Matthew now.

"I have said. I have ze headache."

She sat in sullen silence all tea-time, and then Matthew got up and went out to pen the sheep, which he had left on the knoll outside, guarded by the dogs.

"*Is* there anything the matter, Naomi?" Marion asked, as the door closed behind him. "Besides your headache, I mean."

"Everything is ze matter."

"Are you tired of my staying here? I would have gone on Saturday, but you begged me so much to stay another week—but perhaps you are tired of having a visitor? One does tire of visitors quite suddenly. I can easily go home to-morrow instead of waiting till Friday. I think I'd better do that."

"To-morrow is not practical; they wonder why you come home without writing first. You must stay till Friday," said Naomi ungraciously.

Marion went into the milkhouse with the cream jug and stood there for a moment, looking across the heather through the little window. "What was the matter with Naomi?" she wondered. If it had been possible she would have thought she had overheard that conversation on the hill, she seemed so resentful. She had made a few sarcastic remarks in the last day or two, but only half joking, and then had laughed them off and been friendly again. Why should she have changed so suddenly? Or had it all been working up to this, and had the sight of them sitting on the hill while she did the work genuinely angered her? It seemed absurd, for Marion did so much of the work, and Naomi was always thanking her and saying how she would miss her when she left.

She shrugged her shoulders a little and determined to take no notice. Naomi had always been given to moods, and Friday was the day after to-morrow; she had only a short time to stay.

"It couldn't be Matthew," her thoughts went on, as she tidied the shelves a little. "Till to-day he has never really said anything." Still, she felt a little guilty. They loved each other, and Naomi may have noticed how intensely conscious they were of each other. She did not put it in these words. Marion was not good at putting her vague thoughts into clear conceptions, but the feeling was there. She decided to be very careful and very kind to Naomi until she went home. But she would never come back—not for a long, long time, anyhow. She knew now it wouldn't do. She and Matthew couldn't just be friends, as she had genuinely thought, especially now she knew he still loved her.

She took a last glance through the small window at the stretches of heather in the foreground with the hills purpling behind them in the setting sun, then, taking the empty cream jug, went back into the kitchen to scald it out.

Naomi went out of the kitchen door as she came in, and she saw her go round to where Matthew would be penning the sheep. The next day he was taking some ewes to the station, and would be picking them out and putting them in a separate pen. Naomi must have gone out to speak to him alone. It made Marion feel still more uncomfortable.

By and by the door opened suddenly and Naomi came in alone, her brows black and drawn, her high-coloured cheeks a still brighter scarlet with rage.

"I have given Mattoo a piece of my mind," she shouted, quoting one of Beenie's sayings.

"Oh, Naomi, what are you so angry about?"

"Mattoo can tell you that." She turned and began to revile Matthew in a high, shrill, excited voice, repeating all over again the things she had said before, but with an added venom. He was secretive, she screamed.

"He will not talk—so dumb as his own sheep! But I will make him talk. I will goad him till he talk."

"But what do you want him to talk about? Don't shout so, Naomi. Anyone passing could hear you."

"And who is to pass in zis godforsaken hole he has brought me to, making me work like a slave-woman, while his bitch mother and her sons roll in riches and do him out of his rights: He deceived me. It was not for this kind of life I married ze dumb, callow fool—oh, fool myself to fall in love with him—fool!"

Marion knew by this time that nothing incensed Naomi so much as silence. She saw it was Matthew's great mistake in coping with her—to retire into silence. She was one of those women who love a shrill fight; ready with her tongue, she could always think swiftly of telling answers or bitter insults, and it infuriated her to have no chance to use her genius for retort and for planting her daggers just where they would most surely wound. Without much judgment of character, Marion nevertheless felt profoundly that Naomi, frustrated in her desire for a stand-up fight, was a dangerous woman, one who would act if she thought her words were taking no effect. If she could not goad into speech she might be driven to blows or even worse. She remembered how she had once picked up a large carving-fork and hurled it across the kitchen at Beenie. It went wide and missed the phlegmatic Beenie, who had merely said, "That's right, fling the cutlery about. You'd better try the knife next."

Beenie, however, had usually entered with zest into their wordy warfare, and they would both go on till exhausted and emptied of their venom for the meantime.

Frightened of her violence, Marion still knew it was best to answer her, and kept putting in a word when she paused.

"Matthew didn't deceive you, Naomi. I'm sure he never told you he had money."

"So you know all about what he told me!"

She was off again, reviling Matthew, reviling his mother, his brothers, the "miserly old witch" his grandmother, complaining of her life on the solitary sheep-farm, of having to work with her hands like a servant-girl. She drew comparisons between Bowchester and Goslaw, even insulting Matthew for his youth, his rawness, for not being a man of experience who knew how to treat women. His mother's milk, she sneered, wasn't dry on his lips. But she would break him. She would break him in. She'd put a ring in the nose of the young bull calf and tame him.

Shocked and terrified, dreading what she would say next, Marion let her go on.

"She's blowing off steam," she steadied her quaking heart by reminding herself, but she wished Matthew would come in, while at the same moment afraid of being drawn into a quarrel between husband and wife—a quarrel with all the words on Naomi's side, but more dangerous because of that.

At last the door opened and Matthew came in, white and sullen.

Immediately Naomi turned on him, but he would not speak.

"Oh, speak, Matthew," Marion kept saying to herself. "Shout something at her. Can't you see it drives her mad when you don't say a word?"

At last she could stand it no longer. She went up to him, where he stood leaning his back against the wall, his hands clenched in his pockets, the bones of his jaw standing out white on the brown skin of his face, a nerve ticking in his cheek, sullen and silent.

"Oh, speak, Matthew," she said. "Speak!"

He looked at her and spoke to her.

"Go to bed, Marion," he said.

"Yes, take yourself off!" Naomi turned, and pointed to the door leading to the stairs. "Go! Go!"

Marion looked at Matthew, saw the appeal in his blue, desperate eyes, and went. Upstairs she sat on her bed for a long time, listening to Naomi's voice, wondering what had set her off. She had said nothing directly about Marion herself, but once or twice had conveyed indirect warnings.

She recollected how intimately she and Matthew had sat talking on the hillside, how he had held her hands as they stood up, and remembered that from the kitchen window Naomi could have watched. Had some instinct in the queer, passionate woman revealed to her that Matthew was telling Marion the truth about his marriage? Had she noticed that their love had revived? She remembered other strange words and actions of Naomi's, even before her last promise to stay on nearly a week ago now—how she would not go to the dance after they were all ready, though why, if she suspected anything, she wanted them to go alone Marion could not understand.

At last there was silence down below, and Marion undressed and crept into bed, miserable and shivering with cold. The weather had suddenly changed after tea and grown bitterly cold, with a hint of frost and snow in the air.

Planning to leave on the morrow whatever befell, she lay, shuddering involuntarily now and then, till she fell asleep.

CHAPTER XII

"THE DANCING'S DONE"

THE next day dawned bitterly cold with showers of snow and sleet. Mud and manure were churned up in the yard and pens to a horrible frozen broth mixed with straw and hailstones. Every now and then the sky darkened, and a rattle of hail or a flurry of snow would sweep across the heather and fall in fury upon the little cottage, shaking the doors, whitening the walls, and lashing against the window-panes. Then everything would go quiet for a little while, clouds would gather, and the air would seem heavy and full of threats.

It could hardly have been a worse day on which to travel, but Marion felt determined to get away. She thought it would be better for Matthew if she went, for she was now quite sure that it was mainly because of herself that Naomi had broken into one of her furies the previous evening.

As she dressed she made up her mind that she must see Matthew and tell him that she must get away, that he must take her to the station at all costs. He must yoke Jenny, the old mare, into the light cart if the gig wasn't mended; one of the shafts had been split, and that had been one of Naomi's reasons, she remembered, for keeping her a few days longer. The cart, with straw spread on the bottom, was used for taking calves and young pigs to and from the station across the hills. She must get a word with Matthew and tell him the cart would have to do, as there would not be time for him to mend the shaft before train time.

She did not want to discuss going with Naomi for fear of another outbreak. If she could arrange it and then just tell her she was going it would be better.

Her bedroom window was just over the huge peat-stack at the end of the house, and she noticed as she opened it that the snow, although it was bitterly cold and the hills and moorland were white, was melting on the top of the peats. The road would be passable at all events.

In the kitchen, when she went down, she found Naomi sullen and silent, struggling with the smoky fire, which blew out in puffs when a blast came and shook the house.

Matthew, she knew, would be out just now seeing to the sheep, but he had said he would mend the shaft that day, and would be working at it in one of the outhouses after breakfast. She must try to slip out and see him then.

She had hoped Naomi would stay in bed for breakfast that morning, and give her an opportunity to speak to him, but possibly Naomi had thought of that too, and prevented it.

She was surprised when Naomi turned to her and said in a not unfriendly voice;

"This fire will not go, and you muss be hungry. You had no supper."

"It was all right. I wasn't hungry."

Naomi laughed shortly. "It ees not surprising, eh? A nice tale for you to take home."

That was it, thought Marion swiftly. Naomi was trying to be friendly, so that she would not go back angry with her and tell them at home what had been going on. She would start wheedling her to be quiet about it later on. She knew how Naomi could put on her charm and wheedle promises of silence out of people. But Marion had no intention of talking about their private affairs at home, and said so at once.

"Of course I won't carry tales home, Naomi. How could you think that? You have both been very kind to me, and I shall tell them so."

"It ees not you I blame altogether," said Naomi. "It ees him."

Quickly Marion made up her mind, as Naomi seemed in this friendlier mood, not to wait, but to speak to her now of going home to-day. She would make the snow her excuse. They would both know it was—at least, partly—an excuse, but it would mean they could part on the friendlier supposition that the road to the station might be impassable to-morrow. It would also be a good reason to give at the Falcon's House and Bowchester for her unexpected return. Naomi was quick and clever enough to grasp that for herself without further explanation.

"I think, Naomi," she said, "I will go home to-day. The snow is drifting, and the roads may fill up by to-morrow, and they are needing me at home. There is some trouble with Perry, and anyhow I must be back for Easter."

Instantly Naomi turned, her face flushing darkly.

"You cannot go home to-day. It ees not possible; the trap is not mended. I myself am going to town to-morrow. We can go to ze station together."

Marion was silenced. She was not quick enough to think of another excuse or brave enough to say definitely that she was going. However, she did not give in. She must try to see Matthew and tell him she must go. She felt it was unwise to stay on, and she dreaded any more scenes.

"I think I should rather go to-day," she said, and then, not to be drawn into an argument before any plan was made, she went on quickly, "but we can talk about it later. Do let me try what I can do with that fire. I am more used to old-fashioned, smoky grates than you are. If you see to the other things I'll soon have it going."

Naomi did not answer. She got up from her knees, and Marion, as good as her word, soon had the fire blazing and the kettle boiling.

She had not spoken again, for she felt the air heavy with Naomi's morose anger, and thought it better to pretend not to notice it.

The door opened, and, turning round, she saw Matthew standing there with a sack on his shoulders over his water-proof, kicking the snow off his boots. Silhouetted in the open doorway with the snow-light on his face, he looked very young and for the first time it struck her, with a pain at her heart, how very young he did look beside Naomi, already heavying into middle age, her face at the moment ugly and sallow from anger and sleeplessness. The colour that had once been pretty in her cheeks was now a network of little purple veins.

"Good morning, Marion," he said. "You look as fresh as a daisy."

It was the wrong thing to have said, and certainly very tactless, but he was perhaps tired of thinking of the right thing to say, or it may just have struck him anew how fresh and pretty Marion looked with her fair hair, blue eyes, and milkmaid skin of cream and rose.

"Ha!" sneered Naomi. "She iss not married."

He glanced at Marion, but neither spoke till breakfast was on the table. Matthew had gone and washed, and came in fresh and glowing, his wet hair brushed back, but forming into a funny little untidy boy's twist on the crown that made Marion's heart suddenly ache.

She had never thought of Matthew as young until now; she was so young herself that his youth had never struck her. Now it was suddenly like a knife in her heart. He was just a boy. Love made her see it, made her feel suddenly older than he.

"I must get that shaft mended," he said, and began to try and talk to them both, doing his best to draw Naomi in, but she was sulky now with offence and would not enter the conversation, though Marion and he struggled manfully on with no response, except an occasional sneer or a veiled insult at Marion that made Matthew whiten under his tan.

"Oh, I must go. I must get away," Marion kept repeating to herself, as she tried to eat and appear natural. "Naomi is hating me now. Why will she not let me get away?"

After breakfast Matthew went off to mend the shaft.

"Now," she thought to herself. "Now I must go and tell Matthew he must get the cart ready and drive me to the station."

She waited till Naomi had gone into the milkhouse to make the butter, and then she slipped out. She did not say anything to Naomi, but she went quite openly, with no secret intention except the innocent enough desire to insist on Matthew's taking her to the station, which she felt she could do better without Naomi there.

She did not know why Naomi would not let her go that day, and it puzzled her, but Naomi was subject to all kinds of obstinate moods. Once Marion was away she was sure things would be better between the other two, for she knew the underlying cause of her anger, and that all the rest about the money and Matthew's secretiveness was just flotsam thrown up in the stirring of the mud of her resentment.

The door of the barn where the cart and the gig were kept was open, and she could hear Matthew working inside. She went across the snowy cobblestones and stood looking in.

"Hullo, Marion," he said. "Come in; you'll catch cold standing there."

He was splicing the shaft, and began to speak about it.

"This will have to do till I can get a new one put in."

He was trying to keep to indifferent subjects, and Marion knew it, but she must speak quickly of getting away while she had the chance.

"Matthew," she said, "listen. I *must* go home to-day. I must. It's because of me that Naomi is so angry and upset. Could you take me to the train?"

He had paused in what he was doing and stood looking at her.

"What train? I thought it was all settled you were going to-morrow."

"I feel I must go to-day, Matthew. Please take me. Do take me—to the afternoon train, I mean."

"Of course I shall, Marion, if you want to go. I don't wonder that you do. I'll hurry up with this shaft; it won't take me very long. Does Naomi know you're going?"

"Not yet. I mentioned it, but she would not listen. I thought if we arranged it and I got ready, and then just told Naomi it would be easier. You see, she says the gig isn't ready, but I thought if you would hurry and get it ready it would be all right. She doesn't really want me to stay. So I came across to beg you to hurry and get it finished, and to ask if you could arrange things so that you could take me—there would be time, wouldn't there, before you have to walk the ewes over?"

"I'd make time for you, Marion, if you wanted anything." He paused, then put out his hand and laid it on her arm.

"I know you must want to go. We're making a hell of it for you here. . . . I'm sorry, Marion."

"Don't mind, Matthew, it wasn't you—but, Matthew, I do think it would be better if you would speak when Naomi is cross. It infuriates her so when you don't."

"I just can't, Marion. I know it would be better if I could, but I just can't. There's something in me—you know sometimes when a bottle is too full it won't pour out? It's like that. There doesn't seem anything to say. Words won't cure what is between her and me."

"I know, Matthew, but"—she whispered the last words—"she frightens me."

She began to tremble a little. She felt his hand too shaking on her arm.

"So it's good-bye, Marion—oh, Marion, Marion. . . ." They might not use any term of endearment to each other, and so kept repeating each other's names. The way he said "Marion" in his broken, boyish voice was a caress in itself.

Suddenly he put his arm round her for a moment, gripping her with an iron grip. "Good-bye, Marion," he whispered, his face leaning down to hers. "Do you remember the dance at Peter's when I kissed you? It's all over, Marion, but . . . it's all over and the dancing's done"—his voice broke—"but——"

"*Ah! I knew I'd catch you!*"

With a start Matthew dropped his arm, and they both turned round, Marion involuntarily giving a shrill little cry of terror.

Naomi stood there, her hair wild, her face white, her eyes blazing with wrath. In her hands she held Matthew's old gun, and as they turned she lifted it and pointed it at them. "But

I'll make you pay! I'll make you pay!" she screamed, her voice hoarse with rage, and then a horrible flood of revilement poured from her lips.

Suddenly Matthew came to himself. He had put his arm round Marion again as she staggered back when Naomi lifted the gun.

"Stop that, Naomi," he said, in a stern voice, his manhood suddenly coming to him, his boyhood passing away. "Put down that gun and stop play-acting."

He turned to Marion.

"Don't be frightened, Marion; the gun isn't loaded. She is only at her play-acting stunts again."

"Oh, isn't it loaded! That's all you know! Words won't settle what's between you and me, will they not? You're right. Words won't. I know better than that now! Get out of here, you little——" she screamed at Marion, calling her by a horrible name, "or I'll let you have it too!"

But Matthew, leaving Marion, who staggered up against the wheel of the gig, catching hold of the spokes for support, suddenly leaped across the intervening space, and before Naomi could realize his quickness and agility he had her by the wrists and was forcing the gun of out her hands. Though big and broad, she was no use against his lean, masculine strength. She struggled and kicked him, then put her teeth into his wrist, but the weapon was wrenched from her hands. When she felt it go she turned and made a rush for the house.

Matthew opened the gun, shut it, and pulled the trigger, pointing it upward out of the doorway.

"See, Marion," he said, "it's not loaded. It's empty. She was only trying to frighten you."

He came and put his arms round her. "I must get you home now, my darling. I must get you home!"

She clung to him sobbing while he comforted her and kissed her white cheek, holding her fast, taking out his handkerchief to dry her face. "You're quite safe, sweetheart. Oh, Marion, don't cry—don't cry any more!"

"I'm so frightened. I'm so frightened," she could only gasp, "so frightened for you."

The two young, desperate lovers, little more than children caught in the whirlwinds of passion before they had realized their strength, clung to each other for a moment before they should be swept apart for ever.

Though the daffodils still danced in the little wind-swept garden, tossing their yellow heads and swirling their green skirts, for them youth was over indeed. The dancing was done.

CHAPTER XIII

"HELL HAS NO FURY LIKE A WOMAN SCORNED"

MATTHEW kept Marion beside him in the barn while quickly with shaky fingers he mended the broken shaft. He hid the gun under a heap of straw, telling Marion there was really no danger, because he had run out of cartridges and there were none about the place.

When the gig was ready they went back into the house. Naomi was not to be seen. She had locked herself into her bedroom, and they could hear her pulling things about as though she were moving the furniture or dragging a box from place to place.

Matthew had to see to his sheep, but he would not leave Marion alone in the cottage with Naomi, and indeed she was too terrified to stay, there had been such a madness of hatred in the Frenchwoman's eyes as she pointed the gun. She was afraid for Matthew too now, and was equally terrified to leave him alone with Naomi and go home, but Matthew only laughed at these fears. He could not understand Marion's terror of physical violence to himself.

"Why, Marion," he said, "she's just a woman."

"Are you sure about the gun?"

"Absolutely. There hasn't been a cartridge in the house since you came. I used the last for that hare we had."

"Don't get any more—will you not?"

"Oh, well, I'll see about that. I need a gun, but I'll keep them all well hidden."

He was only comforting her. He had no fear of Naomi and the gun.

Marion went with Matthew up the hill to see to the sheep. There would be just time to yoke the mare and get to the station when they returned. She had packed her things and was ready to leave.

The sheep were just a little way up the hill, in full view of the house, and they walked a little apart, saying very little. After that first clinging together after the shock of Naomi's sudden appearance their natural loyalty to Naomi had returned. She was his wife; to neither of them came any thought of any possibility of breaking that tie. In those days it seemed so much stronger, so much more inevitably for ever—"till death us do part."

So they spoke of her journey, of Easter, of Penny.

"You'll give my love to them all at home."

"Yes, I will, Matthew."

"And you won't say anything about—about Naomi and me. She didn't mean it, you know, Marion. She likes play-acting."

"Ye—e—s." Marion could not think she had been play-acting.

"And you're not to worry about me. I have the farm and the sheep, and you to think about, though I shouldn't do that, and you must forget about me."

"No, I won't do that, Matthew."

They were silent on their homeward way, both wondering in what kind of mood they would find Naomi. She was so incalculable. She might be still in her room, or she might be waiting to attack them with her bitter tongue, or she might have made up her mind it would be wiser to try to part on a friendly note, pretending she had been joking, laughing hysterically. One could never be sure with Naomi.

But when they arrived all was silent in the house and there were no signs of her having been in the kitchen.

"She is waiting till I go," thought Marion, as she put out some bread and cold meat and milk for a meal before they left, while Matthew brought in coals and saw to the animals about the place. The hens were grouped about the door and sitting on the window-sill waiting for food, and the pigs' meat stood in the pails unserved. When the meal was on the table Marion went and knocked at Naomi's door. "Won't you come and have something to eat, Naomi?" she called. But there was no answer.

"Do come, Naomi. I'm just going away."

A harsh laugh was all the answer. Then silence.

They had to hurry, for there was barely time to do everything and catch the train.

"I'll wash up," said Marion, not wishing to leave their dishes for Naomi, "while you bring the gig round. My case is all ready to bring downstairs."

He went out, and she gathered the things together and began to wash them.

Suddenly her heart stopped beating, a feeling of terror made her face blanch. She turned with a wet plate in her hand, her wide eyes fixed on the door. Matthew was coming back, running across the cobbles, a sense of urgency in his very footsteps.

The door burst open and he stood there, his face amazed, his hair ruffled up above his forehead.

"Marion," he said, "the gig's broken up!"

For an instant she felt a flash of relief; some nameless horror had seemed to be approaching her.

"The gig!" she repeated stupidly. She laid down the plate and, drying her hands swiftly on a towel, went towards him.

"The gig's broken?"

They crossed the yard to the barn. The gig was tilted up

on end, both shafts smashed and broken. An axe lay on the floor beside it.

"Has Naomi done it? But why?"

Matthew shook his head.

After a while he said, "I think it's just spite; but how am I to get you to the station?"

Naomi was indeed incalculable. Marion stood trying to make her out. One would have thought Naomi would be glad to get rid of her, they were all so unhappy. Why should she do this? Why? Why?

There was no answer except Matthew's "just spite," it seemed—unreasoning, senseless, bitter spite.

Matthew lifted the shafts and shook his head.

"It will need new shafts," he said.

"The cart?" she asked.

He shook his head. "It's too slow. We couldn't possibly get there in time with Jock to pull it." Jock was the slow, strong cart-horse.

They went back to the kitchen and sat talking in low voices.

"But it won't be ready to-morrow either," said Marion, "and Naomi wanted to go to town; she said so."

He was sitting with his head in his hands staring at the fire. He got up and went and knocked at Naomi's door, but got no answer. He shook the door and called to her, but the only sound that came back was a laugh.

He returned and stood staring into the fire. The day was dull now; the wind had died down, but the sky was grey and lowering, and showers of sleet and snow fell intermittently.

There was no other train that night, but there was one that left early the next morning for the convenience of farmers going into the big cattle market in Breckan, which was held on a different day from the corn market.

"I'll tell you what we'll do," he said at last. "I'll take you with me when I drive the ewes over, and we'll ask Jock to give you a bed for the night so that you can catch the early train. You can ride Jenny."

"But I can't ride. I've never been on a horse."

"You'll manage. You just need to sit on Jenny, and I'll lead her. She's very quiet. Could you take a few things in your small case, and I'll carry it, and send the trunk on? I'm afraid we couldn't manage it."

They arranged to do that, Matthew as eager for her to get away now as she was to go. She went upstairs, opened her trunk, and took out a few things. In it was Granny's box, which she had brought with her because she had promised Granny never to let it out of her hands.

"You take it with you wherever you go," the old woman had said. "Don't leave it about. You never know. . . ."

Marion had laughed, but promised.

She tried to fit it into the small case, but the lid would not close with it in. She tried all ways, and then gave it up. It was impossible to take it. She would have enough to do holding on to Jenny, and she could not ask Matthew to carry it and the case and drive the sheep besides leading the mare.

Anyhow it would look so queer and absurd to insist on carrying a steel money-box that no one had ever seen before, and Matthew would send her trunk in a day or two.

She put it under her other things in the trunk, fastened the straps, and relocked it. She knew Naomi would think nothing of prying if it came into her head to do so.

She wondered if she should go and call "Good-bye" to Naomi through the locked door, and then decided not to. It would be useless; better just go away.

They drank a cup of tea and prepared to set off.

The ewes were taken from their pens and driven outside the gate and the collies set to watch them, Jenny, saddled and ready, was brought round into the cobbled yard, and Matthew was lifting Marion on to her back when suddenly the kitchen door opened and Naomi appeared. As the door opened Matthew put Marion on her feet again behind the mare and ran forward, but stopped before he reached the door, as Naomi started screaming at them, forbidding Marion to go, or, if she went, she must go alone. Matthew was not to go with her; she wouldn't allow them out of her sight together.

She seemed mad with jealousy and suspicion. She shouted that she would take Marion herself to the station to-morrow, but one step together they should not go. "There has been enough of that—too much!" she screamed at Matthew, who, as usual, took refuge in silence.

"Speak to her. Speak!" implored Marion, but it was no use. Naomi came out and drove him backwards in her fury, till he stood against the wall, white and sullen and silent. Only once did he speak during her tirade.

"You think yourself in love with her," Naomi screamed, among her other invective, "and you wish I were dead and in ze grave!"

"I do love her," said Matthew quietly. He did not look at his wife, but at Marion as he spoke.

"How dare you? How dare you?" she shouted, beside herself with grief and fury, for his words were more impressive from their very quietness and the way they were wrung out of his silence.

There was no doubt that Naomi was passionately in love with her young husband, however he might infuriate her. She may at first have wanted one of the Wotherspoons because the family was reputed to be wealthy and because it was supposed they would get the most, if not all, of their grandmother's money; indeed, she had first thought of Mark, but Mark and nature had outwitted her there. Mark would never look at her, and she had fallen in love with Matthew's handsome face, and it could still draw her, however much his temperament infuriated her.

Now his remark stung her as if she had been bitten by a sleeping serpent.

"And what about me?" she flamed. "What about me? You zink I will take that lying down? You think I am one of your sheep? You will find wrong. If you go with her now you come not back! You enter not the door. Love! Love!

It is not love. You are married man. You are married to me; it is——" She used a horrible word, and went on, "I drive you out and make your names stink in the nostrils. I make her name——"

Suddenly Matthew seemed galvanized into action. He sprang forward towards Marion, pushing Naomi aside, and, speaking directly to her at last, his eyes dark with passionate hatred, said:

"Get out of my sight, you horrible woman! I loathe you, if you want to know it. I wish I'd never seen you and never had to see you again. I won't let Marion stay another minute near your filthy tongue. . . ." He had reached the horse, and his final words were lost as he grabbed the reins and with his arm round Marion rushed her out of the yard and through the gate. There he swung her with one quick jerk on to the horse and, holding her on, ran the beast along to where the dogs were guarding the sheep.

Naomi turned towards the house and disappeared as he rushed the stumbling mare on past the dogs and sheep.

"It's all right, Matthew," cried Marion. "Matthew, the sheep! She is away; she has gone into the house."

But he hurried on. Behind them the dogs had started up and were driving on the sheep through the narrow gully made by the burn and a wall which ran for some distance by the burn, enclosing a strip of the haugh for the cows. As he slackened speed the ewes came rushing on helter-skelter and surged past the mare, their hard little feet pattering on the stones, their fleeces rising and falling in their speed.

He called back the dogs and gave them their orders. Looking over her shoulder, Marion saw that Naomi now followed them with the gun, though already hopelessly outdistanced. In her high-heeled shoes she was useless, and kept stumbling among the rough stones partly covered by the snow.

A little farther on Matthew got his small flock into order, and they proceeded more slowly and quietly through the hills.

Marion was crying bitterly now, but trying to control her

weeping and pull herself together. Matthew walked with the reins in his hand, supporting her as well as he could, and so they plodded on through the lonely hills by the running burn.

Once she broke into hysterical laughter, remembering the ridiculous galloping sheep with their grey fleeces rising and falling as they surged past the mare, the barking dogs, the whole hue and outcry of her departure—laughter which had suddenly turned into such frightful sobbing that Matthew had to stop old Jenny, lift her down, and comfort her.

"It's all right now, Marion. You're quite safe, and Naomi will have gone back, and anyhow the gun wasn't loaded."

"It's not that! It's not that!"

"Are you tired? It won't be long now; we're nearly there. You'll see the station when we get round the next bend. I wish I could mount and hold you, but Jenny couldn't carry us both."

"No, no! I'm not tired. I'm all right. Lift me up, Matthew, and let us go on."

But she began to cry again.

"I'm frightened for you. Oh, need you go back to-night? Couldn't you stay with Jock and go back to-morrow when Naomi won't be so angry? Don't go back, Matthew."

"I must go back, Marion. I have so much to attend to. But even if I could stay away that wouldn't do. I'd like to stay and see you safely off in the morning, but you see it wouldn't do, don't you? We must be careful, especially now. Naomi has such a dangerous tongue."

He wiped her face with his handkerchief and lifted her up again and urged the mare on.

"The sooner I get back the better. Try not to cry any more, Marion. Jock's all right, but his wife will wonder if you are crying, and I don't want her tongue gossiping about you."

Round the bend the station came into view. Marion got down again and went and bathed her face in the icy water of the burn. They opened her case and got out the powder which she rarely used, but remembered to have put into one of the pockets when she left home. He solemnly surveyed the result, his young brow wrinkled into furrows of anxiety.

"It's all right," he said. "You look quite all right."

There was no love-making or caresses on that rude, fear-beset journey. A bewildered and goaded boy and girl, they stumbled on, too harassed, too desolate, to think of love or kisses.

At Jock's house Matthew lifted her down and explained about the early train, saying she was needed at home and had missed the earlier one through the gig breaking down.

Then he said a brief good-bye, and went to pen the sheep ready to go into the market the following day, before riding back to Goslaw on Jenny.

CHAPTER XIV

"ABOUT THE DEAD HOUR OF THE NIGHT SHE HEARD THE BRIDLES RING"

JOCK went off to help Matthew with the sheep, and, once indoors, Elsie, his young wife, began volubly to apologize and explain that her eldest sister's baby had been christened that day, and as Jock couldn't get away for the ceremony they had promised to go over in the evening.

"That will be all right," Marion assured her. "I'll sit and read, and then I'll go to bed early."

In her heart she was thankful that she would not have to sit and talk to them; she would be glad to be left alone.

She helped Elsie to dress, and said a glass of hot milk was all she wanted for supper, but Elsie insisted on setting out a cold pie and large cake, on heaping up the fire and doing all she could for the comfort of her unexpected guest.

Then Jock came in, dressed already in his Sunday suit. He would fain have gone in his green corduroy working suit, and that kept them busy arguing for the few minutes before they went off, so there was no time for questions about Naomi or too close inquiries about why she had to go home so suddenly.

Jock had told her that Matthew had gone, and it was just as they left that he suddenly slapped his thighs and said:

"Dod! I've forgotten! There's that parcel of cartridges. I meant to give them to him when he brought the ewes to-night."

"Oh, that's all right," said Elsie. "Willie, the post, took them over. I forgot to tell you." She turned to Marion. "He had a letter for you, so I knew he would be calling at Goslaw."

The farm lay off the more frequented main valley, where there were two or three cottages at intervals, so the postman only went that road if there was anything for Goslaw. A friendly guard, it seemed, had brought the parcel and left it with Jock.

"Well, that's all right then," said Jock, turning to Marion. "I suppose he got it all right?"

Marion was staring at him, dismay in her eyes, but she tried to recover her self-possession.

"I—I don't know," she said; then added, "I suppose he would."

"Ou, aye," said Jock. "Willie, the post, would na forget a parcel. He hasn'a that mony. Weel, lassie"—to his wife—"if you're done titivating we'll get away over to Bella's, but, mind, we canna' bide late. I'll need to be back for the twelve-ten going through, and it's a good step."

"It's just a goods train," said Elsie. "Neddy can see her through."

"Aye, but she'll be stoppin'. There's a wagon o' coals to come off."

They argued for a few minutes about whether Neddy, the assistant porter, could manage, and then went off, Elsie having, as usual, Marion guessed, gained her point with good-natured Jock.

o

With good-nights and directions about supper and bed and "leaving the door on the sneck," they set off, and Marion was left alone.

But she did not take up the *People's Friend*, which Elsie called "a book," to read; she sat down on the arm-chair and began to think.

That parcel—had Matthew got it? And if so why had he lied about the cartridges to her? Was it to keep her from being frightened? Did he know all the time that there were cartridges in the house? But he said at once, "The gun isn't loaded . . . she is only at her play-acting stunts again," and it hadn't been loaded. Naomi *had* been play-acting, as he called it.

She didn't think Matthew was sharp enough to say that at once if he hadn't known it. He was a slow thinker. Still, he must have got the parcel. Perhaps he had put it away and not said anything to Naomi. Perhaps he kept the cartridges hidden and knew that Naomi didn't know where they were. That must be it. He had known that the gun couldn't be loaded because Naomi didn't know he had got the cartridges or where he kept them.

She picked up the paper, but something kept nagging at her brain, and though she read half a column of a story she found that she was only repeating the words to herself; she had no notion whatever what it was about.

She laid it down, wandered round the room, drank some milk, and then picked up the paper again and sat with it open in her hand, the nagging going on in her head.

At last she had it. Yes, that was it—the letter! She remembered clearly Naomi coming in with her letter when Matthew was sitting looking at the newspaper and she herself was stirring meal for the dogs' porridge. There had been no parcel in Naomi's hand, and she had said nothing to Matthew about any parcel.

Had she taken it from Willie and hidden it before she brought in the letter?

But why? That was before the awful scenes had begun.

She puzzled and puzzled over it. Perhaps Willie, the post, had forgotten it and brought it over on his return journey. But there she had to leave it. She had no idea when that might be. If he had forgotten it when he delivered the letter he might have brought it or got some one to bring it over at any time, for all she knew.

But as she thought and puzzled fear had been growing. She was sure now Matthew had spoken the truth, as he knew it, when he had said, "The gun isn't loaded . . . she is only at her play-acting stunts again."

Then she remembered how he had just pushed it under the hay and left it. He would never have done that if he had thought there was any danger. Slowly conviction grew. Naomi had the cartridges. She remembered her laugh and her words, "That's all you know."

Fear mounted and mounted in her terrified heart.

She remembered Naomi running out with the gun, she remembered her threats, her almost insane fury. She had the gun, she had the cartridges—and Matthew was riding innocently back. If he saw her with the gun he would think it was unloaded and he might goad her into using it!

He must be warned.

She glanced at the clock. It was only about half an hour at the most since Jock had come in saying Matthew had just gone.

Could she run after him and warn him? Jenny was old and no great goer at the best, and she was tired, and Matthew had said he was too heavy for her now she was so ancient. Probably he would only walk her back, or, if he rode, dismount at the hills. There was a long, steep hill winding down from the uplands to the station. If she went now she might overtake him before he had got very far and warn him.

He must be warned. She knew that Naomi was dangerous and Matthew didn't know how to treat her. His attitude goaded her so—goaded her into madness.

No sooner had she made up her mind than she slipped on her coat and hat. Her shoes were still on her feet. She stole out, leaving the lamp low and the door 'on the sneck,' and started to run. Luckily the moon had come out and she could see her way. She was strong and a good runner. She sped up the long winding slope.

There was no sign of Matthew when she reached the top, but half an hour was a long start; she could hardly expect to have gained on him yet. She paused a moment to regain her breath, then started to run, speeding along, down hill and up hill, following the winding course of the burn, but cutting at times across the heather where she was sure of the way and could keep the track in view.

Still she saw no sign of man or horse. But now she could not go back. He might be just round the next corner. Several times she thought she heard the beat of hoofs. That would be Jenny! Then the moonlight would show an empty stretch of road in front of her. It must have been the sound of the burn chattering over the stones.

He could not be far now. She had run a long way, slowing at the hills and sometimes pausing at the top, but only to rush on again pell-mell as soon as she had got her breath.

Was she too late? As she began to get nearer to the farm she gave up hope. Jenny must have gone more quickly than she had given her credit for. Still, she would keep on now till she reached the farm. There she would try to make sure that all was well, and then go back without giving any sign of her presence.

It was a mad thing to have done, running to Goslaw after Matthew—a mad episode in her career of which no one must ever know. She must try to run all the way back—all these weary miles—and be in the house before Jock and his wife returned.

They would be late. Elsie had talked of a party and a fiddler. She knew what country folk were when they started to dance. With any luck at all she would be home and into bed before they returned, even if she had to walk most of the way. And she was feeling tired now. She stumbled a little over the outcropping rocks of a deep slope, and then, gaining the top, she paused.

Beneath her she saw the farmhouse lying in the moonlit hollow with the sheep-pens clustered round it.

From the distance it looked very peaceful, lying there among the patches of dark heather and moon-white snow; in one of the downstairs rooms a glimmer of light made an orange square of the window; a chimney threw a black shadow along the roof.

There was no sound, not even the muffled bleat of a sheep or the coughing of a ewe from the pens.

She would just go down, steal quietly into the yard, and listen. The dogs would not bark; they knew her, and, besides, like many sheep-dogs, they were trained not to bark. Then she would creep silently off and make her way back to the station.

This would be her secret for ever—this sight of the lonely farm among the moonlit hills.

A plover rose, called once, and was still.

Then as the silence closed in there came clearly through the quiet air the shot of a gun.

Before she knew she had moved she found herself rushing down the hill on flying feet. She had no time for thoughts, no room in her mind for surmise. Everything was crowded out in one great, black rushing wave of terror.

She had still some distance to go and must have run for at least ten minutes after hearing the shot, but it seemed to her that she was in the yard at once after hearing it, stumbling through the jet-black shadows that lay over the cobbles.

Suddenly she staggered and nearly fell. Her foot had caught against something crumpled up on the ground among the shadows something—soft.

She was on her knees in a moment, feeling along his body, lifting up his young head from the sodden snow and muck in which it lay. She did not scream when the moonlight fell upon his face—his face!

She seemed to have known from the first moment when the

shot rang out among the silent, listening hills—known what she would find.

The shot had caught his face and head, and he had gone down forward, splayed out among the icy broth of snow and filth.

She took her poor small handkerchief and tried to clean his face. She leaned her cheek to his mouth and tried to feel his breath; she put her hands to his heart and felt a slight, fluttering beat. Then the most terrible grief and loneliness of her life came upon her and blotted out the world.

She came back to herself in a few moments. All was silent in the yard. Where was Naomi? The dogs would be curled up in the dog-house at the far end of the pens, where Matthew would have shut them before going on to the house. They were used to guns being fired at foxes in the night-time and would not give tongue. Where was Naomi? Was she in the house? All was quiet and silent there. Had she fled terror-stricken when she saw what she had done? Had she gone for help, flying distrait over the hills to the nearest cottage? Was she waiting to get Marion herself now, peering from some darkened window?

Marion felt no fear for herself, but she could not ask for aid at that house. She did not know what Naomi might do. She still had the gun. She might shoot her too, and Matthew's only help lay in her. There was not a soul to whom she could appeal. Around her lay the desolate, ravelled hills, and empty valleys; only the mad woman lurking somewhere near, or roaming distraught through the trackless heather, might be within reach.

She took off her petticoat, tore it in strips, and bound up his head. Very quickly and quietly she made up her mind. She must get him away by herself.

She put her arms under his shoulders and dragged him as quietly and swiftly as she could over the stones to the barn. It was double-doored, with one door in the yard, the other opening on to the moor. She opened the near door, pulled him in, then closed it and opened the farther one, feeling her way past the cart to do so.

Then she left him and stole quietly round to the stable, where she found and brought out the cart-horse, harnessing him on the moor, where she could see by the light of the moon. She knew how to harness a horse, having often in the days of careless laughter harnessed the pony into the little buggy at Bowchester, and the method was much the same.

Fear beat with her heart-beats, terror breathed with each breath, but grief now lay quiescent; she had no time for grief. Each moment was filled with urgency, with dread of Naomi's discovering them, of making a sound with the heavy chains that would rouse her, of not being quick enough to get away before her return—if she had run off.

But silence still lay over the house and the barn and the sheep-stalls. Only a little wind that was rising came intermittently in quick gusts through the valley, whistling in the bent firs, creaking the wattles that closed the pens.

She led the horse round to where the cart stood facing the door of the barn, and managed, after many attempts, to get the shafts through the chains and to buckle the stiff leather buckles with her small, shaking fingers.

Then came the most difficult feat of all—to get Matthew into the cart. But terror and determination gave her strength. She felt in that hour of supreme anguish and detachment as if she could do anything, as if the utter and ultimate refutation of human weakness or recognition of any limitations ran through her veins like some spiritual essence, taking the place of her blood.

She felt unconquerable. She felt that, if her arms broke, she could still lift him with the jagged bones, that if her heart gave way within her breast, still, with her heart broken, she would raise him and lay him among the straw.

And she did it. First she let the back of the cart down, taking out the iron pegs, then she laid the plank, used normally as a seat, sloping from the cart to the ground, then she dragged him as far up the plank as she could, bound him there with a bit of dusty rope that hung from the rafters, then climbed into the cart and, lying flat, dragged him slowly, inch by inch, with as little jerking as she could, till he lay full length among the straw, strewn there to take the beasts of the field into market.

Her brain was crystal-clear, envisaging everything with penetrating distinctness.

She would need money, a good sum of money, for she knew exactly what she was going to do. She would be in time for the goods train that was unhitching a wagon on its way through from Breckan to Newcastle. There was an infirmary there. They would reach it in an hour or two—goods trains with perishable goods travelled fast—and be there long before the next train left for Breckan. He would get skilled attention there at once. Her urgency drove her on to plan each step. She must pay the guard to take them in the van; she must have money.

She remembered Granny's box and her words that she was to open it if ever she was in need. Had Granny foreseen, with some queer second sight of age, that she would soon be in desperate need of money? She recalled some of her words. Had she thought that she and Matthew might go away together, not like this, but—together; that Matthew would need it too?

The box was in her trunk in the house. She had her keys in her pocket, but how could she get into the house? Baffled for a moment, she stood with her arms resting on the back of the cart where she had just slipped the pegs into their sockets. Then she remembered the window of her bedroom just over the peat-stack. She had left it open in the morning.

She slipped along in the shadow of the barn, stepping as softly as a hunting cat, swiftly crossed the strip of moonlight into the shadow of the gable where the peat-stack stood. She climbed nimbly up and tried the window from the lower sill. It rose easily, with a very slight creaking, and she disappeared through the dark square. Stepping gently on tiptoe, she found the trunk, took out the box, and opened it. She could not see very well, but felt bundles of notes and a little bag of coins on the upper tray; underneath there seemed to be only large papers. She stuffed the bag and notes into the pocket of her coat, relocked the box, replaced it, and locked the trunk. Then, as quietly as she had come, she retraced her steps, closing the window gently after her and creeping back to the barn.

All was silent there, save for the quiet, steady nibbling of a rat among the hay in the corner. Matthew still breathed. She took off her coat and put it under his head. Then she lifted the reins and drove out through the open doorway on to the moonlit moor.

As she did so the rising wind swept down from the hills, rattled the doors of the barn, and went soughing through the pine-trees that stood beside the sheep-pens. She listened, remembering how often they had paused in their laughter at home to say, "The piper in the wind goes by."

Then she drew on the reins and set out into the unknown, following the piper who pipes us all away from the safety of Hamelin.

CHAPTER XV

"THE DAY THOU GAVEST, LORD, IS ENDED"

MARION stood by the little sideboard and waited. She had made the room as homely and comfortable as she could. A big fire blazed in the hearth; he would be able to feel the brightness and hear the flicker of the flames. The table was set, and she had prepared the supper herself, telling the land-lady, a sympathetic soul, that he would be sure to like one of her home-made dishes best.

Matthew had always liked pigeons, so she had bought pigeons. They were not like the wood pigeons at Bowchester, but they would do. She had spiced and seasoned them as they did at home, and put them in the oven in a basin with a plate over it, to serve instead of the brown pots with lids they used at Bowchester and the Falcon's House.

With a fresh stab in her heart she remembered that Matthew would not see them, so that it did not matter about the basin. Her days were full of these stabs now; sometimes she thought her heart must be all stabbed away—all the bits that were left after it broke when she found Matthew shot.

She knew now that it had broken then, because she felt so numbed, as if nothing could matter any more. Nothing, indeed, mattered that could happen to herself; only things about Matthew could stab her still—like the basin that he could not see. She smiled to herself, remembering her father's scorn when she was careless with her language—of course a basin couldn't stab. Ah, well, that was all her father knew.

She had not gone to bring Matthew away from the infirmary herself; he didn't want her to. Indeed, he had begged her to go home until he got used to his first fumblings in the dark.

Every one had wanted him to go home. Mark was coming, indeed, on Friday to take him straight home, as he thought, from the infirmary, but Marion had circumvented that by the simple means of telling them at Bowchester that he was to be discharged two days later than was the case. Marion had her own plans.

She had got him a room in the house where she had lodged in Newcastle herself all the time he had been kept in the ward, while they tried to save his sight and make his face presentable. Both her father and Rachel had come and tried to take her home, but she would not go. Mother Wotherspoon had tried too, but they met a new Marion, a Marion with her mind made up.

She had learned to depend on herself in one swift night. She would never be the same again, easy, listening to others, swayed by what they thought. She and Matthew had been alone in the world that night. They were alone still, because no one could understand. They could not understand that

Matthew could not bear to go home. They thought it was the best place for him, where he would be cared for and looked after. It was all very right and sensible—but Matthew couldn't; he just could not bear to go back to where he had been happy, to be surrounded by their pity, their helping hands.

No one else could understand. But she did.

She shut her eyes standing there. "I feel just the same," she said to herself. "I just have my eyes shut. I couldn't bear either to be treated as if I were something abnormal, something queer and alien to be pitied, to be humoured as some one apart—why, they even lower their voices when they are speaking to him. They shut him out, without knowing they are doing it. It is as if they said, 'You aren't a human being like us any more. You are apart; we must treat you differently. We must always be kind.' How he loathed their kindness, their consideration, their hushed voices!"

A sound made her look round and fly down the stairs to the door. The landlady had wanted to put him downstairs, making changes for the day or two he would be there, and, exasperated, Marion had turned on her.

"Why? He has legs, hasn't he? He can climb the stairs as well as you or me—better than you." She had smiled, winning the landlady back to good humour. "For you know you *are* too fat for stairs, Mrs Laidlaw, hinney." She had picked up the Newcastle term of endearment. "You're as round as a ball."

"'Deed, aye, I could let you have some and never miss it and you'd be the better of it—you're naught but a filleted fish. I like lassies plumped out a bit. . . . I was just thinking he might stumble and fall."

"He's not so silly, and, mind, you're not to treat him as if he was an infant, or had an infectious disease, or was some queer kind of *saint* that had to be treated different from ordinary mortals, or as if he were made of glass and might break. He isn't. He's just an ordinary man like any other man—oh, I wish everybody would stop being kind to him!"

"Well, you're a queer lassie, I must say. You'd think you'd *like* folks to be kind to him."

"Well, I don't. I hate it. I'm not kind to him. I'd loathe being kind to him."

Mrs Laidlaw had departed shaking her head; "the lassie was clean daft."

The sound Marion had heard was the cab stopping. Matthew had come. She ran down the stairs and opened the door. He stood there with a nurse holding on to his arm. The bandages were off his scarred face, but he wore dark glasses to protect his eyes—not that he needed protection from the light now. Matthew was blind.

Totally blind, though the doctors thought that in time he might see a little with one eye—be able to tell when it was daylight perhaps, they had said to Marion—but that might be a long time, and it might be never.

"Hullo, Matthew!" she said. "I thought you were never coming. The supper's just ready."

She put out her hand, took his, and drew him in. Then they both thanked the nurse and bid her good night.

"Take off your coat," she said, "and hang it on the peg. It's just in front of you, and then we'll go upstairs to your room."

She did not offer to help him even when he fumbled for the peg. Love and suffering had made Marion very wise—too wise, and too old for her years, but there it was!

When his coat and hat were off she took his hand.

"I'll show you the way this once, and then you can find it for yourself. Mrs Laidlaw thinks because you're blind you'll tumble down the stairs. I told her you weren't such an idiot, but if you did tumble you could just get up again."

He laughed a little, but she saw he was feeling this first re-entry into the world with terrible keenness, and her own heart sank a little. But she mustn't show it. She was the only one who could rouse him out of his fits of terrible gloom and despondency. In fact, he always had them worst after visits from relatives or friends, especially those from home.

Naomi had gone once to the infirmary and tried to see him, but he had absolutely refused to have her brought in.

"But it's your wife, Mr Wotherspoon."

"That's why," said Matthew grimly, then, recovering himself, "It would be too much of a shock for her to see me like this. I won't look so bad when I've healed a bit."

Nothing would persuade him. He would not see her; he turned his face to the wall and buried his head in the pillows in case they brought her to the door to look at him.

They had told the doctors at the infirmary—and all who inquired—that it had been an accident.

To Mark, who had gone over to Goslaw, Naomi had said it was an accident, and nothing more. To further questions she was dumb. It was an accident, and she had gone for help. "If you want to know more you'll have to wait till he can tell you himself. I do not speak. It was an accident; that is all I say."

Marion had said she found him shot and taken him away. She could say truthfully enough that she did not know how it happened, and to other questions she too was dumb, and indeed they did not pry too closely at the moment into the mystery. "Let sleeping dogs lie," said Mother Wotherspoon, "till you have to rouse them." She knew Naomi had shot her son, but kept her lips tight till she could hear the truth from Matthew. "The day of reckoning will come," she said.

Now Marion helped him up the stairs and busied herself getting supper, talking about the day's happenings, describing the room to him, and telling him what he could see from the window. She had dropped the difficult feat of avoiding the verb 'to see' in all its tenses and aspects; she just used it as she would to anyone else, except where a direct reference to his blindness was necessary, and then she was direct and frank.

"You can see a bit of the new bridge," she told him, and the next minute was saying, "I'll take you all round the room and let you feel everything, their shapes and where they are, and then you can feel your way about. It becomes just as easy as seeing, and people turn awfully clever and develop another instinct when they lose their sight, the doctor says."

"Yes," Matthew said, a little more cheerfully. "You know, I begin to feel that, Marion."

She waited till after supper to divulge her plan, of which he as yet knew nothing.

She had thought it all out and made all her arrangements alone. Of course, she would still have to persuade him, but her determination was so clear, so fixed, that she had no fear of failure. She felt somehow it was predestined, that she was only falling in with what was meant by fate—or the Lord, as Mother Wotherspoon would have said—*Che sarà sarà* (" What is to be will be").

He made an opening for himself.

"Mark is coming on Friday," he said. "I had another letter this morning."

"Yes. I told him it was Friday you were leaving—as I said to you I would."

"It was good of you, Marion, to think of giving me a day or two to get used to the house and stairs and things before going back. But I'm not going home."

"No, I know. Of course you're not going back—not if you don't want to."

"I was thinking I might stay on here for a bit—the landlady seems a decent soul—and go to that place they were telling me about where you learn to make baskets and mats." He laughed bitterly. "Baskets and mats, sitting indoors all day —it's all I'm good for now!"

Another stab at Marion's heart, thinking of Matthew sitting making mats. Matthew! Never! Never! Never!

His own voice sounded beaten enough as he faced the dreary prospect. Rooms in a strange lodging-house, alone and blind, some stranger to take him back and forward from door to door, finding his way perhaps to the tobacconist and the paper shop, tapping on the street with his stick.

Their intense sympathy made them see the same picture together.

"Wouldn't it be better at home?" she asked again, though she knew the answer.

He shook his head.

"No, worse. I just couldn't stand that, Marion, not just now. Oh, God! To have them all helping, all asking questions, all being kind to the poor blind man, a casualty, a burden, a queer, pitiable creature, where I used to be hail-fellow-well-met with them all, an equal instead of a curiosity —staring at my face. . . . I'll get on better alone, among strangers who never saw me any different from what I am. You're the only one out of the old lot I can stand, Marion. I hate them all because they have to be kind to me—all but you." And he put out his hand. "Where are you? You never treat me as if I was a case. How I loathe the word! Oh, Marion, if only——" He stopped.

"If only what?"

"Never mind; I shouldn't have said that." He paused. "I was only going to say, 'If only I didn't mind so much,'" he added lamely, obviously lying.

"I wish you would say what you were going to say, Matthew."

"No, it was just—just silliness, Marion. . . ." He changed the subject clumsily. "You'll be going back with Mark on Friday. That's two whole days I'll have you."

"I'm not going back with Mark," she said.

"Aren't you? What's the matter with Mark? He will be company for you. I'd like to feel you had some one to take care of you on the way. Old Mark's all right. I don't mind Mark myself as much as the others. He just grunts out what he thinks."

"I'm not going back with anybody. I'm not going back at all, ever."

She had come and taken a stool beside him, and sat at his knees before the fire, her feet drawn up, her hands clasped round her own knees, looking into the flames.

CHAPTER XVI

"I SOUGHT HIM WHOM MY SOUL LOVETH . . . I HELD HIM, AND WOULD NOT LET HIM GO"

HE turned his head towards her. His profile was still fine and the unscarred side of his face still boyish-looking, the hair dark as ever, but at the scarred side a tuft of grey hair fell over his brow. The eye socket on that side was empty. That was why he wore the dark glasses, until a glass eye had been made. On the other side the eye looked quite all right, but he could not see with it.

"What are you saying, Marion?" he asked. "What's that? What do you mean? You cannot stay here?"

"No, I don't want to stay here." She hesitated, and then said uncertainly, "Matthew, you know that day on the hill when you said—when you told me—you'd always—like me best. . . ." She paused for so long that he said, "Yes," rather stiffly, and shortly, but she saw the nerve on the uninjured side of his face begin beating. Then before she could speak he went on quickly:

"You must forget that, Marion. I shouldn't have said it. It was just . . . I wanted you to know. I didn't," he went on, desperately trying to explain, "I didn't want you to think about it . . . just to know and then forget it—I can't explain."

"I know what you mean. You didn't want me to think it could make any difference. You just wanted me to know, and put it away—away in a little cupboard in my heart—and shut the door and not take it out and look at it any more."

"Yes." There was relief in his voice at this understanding of what he had meant. He put out his hand gropingly till he felt her shoulder, then touched her cheek.

"That was it, Marion. Now you must lock the door and throw away the key, or"—he laughed a little short laugh—"open the door and take out that confession and throw it away altogether. I shouldn't have said it. I've had a lot of time to think since then. It wasn't fair to you—or to Naomi—but it's you I mind about. Just forget about it, Marion."

"Do you mean—you don't like me any more—love me? Is it Naomi really? Tell me the truth, Matthew—please tell me the very absolute *true* truth. Would you like to go back to Naomi? She does love you. I mean, I can understand now that she didn't really intend to hurt you, that it was rage and jealousy made her fire the gun. I've been thinking a lot too."

He had gone whiter and whiter as she spoke, and now she felt the terrible shuddering that went through him as he gripped her shoulder with unconscious force.

"Naomi! Go back to Naomi? Never! Never!" His voice was hoarse. "I loathe her; she sickens me. It wasn't the shooting; I don't mean that. It's just—it's just . . ." He took away his hand, and, putting both elbows on his knees, hid his face in his palms, shaking so that she quickly turned, edged nearer, and put her arms round him.

"Don't, Matthew—oh, Matthew, I'm sorry. Please don't. You see, I love you so much I want whatever will make you happy, or a little bit happier. I could give you up if you loved her, or anybody, better than me. But if you don't——"

"How could I love anybody better than you? How could I? But I lost you, and if I could be glad of anything now it's that I did—I mean, that you're not tied to me like this, hideous and blind and helpless. A blind and horrible cripple——"

(He called himself a cripple because in some way, possibly from some of his injuries, his shoulders had become temporarily raised a little. She had thought he did not know about that.)

"You're not! You're not horrible or hideous, and you're not a cripple—you're as straight as a reed," she scolded, her eyes wet with tears. "You just *will* keep your shoulders up. The doctor says that will get away with exercises you have to do—oh, Matthew, do you really love me best? Tell me— tell me truly, because I've got a plan if you do—do be *sensible,* Matthew."

P

Her face looked childish again, raised to him in the light of the flames. He could not see it, but he dropped his hands and smiled a little at the scolding and eagerness in her voice, all mixed up together.

"Where are you? Where is your face, you little fighting-cock?"

He put out his hand, and she took it in hers and rubbed her cheek against the palm.

"There it is, there's my face, and I'm not a fighting-cock. I'm a fighting hen. I'm Jane, Hagar's parrot, with my crest standing straight up—feel!"

She pulled his hand over her hair, and he kept it there, pushing back her head a little.

"I can see you, Marion. I can always see you, just as you are. Your cheeks are white, and your eyes have greeny-blue flames like when you throw salt in the fire, and your hair—yes, it would stick up with rage if I didn't keep it down. Love you! Love you! *That* would be sensible, wouldn't it? No, I don't love you. Do you hear? I don't love you. That was just a madness, Marion. You have to forget it."

"It's not. It wasn't. You do love me, and I love you. Oh, Matthew, you're telling lies, aren't you? Big whoppers—you're a lion. You're being a pig with an 'i'—a real pig."

She was back into the language of their childhood, where a 'lion' was not quite so bad as a 'liar,' where a 'pyg' with a 'y' was less of an insult than a 'pig' with an 'i.'

"I'm not."

"Yes, you are."

"Oh, Marion."

"Well, a pyg with a 'y' anyhow."

"Am I? Marion, darling, I have to be."

"Oh, Matthew, please just say it wasn't true; it makes me so miserable."

"It was the biggest lie I ever told, but you've got to believe it. We've both got to believe it. What was it Rachel used to say when she was showing off? *Che sarà sarà.* 'What's to be

will be.' Everything is over and done—'Ah, but the times
that are gone, Nanette, were the best of all.' Do you remember
how gaily we used to sing it? And now it's true. . . . But it
had a merry tune, hadn't it? Come on!"

In a voice a little husky he sang the first verse over:

> "Ah! come guess what there may be?
>   Here in the wood
>   There is a tree,
>   The fairest of all,
> In the wood growing tall."

Bravely she took it up:

> "In the wood growing tall, Nanette!
>   In the wood growing tall.
> Ah! the times that are gone were the best of all!"

He joined in the refrain, as they had always done. A verse
each in turn and then the refrain together.

The merry little tune rang out, and the landlady down below
thought, "How happy they are, poor things. It's good to
be young."

She could not hear the sobbing at the back of their young
throats, or measure the despair in their aching hearts.

Suddenly he put his arm round her, and she took hold of
his hand and held it there while they finished the little lilt,
and would not let him withdraw it when he tried as the
song ended.

"No, Marion," he said. "It's good-bye to all that. I mustn't
love you, and you mustn't love me. You'll go back home
with Mark, and some day you'll marry a gay gallant—and I'll
knock his nose flat to his beastly face if ever I see him—I
mean, if ever—oh, well, keep him out of my way. Isn't it
time you went to bed now?"

"No, I'm going to tell you my plan now."

"What is this wonderful plan?"

"Matthew, listen. Don't speak till I've finished, till I've got
it all out. I'm simply bursting to tell you, but I didn't dare

until I knew—till I knew it was me—you know what I mean. That you hadn't changed, that you still liked me best." She was getting slightly incoherent in her haste to get it all out, to explain. "We are going away together—don't speak, please don't say anything yet. Matthew, we must stick together. We just must. You need me, and I need you, and we can't be here together, or at home. It would shock them all so much, and they would try to separate us—at least, till Naomi divorced you. That's what I mean. We'll go away together, and then she'll have to divorce you, and then we'll get married.

"I've done it all. I've arranged everything. I've got a little cottage. It's in the country. It's near London. And there's a sort of blind school near where they teach you to read braille and make things, not just baskets and mats—not baskets or mats—to make violins and do carpentry. You always liked carpentry and carving. They teach that too, and music—to play all kinds of instruments, but, of course, that will be easy for you—no, don't speak yet; I haven't nearly finished. About money—I've got plenty of money still. You know I told you about Granny. Well, she meant that money for you more than for me. She said so. She said it would have been yours, but she hated Naomi, so she wouldn't let her have any. She wouldn't let her be able to *touch* it, or get any benefit from it. And, Matthew, I think she meant it to help us both somehow from the things she said. She said whenever I needed it desperately to use it with her blessing. I've got a lot left. I have fifteen ten-pound notes and some more.

"Perhaps there was more in the box, but I left it. I think it was just papers under the tray. It felt like that, not crackly like notes and not bundles—something bigger, some sort of paper—perhaps a will saying it was for me in case there was any dispute or something. But anyhow it's in my trunk, and I don't know where that is—perhaps at Goslaw still, but it's locked and my name's on it, so we'll get it some day. We'll have plenty to live on till we can get married, and till you learn to do something to make money and I can get work to do. I'll get a job afterwards, when you don't need me so much. You know, the doctors think the sight will come back a little to the good eye, that perhaps it might come back altogether, but anyhow you'll get used to finding your way about. Dr Markham says it really isn't such a handicap as people think—not being able to see. You develop another sense that does just as well."

She was getting breathless. Suddenly Matthew drew her to him, felt for her face, and put his hand over her mouth.

"Stop, Marion, stop."

She pulled his hand down.

"I won't stop. It's in the country, Matthew—such a dear little cottage. I went to see it. I did. I just slipped off—that time I didn't come for two days and said I had a cold and was afraid to give it to you. I arranged everything—and we are to go to-morrow!"

"Marion! You are mad."

"I love you so much, Matthew. I never thought I could tell you. It makes me so happy just to tell you, because I feel now"—her girlish face was very serious—"I feel I'm not being wicked, not being unjust to Naomi. She had her chance, and look what she did to you!

"Matthew, I feel we don't *owe* anything to Naomi. I mean, we needn't think about her and feel we are being wicked and unkind. Don't you feel that? Do you feel that too? I couldn't bear it if you felt unhappy and wicked about Naomi—you don't, Matthew, do you?"

"I tell you I loathe her. I don't care a fig about her—it's you I'm thinking of. I'm not going to spoil your life, Marion."

"Very well, then, we'll go off to-morrow. Oh, everything's ready, but I've such a lot to do, sandwiches to make—that will be easier for you than fumbling for knives and forks in the dining-saloon—and all sorts of things to see to. It's a blessing all your things are packed. I haven't even opened a case, though they all came from the infirmary this afternoon."

"Hush, Marion, darling, hush! You mustn't do this. I

couldn't. I'd feel such a cad. You don't know what you are doing. Besides, you can't. Your father wouldn't let you. Do be sensible, Marion."

"I can. I'm twenty-one last Monday. You forget all about my birthday, but I forgive you, because you couldn't see the calendar. I've got a cake all packed and twenty-one candles. We are going to have a birthday party in the cottage—just you and me."

"Your birthday! Many happy returns! I'm sorry, darling, dear, little Marion. I must get you a birthday present. We'll go and buy it to-morrow, and then on Friday you will go home, and I will stay here with Mrs What's-her-name. Marion, you *must* be sensible."

"Yes." Her voice was full of scorn. "You see me leaving you, don't you? All alone. Oh, Matthew, think how you'd hate it! No, don't—don't think about it. I can't bear it. All alone, sitting here, no one to read to you, to play games with (Matthew, there's a *piano* in the cottage!), wandering lost in horrible grey streets, learning to make mats"—she shuddered —"coming back here alone—oh, Matthew, how could you *think* you could do it?"

"Oh, well, nothing seems to matter now—except I couldn't go home. You see, Marion, I feel I must go through with it alone at first, till I get used to it. Then perhaps I could go home, but I must get used to myself like this first, fight it out alone. I'm not fit for decent society. Except for you, I feel I hate everybody because they can see. I feel like a bear with the toothache. It's so dark, Marion—oh, Marion, it's always so dark!"

He broke down, and she climbed on to his knees and snuggled up to him, drawing down his head, kissing his cheek, pushing her fingers through his hair.

"I know, Matthew, I know. Matthew, when it's very, very dark I'll shut my eyes and sit with you, both in the dark— they're shut now, Matthew, and you're not alone. We are here together in the dark."

He folded her to him, his arms like steel bands round her choking back the awful sobs that shook him. They cried together, both sobbing wildly in an abandonment to grief that neither had given way to before, that neither could stop for a few minutes as they emptied their hearts together of all the terrible, scalding, unshed tears that had gathered there.

It was Marion who recovered a little first. She felt in his pocket and pulled out his handkerchief, drying her own tears and then his.

"That's done us good," she said, a last little gulping sob catching her voice. "When things are too bad we'll just have a good cry together. Oh, Matthew, it's not so bad when we can share it together, is it?"

"No, no. It's like happiness, sharing it with you. But we must be sensible, Marion. At least, I must. I'm older than you, and I'm a man—at least a sort of one, I suppose," he added bitterly. "Enough not to let you spoil your life for me."

"Who's spoiling my life? Naomi nearly spoiled it for us both, but we're not going to let her. Think how happy we'll be in the little cottage, Matthew! And we'll be good too. I won't want—I mean, I couldn't—I mean, we'll just be good friends till we can get married. I'll be your housekeeper and look after you. There's nothing *wrong* in that, is there, now?"

"And who would believe it? Marion, you mustn't think— you're so innocent—you mustn't think anyone would believe that. They just wouldn't."

"I'm not innocent. I know quite well what they would think. But we must just tell the truth and live the truth and try not to have people believe wrongly about us, but forgive them if they do because they will have every excuse, poor lambs. Now you see how I've thought it *all* out. I've simply faced every single thing."

He laughed shortly, but tenderly, not bitterly.

"You are as innocent as a little yellow chicken just out of the shell; your feathers aren't dry." He put his hand lovingly over her head. "I can feel them all damp. Why, you haven't got feathers yet, just yellow down that sticks up all round your darling face in the firelight. I can see it."

"Don't boast, Matthew Wotherspoon; you haven't got feathers either—just *fur*, brown-black fur like a bear in the Zoo. Oh, Mat, don't you remember the menagerie when we were so hungry, we ate all the monkey nuts we'd bought for the monkeys?"

"Yes, and the bag burst, and we picked them out of the sawdust, and you finished them."

"I didn't."

"You did."

"Well, if I did I was hungrier than you. I was so excited I couldn't eat my breakfast, and then we never thought about food; we spent all our money on the side-shows. Do you remember the fat woman and the midgets? The little man wanted to shake hands with me, and I wouldn't. I just couldn't; he made me feel sick; and I was so sorry afterwards in case I'd hurt his feelings."

"I remember everything you ever did—but this isn't getting us any further, Marion. You know, don't you, it can't be? Do be sensible, Marion."

It was no use. They argued and talked, stopped and started again. Marion had made up her mind. If he wouldn't go to the cottage, then she would stop where they were, and that would be worse.

"You can't get rid of me. Nothing will change me. Oh, Matthew, don't think of any more reasons and things. Think of us getting married. We've just *got* to go through with this. It's the only way. You do see that, don't you?"

"And if Naomi doesn't divorce me?" He was weakening, and she knew it.

"She will. She knows you could never go back, so what would be the use of sticking to it? She's French and very sensible at the bottom. I've often heard her speak of divorce. She believes in it when people don't get on together. But we must go away together and give her a proper, real reason.

Just now *you* are the injured one. She will enjoy being the injured one herself. I know Naomi. You'll see it will be all right.

"Now I'm going to bed. The train goes at eleven thirty-five. I'll have to be up soon. I meant to do such a lot to-night, but you've taken such a lot of persuading."

"But I haven't said yes."

"Yes, you have, in your heart. Listen, I'm saying it for you out loud. 'Yes, Marion, I will.' Now you've said it."

"But——"

She put her arms round him fiercely.

"Oh, I'm so tired, Matthew. Matthew, darling, say yes! Say yes! Say it, say it, say it! My heart's going to break all over again when it was just beginning to mend. Say yes—say yes! Please, please, please."

He put his arms round her and bent to her ear.

"Oh, Marion, it would be such heaven—such heaven. It would make up for it all. I wouldn't mind being blind; it would be worth it. It's like standing at the gate and looking into paradise."

"Say yes—say yes. I'll just die if you don't say it."

"Yes, then, and God forgive me if I don't make it up to you, if you aren't happy, if you regret. But, Marion, I promise if ever you aren't happy, if ever you regret, I'll make you free. I can do that at least, and I will."

She laughed happily, too full of joy to think of what he meant.

"Good night, Matthew. I'm so happy I want to sit up and sing madrigals instead of going to bed."

He suddenly held her close, kissing her passionately.

"My love, my darling, my sweet. But this is our last kiss, sweetheart, until we can be married. You understand, don't you?"

"Yes. We're just going to be friends, though you may give me a friendly one, mayn't you—like you used to? Now and then."

"Oh, yes, I'll give you a hearty, brotherly smack on your

cheek, or your nose. You have such a dear little nose I could bite it off."

Suddenly they were happy. They just could not help it; the sun had got through Matthew's darkness.

"The world isn't all black and dark now; it's full of golden light," he said. "But I should have said no, Marion."

"You would just have kept me up till morning and all to-morrow and all next night and all day till you said yes. Now I'll take you to your room, and show you where everything is. You'll manage, won't you?"

They laughed. They were young and they were together; the world could go by.

CHAPTER XVII

"TIE A GREEN GRAVAT ROUND HIS NECK AND LEAD HIM OUT AND IN"

THERE was a great outcry when it was discovered that Matthew and Marion had disappeared together—completely vanished. Every one wanted to do something, and no one could agree on what to do. They were both of age; they were not children who could be brought back at their parents' bidding. Marion had said in her letter that she would write, and she did write—happy letters about how Matthew was getting on, about their piano, about the kitten, who had been called "Stumpy," after the "hen that had no tail," because she was a Manx cat, about the Airedale who was being trained to take Matthew about, about all sorts of things, except themselves, where they were, what they were doing.

Not a word about coming back or seeing anyone, though Mark put a note in *The Times* offering to come and see them.

"Not yet," was all Marion said. "Not till we get our divorce."

She sometimes asked in a postscript, as though it were something she had just remembered, if Naomi was doing anything about the divorce. When she wanted evidence and particulars she could get them, but until then would they please not try to find Matthew and herself, because they would just have to disappear again. They were happy where they were, but didn't want to see anyone until they could be married and not embarrass the home folk in any way.

"You know we would embarrass you and make things awkward for you," Marion wrote, "so don't bother about us till we are married. We have plenty of money."

She did give them a hint at the Falcon's House about having got some money, but said it was a secret, and she couldn't explain just now, but would tell them some day. At Bowchester they thought Mr Peregrine was helping them, and Mother Wotherspoon often pressed to be allowed to do her share. The Peregrines and Hagar thought that Granny was in touch with them. Old Granny kept her own counsel. She knew nothing of their whereabouts, but thought Marion had her box with her, and chuckled to herself more and more as she grew older and older.

The trunk came from Goslaw, and Hagar and Rachel put it away just as it was. They had no key for one thing, and for another Marion had said nothing about their opening it, so they agreed just to leave it in her room until she should come home.

It seemed to bring her nearer.

But Naomi refused a divorce. No word ever crossed her lips as to what had really happened on the night of Matthew's return. "It was an accident," she repeated to any questions, and shut her mouth like a trap.

She stayed on at Goslaw, saying she was Matthew's wife, and his home would be there waiting for him "when he tired of bread and milk."

Naomi was changed too. She no longer railed against the loneliness of the little farm. She let the hill-grazing for the sheep, but she ran a dairy, and in her clever French way made cheeses—cream cheeses and cottage cheeses and Devonshire cream and other dainties which soon caught on, so that her stall was crowded on market-days, and she even supplied Newcastle dairies and did well as time went on.

Marion had arranged for news to reach her through *The Times* personal column if there was anything they thought she and Matthew ought to know, and she must always have got the paper, as she immediately answered any notice at once.

When they had to put in "N. at present says no" a letter came saying they would wait and see, perhaps she would change her mind, and that Matthew was going to write to her. But if he did Naomi never mentioned it.

They saw very little of Naomi, as she never came to Breckan, but Mr Peregrine went to see her once or twice, and Mark went. She welcomed them, made much of them, and exerted all her charm to please, but absolutely refused to speak of divorce or of what had happened when Matthew was blinded.

Then one Sunday Mother Wotherspoon, dressed in all the magnificence and dignity of her Sunday clothes with the beaded mantle and high, overpowering bonnet, which she wore like a crown tied on under her chin with broad satin ribbons, ordered Luke to drive her over to Goslaw. It was a long way, and they started at seven o'clock in the morning, lunched and changed horses half-way, leaving their own beast to rest and be picked up again on their return. Mother Wotherspoon not only disliked trains, but would not ask the favour of being met and driven from the station by Naomi.

She went for her own purposes, and would not even drink a cup of tea in Naomi's house. Yet she went to beg, and possibly, if the favour had been granted, she would have drunk the tea. She went to beg Naomi to divorce Matthew.

The two women met like seasoned warriors, with a clash of arms.

As Mother Wotherspoon climbed backward down from the gig, showing a length of red flannel petticoat and sturdy legs in grey woollen stockings and elastic-sided boots, Naomi opened the door and came out to receive her.

"How do you do, Mrs Wotherspoon? You are an unexpected guest."

"And an unwelcome one, I've no doubt."

"No, that is not so. I would wish to welcome you as a friend, but I know that you cannot be friends with me. You come as enemy, is it not?"

"I have come to beg a favour of you, Naomi Cuendet. Luke, take the horse away, and amuse yourself till I want you."

Luke grinned at this order of his mother's, given as though he were a boy sent to amuse himself by paddling in the burn while the elders talked, but he saw a fishing-rod leaning on the wall near the window, and went off to try to catch a few trout; the burn was just a few yards from the door.

"I am Naomi Wotherspoon," said Naomi, as they entered the door.

Mrs Wotherspoon sat down and unloosened the strings of her bonnet.

"Aye." She took off the bonnet to ease her head, set it on her knees as if it were John the Baptist's head on a charger, and sat rolling up the broad satin strings. "Aye, Naomi, but it goes hard with me to say it."

They sat for a few moments in silence, and then Naomi said: "You came . . .?"

"I came to put my pride in my pocket, Naomi Wotherspoon, and ask you to divorce my son."

"You call me by my name when you think you can persuade me not to keep it." She rolled her 'r's,' but spoke carefully in the stilted, correct English she could use when she chose and was not excited.

"Aye, that's about it. I was never one to beat about the bush. Will you divorce him? That's what I came to ask, and I may as well ask it at once."

"I answer at once too. I will not."

"Don't be in a hurry to say that. Hear me out first. I didn't come here with my finger in my mouth, without something to suggest or to take a nay-say before I've got it out. Listen, Naomi, Matthew is no good to you. He will never come back. Ye couldn't expect it after what you did, shooting him down in cold blood and blinding him for life——"

"It was not in cold blood. I haf not a drop of cold blood in my veins."

"In hot blood then—hot or cold, it all came to the same thing for him. You must ken in your own heart he will never come back. The thing's no' in human possibility. Surely, woman, ye have as much sense as to ken that. I didn't come here to reproach you. What's done is done. Two women screechin' at each other'll no' bring his sight back or mend his young, bonny face. Ye did it, and how ye'll pay for it is between you and your Maker. But ye can do something for him still—something that might make amends a bit for the sin ye committed against him. Ye might give him his freedom and let him marry the lassie that loved him long before ever you came on the scene."

"He shall never have Marion."

"In God's truth, woman, what's the use of saying that? He has her now, and she has him. Ye canna stop that. Ye can only stand in the way of their being married and living together in the sight of decent folk."

"I am his wife; she is not. He belongs to me. What I have I keep."

"What ye had ye lost. Take thought, woman; he's more lost to you than he'd be if he lay in his grave—more lost than if ye gave him up. For then ye'd have his gratitude and mebbe, for all I know, his forgiveness. I shall never forgive you—no, not if I saw you burning in hell—for what you've done to him. But that's another matter—I'm his mother." She put up her hand and wiped her mouth, round which tiny beads of sweat had gathered.

"If I burn in hell Marion shall burn with me. She stole my husband from me."

"She took back what was her own, or what was left after ye destroyed him. But words about that will get us no further. Think well, Naomi, what you are doing. You do yourself no good. You are only making him hate you. Can you no' be just to him and let him go? Can you no' be merciful? What can you want with the bare letter of the law? You canna' love him or you wouldna' have tried to kill him."

Naomi laughed; a short, bitter sound it was.

"Is that all you know? You old woman! It is because I love him I would rather see him dead than let another woman have him—but I did not try to kill him."

"The Lord knows what you tried to do or whether ye meant it or no, but, oh, woman, ye blinded his young eyes. What do you want with him now? To tie a green scarf round his neck and lead him out and in? To make him follow ye like a dog his master? Or a calf its cow?"

"And if I blinded him who but me should lead him out and in? Who but me should pay by working my fingers to the bone for him? Ah! I teach him what love is. Now he knows that you do not play with the love of a woman like me. Girl's love—poof! Me, I am a woman. I am French. I am not one of your cold-blooded English."

"Aye, that's where ye make your mistake. A fire o' your French tow leaps up and burns with a grand flame, but it's English coal that endures and warms ye all your life—or may roast ye to a cinder once it's lighted up and roused. Don't ye forget that."

Naomi shrugged her shoulders.

"Then I roast, but I keep my husband." Her eyes suddenly blazed. "Do you think I give him up to a raw simpleton of a girl? He tire quickly of that after having known me. He come back to the wine when he has had his surfeit of milk and water. He know it was love made me do it."

"Marion's no raw girl now. She's a woman and has proved it. And it's the real thing between those two. I give you your Frenchwoman's arts—you're a mistress of witcheries—

but what are they against the true, clean love between a man and a lass? Eh, woman, ye are far misled if ye think your sarpent subtleties can win against true love. Take my word for it—it's an honest word and meant for your good as well as theirs—ye've lost him. He'll never come back. No, not till the orange grows on the apple-tree or ye gather figs frae the thistle. Give him up. It's your only chance of salvation in this world and the next."

"Salvation! What ees it? I want my man. I keep my man."

"He's no' your man. I ken nae by what arts ye wiled him away, but no arts o' yours will bring him back." She leaned forward and began to speak in a kindlier tone. "Think well, Naomi. You're nobbut a young woman yet. Ye have a long life in front of you, and you're no' ill-looking. I wouldn't call you bonnie myself, but I'm an old woman. I dare say to the menfolk you're bonnie enough still, and I will say there are times when you have something taking about you. Ye might marry again and have children, make yourself a new life and be happy, instead of withering here among the hills like an auld hen sittin' in an empty coop, like a bird on a nest that's flown. If ye give Matthew up and divorce him I'll help you. Listen——"

"No one can help me. I help myself."

"That's fools' talk—bairns' prideful boasting. We can all help one another. Listen, Naomi, to what I've come here to say. If you divorce Matthew I'll make it worth your while. I have a lawyer's agreement here by which if you divorce Matthew I agree to pay you two hundred pounds, over and above what the court awards ye, a year as long as ye live. Ye could live anywhere on that. Go back to the France ye're so fond of—travel. I'm not the wealthy woman you take me for. It will take a deal of managing to do it, but I'm prepared to do it for Matthew's sake. He can do nothing himself. I don't want to shove it down your throat, but you took away his earning capacity with your own hands. He has to be kept now instead of earning money. But I'm prepared to do that, or meet you with a lump sum. And, what's more, we'd all be grateful to you, Naomi. Eh, woman, think it over."

"I haf thought, and I say no. It is no use, Mrs Wotherspoon. I will not do it."

She rose.

"Let me prepare you a cup of tea now and some bread and butter, and let us part friends as much as we can."

"Friends!" The old woman rose. "There is no friendship between you and me, Naomi Cuendet—his name you may keep to the world, but I deny it to your face—and I would sooner eat out of the pigs' trough than break bread in your house. Keep what you have then, the dry husks and the broken meats, and may your soul starve on them and your heart be eaten by the maggots they breed! God forgive me for entering your door—the door of a——"

Naomi's harsh laughter drowned her last words.

"It is Marion—your beloved Marion—whose name that is now!"

The old woman turned at the door, where the rain was now blowing in.

"My son's beloved Marion!" she said. "Aye, but God will wash it out when He wipes the tears from their eyes."

She walked off, her head high, though her hastily donned bonnet was all awry, holding herself straight, though she could hardly see for the tears in her eyes.

Looking at the proud, upright old figure in the ridiculous bonnet walking away from her door, Naomi had a sudden unreasoning desire to call her back, a longing that nothing could appease to have her on her side. Somehow she felt, though she was inside and the old woman out in the wind and rain, that it was she herself who was outside, locked out and never to be admitted again to warm, homely life.

CHAPTER XVIII

"I HAVE THE SCORPION FOR MY SIGN"

PENNY was standing in the corridor outside the room where Fräulein Trainer was speaking to the doctor. She knew she ought not to listen, but she was too desperate to care about any of those conventions now.

Much had happened through the long months since she had heard of Marion's going away with Matthew. After many discussions Hagar had persuaded Mr Peregrine to tell Penny the truth. With all those sorrows at home Penny had not liked to bother them with her own troubles; after all, she got a certain amount, if not enough, to eat, and the summer hadn't been so bad. It was the winter, after Mallie had been taken ill, that had unnerved her. She shuddered now, thinking of Mallie, of Mallie's fainting turns, of Fräulein's cruelty to her, and of her at last being taken away to hospital, pleading, starved and neglected as she was, to be allowed to stay, terrified of the ward among total strangers, of the stories she had heard of German hospitals for those who could not pay, clinging to Penny's hands.

"You will come and see me, won't you, Penny?"

But Penny had not been allowed to go and see her. Fräulein had been adamant. Penny was delicate herself; she might catch something. Besides, Mallie had behaved very badly in not telling Fräulein she was subject to fits.

"Fits!" But Mallie hadn't fits. She had taken fainting turns. The word terrified Penny, as showing what Fräulein's unscrupulous hatred could do. She hated Mallie for fainting in the shop, for having fainted in the schoolroom—giving her school a bad name! Parents might think they were not properly fed—anything. So Mallie had fits! Penny had never seen Mallie again, and now the friendly maid had gone too, and Mademoiselle was leaving—not that she cared much for

Mademoiselle, who told lies and was not to be trusted, but she had been kind the night Penny's nose had started bleeding and would not stop. On that occasion Fräulein had sent for the doctor, and he had plugged up her nose with cotton-wool and said she was to go to bed.

The bed was icy cold, and she felt frozen. Shivering, she had begged Mademoiselle to get her something hot to drink —just hot water; if only she could get a cup of hot water to warm her a little. But no water came. Mademoiselle had no doubt tried, but she had to walk warily herself, for Fräulein had a long list against her. Stealing down to the kitchen could have so many criminal meanings attached to it.

So Penny had shivered till, worn out, she fell asleep, to awaken still cold.

Then, next day, *she* had fainted at table.

On Thursdays some of the day girls stayed to dinner, because there was a dancing lesson at 1.30, and they had a long way to go home.

There had been a thick mess of lentil soup for dinner, not like the lentil soup at home, but made from whole lentils, like brown peas, with lumps of fat pork among them. Usually she was so hungry she ate it quickly, trying not to feel the soft fat in her mouth, but to-day as she lifted the first spoonful her stomach suddenly turned. She felt as if she were going to be sick, but there was nothing in her stomach to be sick on. Instead she fainted.

It was when she came out of the faint that terror struck her. Mallie had fainted and Mallie had gone off to hospital, and from there—where? What had happened to her? Penny simply did not know. She was too young to argue that her own position was very different from Mallie's, that she had a family, that her father was paying for her, while Mallie had been earning her own living and was alone in the world.

But, apart from the hospital, she remembered how Mallie had been treated for fainting, the insults, the innuendoes, the punishments, how Fräulein said she needed air and forced her to walk up and down before the window in the bitter cold, how she said that Mallie had softened herself at the stove and forbade her to go near it, how she had said, and said now, that Mallie had fits. She might say that Penny had fits.

She was frightened. The doctor had returned to see how she was, and was now closeted with Fräulein, and Penny was listening to see if she could hear what was said. At the slightest sound she started, trembling like a leaf, ready to slip into cover. But the confidential voices were not raised. She could hear nothing.

It was later that Fräulein said to her, "The doctor thinks it would be the worst thing in the world for you to go back to the fogs and cold of Scotland in the spring. It is my own opinion too, but of course I have said nothing. However, I shall write and let your father know what the doctor says and repeat his warning. That is my plain duty."

"Oh, please——" The words pleading for silence were trembling on her lips, when she met Fräulein's cold little blue eyes—like a pig's, Penny always thought—and she kept them back. She was learning better than to show any outward sign of what she felt. Fräulein had such subtle ways and means of venting her displeasure.

But despair seized her—despair so great she could scarcely bear it. Never, never, had she dreamed she might have to stay on beyond the year. She had made up her mind to endure for the year; her little secret calendar was scratched day by day, even to the hours and minutes, and counted over and over. Now her escape was threatened she might have to stay on for weeks—months—indefinitely, if her father thought it would injure her health to go home. And if the *doctor* said so what could he think but that it was true?

That night she lay curled up in her bed like a mouse, unsleeping, thinking. Fräulein von Schell slept in Mallie's bed now, but Fräulein, though kind enough, was cold and distant. If she had some money! She had absolutely none. Her pocket money was not given to her. It was kept in a little box by Fräulein, and doled out to the governess who went with her to spend on any little things she needed, toothpaste, darning wool, soap, always a sixpence once a week for sweets. She chose the sweets, but the governess paid. It had begun with Fräulein Trainer's "not wanting her to be cheated" when she did not understand the value of German coins, and had just gone on because Penny was too timid to make any protest.

At home they had always thought Penny as bold as a little lion, but a little girl, frightened and alone in a strange country, soon becomes timid.

If only she had some money to buy a stamp—it cost twopence halfpenny—she would write home and tell her father she was quite well, very, very strong, and please, please—on her knees she would beg him—please to come and take her home.

But where could she get twopence halfpenny?

Suddenly she remembered. They had gone out that day, and Fräulein had given Fräulein von Schell two marks of her month's pocket money to buy some odds and ends, but they had just come to one mark sixty-five pfennigs. There was thirty-five pfennigs of her own money in the bag, and it was lying on the dressing-table. Suppose she took it? She could write a letter to her father, give it to one of the girls to post with twenty-five pfennigs for the stamp.

But Fräulein von Schell would miss the coppers. She would be returning them to-morrow after tea. There was never any time before that for anything but lessons and work. She would have time to get the letter away. It would be away. . . .

She did not give herself time to think. She was too desperate. She stole out of bed, tiptoed across the moonlight, lifted the bag, and was about to open it when an awful voice from the bed said:

"What are you doing there?"

She dropped the purse, staggered, and fainted clean away.

Next morning she was kept in bed. Fräulein von Schell had not spoken to her, had not even bid her good-morning or asked how she was.

She lay staring at the wall, seeing herself branded as a thief, seeing herself staying on and on at Das Glockenhaus, seeing home recede farther and farther away.

When the house was all quiet, and she knew lessons would go on till one o'clock, she sat up in bed. She was safe till one o'clock. With her reduced staff Fräulein Trainer had not a moment to herself all morning. She would wait till one and then come up and see the culprit.

Penny got out of bed and dressed, as quickly as she could, though her knees shook so she had sometimes to steady herself by holding on to the dressing-table. She put on her coat and hat and shoes. She dared not seek her little case, so she rolled a nightdress and her toothbrush in a piece of newspaper she took from the bottom of a drawer.

In her handbag she put the little odd pieces of jewellery she had, including Anthony's locket. As she did so she opened it to take out the tiny ring he had given her out of the Christmas pudding. She had kept it there for safety. Now she would put it on her finger. Thin as her hands were, it was too tiny for any but the little finger.

As she was about to shut the locket she noticed that the rim at one side looked loose. She pressed it; the rim came out altogether and with it the tiny round plate at the back. Behind it she saw the half-sovereign. Quickly she found the other.

She stood for a moment staring at them. Anthony had sent her a sovereign. It had been there all the time. Anthony! Anthony! Oh, if only Anthony knew *he* would save her. She thought quickly. With a whole sovereign in her possession she could do things! She had been going to run away, but it had all been hazy in her mind. Now she stood and thought definitely and clearly, making a plan. She knew where the exchange was—next to the post-office. She would change the sovereign, then she would go to the post-office and send a letter to Anthony, then she would go to Biebrich and take the boat to Cologne and go to the Dom Hotel there, give them what money was left, and ask them to let her stay till Anthony came for her—no, she would say her father. It would not matter when he came that it was Anthony.

All her thoughts were fixed on Anthony now. He had sent her the sovereign. It was like a message to say he would help her.

She slipped down the silent stair, ran round to the side-door, and let herself out into a quiet part of the garden. Then she ran swiftly down to the little gate and took a short cut to the town. She was away! She was free! All went as she planned with remarkable ease. The sovereign was changed. She had slipped an envelope and a sheet of paper into her bag. She wrote a hurried scribble standing in the recess where the telegram forms were, bought a stamp, and posted it. It was still only ten o'clock. There was a ten minutes' break at eleven o'clock, but Fräulein would be too occupied getting her cup of coffee to go upstairs.

She took the tram to Biebrich, and caught the boat that was just leaving for Cologne.

CHAPTER XIX

"THEY SHALL FIND HIM WARE AN' WAKIN'"

HAGAR looked up from the letter she was writing as Mark came into the parlour. Not for worlds would she have given away the fact that at the sight of his tall, lean figure her heart beat more quickly. Her Yorkshire pride had been wounded by Mother Wotherspoon's hints that Mark should look higher than a housekeeper for his wife, that she was setting her cap at him.

Mrs Wotherspoon's failure over Marion and the news of Perry's refusal to go into the business had made her more determined than ever to marry Mark to Rachel. Mark was unsatisfactory at Bowchester. "No farmer," she said, not

being able to see he was more deeply a farmer, more wed to
the land, than any of them. Her businesslike mind could not
conceive a farmer who was not determined above everything
to make the farm pay. "A dreamer," she called him, because
he was the only one at Bowchester who ever read a book for
pleasure and loved animals and flowers and country things
for their own sake. Now she had got it into her head that if
he married Rachel and they came in for the business it would
suit him better than farming, and leave her and her younger
sons to do as they pleased about Bowchester. She wanted to
be rid of Mark, not because she wasn't fond of him, but he
stood in her way. Not only that, but, according to her clear,
businesslike head, in his own way and that of his brothers
also. He was so stubborn.

If Perry did not go into the business—Mr Peregrine was
beginning to see that Perry, who had shot up in a month or
two into a slim, manly-looking, and determined youth, was
older than his years and had very definitely made up his mind
about his future—then the only one in the family who might
carry on the business was Rachel—and her husband.

Anthony Truett was no connexion, and Penny was a child.
Anyhow, that affair had blown over. She had heard Anthony
and Hagar were very friendly nowadays—a very suitable match;
she'd give them a really good dinner-set when they married.

Hagar, whom Mother Wotherspoon left in no doubt of her
intentions, was determined she would not stand in Rachel's
way. No, indeed, hadn't Naomi, the previous housekeeper,
stolen Marion's sweetheart, a Wotherspoon too? Her gorge
rose at the thought that Mother Wotherspoon had compared
her with Naomi.

Yet she could not forbear a smile as she thought of Mark.
Like a sheep (though anything less like a sheep could hardly
be imagined) with the collies at her heels (herself and Mother
Wotherspoon), he was being determinedly, though quietly,
not to alarm him, shooed and wooed and guided along to the
pen prepared for him.

The same process was going on with Rachel, but even more care had to be taken with Rachel, who had the wild look in her eye of the sheep who has got wind of the fact that its freedom is threatened.

Mark had no wild look in his eye. To continue the metaphor, he quietly went on in his own way, stopping to nibble a few blades of grass here and there and giving no indication that he was aware of any pen, even approaching it, walking round it, and then going leisurely off, as if he had never seen it or the watching collies alert to every movement; whereas Rachel would have been hell-for-leather across the field and over the hedge in the blink of an eyelid.

They were a difficult pair. No wonder Mrs Wotherspoon sometimes sighed impatiently and wished she could knock their heads together!

No wonder Hagar occasionally indulged in a good laugh.

"Thank heaven I can still laugh!" she said to herself. "Even if it twists my mouth it doesn't twist my heart up as it used to do—'Werena' my heart licht I wad dee.'" Then she would sigh a little. There was something terribly taking about Mark. In fact, she couldn't understand Rachel, and wondered sometimes if she were standing out of her (Hagar's) way and both of them at cross-purposes, for she had no illusions about Rachel's heart being broken over Matthew. It had had a good dent, but his blindness and all the storm over his disappearance with Marion had completed the cure.

Without wanting to, Rachel rather shrank from Matthew; like others who were fond of him, she couldn't bear to see him blind. She hadn't Marion's love that "endureth all things," that "many waters cannot quench . . . neither can the floods drown," by which his blindness was utterly contemned. Her love had just taken it in its stride, overleaped it, and gone on. Her last letters were happy ones in spite of the doubt that had crept in about Naomi's ever divorcing him.

Hagar was alone that Saturday evening when Mark came in. Rachel was out seeing Granny Wotherspoon, whose life still hung on its frail-seeming thread, and Perry had gone to see some aeroplanes that were giving stunt flights, determined to try to wangle one for himself.

"As daft as a brush," said Beenie. "If the Lord had meant us to fly wouldn't He have given us wings?"

"Well, you used to ride a bicycle," retorted Perry, "and He didn't give you wheels," and for once Beenie was nonplussed. She couldn't with the best will in the world produce wheels. Luckily Penny wasn't there to have carried the argument still further; nothing would have delighted Penny more than to have gone on to fins, flappers, paddles, and other modes of progression till Beenie was not only utterly flouted, but both *en*raged and *out*raged by the challenge to produce them for inspection.

But poor Penny, could they have but known it, was far now from flouting or challenging Beenie to war. Fräulein Trainer believed in breaking spirits while the heart was young.

Hagar left her letter, and invited Mark into the kitchen while she prepared tea, as Beenie was out.

He followed her and stood leaning by the mantelpiece as she put the cups on the tray.

"I have some news, Hagar," he said.

"Good ones, I hope, Mark."

"Hardly." He paused a moment. "An ultimatum, in fact. Mother's given me the choice of letting her and the lads run the farm as they want to, or she's taking her money out and leaving."

"But—you can't run Bowchester without money."

"No, she knows that. That's where they win."

"Oh, Mark, but that's cruel. I didn't think they could be cruel."

"All Wotherspoons—or, at least, all Waughs—can be hard where money is concerned."

"But it would ruin you!"

"Mother doesn't think that. She thinks we'll all make our fortunes—mine too—with these new intensive schemes." He gave a short laugh. "Plough out all the pasture land and reclaim every waste bit, put every hen in a separate little wire cage—a foot or so square—for life, as long as it can lay an egg to fall on the wire netting and roll into a little drawer. No pity for the poor caged brutes—no freedom. By God, I couldn't stand looking at them! I'd rather go and drown myself in the curling pond they're going to drain—a nice find for them that!"

"Oh, Mark, they couldn't surely do that to the poor hens!"

"Couldn't? They are starting on the cages. They have the money——"

"I hate money—it's a curse!"

"Aye, but a man can do little without it, and I can't turn my own mother out of the farm, even if I could run it alone —but it's too big. I can't turn my mother out, and I can't ask a girl to marry me."

"Rachel——" she began, but he interrupted at once.

"Who's talking of Rachel? What's young Paul doing now?"

"He's going to South Africa almost immediately. They need him out there."

"It's a pity he hadn't been older. Hagar, what's this I hear about you and Anthony Truett?"

"Me and Anthony? Goodness, what do you mean?"

"Mother tells me——" He paused, for she had turned and was positively glaring at him. "It's all right, Hagar. I really didn't believe it—at least, I didn't want to."

"I should think not indeed! Anthony adores Penny. She may be just a little girl, but he's the faithful dog kind, and Anthony knows how to wait. And I love Penny—*love* her. Oh, I'm sick of being suspected of luring away other girls' men! Rachel's, and now Penny's, just because I have tried to cheer him up a little, given him some flowers out of Penny's garden as she asked me to and a cake now and then because I promised her. I suppose it's that mean old curmudgeon of a landlady——"

She suddenly sat down, white and exasperated, putting her hand to her mouth.

He went over and, taking hold of the hand she lifted to push him back, he raised her chin, gently moving away her hand.

"That scar by your mouth is nearly all gone," he said, smiling slightly. Then he stroked back her hair from her brow. "And so is the one on your brow. Don't grow any lovelier, Hagar—you are too lovely for me already. Hagar, if——"

"Don't," she said quickly, jumping up and pushing him aside. "Please don't, Mark. Don't say any more."

"Don't you want to hear what I was going to say?"

"No," she said ruthlessly. "I don't. . . ." The boiling of the kettle gave her an excuse to get busied with the teapot. He came over and stood watching her as she filled it, a frown on his forehead.

"I wish I knew what is going on in that small head of yours, if I'm really . . ." He hesitated, frowning more deeply.

"You're bothering me," said Hagar, brusquely. "I do wish you would not——" She turned away to hide the tears which had sprung to her eyes in spite of herself, but he did not see them, for at that moment Mr Peregrine came through the hall and into the kitchen, looking very agitated.

"What's all this? What's all this?" he asked, all his pretences and play-acting laid aside for the moment.

"All what?" asked Hagar, gazing at him with the teapot in her hand.

"Truett's gone."

"Anthony?"

"Yes, of course Anthony. There's no other Truett, is there? But that's not it. What's this about Penny?"

Hagar stood startled, paling. She had never been happy about Penny.

"Penny! What is it, Mr Peregrine? What has happened to Penny?"

"That's what I'm asking you. Where's Rachel? Have you

women been keeping things from me? Rachel had a letter yesterday, hadn't she? Penny was all right then?"

"Yes. Rachel read it to you. I read the letter. Penny seemed all right."

"Then what's the meaning of this? Anthony has sent it over. He might have come and explained to me. Keeping me in the dark! Eh? What's it all about? What have you all been keeping from me about Penny?" He shook a piece of notepaper at Hagar. He was frowning till his thick dark eyebrows met above his penetrating little eyes. For the first time Hagar saw Mr Peregrine looking really angry.

She took the paper and read it.

I am catching the two-twenty and going to Germany. Penny has run away from school. I had a note from her saying she was going to the Dom Hotel at Cologne. That's all I know.

ANTHONY TRUETT

"He couldn't come," said Hagar at once. "He must have got the letter when he went at one-thirty for lunch. He's always later on Saturdays too. He'd just have time to catch the train."

"Of course *you'll* stick up for him!" said Mr Peregrine, so agitated he had to turn on some one. "I expect you know all about it—you and Truett are as thick as thieves. Has he been writing to Penny?"

Hagar's face flamed scarlet. Mark stood aside watching, his face dour and drawn with what seemed a mixture of concern and anger.

"No, he hasn't," said Hagar quickly. "Anthony wouldn't do that. He isn't underhand. Penny must have written to him in desperation. Oh, what are we to do?"

Just then Rachel came running in. She had called in at the shop and heard the news, for it seemed Mr Peregrine had gone off in an explosion of wrath, surprise, and dismay when he opened the note.

In the scene of consternation and grief that followed Mark could do little but try to comfort Rachel, who immediately burst into sobs and wild recriminations over Penny having ever been sent to Germany.

"I knew she wasn't happy! I knew! I knew!" she exclaimed. Then she turned on Hagar. "Why has Anthony gone alone? I should have gone with him—I'm going! Did you know she was unhappy? Did Anthony tell you? Is that why you've always kept saying you weren't happy about her? Did you and Anthony know?"

For once Hagar lost her head. Furious at these accusations, at Mr Peregrine and Rachel, who made them, at Mark, who stood there staring at her, she turned on them all.

"If that is what you think," she fumed, "then I'm going away. I am going away at once. If you all suspect me of being underhand I am no use here. I couldn't bear it—I'm going!"

She made for the door, but Rachel rushed to her.

"Oh, no, Hagar—no, I don't mean it. I only thought with you and Anthony being so friendly——" She stopped as Hagar pushed her aside.

"They need you just now, Hagar," said Mark quietly.

That pulled Hagar up. She remembered her own philosophy that words spoken in anger were never meant and should not be taken seriously, and Mark was right. They did need her.

She stood there uncertainly for a moment. Then she turned and put her hand on Rachel's arm. Rachel was now sobbing again, quite distraught, while poor Mr Peregrine, utterly taken aback by Hagar's anger, for he too had never seen her angry before, was babbling out assurances that he had never meant what he said, that they couldn't do without Hagar, couldn't bear the possibility of her leaving them—she was one of the family.

"All right," she said, pulling herself together. "We are all upset. We can't do anything for the moment; the train's gone, and there's not another till eight o'clock. Let's have tea and decide what to do. Anyhow, Anthony is off—he's on the way; and I'd back Anthony to do the right thing and find her and bring her home better and more quickly than any of us."

They all agreed to that. Anthony had not waited to talk or discuss things. Anthony had wasted not a moment. If anybody could rescue Penny from whatever mischance had befallen her Anthony would do it.

CHAPTER XX

"THE PIPER IN THE WIND GOES BY"

ANTHONY, still wearing his shop clothes of black morning coat and striped trousers and looking rather like an untidy stork with his long legs, and dark, untidy hair, got out of the train at Cologne, carrying his old-fashioned black bag in his hand. He was hatless, having lost his hat crossing the Channel, and having neither time nor thought to spare to buy another.

The Dom Hotel did not take much finding. There was rather a crowd in the vestibule, but he fought his way through, looking so determined and distraught that people quickly moved aside for him.

He lost no time in preliminaries.

"Is Miss Peregrine staying here?" he asked.

He knew a little German, but the clerk spoke English.

"Miss Peregrine?" He sought through his book.

"No," he said.

"Yes, she is," said Anthony. "A young girl—English."

The man shook his head and consulted with his superiors, who came forward.

"Did you expect ze lady to be here?"

"She is here," said Anthony determinedly. "Where is the proprietor?"

But no one knew anything of Penny. At last an underling was found who said a shabby little girl had come and asked if she might stay, but he thought she was German. She spoke German like a German, and he had thought she did not look at

all like the Dom Hotel. He had recommended a cheaper hotel
in another *Strasse*, and she had gone away.

"Did she leave no message?"

She had said she would come back. He had thought she
might be expecting a letter. No, she had not given her name
—but she was not an English mees; he was sure of that.

Anthony went to the hotel. Yes, a girl had stayed for the
night. She had spoken German, very high-class German, but
had gone away next morning in a great hurry without having
any breakfast.

For days Anthony hunted round every inn and lodging-
house he could find, returning to the Dom Hotel at intervals,
thinking she might come back to look for him, staring at every
girl he met in the despairing hope that it might be Penny.

They tried the hospitals, for he got the police to help him,
but she was not there.

Fräulein Trainer was distracted. He went to see her, for she
also was on the hunt—had been ever since Penny left—but she
had gone off on a wrong clue, thinking Penny had heard
where Mallie was and was making her way there.

Anthony had come in one night in despair, and was sitting
in front of an untasted supper the waiter had brought, when the
lad who had last seen Penny came in and spoke to him.

He thought he had heard of the girl. There was a little girl,
very ill in a certain street in Cologne. The people of the
house had had trouble with the police, and were lying low at
the moment, so had said nothing about her.

He was still talking when Anthony seized him by the arm
and rushed him out of the hotel door. . . .

When Penny, very shy and strange, had been turned away
from the door of the Dom Hotel she had sought out the inn
the lad had directed her to. She thought it was rather a poor-
looking place, but went in and asked for a room. She had not
much money left, but thought she could sell some of the small
bits of jewellery to make it spin out. At the Dom Hotel she

had thought that, as she had stayed there with her father before, they might have remembered him and have let her stay until Anthony came for her, even if her money ran out; but it was different in this strange place, and she had not had courage or experience enough to ask to see the manager.

But she had a fright through the night. There had been some mistake about the rooms, and she was awakened by a loud beating on her door and a man's voice demanding entrance. She would not open it—she was too frightened; and at last a maid had come and opened the door with another key and angrily explained to her she was in the wrong room. She had shown a ticket they gave her with the number of the room on it; then they had demanded if she hadn't seen the luggage in the corner. She had, but, being utterly unused to hotels, had thought it had just been left there for some reason by the last guest.

At last another room was found for the man, the luggage removed, and Penny left in peace, but she was terrified, and felt she had made them all angry with her. She was always afraid of blustering German anger. She sat up shivering in bed all night, and went off as soon as she had paid her bill in the morning.

She wandered about all day. She had reckoned that it would be at least four days before Anthony could get her letter and come to Cologne, and she was terrified of Fräulein Trainer's finding her.

In the Dom Hotel she would have felt safe, but wandering about with nowhere to go was a different matter.

She bought rolls and butter and ate them in the cathedral, where she rested for a long time in a dark corner.

Then she went out to seek a place to spend the night. She found a cheap-looking inn, went in, and asked for a room. She was asked to pay in advance, and did so for two nights, which took all her money except a mark, but she wanted a room where she could stay in hiding.

No sooner had she done so than she regretted it. There was a horrible smell about the place. She did not know if it was in

R

her room or in the house, but her very food seemed impregnated with it, so that she felt sick and could not eat the mess of fried potatoes and some kind of sausage they gave her for supper.

By this time she was weak from lack of food, from strain, and from terror. She was in any case in a very low state of health from underfeeding, from her lungs being delicate, and the terrible nose-bleeding, and ought to have been in bed being carefully nursed. Terrible fits of coughing seized her, and she was in constant dread of everything—of the house, of the people in it, of Fräulein Trainer's finding her before Anthony came, of another fit of nose-bleeding, and she was desperately lonely and in a state verging on collapse.

She lay awake most of the night, listening and starting at every sound, sick with the smell, but she could only retch, for she had eaten nothing.

At last morning came, and with the dawn she felt she must get away. Anthony would be coming next day. Perhaps—it had never struck her before—the proprietor could send a telegram to her father. Was there a cable under the Channel? Would it cost an awful lot of money? She had no idea, but she could offer him her little locket to keep till Anthony could buy it back for her. Anyhow she could not stay where she was—no, not if they did tell the police and Fräulein Trainer. She felt so terribly ill.

She was trembling so much by this time she could scarcely stand to dress herself, but at last she was ready, all but her coat, and she sat down on a chair at the window to wait till the town was stirring. She looked at her watch. At eight she would go.

At last, feeling desperately ill and faint, she got up to put on her coat and hat, but she could not find her hat. There was a huge double wardrobe, and she had put her coat and her hat too, she thought, in one division. She was sure she had not even opened the other door. Still, she might have done so in mistake when she put her hat away. She went forward, stopping to hang on to the washstand while a fit of coughing racked

and shook her; then she opened the other side of the wardrobe
and was met by the frightfully sick smell. Hastily she looked
on the hooks, but her hat was not there. At the bottom of the
wardrobe was some brown paper, with something dark behind
it. She put out her hand to touch it, and then drew back with
a shrill scream of horror, which she stopped at once, hands
against her mouth. It was the body of a tiny baby.

Horror glued her feet to the floor. She had hastily banged
the door of the wardrobe shut. Now in the mirror she saw
herself wavering in its greeny depths like a disembodied ghost;
she saw her white face, looking mere bone with the white skin
stretched over it, her great horrified eyes staring over the two
hands clasped across her mouth.

She turned to fly, to get away—anywhere out of this terrible
place, out of the gruesome, frightful room.

She fled across the room, rushed over the landing, treading
lightly in her desperate urge to escape without being seen; she
had nearly reached the top of the stair when a board in the
rotting woodwork creaked. She heard a door open behind her,
and went headlong down the stair. Half-way down her foot
caught in the tattered oilcloth, and she plunged forward with a
wild, mad scream and collapsed unconscious at the foot.

Anthony found the fat landlady full of woe and excuses.
Yes, the *junge Mädchen* was there, but she was unable to get up.
They had done everything for her, but a doctor—well, no. . . .

She plunged into explanations in German, but Anthony did
not listen. The *Mädchen* had fallen down the stairs—yes, but
there were no bones broken. A day or two's rest in bed . . .

He climbed the stair after her and went in. At first he
thought, "It's not Penny after all," his heart going down; then
it leaped—and seemed to stop. Yes, it was Penny—but what
had they done to her?

What in God's name had been done to her to break her
like this?

She lay so flat and small there was scarcely a ridge in the

bed; her face was like a skeleton's, with the hair combed back and so damp and soiled it did not look like Penny's fair, sunny mass of floss, but like some older woman's thinning, dank, flattened-out hair, showing the shape of the skull.

She was talking, muttering to herself, and hardly seemed to know him when first he put his hands over her restless, moving ones, but as he bent he heard one or two words, "Anthony" and "home." The rest was all in German.

Instantly he was convinced of one thing. To save her—to save her mind as well as her body—he must get her home. There must be no delay, even if he carried her in his arms all the way—he must get her home.

He stooped over her and spoke.

"Yes, I've come to take you home, Penny."

Her restless muttering ceased for a moment, the light of reason came into her eyes.

"I knew you would come, Anthony. Oh, take me home!"

He heard the fat woman talking about things that seemed absolutely without any sense: of a wicked woman who had stayed in the hotel and left a parcel, of ruin if he got in the police, of her being a widow, of a wardrobe . . .

"Tell her," he said to the German lad, who was now in the room, "that I'm not going to ruin her, that I want nothing to do with the police, that I want her to go out and buy a clean blanket and warm dressing-gown as quickly as she can, and then I shall pay her and go, and that is the end—and you get me a cab."

He put Penny into the dressing-gown and wrapped her in the blanket himself, and started with all the speed he could to take her home.

He knew that every one would want to put her to bed and get a doctor—that it would be considered the only sensible thing to do; but somewhere, deep in his consciousness, he knew better. He knew the only hope was to get her home.

He took the train that night with her in his arms and, except for a few minutes now and then when he laid her on cushions or in a berth, he literally carried her home, sitting with her in his arms, lifting her from train to cab, from cab to steamer, holding her night and day, never sleeping except when he dozed still clasping her against him. She was as light as a feather, and so worn and thin he wondered how she still lived.

He cabled all arrangements, and Hagar met him with a hired car at the dock. He had said that Hagar must come. He thought she would stand the shock of seeing Penny better than Rachel.

At last he walked into the Falcon's House with her in his arms and straight up the stairs to her own room, where everything was ready for her, her things just as she had left them, the first pussy willows and primroses on the window-sill, a great bowl of scillas, hepaticas, crocuses, and purple iris on a little table by her bed.

Suddenly she stopped her endless muttering, and the tears ran down her face.

"Am I home?" she asked, as if she could not believe it.

"Yes, my darling," he said. "You're home, Penny, sweetheart, and now you'll get well, won't you?"

But time passed and Penny showed no signs of getting well. In spite of all their love, of all Dr Merriman's attention, she lay utterly broken, racked by her cough, disturbed by awful dreams, unable to swallow more than, as Beenie said, "would keep a bird alive." They kept giving her spoonfuls of milk and brandy. They brought her Jane the parrot and Mrs Brown and Robbie to waken her interest; even the robin was tempted inside her window-sill by meal worms, but it often seemed to them that something was broken in Penny, some will to live, and that she would just slip away out of their lives quietly and softly and utterly unlike the gay, obstreperous, high-spirited Penny they had once known and loved so dearly, whom they loved more dearly than ever now—loved with aching, regretful, self-accusing hearts.

Mr Peregrine visibly aged; his black coat took a sloping, rounded line as he crept, more like a black crow than ever, through the garden, where spring was rioting and the birds singing, where the little ghosts of May-time seemed waving farewell to Penny.

In the meantime the world went on. Things were moving at Goslaw and Bowchester, and with Marion and Matthew too.

Granny Wotherspoon's money was evidently giving out, and they had had to leave the cottage so that Marion could take a job. Letters came from London which said she was working, but gave no indication of what she was doing; one came from Paris, and then they seemed to be always on the move. There was never any complaint, but at home they gathered that times were occasionally hard with them. Marion never gave any address; indeed, most of her letters were written when, it seemed, they were just moving on. At first she had mentioned the divorce in every letter, but gradually that ceased. She seemed to have given up hope of Naomi's divorcing Matthew.

Naomi herself said nothing, but it seemed that she too had given up hope of Matthew's return to her. She had always said his home at Goslaw was waiting for him when he should return, but now they had heard that she was leaving Goslaw and going nearer Newcastle, and though some new home might still welcome him it had less significance. They thought so at Bowchester in any case, and surmised that she was realizing that he was gone for good. But she would not speak of divorce, and indeed they had ceased their efforts to persuade her. If she could not have Matthew back at least she had her revenge, for Matthew and Marion could never return to the district, or home, but must remain "outcasts on the face of the earth," as she had said.

One night when Penny was very low and Anthony sat holding her hand he was thinking of what Beenie had said when the last north-east wind had swept the town. Every now and then in Breckan in the spring a bitter wind would come blowing from the melting icebergs in the north, causing the fishermen to repeat their old saying that when the icebergs

broke away in the Polar regions the wind pierced your bones
at Breckan. Penny had almost slipped away in the last north-
easters, and Beenie had said the next north wind would blow
her away, and now the wind was rising, shaking the last late
blossoms off the fruit-trees and moaning through the stone
wings of the turtle-dove and the feathers of the falcon on
the roof.

"Blow slowly, wind," his thoughts were saying. "Blow
slowly over the world, for the day comes when you will blow
her away from me."

It was as if Penny had read his thoughts, for as they listened
she suddenly turned to him and smiled. "Do you hear him?"
she whispered in her weak voice. "Rachel says he always
brings changes when you hear him clear like that."

"Hear what, darling? Hear who?"

"The piper. Listen, Anthony! The piper in the wind
goes by."

BOOK III

*So he made it again another vessel, as it seemed good
to the potter to make it.*

CHAPTER I

"N'Y TOUCHEZ PAS, IL EST BRISÉ"

THE crocuses flamed and sank and withered, the cherry-tree
bloomed and took off her bridal veil in a night, the chestnut
candles, pink and white, were lit and blown out, and still Penny
lingered on. The old doctor came every day, looked at her, and
shook his head; there was nothing more he could do, because
there was nothing intrinsically wrong. If only they could get
her interested in life again, if only the strong will to get better
were roused, she might still come round, but, while everything
seemed to please her—the sun coming in at the window, the
shrill song of the wren, the branch of cherry-blossom brought
in from the garden and stuck in the Chinese vase, the lace on
her new bed-jacket, the kittens that Mrs Brown offered as her
own inducement and that were brought up to her room in a
blanket, mother and all—nothing seemed to really rouse her
enough to give her the power to go on. She was happy and
seemingly content, but made no progress. If one day she
seemed a little better she was weaker the next, and she never
seemed to want to get up.

"I'm so tired," she would say. "It's lovely just to be
home."

Perry had at last got permission to leave school, after
working like a nigger to take his leaving examination, and
there was talk of his going to Cambridge to take his B.Sc. on
the engineering side, as he was interested in the making of
'planes as well as in flying.

It saddened Mr Peregrine that he would not go into the business, but he ceased to press him.

Paul went off to South Africa, and word came that Naomi was leaving Goslaw immediately and going to live nearer Newcastle, and on the top of that came the news that Mark and Mrs Wotherspoon had had a bitterer quarrel than all the rest, and that she was buying another farm—High Seaton—lying some distance to the west, and taking everything away from Bowchester.

Mark had almost given up coming to the Falcon's House. They hardly ever saw him, and it was from Luke they heard the news.

"But what will Mark do?" Rachel had asked.

"Go to hell!" said Luke, who was exasperated beyond control.

"To prepare a place for you," said Mr Peregrine, unwittingly quoting the New Testament instead of the Old, as was his habit. If he had thought he would not have used words he considered sacred, but he was exasperated too, and was all on Mark's side.

Hagar thought a lot about Mark, crying sometimes into her pillow at night and often wishing now that he would come back and talk to her. But since that Saturday when they had all so cruelly, as she felt, linked her name with Anthony's she and Mark had never had a word alone together.

Then they were all so taken up with Penny at the Falcon's House that sad spring, so grieved about her, so helpless, there was not much visiting going on except to see her.

Mallie had found out a great deal from Mademoiselle about Penny's running away, and had written from France, where she had gone to take a similar post and was very happy. A long, rambling letter had also come from Mademoiselle, and Fräulein Trainer had written, when she sent back her things, saying Penny had ruined her by running away, and she had to leave Das Glockenhaus, and was starting afresh in Baden-Baden. It was a whining letter, but rather frightened, and ended by saying she hoped they would let the matter drop, and that Penny was really not normal and should never have been sent away from home.

"The beast, the hateful, subtle beast!" exclaimed Rachel, throwing the letter into the fire.

But they were all too sad to take much notice or bother about Fräulein Trainer, for Penny seemed just then to be sinking, and they had little hope left.

Anthony spent every spare moment with her, bringing her wild flowers, sitting patiently peeling the largest and bloomiest hot-house grapes he could buy and taking out the seeds before popping them into her mouth, trying to make her smile, wondering if after all he had done right to bring her straight home, but, "Yes," he always concluded. "Penny would have been gone now if I hadn't brought her home."

Then one day, when they were all in despair about her and he was not far from it himself, Anthony went out to sit in the sun and think over again what he could do for Penny. It was his weekly half-holiday, and he was going to see Penny. Every spare minute had been spent with her recently, but after the meagre lunch that Miss Gunter took so little trouble over, since Anthony never grumbled about his food, he took his way across the bridge and up the burn where he and Penny had so often strolled among the wild mint and alders, watching the water-voles, finding the nests of the moor-hens, stalking the otter, following the tracks of stoat or weasel, of heron or ousel, to their homes, vying with each other in finding rare flowers or birds, laughing through the summer afternoon as they built their fire and picnicked by the chattering burn or under the old pine on the hill. Even in the soft summer rain they had picnicked, where he made a little house for Penny under the whins or by hanging his waterproof on the branches of the firs.

They were so easily pleased, so happy together with the simplest things, in sunshine or in rain, so deeply interested in the finding of a feather, the call of a bird, the way the vole ate the water crowfoot, the plover made its nest, or the wasp bit the dry hemlock to make its home. Would she never wander with him again, never watch the grasses bending under their drop of water after the rain, count the nuts in the squirrel's hoard, listen to the larks carolling—carolling?

He sat down on the warm turf under the lee of an old wall, playing with a few pebbles he had picked up, dropping them from hand to hand, thinking of Penny, his child love, his meaning to life, the latchets of whose little shoes he felt himself unworthy to unloose—his Penny, for whom to have laid down his life would have been as simple as to lay down his cloak in the mud that her feet should not be soiled. Penny, whom he could do nothing to save—do nothing but ride gently with her to the grave, who might have said:

> "Ride hooly, hooly, gentlemen,
> Ride hooly, men, wi' me!
> For there was never a wearier burd
> Rade in your companie."

They were the words of one of the Scots ballads he had been reading to her the night before. They both loved the old Scots ballads.

As he sat, dropping the pebbles from one slender hand to the other, looking so indifferent to all the world, a movement caught his eye, and, turning a little, he saw a tiny baby leveret crouched in the grass.

He watched it for some time, wondering at its being there alone; then he rose, picked it up, and held it in the palm of his hand, stroking its back with one finger and wondering how it came to be there, when, glancing about, he saw the solution of the mystery. A dead hare, worried by some dog, lay behind a tussock of grass. The leveret's mother was dead.

Not knowing what to do about it, he put it gently in his coat-pocket, as he had so often with findings of Penny's, half-dead redwings, tiny fieldmice, forsaken nestlings, broken-winged birds, all of whom she would nurse and try to heal and bring back to life. Thinking how interested she would have been, how she would have loved to coax and wheedle the little leveret into feeding from her hand, how happy she would have been trying to bring it up, he turned towards home, remembering how many tiny creatures she had nursed and brought up and then set free, how many too, alas, had died in spite of all her care and been the source of tears, howls, and recriminations against anyone who could possibly be blamed, even the Lord, Whose will, Beenie would ungenerously remind her, it was if they died.

Suddenly then the idea came to Anthony; he would take the little leveret home to Penny and tell her she was the only one who could save it—that its small life depended upon her. It might just give her that tiny interest in life the doctor had spoken of, awaken, however slightly, that will to live that was somehow gone. For Anthony knew too that there was no real disease; her lungs were not yet seriously affected—in fact, her cough was almost gone. It was some broken cord that needed mending, some well-spring of life that had ceased to bubble up from beneath the surface.

He carried the little creature carefully back to the Falcon's House, and, going up to her room, he gently took it from his pocket and put it on the bed beside her, where it lay quite still, its bright eyes full of fear.

"It's mother's dead, Penny," he said. "A dog had killed it. I brought it to you because you're the only one who could do anything for it. It will die if you can't save it."

She put out a finger and stroked its soft fur. It lay still for a moment, then suddenly it made a little movement and scrambled in beside her.

She smiled and tried to sit up.

"Oh, Anthony, it likes me. It's come in beside me."

"It must be starving," said cunning Anthony, "but I don't know how to feed it."

She continued to stroke it. Then she whispered, her voice very weak, "A doll's bottle and some warm milk. Sally Gibson has dolls' bottles."

In a few minutes Anthony was back with a doll's feeding-bottle from Sally Gibson's toyshop. It cost twopence, but he would have cheerfully given a thousand pounds, or all he had, for that ridiculous little toy.

He sat behind Penny on the pillows and supported her as she coaxed and wheedled the little creature, guiding her hands when they trembled with his own long, slender fingers, supporting her arms when they tired. At last, after many futile attempts, she got it to suck the milk, and in two shakes it had emptied the bottle. At that suddenly, happily, Anthony and she both laughed—a real laugh! Though Penny's was but a faint little giggle, it was the first sign of a real interest. Anthony felt as if she had taken hold of a slender gossamer line that might draw her back to life, but, though his heart leaped, he was afraid to hope.

The hare snuggled in beside her, and had perforce to be fed again in an hour or two, and nobody but Penny could feed it, but by this time the tiny morsel of fur had wound its way into her heart. All birds and animals had always had confidence in Penny; she had the gift of securing their trust. The little hare burrowed in beside her, and whenever anyone came into the room she could feel its small heart palpitating as it scratched in nearer to her with its sharp little claws. It trusted her and depended on her, just a scrap of unregarded life, a fragment of fur, but it supplied the end of a thread to which stronger and stronger cords of life were tied. If only it held till her fingers had grasped the little-stronger string!

It would have been comical if it had not been tragic too, the way the household gyrated about the little hare. They were terrified it might die. Books were consulted about bringing up wild animals; the town naturalist's opinions were sought and gravely considered; the vet was called on by Perry on the subject of diet. The first question every morning was about the hare—was it still alive?

For Penny roused herself to attend to her pet. She struggled up to a sitting position to feed it, and each day would sit upright a little longer to play with it, for the little creature throve and soon became mischievous, forcing her to move about, to laugh, to forget the nightmare she had been through.

Slowly, gradually, with many setbacks, Penny began to take the turn. Warned by Anthony, no one else attempted to feed or do anything for the hare, no one tried to gain its confidence. Penny had to look after it or it would die.

Faintly at first, then happily and eagerly, Penny made the effort. The tiny leveret lived in her bed against every rule of good housewifery. Even Beenie forbore to grumble about soiled blankets and milk-soaked sheets. Rachel made and lined a little basket for it, and Hagar constructed a snug nest out of an old fur cap. Every one seemed, indeed, more concerned for the comfort and progress of the baby hare than for Penny's.

Perhaps they had concentrated too much upon her, stifling some life force by their very terror that she would die. Now they were terrified the hare would die or some accident befall it, and that took their thoughts off her and gave her, as it were, more natural air to breathe.

Already she looked very different from the day that Anthony had found her. A faint shell-pink began to come and go in her cheeks; her hair, carefully washed and tended by Hagar and Rachel, had lost its flat, dank look, and stood out in a shining aureole round her head; the deep sunken lines from nose to mouth had gradually begun to disappear. Cups of broth and invalid food began to go down empty to the kitchen, where they were almost washed with Beenie's tears of joy.

When a willow-warbler nested at the foot of the rockery, and a chaffinch in the lichened crook of the apple-tree bough, Anthony rolled her in a rug and carried her down to see them, and after that she had to be carried round the garden every warm and sunny day to see how things were progressing, how the gooseberries were swelling and the rosebuds showing pink, how another blue egg was in the thrushes nest and the first swallows building in the eaves.

Anthony was her slave, and the rest of the family not much behind. If Penny had been spoilable she would have been spoiled then, for they were all ready and eager to rush and fulfil her slightest wish. But there was something intrinsically sweet and lovable about Penny; she would not spoil.

Then other things began to happen as she gradually came round and the house began to resume its normal course.

CHAPTER II

"IN THE SWEET BY-AND-BY"

IT was raining, and the wind was cold, though summer had come, and the streets of the town were shining and wet under the lights from the shop windows and the flare of electricity.

The music-hall was crowded, and people were whispering as they waited for the curtains to part for the next item on the programme—No. 4.

"It's those singers," said one man to another. "There's a mystery about them."

"Why more mystery about them than any of the others?"

"Oh, I don't know. You'll see, they give you that impression."

The curtains began to part just then, and a girl came in leading a man who was evidently blind. It was Marion and Matthew. Marion had never expected that Granny Wotherspoon's money would give out before Naomi got her divorce. It had really never dawned on her that Naomi would get her own back and punish them by not divorcing Matthew. It may have been foolish, but she was young, and even Matthew had not seriously believed it when he said that night in Newcastle, "And if Naomi doesn't divorce me?"

Both of them had been quite sure that in going away together they were doing the right thing to get a divorce, and when it was all over they would marry and go back home. There might be a good deal to live down, but they had been prepared for that. Naomi would naturally leave Goslaw, for she hated it and loathed the country, apart from the house being Matthew's, and Goslaw was away in the hills, where they could live quietly, with a good shepherd in the near-by cottage to look after the sheep.

But all these dreams had gradually faded away as it became clear that Naomi had no intention of divorcing Matthew, that their money was running out, and something must be done.

Neither of them could bear the thought of asking those at home to keep them. No, they had taken their fate into their own hands and burned their boats. They must find some way of making money.

They had tried many ways. Matthew could read Braille now and do a number of things, but there was not enough money to be made in any of them to keep them.

They had tried typewriting. Marion had taken situations as a typist and clerk, but she was not very good at any kind of clerical work, and the weekly wage she could command was very small. The same with jobs as an assistant in a shop—well enough for young girls, but hopeless for a woman—Marion called herself a woman now—with a blind man to keep.

Then Marion had tried various strange ways of making money. She had been a fortune-teller, having got the idea when she was working as a typist and clerk in his show for a showman in London. That had been a success for a while, but she had been visited by the police and got a fright, though the fortune-telling was the most innocent affair, depending mostly on a sort of gipsy get-up with shawl and curtain rings in her ears, and a knowledge of reading teacups, or hands, or the cards, from old times at home when they spent many an evening telling one another's fortunes.

It was then that she thought of singing. They had practised together, and gone out and sung in the streets to "try it on the dog," as Marion said. Then in a rather low-class restaurant they had got a start as a 'turn,' and from that had got rather better 'turns' in music-halls in various provincial towns.

Their present engagement had been rather successful, as they had hit on the idea of singing together the most simple of old-fashioned songs and even hymns. Nobody else did it, and in the midst of the blare and the lights, the vulgarity and the suggestiveness, the cleverness and smartness, the sudden change to absolute simplicity and homeliness had caught on in a mild way. They made enough to live above the poverty line. If only it might last!

Though Marion had to lead Matthew in, the doctors had been right, and the eye was improving a little. He could tell light from darkness, and he did not wear the dark glasses; he had a glass eye now so perfect no one could guess it was not real, and the dark glasses impaired the slight sight in the other eye.

Perhaps his tall figure, slightly marred still by the stoop, which gave it a certain distinction nevertheless, his young Apollo face, and his blindness had something to do with their success, not to speak of Marion's fair and youthful face. Happiness had made Marion plumper, for all her privations; for the two were immensely happy in spite of everything. They understood each other; they had the same sense of fun, and liked the same things. A treat shared was a real treat. They made a feast of a dish of fried liver and bacon and had laughter for sauce when bread and cheese was all they could buy—"better is a dinner of herbs where love is, than a stalled ox and hatred therewith."

Matthew usually played the violin or the banjo. To-night he sat plucking at the strings of the banjo, while the rich low notes of his voice made the perfect accompaniment to Marion's sweet high soprano. They sang as the spirit moved them, and somehow it was effective, though all the songs were old-fashioned and simple. They most certainly would not have been a success in a highly musical gathering; their appeal was

s

to the homely folk of provincial towns away from the more musical centres.

To-night they sang their old favourite, with its funny, absurd little story of the tree in the wood.

> "Ah, come guess what there may be,"

sang Marion, in her merry lilt, and then came the sudden change when Matthew's deep, mournful voice interposed:

> "Ah, but the times that are gone, Nanette,
>   were the best of all,
>   Were the best of all."

> "In the wood there is a tree,
>   And on that tree there is a branch,"

trilled Marion's happy laughter.

> "Ah, but the times that are gone, Nanette,
>   were the best of all—
>   Were the best of all,"

came the sad echo.

And so through the story, Marion adding a line each time about the nest and the bird and the egg and so on. There was no sense in it, no meaning; it was just at one moment the child trilling laughingly, gaily, about a bird's nest in a wood, and the next the old man remembering—remembering. . . .

But it caught on. They had to sing it all over again.

Then they sang *Madam, Will You Walk?* Then a quaint old Scottish nursery rhyme about a frog, when to Marion's gay and ringing invitation,

> "Ho! Miss Mouse, will you marry me,
>   And sit for ever on my knee?"

the laughter echoed through the hall. She saw the fun of it and they saw the fun of it, made funnier still by Matthew's booming "Um-um" underneath with its note of reflective doubt on the wisdom of poor Mr. Frog's gallivantings.

Last of all they sang *In the Sweet By-and-by* to an old setting for two voices, where Marion's, clear and sweet, hung on the long-drawn sustained notes "In the sweet by—and—by" like a bird winging over the marshes, while down below, short, deep, staccato, Matthew accompanied her, "like a frog croaking in the bog," he said himself, and somehow that caught on too, for, however smart, however sophisticated we may be, we all have some wistful hope of a sweet by-and-by.

"It went all right to-night," said Marion, as Matthew tucked her hand under his arm and they set off with Mike the Airedale for the room they called 'home,' hurrying through the mist and rain that had settled down with that persistency it has in the west.

"They can't help loving you," said Matthew. "That's what does it."

"Not on your life! Nobody cares about plump women like me; they like them lean. No, it's your looking so frightfully handsome that does it. I saw all the girls eyeing you and wondering if 'The Nightingales' were married folks or brother and sister or what."

They had called themselves "The Nightingales," partly because they usually sang at night, partly because Matthew had taken 'Gale' as a surname in case of any publicity. Matthew had strenuously objected at first to being called a nightingale, but Marion had learned a great deal since she was thrown, as it were, to the lions; she knew the value of a taking name that was easily remembered and conveyed an idea, and "The Nightingales" they became, much to their own amusement.

The room was cosy with a banked-up fire ready to burst into flame at the touch of the poker, and Matthew set the table while Marion cooked and made the sauce for the fish.

Matthew could do all sorts of jobs in the house now, and go almost anywhere with the aid of Mike. Mike, trained to lead the blind, had cost a large sum from Granny's store, but he was worth it. He adored Matthew, and was almost uncannily wise where he was concerned. For Marion he had a good-natured tolerance, and the rest of the world had to leave him alone. He never bit, but he had a way of showing his teeth that was sufficient, and he loathed being touched except by Matthew or Marion. "Don't pat him," was for ever on their lips. He was so handsome and clever every one wanted to pat him and fuss over him, while his whole concern was to look after Matthew.

After supper Marion saw Matthew settled with his pipe, refusing all offers of help with the dishes and going off to wash them on the landing, where the communal sink and hot-water tap were placed.

She had given him a book in braille type, but when she came back he was gazing into the fire, with his hand on Mike's head.

"Happy, Matthew?" she asked rather doubtfully, as she sat down on a stool and put her arm across his knee.

"Quite happy, Mingie." He had lots of pet names for her. They both sat looking into the fire for a while in silence.

"You're thinking of Goslaw?"

"Well, it was the sheep—there must be a mart here to-morrow. I heard them bleating as they went by."

"Yes, I expect there is." A long silence, and then she said, "But, Matthew—you couldn't manage sheep now."

He gave a short laugh. "Aye could I. Mike and I could manage a flock o' sheep, couldn't we, Mike? With maybe Tyne and Tweed [his old sheepdogs] to scour the hills. But it's no use thinking of that!"

"Matthew," she could not refrain from asking, "would you like to go back to Goslaw so much? Are you homesick for it?"

"We can't go back. You know that, Mingie—not till Naomi divorces me."

There was nothing to be said about that; they had threshed it all out long ago. They could not return to the neighbourhood and live together unmarried among their friends and relatives. It was impossible—not to be considered. Matthew hated towns and pined for the country, but there was no way to make a living in the country, and they were both determined to make their own living. They had gone against all their friends; they were living to all appearances together under their strong disapproval—under their own, for that matter, since Marion knew really that not only evil, but "the appearance of evil" should be avoided. No one knew what Marion suffered because of their anomalous position. Every day and hour something gave the knife a twist in her heart. She was always praying for forgiveness, and reminding God she hadn't meant it to be like this. She still meant to "be good" and just look after Matthew and be his housekeeper till they could be married, for she couldn't leave Matthew as long as he was so blind. He depended so much upon her; his blindness made him so helpless without her because she had been with him from the first and knew as no one else could ever do just how to help him. So they just had to go on as they were at present.

"No," she said at last. "But I sometimes wonder if—if there is *nothing* we could do in the country. Oh, Matthew, do you remember how the hills rolled away up to the sky, all pink with heather, and the sound of the bees in the ling, and sitting among the yellow tormentil on hot days, and hearing the hill larks rising and singing, and the curlew calling?"

"And the burns tinkling among the ferns and the bracken," he went on, seeing it all behind his blinded eyes. "and the way the green turf came right up to the door at bonny Goslaw, and the mist going off in scarfs from the hill-tops in the early morning when the sun struggled through. . . . Aye, Mingie darlin', I cannot but remember such things were. . . ."

They sat hand in hand looking into the fire.

"Mike would like fine too to stretch himself across the moorland and splash through the bogs—wouldn't you, Mike?"

"Perhaps some time—some time we might go back," said Marion. "Perhaps Naomi . . ." But her voice was without hope.

They had so often said, "Perhaps Naomi," but Naomi was as bitter as ever; against hate like that there seemed no appeal.

Matthew laughed. "In the sweet by-and-by," he said, his voice rough with regret and pain.

CHAPTER III

"I WILL ARISE AND GO NOW"

GOSLAW's empty now," said Rachel. "Naomi has gone, and there's nobody in it. I wonder where she is exactly? She never told anybody where she was going—just said it was near Newcastle, a sort of partnership with a widow who has a dairy there. Well, she'll make it pay; she's clever."

They were sitting in the garden at the Falcon's House in the late September sunshine. Penny was lying in a hammock stretched between the trees; she was still very delicate and still looked as if the wind might blow her away, but she could walk about a little now, and her old gay spirit was returning, tentatively and in fits and starts, but showing itself in sudden chuckles of laughter, in teasing Beenie, in measuring herself once more against Anthony's slender height and scolding him because she said he had grown another inch surreptitiously and behind her back.

"I'll never be able to marry you," she said, "if you go on like that!"

"Am I jilted?" asked Anthony, smiling his slow, whimsical, patient smile.

"Not till I tell you," said Penny.

Rachel had been reading a long epistle from Paul, who had taken to farming in Rhodesia like a duck to the water. He had asked about every one, Naomi included. "There's a man here," he said, "called Jourdain, who was asking a lot about her, so don't forget to tell me what you know." Then he had gone on to describe the life and to assure Rachel she would love it. "I've chosen a spot where I'm going to build a house," he announced, "when I've got my own farm," and then came a long dissertation on the site and the kind of house he was going to build when he was older and had his own farm.

"How old is Paul?" asked Hagar, who was busy knitting a yellow jumper for Penny.

"Eighteen—and I'm nearly twenty now," said Rachel, and then flushed as she realized she had joined their names together. "Just a boy," she added scornfully—"him and his house!"

"Paul always seemed so old for his years," said Hagar. "He isn't tall, but he has that broad, set look, and he's so sensible."

"Not like Perry," said Penny. "Perry will never be sensible; he's not made that way."

"There's not much we can tell him about Naomi," Rachel went on musingly, "except that she's left Goslaw. I suppose he'll expect us to say how small the world is and all that sort of thing, but the only thing that surprises me is anybody wanting to know anything about Naomi, especially when you'd got as far away from her as South Africa."

Just then Mr Peregrine came in for tea, which they were having in the garden. He seemed rather perturbed, but at once began to quote as usual. "Ah, the cup that cheers, but not inebriates. I feel I need cheering."

"I feel I need inebriating," said Rachel. "We've been talking of Naomi Cuendet."

With a sort of stubborn, stuck-in-the-sand attitude none of them would now give Naomi her married name.

"I was thinking of her," said Mr Peregrine—"that is to say, of Bowchester. I hear there have been more—ah—words over at Bowchester, and Mark has gone off."

"What has that to do with Naomi?" asked Rachel, not noticing Hagar's face, which had paled a little as she stared at Mr Peregrine.

"Correlation of ideas." Mr Peregrine was never to be hurried. "Let me see now. It appears Mrs Wotherspoon's latest—ah—weapon against Mark is that she needs more money to try to buy Naomi off—not that anyone believes she can be bought off, but there it is, and they have quarrelled again. This time it's over the curling-pond and the long spinney. She is going to sell the trees to a contractor who is bringing in a steam-saw—I do not know if I have got the right term—to cut them up. Mark went off last night, and no one knows where he is. They are, I gather, a little—ah—anxious. In fact"—he suddenly turned in that disconcerting way of his and stared at Hagar, his clever little eyes blinking at her through his bushy eyebrows—"they are a little nervous about something he said about the curling-pond."

"What?"

Rachel and Hagar both turned quickly to him, but it was Rachel who spoke. Mr Peregrine had not noticed Penny, who had been lying deep in the hammock, covered with rugs. She sat straight up, her eyes wide with apprehension, and Hagar ran to her just as Beenie arrived with the laden tea-tray and planked it down on the table.

"What's this I hear?" she asked, putting her hands on her hips. "What's this I hear about Mark Wotherspoon? If that laddie has drooned hissel in the pond——" She caught a glimpse of Hagar's signals and stopped.

"He hasn't! He hasn't!" screamed Penny wildly.

"Eh, now, what are ye upsettin' yersel' aboot?" Beenie began at once to climb down, remembering too late that Penny mustn't be upset. "It's naught but auld wives' clashes. Mark's as right as rain. It's that wifie Turnbull comin' to door with a face as long as Leith Walk that pit me aboot. There now, my dawtie. Dinna you upset yoursel' about anything auld Turnbull said. She's just a fair clash-me-claver!"

But it took some time to calm Penny, and Hagar, with her heart suddenly torn with fear, had to pull herself together and pretend she knew that Mark was perfectly all right, while some words of his kept ringing in her ears. "I'd rather drown myself in the curling-pond they're going to drain—a nice find for them that!"

She did not believe that he had meant it—it was only a manner of speaking; but Mark was such an unknown quantity,

so dour and silent at times, so passionate at others, she could
see him walking off in speechless rage, his shoulders up, his
face strained so that every bone stood out. She just didn't
know what he might do if driven beyond a certain point.
After all, none of us know what we might do if driven to the
ultimate bounds of what we can bear. And there had been
the story of the dog too.

When Penny had gone Mr Peregrine had told them what he
knew. There had been a terrible scene when Mrs Wotherspoon had told Mark she was selling the trees and draining
the pond. Hagar did not quite know if she even had the power
to do that. Bowchester was to be Mark's when his mother
died; that was plain enough, but the rest was all vague to her.

In any case, while they were arguing a puppy of Sally's,
brother to Hagar's Samuel, had got into some of the new
machinery and been mangled to death. That had been the last
straw, and Mark had gone off—just walked out of the house
as he was—and no one had seen him since or heard anything
about him. That was last night, and they were still without
news, and John had come over to see Mr Peregrine and ask if
he had been there, and had mentioned that in the heat of the
quarrel Mark had said he would rather drown himself in the
pond than let them destroy it and the whole place, as they
talked of doing.

John was less pigheaded than Luke and his mother about
making money, and admitted he'd be sorry to see the trees
cut down and the pond drained. "We've had such fun there,"
he said. "It would be a pity if the village had nowhere to
skate and curl. We always sent a team to the bonspiels from
Bowchester."

Not only that, but the Wotherspoon men were all noted
curlers themselves. To Hagar this craze to turn everything
into money was inexplicable, especially as Mother Wotherspoon had so much goodness and kindness in her make-up.

When at last tea was over, and Mr Peregrine had gone back
to the shop and Rachel was upstairs with Penny, who still went

to bed very early, the fire always being lighted in her room and the girls or friends sitting there and playing games with her or reading aloud, Hagar, instead of going up to join them, stood by the French window looking into the garden, afraid and terribly distraught over Mark, wondering what she could do. Where was he? If only she could find him and help him!

She would not think of the pond. Mark wouldn't do that, she assured herself. No, he wouldn't, he wouldn't!

Just then she saw a white shape in the garden and, thinking it was Samuel, who was a big puppy now, she opened the window to call him in. But it wasn't Samuel.

It was Sally!

Sally! But Sally never left Mark. What was she doing here? She stood looking at Hagar, one ear drooping, the other cocked straight on end. Then Hagar saw that she was covered with mud and panting. She drew her in and gave her water, which she drank eagerly, and then she hungrily devoured the remains of a stew which Hagar brought from the pantry.

As Sally stooped over the dish Hagar noticed that a scrap of greenery was caught in her collar, and, pulling it out, she saw that it was heather. Heather! There was no heather in the immediate vicinity of Breckan. She must have come from some distance—Goslaw!

At once in her mind's eye Hagar saw the little sheep-farm lying in a lirk of the hills with the heather all around it and coming almost up to the door.

But there was no one at Goslaw. The house would be empty and shut up. Naomi had been gone for a week and more. What could Mark do at Goslaw?

Sally had finished the stew in a few gulps, and now made for the door, which she tapped gently with her claws. She had been trained not to scratch the paint. Hagar let her out of the kitchen, and she went straight for the French window. Let out again, she went down the garden, and then stood looking back.

"Woof!" she said.

"Oh, Sally," said Hagar, "if I could only speak to you! Of course I know what you want. You want me to follow you, but where? I can't start off to Goslaw, if that's where Mark is, and follow you all the way there."

For by this time she was growing certain that that was where Mark was.

Had he forgotten the house was deserted and shut up?

No, he would never have gone near the place if Naomi had been there. He could not bear Naomi. Had he just gone to look at the place, to see if he could make anything of it? Or just perhaps in desperation for somewhere to go—away from his mother and brothers, away from Bowchester, away from the screams of the puppy? But why had Sally left him? And what should she do? What could she do?

Goslaw was miles and miles away. She looked at her wrist-watch, remembering the trains they had looked up when Marion went to stay with Matthew and Naomi. There was one about five. She could catch it, but even if she did it was miles from the station, and, though she had been there once with Rachel to see if they could persuade Naomi to get a divorce, she was not sure if she could find the way.

Then she remembered Jock, the stationmaster, had lent them a round, fat barrel of a white pony, which they had ridden by turns, astride in their petticoats, for there were no side-saddles there.

Suddenly she made up her mind. She would go to Goslaw.

Beenie was busy in the larder—the milkhouse, as she called it—sorting the jam shelves and putting away the plum and greengage jam they had been making. She would confide in Beenie.

She went in and told Beenie about Sally.

"That's whaur he is," said Beenie at once. "But you canna' go there; ye'd never get back the night."

"I'm going," said Hagar. "If I can get there I can get back, as far as the station anyhow. Jock can put me up for the night." They had all got to know Jock and his wife slightly, through Marion having stayed there.

"Weel, ye ken yer ain ken best. What am I to say?"

"I'll just slip off. I don't feel like explaining or arguing about it. You see, Beenie—I just must go."

"Aye, fine I ken. I wonder the pair o' ye haven't brought it off afore now. As fine a mon as there is in the kintra-side, and as daft about you as you are about him."

"Beenie! I'm not daft about anybody."

"Don't stand argy-bargying there or ye'll miss your train. Daft or no daft, he's your man, and well ye know it—all this about Rachel! Rachel! He's never cast an eye on the side the road she's on."

Hagar left her talking away to herself and flew up the stairs to put on her hat and coat. She took her large shopping hand-bag and stuffed one or two things into it, saw that she had plenty of money, and flew swiftly down the stairs again, not making a sound. She could hear Rachel's voice reading *Treasure Island* and their laughter as she and Penny enjoyed some joke.

Beenie was at the kitchen door with a basket in her hand, the lid firmly shut.

"What am I to say, then, if I'm asked about ye?"

"Just tell the truth. Say I didn't want to talk about it, and ask them not to. He may not be there, but it's a chance."

"Well, here's something to eat. Never neglect your meat. Ye'll be fair clemmed or you get there, and there'll be nothing to eat in that godforsaken hole, as far as I can make out."

"Oh, thank you, Beenie. I never thought of that."

She took the basket and went out by the back door; then she remembered Sally and looked in the garden. She was still standing there watching the door, and came to Hagar when she called. She knew Hagar well, and had evidently made up her mind to trust her. She trotted after her, and made no fuss about getting into the train, which cheered Hagar a little. It looked as if Mark had gone by train and taken Sally with him. She was so sharp she would understand this was the way to go back.

"You're a queer dog, Sally," she said to her, remembering

Mark's conviction that dogs did not so much listen to what you were saying as read your mind in some way.

A peculiarity of Sally's was that if an order was strange she did not obey it at once; she would sit looking puzzled, or at times just solemnly stupid; then she would suddenly go and do exactly as she had been told, possibly five minutes or more later. Was she thinking? Or did it just take some time for her to get at what was wanted by some way one did not understand? Hagar did not know, and, tired out, Sally had curled up and gone to sleep.

CHAPTER IV

"WAKE ANY, WATCH ANY, HERE IN THIS DWELLING?"

HAGAR got out at the little station, followed by Sally, and looked round, but before she was well on to the platform Sally was off through the gates and down the road.

In a moment Hagar saw her again streaking up the hillside and over the heather. It was only for a moment that she saw the white speck moving, then it was lost on the heathery hill.

Jock came forward and bade her good-evening, trying not to look curious as he remarked on the weather and made comments about the crops. Hagar had decided in the train to say as little as she could about Mark, and now she felt sure from Sally's actions that he was at Goslaw thought it better just to take it for granted that Jock knew Mark was there. She was glad now of Beenie's basket; it gave her some kind of excuse for coming, even if it was a curious hour to arrive.

"I've brought over some provisions for Goslaw," she said. "Could I have the pony to ride over?"

"Eh, miss," he said, "the last up-train went an hour ago. You'll no' get back the night."

Instantly she took the cue.

"But there's one about eight, isn't there? We thought I'd just have time to ride over with the basket and get back."

"No' the night, miss. There's a late train on Saturday nights goes through frae the market; ye'd mebbe be thinkin' on it." He paused. "And then there's the 'Fish,' but she's a goods. . . . Still, Andy MacBriar might take ye in the van, if so be that ye were wantin' to get back the night."

"Oh, yes," said Hagar carelessly. "I have to get back to-night."

"Aye," he smiled, "town folk aye think there'll be trains—but you'll make the 'Fish,' miss. She doesn't get in till eight-thirty. Is Mr Wotherspoon biding in bye?"

With the hill people 'in bye' meant anywhere in the hills, 'out bye' was anywhere away from them.

"Well, we don't know. He came to look over the place and hasn't come back, so his mother thought she'd like to send some food over and hear what he's doing; but both the lads are away, and she's alone at home, so I came off with the basket."

She smiled as she held it out. After all, he knew very little about the families at Bowchester and the Falcon's House, and was not likely to know anything about her. He'd just seen her with Rachel, and didn't even know her name.

"Aye, ye'll need the powney for that. I'll have him here in a jiffy."

Hagar sat down in the little waiting-room, and in a few minutes she heard a hail and went out. He helped her into the saddle, telling her how he'd bought the "powney" after he was married for his wife to ride over the hills to her own home and that of her married sister.

"Ye'll be a Wotherspoon," he remarked, as he settled her basket in front, but luckily at that moment the pony decided it was time to be off and started with a jerk which saved Hagar from the need to reply. It took her all her time to grasp the reins and get away without mishap.

"I'll no' be here when ye get back," he called to her, "but Jimmy'll see to you."

Evidently the pony knew the road all right, for he set off up the hill without further direction, and after that there was only the one track till they came to the fork leading to the two valleys, and she knew that Goslaw lay to the left.

Once started, she began to worry again. She had not wanted to ask Jock any questions, and, besides, she felt sure that he knew nothing or very little about Mark or he would have told her. He was a garrulous, simple soul, and anything that was in his head came out.

She was sure now that Mark had gone to Goslaw, and that Sally had left him there, but why *had* Sally left him and come all that distance alone?

Vague apprehensions seized her and made her shiver. The place was so lonely too. Once she had got away from the station there was nothing but the rolling hills and the intense solitude of the narrow valley with the burn, silent as it slipped through the heather, or talking secretly to itself as it wound about among the stones.

"I don't like it," she thought, "and I'm sure Mark wouldn't either. I don't wonder that Naomi had to leave. How could any woman live alone in a place like this with its eerie quietness as the night comes down, and its secretiveness—there's not even a bird calling to its mate."

Just then she was startled by a plover rising from the heather beside her and giving its mournful cry:

Weep—weep . . .

The pony was startled too, and went clattering down into a ravine full of shadows and through the water of a little stream that crossed the track to join the larger burn.

It seemed a long way to Hagar, much longer than she remembered, but then she had not been alone, and it had been a sunny forenoon in spring, not the evening of an autumn day. Then, too, she had not been racked with anxiety or filled with vague fears and forebodings.

At last she topped the rise and saw the little farm with its sheep-pens lying below her from the point where Marion had paused in the moonlight nearly a year ago now.

It looked very still and lonely in the deepening shadows. The sun had sunk behind Goslaw Rigg, but there were red patches among the black reeds of the swire where the wild geese used to flock and still came in winter when driven forth by the snow from the far north.

She looked, as the pony took the downward slope, to see if there was any smoke coming from the chimneys, but there was none. All was quiet and very still. The fir-trees at the end of the stall stood sentinel over the empty pens, from which came no sound, no bleat of sheep, no coughing of the ewes.

She wished, if Mark were not there, that she had been and gone, had turned her back on it and was on her homeward way. And now it looked so deserted, so void of life, that she could not think that Mark was there. There was no sign of Sally, or any other creature, except that as she passed through the gate a rat ran out from the barn and, crossing the pebbles in front of her, disappeared among the forsaken outhouses.

She dismounted and tied the pony to the iron handle of the barn door, where it could crop the short turf, and then, taking the basket in her hand, she went to the door and knocked.

There was no answer.

She knocked again, and then from the inside she heard Sally's tail thumping on the floor. There was a sort of scraping noise and the sound of feet crossing the floor, the door opened, and Mark stood there!

For a moment neither of them spoke, and then a light leaped in Mark's dull eyes. "Hagar!" he said. Then, as if he could not believe his eyes, "Hagar!"

Her relief was so great that immediately she began to scold. "Hagar!" she repeated. "Hagar! Yes, it's Hagar, and is that all you have to say after frightening me out of my wits and bringing me all the way here to this horrible place? I've a good mind to give you—a bat on the head!"

But he had put out his arms and drawn her into them. He lifted her up and, carrying her in, basket dangling from one hand and her absurd shopping bag from the other, set her on the only place there was to sit, the high window-sill of the little window looking up the valley from near the fireplace. Then he put his arms round her again and drew her close; her head dropped on his shoulder, and she began to cry as she had not cried for ages, as she had not cried since she had to stop crying because it opened the wounds on her face.

"Oh, you bad man," she scolded ridiculously amid her sobs. "You bad, bad man. You've nearly killed me!"

All the terror that she had mastered, all the fear that he was lying in the mud in the curling-pond or had come to this lonely spot to do away with himself, now rose from the depths where she had forced them down, not allowing them to overcome her, not allowing them to rise, from sheer terror of what it would mean to her if she permitted them to surge up in all their black horror—not allowing herself to think of what it would mean if Mark were no longer there.

"Hagar!" he said again. "Hagar! Did you come to find me? Did it mean so much to you? Did you care what has become of me?"

"Care? Of course I care—of course! Of course. . . ."

Her voice was lost in sobs. She sobbed and sobbed, while he held her, kissing her hair, comforting her, laying his cold cheek against her hot one as he pressed it to his shoulder.

"I didn't know," he said. "Why didn't you tell me? I thought it must be Anthony."

"You're silly—you're just plain silly. How could it be Anthony? You knew it was *you*. I nearly told you!"

There was such indignation in her last confession that he laughed outright and shook her.

"Nearly! Nearly! What good is that to a man, and what do you mean by 'nearly' telling me? Turning me out of the house? Shooing me into Rachel's arms? Poor Rachel!"

She was drying her eyes by this time.

т

"Well, it would have been a very good match," she said, sniffing.

"Excellent," said he. "You didn't let me forget that either."

"Where have you been all this time?" she demanded severely. "Do you know they are going to drag the curling-pond?"

At that he went into a shout of laughter. "Drag the curling-pond? You're joking, Hagar."

"No, I'm not—at least, that's what Beenie said. Anyhow, everybody is in a state about you—*every one*. I'm not the only one."

"You're the only one that matters. I'm sorry I frightened you, Hagar, darling—at least, I'm not really, if I've frightened the truth out of you—but I never thought of frightening anybody. I'd said I'd throw up Bowchester and come to Goslaw if they went on as they were doing."

"But there is nobody here. The house is empty. What have you been doing?"

"Well, I got here late last night, and to-day I've been going all over the boundaries and looking at the house and outhouses, seeing what they need, what can wait, and what must be done at once. That took some time, and then I found I'd missed the train, and was just sitting thinking I'd walk over and catch the 'Fish.' By the way, had you a visit from Sally?"

"Yes, it was Sally made me think of Goslaw. There was heather sticking in her collar."

"Good lass!" he said, speaking to the dog. "You see, I'd nothing for her to eat, so I told her to go home and get a meal and come back, but evidently she thought she'd try you first before going on to Bowchester."

"She wanted me to come," said Hagar. "She waited for me."

He clapped Sally again, who sat looking as solemn and mournful as if a judge was about to put on the black cap and condemn her. "Sally's a marvel," he pronounced.

"Fancy sending a dog all that way to get something to eat! I think she has more sense than her master."

"Well, she won't eat raw meat, and there's nothing here but rabbits, which she just kills and buries, so I said, as I've said a thousand times, 'Go home and get your dinner,' and she went home and got her dinner. But you know you always give her a much better feed than she gets at home, where she has to share the porridge with the other dogs—she tried you first. At the same time, I must confess I did mention you. She knows your name, you know."

"What were you saying about me?"

"Ask Sally."

He had lifted her down from the sill and drawn up the old wooden box he'd been sitting on. He sat down on it now, took her basket and bag, and put them on the floor.

"There's only room for one on this box, and it's pretty hard," he said, lifting her to his knee. "Now, shall I tell you what I said to Sally? I said, 'You know that girl called Hagar over at the Falcon's House? She's——'" He proceeded to tell her all he had told Sally, with doubtless some additions as he rose to this marvellous opportunity of just letting himself go, while he held her close with one arm and with his other hand stroked her hair, tucked it behind her ears, ruffled it up, kissed it flat again, held her chin up to kiss her, or pressed her head gently back into the crook of his shoulder.

"You must have taken all day to say all that," said Hagar at last, beginning to recover herself.

"That's only the beginning," he said. "After that I told her you were a witch, and if we didn't look after ourselves you'd put a spell on us and turn me into a mouse and herself into a rabbit, which she despises above all creation—in fact, I said I was turned into a mouse already, terrified to make a movement in case you were off."

Hagar laughed out loud. "You're getting your metaphors mixed, as Mr Peregrine would say. It's the mouse that would be off."

"Who cares about metaphors? Hagar, do you think you could bear to live here? I think I'll have to leave Bowchester, and Matthew has written and asked me to take it over and pay him a rent when I could, now that Naomi's gone. I think I could manage to stock it and furnish the house plainly. I've been going all over it to-day—that's how the time flew past."

She jumped up.

"The time! Oh, Mark, I mustn't miss the 'Fish' train."

"It's all right. I'm going back with you. We have ten minutes." He drew her back. "Listen, Hagar. Do you think you could bear to come here and be a poor man's wife? I have so little to offer you. I kept thinking something might be arranged at Bowchester—I didn't want to leave it, and we could have had Redbarns"—Bowchester had originally been two farms, and there was a smaller farmhouse, Redbarns, on the estate—"but I couldn't ask you till something was settled, because I might find myself turned out without a penny unless I agreed to everything my mother wanted. Then when I had made a plan and sort of saw my way you completely turned me down, and I thought the reason was Anthony Truett."

"Anthony Truett indeed!" Poor Anthony was dismissed with scorn. Then, being Hagar, she added immediately, "Anthony's a darling!"

"What's that?"

"Anthony's a darling—go on about the house."

"It's your turn. Would you, Hagar? Would you live here?"

"With you?"

"Of course with me. Who the——"

"But you haven't asked me to marry you yet."

"Asked! I've begged, pleaded, gone down on my knees——"

"Bullied," she put in.

"Bullied! Does one bully a wasp?"

"Oh, I'm a wasp!"

He caught her chin in his large brown hand.

"Have I to begin and tell you all over again what you are— you're a witch and a darling love, you're a bird in my heart with its little wings closed, and you're——"

She put her hand over his mouth and, drawing it away, he said:

"Will you marry me, Hagar?"

"Take back about the wasp?"

"I take back about the wasp. I meant a—a——"

"Never mind, I am a wasp; I know I am. Now go on about the house.

"Could you live here, Hagar?"

"I don't like it very much, but I think I could—with you. . . . Where shall we put the dresser?"

"The dresser?"

"Yes, we must have a Yorkshire dresser with blue plates——" She was off; the house was furnished in two ticks.

"Some day," he whispered, "some day, sweetheart, if you'll just put up with this now, you'll have Bowchester."

"Oh, I love Bowchester! I think I love it even as much as you do." She sighed. "Will *you* mind terribly, Mark?"

He did not answer. He sat holding her, looking out of the window.

"It's mine," he said fiercely. "It's mine. If only I had the money to run it I'd make them go now—now I see what they'll do to it. None of them care two straws about it—only the money it can make. I used to think Mother loved it, but she doesn't—she doesn't care. She's a Waugh, you see, not a Wotherspoon. It's not her blame, it's not in her blood. Luke and John are Waughs too."

"Oh, why don't they go away and leave it?"

He said patiently. "It's the money, Hagar, sweetheart. You can't put it in two places at once, and Bowchester is so big."

"Very well, we'll live here. I don't mind very much except for you, Mark—only you won't have to leave me alone at night, with the hills coming up to the door and the wind woo-wooing round the house. I'd be frightened."

"I won't leave you alone at night. I'll tuck you in and hold you close. I've only to shake my fist at the wind and the hills with you in my arms—and off they'll go!"

"You are a goose! It's a good thing nobody else can hear

you. They'd think you were just plain silly." She held his hand tight. "They wouldn't know it was true. And if you hold me I'll shake my fist at the wind and the hills too, and they'll go flying over the world like frightened bullocks with their tails in the air."

Having approved of this meek and unassuming statement in his own way, Mark caught sight of the basket.

"What's in that basket?"

"I don't know. Beenie gave it me—but I don't think it's a kitten!"

"I'm as hungry as a horse—I've had nothing to eat since yesterday, now I come to think of it, except a bit of bread and cheese I put in my pocket."

"So am I—but we've no time. We must go."

However, they had time for a huge sandwich each, and then Mark lifted Hagar on to the pony, and, running beside it on his long legs, made it gallop as it hadn't galloped since it got the middle-aged spread; they went gaily lolloping back through the hills, up hill and down dale, and caught the 'Fish' just as it swam into the station puffing—to keep to Mr Peregrine's appropriate metaphors—like a whale. In the van they sat on boxes of smelly fish and finished the contents of the basket, Mark sharing the large bottle of beer with Andy, the guard, and all of them blessing Beenie and her forethought.

CHAPTER V

"BUT THE LOWLANDS FOR ME"

THE pond had not been dragged for Mark. In fact, much of the fuss was all imaginary on Beenie's part, or perhaps on the Widow Turnbull's. They had certainly been worried about his disappearance at Bowchester, but it hadn't come to pond-dragging. They were just making inquiries.

"I must be really in love," said Hagar to herself innocently (for all her common sense and twenty-seven years, Hagar could be as slow in the uptake as any of us), "to get into such a paddy about nothing." She heaved a sigh. All the same, it was very nice allowing herself to admit she was in love with Mark.

She had had to confess it when she and Mark and Sally and the empty basket had been deposited by the 'Fish' on the platform of Breckan, to be met by Mr Peregrine, who had really worried about Hagar, and at once took Mark to task.

"What do you mean, young man"—blinking under his eyebrows—"worrying us all about our Hagar? Can't be done—can't be done. Much too precious."

"I'm terribly sorry, sir," Mark said at once, "but—but—well, you see we are engaged."

Mr Peregrine did not look in the least surprised. He took the shopping bag in one hand and Hagar's arm in the other, and she was escorted down the quiet main street between them.

"I congratulate you, Mark," he said, when they were out of the station. "You are, at the moment, the luckiest man I know—but what are *we* going to do without Hagar?"

It was the question they all asked, for Hagar, still a little doubtful about Rachel, had thought it kindest to announce her engagement at once, especially as Mark was not to be silenced on the subject.

But Rachel was grown up now and much older in every way than when Hagar had first arrived at the Falcon's House; with Beenie and perhaps a little maid to help, there was no reason why she should not manage, especially as Penny was getting stronger every day. Penny would never be robust, the doctors thought; she was too highly strung, her nerves too sensitive to every emotional wind that blew across them. But, given happiness and quietude, she would be all right, and she was naturally of a happy temperament, pleased with so little.

So it was arranged that Mark and Hagar would be married in a few weeks, and that they would live at Goslaw. Mark hated leaving Bowchester, but, as Rachel repeated, "*Che sarà*

sarà"—what was to be would be. His mother and brothers had been considerate enough to stop all their alterations and plans in the meantime when they knew he was going to be married and leave Bowchester so soon.

"I'll never go back to look at it," he said to Hagar in the bitterness of his heart, and she felt too that it would be better if he did not see the despoiling of the place he loved so dearly. Neither of them really cared very much for Goslaw; although Hagar loved the country, it was the softer lowlands she loved, and so did Mark, and Goslaw was a sheep-farm. It was Matthew who loved the sheep and the rolling uplands, the distances, the cry of the curlew, the solitudes, and the plashing of the peaty burns, and Matthew was banished from all that, from all he loved—*che sarà sarà*.

Still, Hagar got great fun out of the furnishing of the house. She loved houses and housework, and was never happier than when arranging them. Some alterations were made, a bathroom put in and a hot-water system. Old Granny Wotherspoon had gone up in flames of wrath when first she heard that Mark was leaving Bowchester and going to Goslaw. No one understood why, as she had always taken the side of Luke and John, but it seemed she considered that as Goslaw was Matthew's he ought to come and live there. They never knew if she quite understood about Naomi and the divorce. And then, though Matthew had been her favourite, before the quarrels began she had seemed very fond of Mark too, and she now said Mark ought to stay at Bowchester and farm the place "properly." "What's a few trees?" she asked. "What's a curlin'-pond? Hens! Poof! Hens have no feelin's. Soft! That's what Mark is! Let him stay at home and farm his own place. What's he going to do among the hills? It's mixed farming he was brought up to."

She was right about that. It wasn't any intensive kind of farming Mark loved; he liked all the routine of a mixed farm with its sheep and cattle, its pigs and hens and geese and ducks and turkeys, its cart-horses, with one or two for driving or hacking or following the hounds. He was interested in breeding and in the dairy, and he was a splendid farmer. That was what annoyed Mother Wotherspoon. He might be a wealthy farmer, and he just wouldn't, with his old-fashioned ideas. Yet sometimes in the watches of the night she wondered what his father would have said—if she was really justified in putting herself against him. Then she would comfort herself by the thought of how badly they needed more money. The lads and she would make Mark's farm prosperous for him, and he'd benefit by it in the long run. If you didn't keep up with new inventions, if you weren't as hard as nails in these days, you got left behind.

Granny Wotherspoon, once her anger had subsided—and it subsided as quickly as it had risen—came down handsomely over a wedding present and was doing up the house and buying the furniture. No one knew how much money the old woman had. She was Yorkshire through and through. "Say nought," was her motto. It was from her mother Mrs Wotherspoon had her love of money and keen business mind.

The kitchen, when Hagar had finished with it, was charming. She had the North Country love of a real kitchen. None of your 'kitchenettes' or 'living-rooms' for Hagar. You lived and worked in your kitchen and called it a kitchen. The walls were cream, the floor covered with a cork material that suited stone floors, in blue and cream squares, the woodwork painted blue, a bright, gay blue. There was a dark oak dresser with blue dishes, as she had said, and there was a "long settle" covered in clear petunia to match the curtains, and a great scrubbed table to work at and have your meals at, and a smaller table to sew at or lift near the fire on winter nights when the thick curtains would be drawn and the flames from the open hearth leaping up the chimney.

But Hagar did not despise modern improvements. She had the best oil-stove to be bought and the best lamps. The 'parlour' was a country parlour, with gay washing covers on the chairs and a piano and corner cupboard, but the deep walls on each side of the fire had built-in bookshelves, and she had a trolley to wheel in the tea.

"When we have visitors," she said, "they'll dine in the kitchen, with no pretence about it, but we'll have tea over the parlour fire."

The big dairy, as big as a good-sized room, was re-shelved, but the slate shelves left for the milk, the 'back-kitchen' walls re-cemented and distempered and the room made into the 'little kitchen' of Northern farmhouses where the rougher work could be done.

"I just love it," she said to Mark, when it was all finished and ready for them to go into, down to the last dish and towel. "I'm simply dying to be married!"

They had come over to put in the last finishing touches. Rachel was there too. She had brought some lovely old bowls and vases from the Falcon's House to be ready for flowers, and other bowls filled with hyacinths, tulips, and suchlike spring bulbs, as it would be too late for Hagar to plant them. The pantry shelves were filled with home-made jams, chutneys, pickles, curds, and bottled fruits. Home-cured sides of bacon and hams from Bowchester hung on the large hooks in the ceiling with bunches of dried herbs and onions.

At Bowchester crates to be filled with Mother Wotherspoon's best Rhode Island Reds and Runner ducks were ready to be sent over, and Mark had already bought some of his stock, to come in after they were married.

"Everything is ready for the wedding bells," said Rachel, looking round before they locked the door. "I'm simply dying with envy, Hagar—I wish I'd set my cap at Mark. Would you have had me, Mark?"

"Couldn't have spared you," said Mark. "I need a sister; we never had any sisters but you girls. I wouldn't change you for all the tea in China."

"That's what I call a real diplomatic answer—you're cleverer than I thought you were, Mark. The plain truth is you're head over ears in love with Hagar."

"That's so," said Mark, turning the key in the door, and then, linking each in an arm, he ran them to where the new dogcart was waiting. If he sighed a little, looking at his new domain, no one heard it. He was determined Hagar would never know how his heart ached for Bowchester, how sometimes he could hardly bear to look at all the new furniture, the gay walls.

While Hagar, looking round the lonely hills, was thinking, "I do love it; I do. I'll soon get used to nothing but heather, and Mark must never, never know I'm not as 'country' as all this."

The wedding day had been fixed for a Tuesday, as that was a slack day at Bowchester, and then, two days before the wedding, something happened.

CHAPTER VI

"TO WHINNY-MUIR THOU COM'ST AT LAST, AND CHRISTE RECEIVE THYE SAULE"

RACHEL was trying on her bridesmaid's dress in her little tower room. Penny had wished to be a bridesmaid too, but she wasn't strong enough yet. Hagar had wanted a quiet wedding, but neither the Wotherspoons nor the Peregrines were people who liked to do things quietly. The latter especially liked large family gatherings and feasts and merry-makings, and they had had so few opportunities with Rachel declaring she was going to be a spinster and showing no sign of interest in any young man, and Marion's tragedy, and even Penny's delicacy, which forbade any thought of marriage in the family for years to come, so they all decided that Hagar must have what they called a real wedding, with veil and orange blossom and a grand luncheon and champagne and so forth.

Mr Peregrine himself was the prime mover in all this. The

child in him loved display, and he liked to see himself as the head of a family. He would dearly have loved to sit at the top of a table every Sunday and carve roast beef for eight to ten grown-ups—daughters and daughters-in-law, sons and sons-in-law, with a table in the window full of grandchildren and a cradle on the hearthrug with the youngest baby!

So Hagar and Mark had to give in, and the preparations were going forward. The dressmaker was kneeling at Rachel's feet with her mouth full of pins, Hagar was busy straightening out the sheet laid on the floor to keep the delicate material clean, and Penny was watching from the divan, when Beenie's feet were heard pounding up the stair.

"Eh!" she cried, bounding in. "The Lord preserve us all! There's been an accident at the Brae House and the auld leddy's gone."

Yes, old Mrs Waugh—Granny Wotherspoon—was gone at last; but that wasn't the worst. Old Granny's death had been expected for months, not to say years. She was so old and frail that her death at any time in the last two years would not have surprised anyone. Indeed, the surprise was rather how she hung on so long. She had been neither better nor worse lately, so the suddenness of her end was a surprise, but it was the manner of it that caused the most dismay.

Her daughter, Mother Wotherspoon, had gone to see her that afternoon, and Granny had insisted on getting out of bed and going across the landing to see a new bed that had been installed for the woman who looked after her, a Mrs Peach.

Granny took a lively interest in everything that went on in the house, and wanted to see the new bed. Mrs Peach and the doctor had both said she shouldn't leave her room, as the weather was rather chilly, but Granny chose to suppose that Mrs Peach didn't want her to see the bed because it was grander than the old lady might consider necessary for a "nurse body." Granny had said a single bed was quite sufficient, but Mrs. Peach was portly. . . .

As soon as Mother Wotherspoon had settled in for an hour

or two and Mrs Peach was safely off for her walk, Granny had insisted on getting up. She had been so determined that Mother Wotherspoon thought it would be better to let her have her own way and content her. She had warmed her slippers and her dressing-gown and wrapped her in a shawl, and, with her stick in one hand and supported by her daughter, she had safely made the short journey across the landing, but, coming back, she had put her stick on the polished wood at the edge of the carpet, and it had slipped. They were just at the head of the stair, and in trying to save her mother from falling Mrs Wotherspoon had slipped herself and fallen down the stair. She had saved Granny from going over—the old lady had subsided on the landing—but Mrs Wotherspoon had broken her leg, and the old lady had died shortly after being lifted into bed.

Beenie's news spread consternation and dismay. The brides-maid's dress was slipped off, and Hagar and Rachel hastened off to the Brae House.

There they found Mother Wotherspoon in bed. She was a big, heavy woman, and was suffering badly from shock, not only from the fall, but because of her mother's death, which she blamed herself for bringing about by allowing the old lady to get up.

Preparations for the wedding were, of course, all stopped. There was some talk of a quiet ceremony, but it was too near the funeral for even that, and after some discussion Hagar saw they would all be happier and it would be easier for them to postpone it for a week or two. Rachel had gone over to Bow-chester to help there, and Hagar was needed at the Falcon's House.

The day of the funeral was dull and wet. Hagar went over to Bowchester to sit with Mrs Wotherspoon and allow Rachel to go to the Brae House. Mrs Wotherspoon had been sur-prisingly gracious to Hagar once her engagement to Mark was an accomplished fact. She was never one to cry over spilt milk, and she had done all she could to help with the preparations for

Goslaw. She seemed to think, however, that she needed to explain herself a little, for she said, wakening, as Rachel and Hagar exchanged places, from a little nap she had been taking:

"Is that you, Hagar? I've been wanting to have a word with you."

"Yes," said Hagar. "How are you feeling, Mrs Wotherspoon?"

"I'm all right, if I could just get up. The leg's all right. It was a clean break, and we Waughs are good healers—good, clean Yorkshire blood—like your own!"

Hagar laughed. "My mother was a Northumbrian," she said, "but my father was pure Yorkshire. We *ought* to get on together, Mrs Wotherspoon."

"Aye. Mind, I'd no personal feeling against you when I set myself against anything between you and Mark. You're a good lass, and will make him a good wife—I see the difference you've made at the Falcon's House—but—well, you see, James and I"—she called the late Mr Wotherspoon James—"wanted a match between Peregrines and Wotherspoons, and after Marion I set my heart on Rachel. However, it was not to be. She tells me she could never have done with Mark. I don't blame her," she added fiercely. "A dour, determined devil, if he is my own son."

"I like them like that," said Hagar, laughing, and then to comfort Mother Wotherspoon a little she said, "But perhaps it will all come right in the end with Matthew and Marion. I think it will; they are both so good."

"They took the law into their own hands, and the Lord will punish them," said the old lady severely. "They made their bed and mun lie on it—not that I wouldn't give them some down from my best ducks to make it softer," she added, with a glint of humour in her stern brown eyes. She turned and looked at Hagar. "That's what I need money for—I think still Naomi could be bought; that sort aye has a price. She's stickin' out because she wants more. She thinks we're rolling in money."

Hagar could not agree to that. She knew that when she and Rachel went there was no sign of anything of the kind about Naomi. But she understood that this was a sort of apology for Mrs Wotherspoon's treatment of Mark and said, "Yes, I can understand how you feel about that, Mrs Wotherspoon," and changed the conversation. She was rather wondering about Granny's money. If Granny had left her money to Luke and John surely they might use that to try to buy Naomi off? Well, the will would be read to-day, and they would know for certain.

But when they all came home from the funeral it seemed that things were not so satisfactory as they had supposed.

The lawyer had read a will right enough, and there had been even more money than they had supposed—quite a large fortune, which was for the most part divided between Luke and John, though Mark and Matthew were not forgotten. But some papers had gone a-missing, and among them a later will.

They might have supposed that Granny had destroyed the later will—she had made and destroyed a number of wills—but as these very important papers had completely vanished as well, it looked as if she must have put them away together in some secret hiding-place of her own, and nothing could be done until a thorough search of every corner had been made.

No one knew anything of the contents of this rumoured will, except, of course, the lawyer who had drawn it up, but it was generally supposed in the family that Granny had altered it to give more to Matthew after he had become blind. She had been such a secretive old lady, however, about money that not even to her only child, Mrs Wotherspoon, had she ever disclosed anything.

Hagar felt rather in the way among all the discussions that were going on, and slipped away as soon as she could do so unobtrusively.

CHAPTER VII

"WHAT I KEPT I LOST"

A NOTICE of Granny's death was put in *The Times*, and another message to Marion and Matthew in the personal column saying the will was lost, and asking Matthew to get into touch with his family, as it was very urgent he should do so.

They put in about the will, as they did not want to raise their hopes too much of an immediate settlement. The papers had still not been found, and things were more or less at a standstill.

Marion read the notice to Matthew, and they discussed it far into the night, deciding that now Naomi would not divorce Matthew, they might as well let their families know where they were. It had seemed all right to keep their secret when there was a hope that the separation was just for a short time and had better be complete to make it easier for them all, but Naomi's attitude made a difference. Matthew had written to her again and made another appeal, but got no answer so far.

It was not till the next morning that Marion remembered something.

She was reading over the notice again while Matthew sat writing. She was hoping there would be some money for them when the will was found; their engagement was at an end, and they were living on their scanty savings till they could fix up another, which, so far, had not materialized. Not that Marion allowed herself to worry too much; her vagrant life had not only ripened Marion early, but made her quick and clever at thinking out ways and means of bringing grist to the mill. She had no pride of position left—all that was long gone to the winds. She had been what they would have called at home "an adventuress," making money out of fortune-telling and cards, singing for money in *cafés* and in the street, making pence in all sorts of queer ways in vulgar, garish shows in which the people at home would never have set a foot. She had loaded rifles for firing at bottles and taken pennies on a switch-back railway. She laughed sometimes, thinking of their horror if any of them had seen her in their worst months, before they had thought of singing together, but she was proud that they had held out and never begged for help from home.

"Granny was always hiding things," she said to Matthew. "You know that time——"

She stopped dead; her eyes widened in sudden thought. She put out her hand and caught Matthew's arm, causing his pen to splutter.

"Matthew!"

He put his hand over hers and turned to her smiling.

"What is it, Feather-top? You've spoiled my good paper, and I haven't much left."

He had special paper, on which he could write quite well.

"Matthew!" she repeated excitedly. "I never thought of it—the box!"

"What box, darling?"

"Granny's box—the one she gave me with all the money on the top. There were papers under the tray. I never looked at them, but they were there—thick papers. I felt among them to get all the money."

He had put down his pen now and turned round to her.

"Are you sure, Marion?"

"Of course I'm sure. There were papers there. They seemed to be what you call parchment, like deeds or something." Marion's ideas on 'parchment' and 'deeds' were somewhat vague. "Oh, Matthew, perhaps the will was among them."

Matthew didn't look too jubilant.

"Perhaps . . ." he said. "Still—I hope not, Marion."

"Why?"

He paused a considerable time before replying, then, "Greed!" he said. "Sheer greed—only it's for your sake mostly. I hoped that she had made it *after* I was blinded—you

U

see, she might have thought, 'Poor devil, I'd better leave him
something to keep him alive, now he's a broken pot, thrown
out on the scrap-heap, with a woman keeping him.'"

The bitterness in his voice was terrible to her, revealing so
much they usually kept hidden: his hatred of his dependence
upon her, of the work she had to do, of her exposure to a
world from which he should have protected her, of her
working for him, of her looking after *him*—while he should
have worked for and protected her. His whole wounded,
masculine soul, the pride of his manhood, revolted against
it with such bitterness that his voice sounded rough, angry,
and hard.

But Marion had been through times like this before. She
knew it was best not to give way. She would have liked to
throw herself into his arms and weep and be comforted, but
that was for other women, not for her. She must be the strong
one always—however tired, however despairing; for Matthew
was blind.

"A scrap-heap! Is that what you call me?" she demanded.
She ruffled up his hair. "Oh, Grandmother, what a large, huge
hump of unappreciativeness"—she stumbled over the long
word—"you've got. I will not be called a scrap-heap. Anyhow, you're digressing, and you don't know what may be
in the will. Granny told me she loved you best. She did. . . .
But what about that box? Put on your thinking-cap, instead
of growling like an old hairy bear, and tell me what we're
to do."

"You know I didn't call you a scrap-heap." He took hold of
her hand and rubbed it over a large bump he had got the day
before venturing into the low coal-cellar when she was out.
"That's come up since yesterday; it's more love for Marion.
There was so much in my heart already there was no room for
any more, so it came out in a bump on my head. Where is
the box?"

"Goose! . . . I don't know. I mean, it's in my trunk, the
one I left at Goslaw with clothes and things. I suppose Naomi

would sent it home——" An awful thought struck her. "She wouldn't *keep* it, would she?"

"Lord knows! Did they know about it at home—did Hagar know?"

"Of course she did. Hagar and Penny together helped me to pack."

"Then it will be all right, you bet." He laughed, remembering her descriptions of Hagar's efficiency. Doubtless she would have run down and unearthed Marion's trunk like a dog on the scent of a hare.

"It will be at the Falcon's House." He picked up his pen again. "Now you be quiet till I get this letter written. I'll tell them—no, you write to Hagar or Rachel about the trunk. That will be better—and it will keep you quiet."

In a few minutes they were both scratching away with their pens.

But when Marion's letter arrived at the Falcon's House it got at first but scanty attention, for another and much more reverberating bomb had fallen from another letter.

"It never rains but it pours," said Penny later, referring to "events that seemed to be falling over each other's heels," as she put it, thereby giving Mr Peregrine a task of sorting out metaphors that was almost beyond him.

The letter was from Paul and had "Urgent" on it, which wasn't much good, as there was no air mail in those days, and even Penny would hardly have expected the Union Castle liner to plough at full speed, snorting like a porpoise, through the waves because of that tiny "Urgent" on the corner of an envelope. So it arrived in due course, a month after it was written, and anything might have happened in the meantime.

I'm writing this at once [he said] and getting a runner to take it to Salisbury to get it off as quickly as possible. In fact, I thought of cabling, only I haven't the money, and it would take so much explaining. That man I told you about who knew Naomi Cuendet says she isn't Naomi Cuendet at all. That's her maiden name, and she is married to a man called Regnard who's

still alive and in South Africa, but he thinks she may have
thought he was dead, because he left her and went off and disappeared. He says he wrote and told Regnard about her being
married to a man with lots of money, after he had squeezed all he
could out of me. I didn't say Matthew had a lot of money, but
I did say the Wotherspoons were wealthy, he kept asking me so
many questions. I don't know what he's doing all this for. I
don't know him very well, and I just thought he was interested
in Naomi because they were brought up in the same village. I
told him about Matthew's being blind, and he said he was sorry
for the poor chap because Naomi was a "bad 'un," but I wouldn't
be surprised if he thinks there's money in it for himself. Anyhow,
he's gone off, but he said he was "seeing about things."

I think it is right enough. He said he was at the wedding, and
can tell us the *mairie* or something where it was and where there
will be papers.

I don't know what to do about it, but I'll send you his address
as soon as I get it. It's no use writing to him here now, as he has
gone off. I think he'll be wanting money; he's hard up, and perhaps wants to keep me out of it now he's got all he can out of me
—silly bounder! As if I'd want money for helping our Marion!
But I can do so little away here in what you'd call the backwoods,
but I expect you'll be hearing from him. He wouldn't give me
any addresses, but he said it would be all right, so that's why I
think he wants to get money. He knows I haven't any, so
wouldn't give anything away to me.

He went on with some more details, but that was the gist of
his letter.

At first they all sat speechless as Rachel read out her letter.
It was such a tremendous surprise and shock that at first it
seemed as if they had nothing to say. And then it took some
moments to readjust themselves to the news and all it meant.
It was Penny who spoke first. Penny was down to breakfast
for the first time, sitting propped up with cushions beside her
father.

"Then," she gasped, staring joyfully round the table,
"Marion is really married!"

There was a pause, and then Mr Peregrine said:

"Not yet, Penny, but if it is true she and Matthew can be married at once."

If it were true! Hagar and Rachel drew in deep breaths—if only it were true. If only they could know at once!

"Oh, thank God! Thank God!" said Rachel softly, the tears running suddenly down her cheeks. "Oh, I will thank God all my life, every day, if only it is true. Oh, poor Marion! Poor Marion! What are we to do? How are we to let her know? She must know at once. I can't wait till we hear from them."

Mr Peregrine had not looked at his own letters, which lay in a bunch by the side of his plate.

"We mustn't tell her till we know," said Hagar quickly. "It would be so terrible to raise her hopes and it not be true after all."

"It is true! It is true!" announced Penny desperately. Penny's arguments were always asseverations, so to speak. She always seemed to believe that if you asserted anything quickly and desperately enough it must be true. "It must! It must!" she added quickly.

"Oh," said Rachel joyfully, as if she must repeat it over and over again. "Marion can be married. Dear, darling, lovely Marion can be married. She can come home, and we can all love her and make it up to her for all the misery—oh, I wish I could fly away this minute and put my arms round her and tell her. Oh, why don't we know where she is? What shall we do? What shall we do?"

"I think I shall go over at once to Bowchester," said Mr Peregrine, rising.

Hagar had been thinking hard, her heart like to burst with happiness for Marion, but terrified lest they were building too much on Paul's letter. Yet Paul was so sane, so sensible. Paul wouldn't have raised their hopes if he had felt there was any doubt. Dear Paul, so slow and sure! Gradually her confidence in Paul was ousting her doubts, and—if it were only true! A wave of joy swept through her, her cheeks went scarlet with excitement—Marion's banishment was over. Dear, lovable Marion. It would be all right for her at last. Hagar had known better than anyone what Marion must have suffered, Marion the home-loving, the accepter of things as they were. She was not like Rachel, who would have fought with anger, with her head in the air, with defiance. Marion had made no revolt against marriage; to her marriage was right, and, though a great love had made her defy convention and put herself wrong in the eyes of the world, she had kept her integrity. But Marion had been shamed, and had accepted shame as her portion.

"No," Hagar went on. "Let's talk it over together first before you go to Bowchester, Mr Peregrine. We haven't really grasped it yet, or thought of what we should do. For one thing, I think we should cable at once to Paul. He may know more by now. He may have written again, but letters are so slow. If he has the address of the *mairie*—I think he means the mayor's office; isn't that where people are married in France?— or the address of that man, he could cable them. We can't do anything until we find out if it is true."

"We must tell Marion," said Rachel. "I can't bear to think of our knowing and not telling her at once—even if it's just a hope."

Mr Peregrine was standing at the breakfast table, still considering, his shoulders hunched almost to his ears, idly turning the other unopened letters over in his hand, but hardly glancing at them.

Suddenly he dropped the bundle, which scattered on the table and the floor, all except one, which he held up to his eyes.

"Surely," he said, "surely that's Marion's writing!"

Rachel flew to him and grasped it.

"It is! It is!" she cried. "Open it, Daddy!" She had not called him "Daddy" for years, but excitement had overcome her. "Open it—quick, quick!"

She had seized a knife from the table. He took it, but his

hands were shaking so much he suddenly sat down and handed
it to her. "You read it, Rachel," he said. "I—I . . ." He
slumped down on his chair, and Hagar, seeing how white he
was, ran off for the brandy.

"He hides his feelings too much under all that play-acting,"
she thought to herself. "He must have been grieving terribly
about Marion, and sometimes—God forgive me—I've almost
thought he was a little indifferent. It's just a façade he puts
up to hide his sensitiveness."

She was over to him in a minute with the glass of brandy,
but his hands were shaking so much she had to put her arm
round him and guide it to his mouth. As she did so she
realized that she really loved this queer, strange, elderly man,
for he seemed old to her, though he could not be more than
in his fifties—loved him in something of the way she had loved
her father, but with it was now born a protecting tenderness
the stern old Yorkshireman had never called forth.

"Drink that," she said, and, seeing some of it had run over
his chin, she took his handkerchief and wiped his face, holding
him with her strong young arm and laughing gently. "Oh,
Daddy Peregrine!" she exclaimed involuntarily. "Wasting
that good brandy!" And "Daddy Peregrine" he became from
that minute.

Gone was the slight awe with which she had always regarded
him, faded the puzzlement and the sense of something guarded
and almost alien between them. From that moment she loved
and bullied him in something of the same way as she was to
love and bully Mark, if a sparrow can be said to bully a brown,
good-natured bear.

By the time he had recovered Rachel had read Marion's
letter, which was mostly about the box, but which to Rachel
contained only one item of importance—her address. She
made up her mind to go to them at once.

Within an hour she was dressed and ready for the road,
a copy of the letter in her pocket. There had been some
argument, because her father wanted to take it with him to

Bowchester, so Hagar had settled it by sitting down and making a copy.

"What's all this about a box?" she said to Rachel, handing it to her. "A box, and Granny's will?"

"Oh, yes," said Rachel, "a box—I don't know about any box. Will Naomi have it?"

"Don't you remember we brought a trunk home and hadn't a key and just left it, thinking Marion would soon be home? She says it's in it, but she doesn't say anything about the key."

"Oh, well, I'll ask her about it, but I expect it's all nonsense. Granny would never give Marion a box with her will in it. It doesn't make sense. People are awfully careful about wills. I expect it's some old letters or riff-raff. Granny was always hoarding trumpery, and expecting us to be interested in things that happened before the Flood."

And with this dictum she went off. But Hagar went up to Marion's room, got out the small trunk, and had a look at it. It was there all right anyhow, and if Marion had put the box in it the box was also there—unless . . . But Naomi had never had the key!

When Mr Peregrine arrived at Bowchester he was taken up to Mrs Wotherspoon's bedroom. That redoubtable woman was up and on a sofa, having insisted on being dressed by the cook, an elderly woman like herself, and then lifted to the sofa by her sons.

What was the use of sons, she had asked, if they couldn't lift their mother about? Hadn't she lifted them about when she was young and they couldn't use their legs? Very well.

On the sofa she was, in a bright purple dressing-gown and an old mangy fur cape.

"How are you, Martha?" asked Mr Peregrine.

"Very well, James, considering. What's brought you over here in the middle of the week? How did you manage to leave the shop?"

"Anthony Truett can manage the shop. In fact, I sometimes think he can manage it better than I can."

"Stuff and nonsense. You're the business head of Peregrine and Turtleton's, and well you know it. Anthony Truett's well enough, but he lacks grit. What about him and Penny, James?"

"We'll see, we'll see," said James, not committing himself. "Penny's still a child, and the doctor says she'll never be strong."

"Well, it oughtn't to be a bad match later on, but there's plenty of time. I hope there's nothing wrong. Did you come over about Mark's marriage? I'd like to be on my feet before the wedding, but I suppose they'll be wanting to get settled."

"No, I didn't come over about the wedding. We all hope you'll be able to be there. No, it's something—I was going to say more important, and to tell the truth that's how I feel about it. It's about Marion. Rachel had a very strange letter this morning."

He then proceeded to tell her all about Paul's previous letter, and then read out the one they had received that morning.

Mrs Wotherspoon sat and listened, nodding her head and saying nothing until he had finished.

"Aye," she said then, and sat silent for a few minutes. "To tell the truth, James," she said, "I know something about this."

"You?" He was amazed. "You know about it?"

"I know a little. Here's my keys. Open the top little drawer in the left side of my wardrobe, and bring me some letters you'll find there."

Mr Peregrine did as he was bid, and then she told him her story.

It appeared that some weeks ago she had had a letter from a Mr Jourdain, a Frenchman, who had said he had some information of great interest to her, but that he was a very poor man, and naturally, etc., etc., all boiling down to the point that he needed a great deal of money. He was a married man, with a delicate wife and large family, and also delicate himself, and in his struggles he had got badly into debt. He understood that Mrs Wotherspoon was a wealthy lady, and, as no one but himself knew the facts about a Naomi Cuendet, she might be willing to enter into negotiations with him, in strict privacy and secrecy—otherwise he would simply disappear.

There was more than one letter, and the last were from France. Mrs Wotherspoon had said nothing. She had thought at first she was simply being gulled, but his last letters had gone so far that she had bluntly asked how much he wanted. The sum was so large that she had gasped. Still, she had been prepared to buy Naomi off and undertake all the expense of a divorce. She saw that in either case she would need a lot of money, for she had no way of forcing this Frenchman to divulge what he knew. That was why she had sold the wood —or, at least, entered into negotiations about it; it wasn't actually sold yet.

"But surely you've plenty of money, Martha?"

"Not as much as you may think, James. I have money, no doubt, if I could realize it, but it's mostly in the farm, and times have been bad. I have large sums laid out that I can't call in just now. You know yourself your business may be big, but ready money hard to come by—and now there's all this trouble over Mother's will."

"Well, we must put our heads together and do something," said Mr Peregrine. "The old folks must save the young."

For the rest of the forenoon they put their heads together.

CHAPTER VIII

"THERE IN THEIR OWN DEAR LAND"

THINGS happen so quickly," said Penny, one morning later. "I have to run to keep up with them."

Things indeed had happened quickly. Mother Wotherspoon and Mr Peregrine together had settled with Monsieur Jourdain and got all the information they needed. Mr Peregrine had been a little dubious at first about his demanding more later on, but, as Mrs Wotherspoon quickly pointed out, there was nothing to hide on their part that he could demand more money for. All they wanted was certain information and proofs. Monsieur Jourdain turned out not such a bad soul after all. He met them as to price, and did all that was necessary in France, putting them in touch with the mayor of the little town where the marriage had taken place, and helping about copies of documents and so forth. They even got Mallie, who was still in France, to go and see him. For both the old people were determined to have no mistakes this time.

Naomi took it all with a sort of hard common sense after the first passionate denial and furious outbreak, and when she saw there was nothing to be gained by fury and obstinacy. She said she thought her husband was dead, and produced a letter in support of her statement telling her he had died in South Africa. On hearing from M. Jourdain that he was not only alive, but doing well, she coolly asked Mrs Wotherspoon to pay her fare out there and give her a hundred pounds to help her till she found her husband, which Mrs Wotherspoon promptly did, glad to see the last of her. In fact, she gave her more, but kept that to herself, and Anthony, the ever-useful Anthony, went to Southampton and saw her off in the liner, partly to make sure that she had gone, and partly because they were all rather sorry for her now, as Mark said, "her teeth were drawn."

Marion and Matthew were quietly married by special licence, and were coming home that day, bringing the keys of the trunk. For Marion had remembered her promise to Granny about secrecy, and she and Matthew both thought that Marion should open the box and look over everything in it herself first, before letting anyone else into Granny's secrets, whatever they might be.

They were coming to the Falcon's House in the meantime to stay there till something was arranged for them. Marion was longing to come home, and they were all eager to have her with them again.

Mark and Hagar were to be married just before Christmas, and excursions were made over to Goslaw every few days to light fires and keep everything aired and in order.

Perry had come home from Cambridge, where he had gone to take a course in engineering and get his B.Sc., for when it came to actual flying Mr Peregrine and all of them wanted to put it off as long as possible. It seemed he had now made up his mind to join the Army and go into a flying corps. However, that was still in the future, and they were all happy at the prospect of a Christmas together.

It was to be spent at the Falcon's House, and everybody was to be there, Mother Wotherspoon with Matthew, Mark, Luke, and John, Anthony Truett, Marion, Rachel, Perry and Penny and Hagar, and last—Mallie. Mallie was coming back from France, where she had helped them about Naomi's marriage, to spend her Christmas holidays at the Falcon's House, and Penny had been promised that, if the day were fine, she would go in the cab to meet her beloved Mallie, whom she was dying to see.

Hagar had been, and was still, so busy getting forward the Christmas preparations that she had very little time to think of her wedding—except in bed at night, and then she was so tired she usually fell asleep just as she was going to indulge in her own dreams of happiness.

Now everything was ready to receive Marion and Matthew. Mr Peregrine, leaving Anthony in charge, had gone to the station with Perry and Rachel, while Hagar and Beenie finished setting the table and kept the kettles boiling, and Penny, in the arm-chair with Mrs Brown on her knee and Robbie and Samuel at her feet, toasted and buttered the tea-cakes, of which they needed a large supply, for Mark and Luke were to be there too, while John kept his mother company at home. Mrs Wotherspoon had made a remarkable recovery, and could now get about a little with the aid of crutches, which she loathed, but was at the same time glad to make use of. She was coming to the wedding. A wheeled chair would be used for her in the church.

When the time drew near to expect them Penny stationed herself at the drawing-room window to watch and give the signal for the doors to be opened and the tea to be "mashed," as Beenie called it.

But at her wild shriek of "Here they are!" Beenie left her teapots and flew with Hagar to the door to welcome her long-lost darling.

A scene of laughter and tears followed, Marion being handed from arm to arm to be kissed and hugged, laughed over and cried over, while she laughed and cried herself and strained them to her as if she could never let them go.

They had all been a little shy and even frightened about Matthew, so afraid they would do or say the wrong thing, and were expecting a tragic figure in whose presence they would, so to speak, have to walk softly all their days, but Matthew was a revelation to them. Marion's swift understanding of how to treat Matthew in his blindness had borne fruit. She had absolutely refused to regard him as some tragic figure who had to be treated as a sort of child and any reference to his blindness to be forbidden, as though it were something to be ashamed of or too delicate a matter to mention. He was so used to Marion's frankness about it that he was quite as frank himself, and so inordinately happy to be married to her with everything open and above board that he was just the simple, gay Matthew they had always known. He was used to his blindness now, but on their way through Newcastle they had called to see the famous oculist who had treated him, and he had given him hope that the one eye was gradually recovering and that he might see fairly well with it one day, though at present he could do little more than recognize daylight from darkness—so that made him happy too.

He hugged everybody and kissed everybody, and made them all laugh by hugging and giving Mr Peregrine a resounding

kiss and then saying that, being blind, he took him for
Beenie. Beenie roared with joy at this joke, and ran and
hugged Matthew herself, declaring he was only pretending to
be blind and could see as well as any of them, at which he
actually winked at her and asked her not to give him away.
The only way, he declared, that he could keep Marion under
his thumb was to keep up the pretence. And, indeed, like all
blind people, he was so clever at getting about and "doing
for himself," as Beenie put it, they could hardly believe sometimes that he was blind. He talked about seeing as naturally
as they did, so they soon stopped beginning sentences like "Oh,
Matthew, you should see——" and then stopping confused.

"Well, tell me what it's like, and I'll see it," he would say,
and they got into Marion's way of describing everything to
him quickly and simply, and even copied her "Oh, dash, I
forgot you were blind and couldn't see it."

Matthew had ripened under his blindness too, and now
instead of resenting people's attitude he had learned to sympathize with it. He understood that it made them awkward
through sheer nervousness and pity and the fear of hurting
him through drawing attention to it, so instead of bitterly
resenting it he tried to help them—thought, in fact, less of
himself and more of them, and the result was an easing of the
tension and more freedom and happiness all round.

Mr Peregrine, with his queer instinctive cleverness, had no
need of any hints. He never seemed to remember that Matthew
was blind, but never a hint of awkwardness revealed itself
when he was there. He seemed so quick to know just where
Matthew needed a little help and where he could manage for
himself, and his help was so unobtrusive it was never noticed.

But perhaps an even greater surprise was Marion. She had
left them a raw, innocent, pretty, slightly stupid (it seemed in
comparison with Rachel's quickness) girl; she was now a
plump little poised woman of the world with a delightful
out-of-the-way humour of her own and a self-assurance and
air of experience that made Rachel herself feel raw and girlish

beside her. She was quick at repartee, and seemed to know so much—as indeed she did—that Hagar laughingly summed up her impressions by saying, "Marion could dine with the Queen, the Prime Minister, and the Shah of Persia without turning a hair."

On her side, Marion saw changes too. Hagar looked years younger, and so pretty and happy she hardly recognized the pale, determined, scarred little face that had appeared out of the snow almost two years before.

Rachel had lost her air of brooding, and, though her tongue was still sharp, it was less acrid and could be witty at her own expense as well as that of others.

Perry had shot up into a slender, red-headed youth, but had changed least of all. He was still the dreamy boy, thinking of aeroplanes and coming out with extraordinary items of information, if not on *Helix pomatia* and the results of mating black rabbits with white down to the fifth and sixth generation, on equally abstruse theories about, as Penny innocently remarked, "the mating of engines and their insides." Off Penny Marion could not keep her eyes. To the others, who had seen Penny as she came home, she looked almost her old self again, except that she was thin and, of course, delicate-looking; but to Marion it was a wraith of the small, sturdy Penny she had known who sat propped up with cushions beside her father.

"Penny looks exactly like my childish idea of an angel," she thought, half smiling at herself for the sentimentality of the notion, "so ethereal, so light, so terribly frail." And suddenly she remembered Anthony saying he would be there for Penny till the wind blew her away from him, and she had to force back the two hot tears that were welling in her eyes as she prayed, "Oh, don't let the wind blow Penny away—don't let the wind blow darling, dear little Penny away."

But, except for this momentary pain in Marion's heart, it was a gay tea-party that gathered round the huge mahogany table, into which two or three leaves had been added to make it big enough. Mr Peregrine was in his element as he sat at the top, thoroughly enjoying being the head of such a fine and handsome family. There was no doubt about it, his own girls were pretty, and Perry, though so slender still, would broaden out into a good-looking youth, with his long, aristocratic face and tumbled hair, and Hagar was growing prettier every day—happiness had wonderfully improved Hagar's looks. "The puss!" he thought. "She's beginning to rule me, but I like it. I could have done quite well with an eldest daughter like that. . . . Well! Well! She *is* my eldest daughter. I've adopted her as such."

The Wotherspoon men were all good-looking in their gaunt, hardy way, and Anthony—who had run over for tea—was so intensely aristocratic with his slenderness, his slight sideboards, and his haughty nose that he made a striking contrast to their rougher, harder strength.

"A table to be proud of," Mr Peregrine said to himself, and he was proud, and his small, clever eyes blinked more than ever, as he shot out his sudden, cryptic remarks, and hospitably saw that their plates were piled and their cups filled with the good, creamy tea he loved.

After tea the house had to be gone over and the large room admired which Penny had once told Hagar was waiting for its ghost. The Nottingham curtains and the chilly aspect were gone. Hagar and Rachel had been as busy as bees, and now with its sunny yellow walls and crocus-purple curtains drawn right across the windows, its poster bed and gleaming furniture, the fire roaring in the old-fashioned round grate, no one would have recognized the cold, grey room Hagar had peeped into.

"We gave it to you and Matthew," Rachel explained, "because it is the biggest room, and your own is so small. But we changed it completely—you do like it, don't you?" She drew the curtains so that they could see the moonlit garden.

"Oh, I love it," said Marion. "I can see the garden, Matthew, and the apple-tree. . . ." She described all she could see quickly.

"That's how to do it," thought Rachel, and immediately chimed in, "And we papered the walls yellow, and the curtains are purple, and the old nursery screen is enamelled yellow and put by the fire—here it is!"

She took his hand and went round the room with him, while Marion looked on, her heart full. They were all so kind —so kind. . . .

The trunk was standing in a corner, but they left it till after supper to continue the round of the house, gaily racing up and down the stairs, banging the doors, teasing Jane the parrot, who was sulking because she hadn't been taken into the dining-room for tea, and lastly raiding the kitchen, where Beenie was baking a Yorkshire ham, covered with paste, and preparing roast chickens for supper, which was really to be a dinner, because Marion had always adored roast chickens stuffed with a special Yorkshire stuffing.

It was not till late that the trunk was brought down to the drawing-room by Matthew, who ran up the stairs as if he could see as well as any of them, but, of course, he knew every inch of the house, having played "dark hide-and-seek," when every light was put out, hundreds of times in their childhood.

Marion exclaimed over her almost forgotten dresses and undies as they came into view, and then they took out the small steel deed-box, and Rachel and Hagar slipped away to help with the dinner, leaving Matthew and Marion to examine its contents alone. Penny was already in bed, propped up with cushions, her books and the lamp on the table at her side, and the door open so that they could run out and in, and she could hear all that was going on. Mr Peregrine and Anthony were back at the shop, for they were terrifically busy with Christmas close at hand, and Mark had gone with them to give a hand with some packing.

They were all going over to Bowchester the next day, which was a Sunday, Matthew and Marion immediately after breakfast, and the rest later on.

Marion took her key and opened the box, with Matthew

x

sitting beside her smoking and gazing dreamily into the fire, his long legs stretched out, Samuel at his feet and Mrs Brown on his knee.

Robbie Burns was not there; he was ensconced on Penny's bed, his nose on his paws, his bright eyes watching her every movement. Since her return Robbie was more than ever Penny's dog. He put up with Samuel in the rest of the house, but there was a battle royal with fur and hair flying if Samuel as much as put his nose in Penny's room, ending, unless separated quickly, in both of them rolling in a black and white ball of fury down the stairs. The hare had grown up and been let loose in the meadow where Anthony found him. Penny would never put a wild animal in a cage or even a run like the guinea-pig's.

The tray on the top of the deed-box was empty, and Marion lifted it up and put it on the table. Beneath it were several papers tied round with pink tape. She lifted them out one by one and looked at them, but they were all legal-looking documents that she could not understand at a glance and was not very interested in. As she lifted the last she read its inscription out to Matthew:

"Last Will and Testament of Marion Waugh."

"Of course, you were called after her, I remember," said Matthew. "They said it was because your own mother was partly brought up by Granny."

"I suppose that's why the Peregrines and Wotherspoons have always been so closely connected," said Marion. "My mother and your mother must have played together like we did. Do you think I should read the will?"

"I think she must have meant you to—do you remember what she said?"

"Yes, but it was all about the money for me. She never mentioned the will. Do you think she can have put it there and forgotten about it? She was always hiding things."

"Very likely—she was getting old. I'll tell you what. I

know where old Davis the lawyer lives. I'll go over and ask him. Mike and I could do with a stretch anyhow."

"Take the box." She wrapped it up in a piece of brown paper and looked at the clock. "We are not having supper till nine, when Father comes in. Anthony's coming too. You'll still have plenty of time, and I'll go and help Hagar and Rachel."

He went off, and Marion danced down into the kitchen and flung her arms round Rachel.

"Oh, it's so lovely to be home! Matthew and I must get a little cottage near Breckan where we can keep one sheep to please him. Isn't it queer to like sheep?" She gave a sigh. "But how we're going to live I don't know! I've found Granny's will, but it won't make any difference to us, as it was made before he became blind, and Matthew and I got our fair share, but I do hope"—she turned to Hagar—"that Mark gets some, Hagar, to help him at Goslaw. Oh, how I loved Goslaw! There's no place in the world like Goslaw. You'll love it, Hagar," and she was plunging into descriptions of the hills and the burns when Rachel said:

"Didn't you read the will?"

"No, I didn't like to. You see, I think when Granny gave me the box she just remembered the bundles of notes on the top tray and forgot all about the papers underneath. Matthew has taken them over to Mr Davis, so we'll soon hear about it, but I think they ought to know first at Bowchester, seeing Granny was *their* granny—don't you?"

"I suppose so," said Rachel, "but I'm dying to know what's in it. I don't think it's fair for Luke and John to get so much."

"Oh, well," said Hagar, "it was the old lady's money, and she could do what she liked with it. Come on, Marion, and make the bread sauce; you were talking about learning French cookery when you were in France, so you can just prove it wasn't sheer, uppish boasting."

"Besides," said Rachel, "when we've killed the fatted

chickens for her she can jolly well help in their preparation. Oh, Marion, it's so nice to see you in an *apron* again! I'm glad we found that one in your case."

And chattering like magpies and shouting news of the progress of the dinner up to Penny, they filled the kitchen with mirth and love and glee.

CHAPTER IX

"O HAPPY EYES"

WHEN they all arrived at Bowchester next day it was to find that Mr Davis was there too. He had come over to lunch, and was to read the will when they were all gathered together.

Marion and Matthew had driven over early. Luke had come over for them in the dogcart, and Anthony, as in the old days, was driving the rest over in the big wagonette hired from the Red Lion. He had suggested staying at home and Perry driving, but no one would hear of it. "Where we go Anthony goes," was the order of the day, and any suggestion of his being *de trop* in family conferences immediately quashed.

"You're going to be one of the family when you marry me," said Penny, and that settled the matter.

When the family was called into the drawing-room to listen to the will Hagar and Anthony were both for staying where they were, but Mrs Wotherspoon insisted on their joining the rest.

Hagar was going to be married to Mark in a few days, and "as for Anthony," she said, if he saw how he was going to escape from Penny's clutches it was more than she did, so he might as well be there too.

Mrs Wotherspoon had a great regard for Anthony in one way. She could never forget that his father had been 'county' and the master of the local hunt, and that he was socially far above them, though he was so quiet and apparently content to be an assistant in a bookshop, and now that Mark was marrying Hagar she thought it would be quite a good thing for Anthony to wait for Penny and come in for the business. Of course, there was Rachel, but Luke and John were both taken up with other nice girls, even if Rachel had ever cast an eye over them, which she most decidedly had not, while they would just have laughed at the idea of any sentiment between them and "old Rachel," as they called her, being a few months younger, but she had always taken advantage of these few months and slapped and kept the twins in order in their younger days.

Mr Davis was stout and fussy, and made a little speech before reading the will; then took his spectacles out of their old leather case, cleaned them on his silk handkerchief, and began.

To say they were all amazed at the contents hardly expresses their thunderstruck surprise; for Granny had completely turned the tables on them. The bulk of her money was equally divided between Mark and Matthew, the two elder sons, while Luke and John got a bare thousand pounds each.

Matthew's money was tied up in such intricate ways by the wily old lady that Naomi could have benefited very little by it—in fact, it looked as if the old woman had banked on a separation or divorce, or had known more than she ever divulged. As Matthew, however, had never been legally married to Naomi all these clauses were so much wastepaper and the money was his with no restrictions whatever, and his share was as much as they had guessed she had altogether.

Rachel and Penny and Perry were all remembered, and the lawyer had discovered that in the box were other papers making over shares to Marion which would have brought her in quite a nice little income after she and Matthew went away together if she had ever looked at them, but by then Granny herself had been too old and worn out to bother or make inquiries. In fact, if the will had been dated later it might have been contested on the grounds that she was not mentally in a condition to make a will, so she had been far-seeing there too. Not that any of them would have wished to do any such thing as contest the will. After the first shock of surprise they all admitted that it was absolutely fair. Mother Wotherspoon had enough, as Granny mentioned, to divide between her two younger sons.

The surprise was that Granny, who had despised Matthew for marrying Naomi and hated Naomi, and to all seeming had been bitterly angry with and opposed to Mark's ideas and all in sympathy with the twins and their mother, had yet divided her money between the two with whom she had quarrelled.

"She told me she'd never leave me a penny after I married Naomi," said Matthew.

"She told me the same thing," said Mark, "when I refused to knuckle under to her."

The old humorist, they agreed, had taken them all in, and no doubt enjoyed many a chuckle at their expense.

She had left various small sums, pieces of property and one thing and another, to other friends and relatives. Mother Wotherspoon got the little Brae House and all its contents, the old family silver, china, portraits, and suchlike, which were to be divided at her death among her four sons. There were a great many valuable antiques among them. Even Hagar was remembered with a hundred pounds "for being kind to an old woman" and a little sewing-table in mahogany that she had often admired.

They all had a rather quiet tea together, for the lawyer was invited to share the meal before he left, and then they all drew up their chairs round the drawing-room fire and amicably discussed the pros and cons of the new state of affairs.

Luke and John congratulated their brothers and said they were "jolly glad," as they had been wondering about Matthew and what to do for him, and now he could do as he pleased, for he had plenty of money, and the same with Mark. It appeared they saw immense possibilities in High Seaton, which was near a big industrial district and was perfect land for potatoes, with acres of new hen-houses for intensive egg production just put up by the owner before he was killed in an accident.

Bowchester, it seemed, had been something of a white elephant to them, as they could neither get rid of it nor run it without a great deal of money, and then there had been Mark's opposition to all their bright new ideas and modern ways. High Seaton was still on the market, and before many minutes had passed Luke and John were deep in discussions of what they could do there. Like Bowchester, it had been originally two farms, and there were two farmhouses if they wanted to marry, but in the meantime they immediately proposed that Mother Wotherspoon should take her money out of Bowchester, which Mark would now be able to run, buy High Seaton, and go there with them, leaving Bowchester to Mark and Hagar.

No sooner was this agreed on than Matthew turned to Mark.

"You won't want Goslaw then, Mark. I'd like to go back to Goslaw better than anywhere in the world. I know it and could find my way blindfold—or blind," he corrected himself smilingly, "from end to end. With a good shepherd and Tyne and Tweed I could manage the sheep—and Marion loves it too, don't you, Marion?"

"I adore it," said Marion. "It would seem too good to be true, but—there's Hagar. She's just made the house into a lovely home for herself and Mark."

Hagar turned—she was sitting next Marion—and quickly took hold of her hand.

"Oh, Marion, I'd just love you to have it—to walk into it as it is. Surely we can arrange that?" She turned to Mark and Matthew. "Couldn't we? We'll go over and see it to-morrow. I'm sure Marion will just love it—if it's not too small."

She suddenly felt as if she were selfish, accepting with such a rush of joy the thought of Bowchester for Mark and herself, while the house at Goslaw seemed so small in comparison for Marion. Still, they had as much money as she and Mark, though Mark, being the eldest son, had Bowchester as well. Marion and Matthew could do as they wished—in fact, they would have more 'spare' money, as Bowchester would need a great deal of stocking.

"Too small? What an idea!" said Marion. "Why, Matthew and I will think it's a palace after living in one room and washing up and cooking at a gas-stove and sink on the stairhead. Oh, I simply can't bring myself to believe we'll go and live at Goslaw!" And the tears ran down her cheeks while she laughingly dried them up, saying, "I'm not crying! I'm not crying! I'm laughing with joy! If it can possibly be. . . ."

"Nothing to hinder it," said Mother Wotherspoon, "but we can't arrange everything in a night. There's lots to think over and go into."

But in spite of her words they all talked and talked, talked till supper-time and through supper and far into the night. Penny was staying all night and was at last persuaded to go to bed, though she was as keen and excited as anybody and wanted to hear every word that was said.

However, after Rachel and Hagar and Marion had all promised to tell her every word of what passed she was finally persuaded to go to bed, and Anthony carried her upstairs, with Luke and John following with their arms full of cushions, and Rachel and Hagar to help her undress and tuck her up.

By the time they piled into the wagonette a great deal had been provisionally decided.

Marion and Matthew were to go over and see Goslaw and all the improvements the next day, and then to move in as soon as they liked, as Hagar said it wouldn't be nearly as nice for Marion if some one had lived in her new home first.

After their wedding Mark and she were to have a few weeks' honeymoon—they had been going to go straight to Goslaw— and in the meantime Mother Wotherspoon and Luke and John would settle about High Seaton and start to move in. The big farmhouse there was empty and in first-rate repair. There was plenty of furniture at Bowchester, which was a big, rambling old place, filled with the collections of over a hundred years, to leave a room or two furnished for Mark and Hagar till they could look round and buy more of their own and gradually refurnish the house.

It was a happy party that crowded into the old wagonette, and as happy a one that stood crowded on the doorstep waving them good-bye.

As they drove away Matthew suddenly began to sing softly,

"O happy eyes, for you shall see . . ."

Soon they had all joined in:

"O happy, happy eyes,"

and so they went singing home as they had so often sung before. . . .

"Ho! Miss Mouse, will you marry me,
And sit for ever on my knee?"

heard Beenie, as she turned over in bed to the sound of the gay lilt as the wagonette drove up in the moonlight.

"Nothing will daunton that lot," she said to herself. "Ye may smash them to bits, but the Lord aye sticks them together again."

CHAPTER X

"THE PIPER IN THE WIND GOES BY"

CHRISTMAS was spent at the Falcon's House.

Mark and Hagar were married, and had returned from the first part of their honeymoon to join in the festivities. Mallie had arrived and been at once adopted into the household, as she had no home of her own, and the Falcon's House always seemed ready to take another—in spite of Mr Peregrine's war against mixed metaphors—into its hospitable arms.

Of course, she would follow her career, but now she had

somewhere to call 'home' and to spend all her holidays, for they all took to Mallie at once, besides being grateful to her for all she had done for Penny.

All the Wotherspoons were there in high spirits and, needless to say, Anthony, who was introduced to Mallie by Penny as her future husband, "only it's a family secret."

Matthew and Marion came over from Goslaw, where they were already settled in, being too excited and enchanted with their "dream come true" to wait, and having also the excuse that, what with the wedding and visitors for Christmas, the Falcon's House was just about crowded out.

It was at any rate full to overflowing on Christmas Eve, when they burned the Yule log and told hair-raising ghost stories, which made them so hungry Luke and John fried bacon and eggs at two o'clock in the morning and then went out with Mallie and Rachel and snowballed one another in the garden "to shake it down," as a light snow had begun to fall late in the afternoon to give the last perfect touch. Mallie came back to make the others come out to see the house, which looked exactly like a Christmas card, with all the windows glowing orange in the lightly falling snow, the roof and the little towers already white, the falcon and the turtle-dove black against the sky.

On Christmas morning Mother Wotherspoon arrived in the gig, looking larger and more solid than ever, and Anthony walked over laden with parcels and flowers and sniffing loudly at the turkey, which was already in the oven, and which he declared he had smelt as soon as he shut the front door of his lodgings.

Mr Peregrine was in his element, welcoming the menfolk to his parlour for drinks and a quiet smoke whenever they needed it. No woman was allowed in there, he said, except Jane the parrot, who liked a quiet life. Mr Peregrine and Jane were great pals, and enjoyed each other's company immensely.

Hagar took on the wand of office once more, and packed them all off to church while she and Beenie prepared the dinner and did their best to keep Penny in bed so that she would not get over-tired later on with all the excitement.

It was a joy to Hagar to hear their laughing voices as they came trooping up the garden, kicking the snow off their shoes on the doorstep and calling up to Penny at the window—Luke and John 'serenading' her with a carol while they pretended to be "Spanish hidalgos," whatever that might be.

All their differences with Mark were made up. They had none of his intense love for Bowchester, and were as keen as mustard about High Seaton and all they were going to do there with a free hand. Mark could "grow lichens all over him" if he liked at Bowchester. Mother Wotherspoon too was thoroughly enjoying all the bustle and activity of changing house, the newer house at Seaton with its electric light and modern conveniences suiting her much better than rambling old Bowchester with its lamps and inconvenient bathroom. Her happiness over Marion and Matthew had softened her too, so she was in high good humour.

The turkey was declared, as it no doubt was in a million other homes, to be the best turkey that ever appeared on a Christmas table, a compliment to Mother Wotherspoon, who had reared it, and to Hagar, who had cooked it. The plum-pudding was greeted with cheers which increased to gales of laughter when the sprig of holly, caught by the blue fire, went up in flames as well and appeared on the table as a forlorn black stick.

Nothing could dampen their enthusiasm, for they were all happy.

Rachel was enjoying her new status as mistress of the house, sitting opposite her father and hospitably pressing food on her guests and being the good hostess. Hagar, as the bride, had the seat of honour on Mr Peregrine's right, and both enjoyed their new teasing, familiar relationship as father and eldest married daughter.

When the toasts were in full swing Mr Peregrine brought down the house by introducing Anthony as his new partner in the firm of Peregrine, Turtleton, and Truett, Perry being loudest in his acclamations, while he privately wondered how anyone could bear to be shut up in a shop when he might ride on the wings of the wind. But "to each man his fate, to each as He saith." Anthony, looking at Penny's glowing face, was happy to see that she could now pick at a wafer of turkey breast and make it disappear, that the frail hands could ply knife and fork and spoon without growing tired, knowing with a joy that was almost pain that it was to him she always turned for help, praying that he would always be able to keep his own passionate love well in hand in case in any way it should disturb her. Yet no one could have guessed from his quiet face that anything perturbed Anthony. Rachel, indeed, sometimes wondered if he were anything more than amused in an affectionate older-brotherly sort of way at Penny's open adoration.

She had not read Browning's dictum that a man "boasts two soul-sides, one to face the world with, one to show a woman, when he loves her," nor quite appreciated the fact that Anthony had to wait a long time before he could show the second; he had to keep it well turned away, and only show the other, even to Penny, who was not only too young, but too frail for anything more than a humorous brotherly care and kindness.

Hagar at the moment was thinking of Penny too. She must have her over to stay with them at Bowchester. Mark must get a little quiet pony, and Anthony could teach her to ride; he was so good with horses, and loved riding himself. They'd lend Anthony a horse too. There were several at Bowchester, and Mark had said he was going to go in for breeding hunters. Anthony and Penny could go riding together, she was so safe with Anthony. . . .

No one would have guessed, either, that under the tablecloth Mark was holding her hand and giving her finger little secret pinches that meant all sorts of messages. They were a most sedate and orderly couple, and Rachel was thinking, "Fancy

anybody wanting to marry Mark! I'm sure he hasn't the first
notion of how to make love!" But then she never had seen
Mark 'making love.' He was another who kept one soul side
for the world.

As her glance left Penny and she looked round the table
now Hagar was remembering her old parson father's quotation
about the Potter and the vessel of clay. "How many of us,"
she was thinking, "have been broken in the hands of the Potter
—even before the clay was quite dry—and then put on the
wheel again and moulded into other vessels. . . . There's
Matthew, terribly smashed up, but turned from rather a handsome weakling into a wise, humorous philosopher, contented
with his lot, making do with what he has, and thinking of
how not to make his blindness a source of awkwardness or
discomfort to others. And Marion—she not only came a crash,
but was ground under the wheel, reduced bit by bit till she
was an outcast in strange cities, glad to take dirty coppers in
her bare hands from clodhoppers at a penny show. Now she
is the rarest and most finely finished of us all. Not young-
looking or pretty any more, a rather short and sturdy little
woman, but with nevertheless the distinction of a duchess.
Nothing will ever overcome Marion again.

"Rachel has only had a little dint so far—I'll leave Rachel
out; and Penny is only slowly creeping back into life after the
smash. She is of such fine clay she will never make a strong
pot, just a lovely delicate bowl that will need careful handling
—*n'y touchez pas, il est brisé*; do not touch roughly, the vase is
cracked. Darling, lovely Penny. I'm so glad she has Anthony.
We know nothing of Anthony's fall; he must have come a
cropper too when they were ruined, but Anthony never speaks
of himself. But he'll understand Penny; he's made of the same
finer clay.

"And there's Mark. He didn't fall so much as get crushed
between the wheels till he was a different shape altogether
from what he was meant to be, a dour, stiff lump—bless his
heart!" She had loved him even at his dourest because he'd

let her see bits of the real Mark now and then. Now his mother
was asking what she had done to him he was so changed.
"Perry and Luke and John," she thought, "are all whole pots
still, and Mother Wother and Daddy Peregrine are old, well-
battered pots, and lastly there's me. Well, I was well smashed
up too, and from a pretty vase moulded into a useful crock
for carrying the spring water from the well or holding the
daily bread, a good sensible pot to make a wife out of and,
I hope—a mother. I hope Mark and I have a large family
of sturdy little pots. Daddy Peregrine will have to be the
grandfather. He'll enjoy that, bless him! I must tell Mark we
must have at least seven to fill up all the holes and corners
at Bowchester——"

Her thoughts were interrupted by a cracker going off, and
from that moment her day was too full for any dreaming.

The old folks and Penny rested in the afternoon, while the
rest played boisterous games as if they were children again,
racing about the house in hide-and-seek and catching Beenie
and sliding her down the stairs on a tray.

All their fun and teasing cleared away their last sensitive
shrinking over Matthew's blindness, for Matthew came completely out of his shell and was the most boisterous of the lot,
boasting of his prowess in blind man's buff, and then being
thoroughly trounced by Mark, who beat him, as he said, "on
his own ground."

Marion was almost fey with joy all day because Matthew had
said that morning that he could see her shadow when she
passed between him and the window. She had run and hugged
him till he had to loosen her arms by main force.

"Do you want to choke me, you little baggage?"

"Oh, Matthew, you'll see again! I know you will! I can
see you coming down from the hill behind Goslaw, driving
the sheep before you!"

At night they had a cats' concert, and if you don't know
what a cats' concert is it's time you did. A cats' concert is an
entertainment got up on the spur of the moment, in which

every single member of the party must do a turn. No excuse
of any kind allowed. As they were all more or less musical
they all sang.

Mr Peregrine sang *Mr Mulligan's Birthday Pie* and Mother
Wotherspoon an ancient ditty called *Bother the Men* with such
gusto that they all sang it over again. Matthew and Marion
sang an old song from their concert repertoire, *Believe Me if All
those Endearing Young Charms*. Even Beenie came in and sang,
Sair failed, Hinny, Sair failed Now, and Mallie sang, *Malbrouk
s'en va-t-en Guerre*, in which Luke and John supplied the
band with the poker and a penny whistle from a cracker—
"Mironton, mironton, mirontaine!"

As she finished Mr Peregrine looked up and said:

"As you're the travelled one of the party, do you know
where Serajevo is?"

"No," said Mallie. "Never heard of it."

"Why?" asked the others.

"Oh, I've just read that some Austrian royalty is going
there in the spring."

"I'll fly there some day," said Perry—"not knowing in any
wise the mind of Allah. . . ."

At last the time came for the party to break up, as Mark and
Hagar were catching the midnight express for London *en route*
for the Alps and a holiday of ski-ing and skating.

On the doorstep, to Rachel's surprise, Mark picked Hagar
up, swung her to his shoulder, and challenged Luke, John,
and Perry to a race to the garden gate—and won it!

"Long legs should be penalized," said Perry. "They're
not fair."

The others had wanted to go to the station, but were
absolutely forbidden by Hagar, who had come on a packet
of rice hidden under a coat. (No horrid French confetti was
allowed at Hagar's wedding; it made such a mess, whereas
good old-fashioned rice was soon picked up by the birds, who
thereby—as Penny pointed out—also enjoyed the wedding.)

So Mark tucked Hagar's arm beneath his own, and, holding

her hand tightly and warmly clasped in his, they went off through the almost deserted streets.

In the distance through a thin veil of blowing snow they heard the faint, plaintive notes of a tin whistle rising and falling under the sickle of the moon, which appeared now and then above the old town-hall. It sounded like the calling of the wind.

"Hark!" said Hagar, tightening his arm against her side. "The piper in the wind goes by."